PRAISE FOR KIT ROCHA

Praise for *The Devil You Know*

"The stakes are high, the danger is imminent, and the sexiness is through the roof."

—*BookPage*

"This sequel has all of the action, smolder, snark, and surprising warmth of the first, with more development of a postapocalyptic Atlanta that is slowly finding its feet again—with the help of the Mercenary Librarians."

—*Booklist*

"This series entry begins to peel back the layers of the characters that make up the Mercenary Librarians and the Silver Devils, while giving hints to deeper secrets and conspiracies of the corrupt TechCorps and its plans for control."

—*Library Journal*

Praise for *Deal with the Devil*

"A full-throttle read! I can't wait to see what happens next!"
—Jeaniene Frost, *New York Times* and *USA Today* bestselling author of the Night Huntress series

"Hard hitting, unflinching, brutally, beautifully written, and surprising even in the last act. It pulls off a few tricks I would have called clichés past redeeming. I am SO impressed."

—Seanan McGuire, *New York Times* bestselling author

"A roller coaster of nail-biting thrills combined with top-notch world building, palpable heat, and real emotional stakes. You're going to love it."
—Gwenda Bond, *New York Times* bestselling author of *Stranger Things: Suspicious Minds*

"High-stakes action and plenty of chemistry, *Deal with the Devil* absolutely crackles!"
—Chloe Neill, *New York Times* and *USA Today* bestselling author

"The sizzling sexual tension is simply the icing that makes *Deal with the Devil* one of my favorite SF reads ever."
—Alyssa Cole, award-winning author

"My advice? Cancel your plans so you can get swallowed up in Kit Rocha's exciting new world."
—Thea Harrison, *New York Times* and *USA Today* bestselling author

"An exhilarating start to what promises to be a compelling series . . . bring on the next Mercenary Librarians adventure!"
—Nalini Singh, *New York Times* bestselling author

"Complicated characters, complex stakes, and world building on a grand scale—I loved this book. Preorder—and get multiple copies for friends too!"
—Melissa Marr, *New York Times* bestselling author of the Wicked Lovely series

"Nina is everything I love in a heroine—smart and badass, but with a core of hope and kindness. And Knox is jaded, honorable, and so very conflicted. I loved it!"
—Jessie Mihalik, author of *Polaris Rising*

CONSORT
OF
FIRE

CONSORT
OF
FIRE

Bound to Fire and Steel Book 1

KIT ROCHA

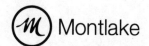 Montlake

Text copyright © 2023 by Kit Rocha
All rights reserved.

Published by Montlake, Seattle

www.apub.com

Amazon, the Amazon logo, and Montlake are trademarks of Amazon.com, Inc., or its affiliates.

ISBN-13: 9781662513183 (paperback)
ISBN-13: 9781662513190 (digital)

Cover design by Hang Le
Cover images: © Darren Woolridge / Shutterstock;
© BERNATSKAIA OKSANA / Shutterstock; © Olga Nikonova / Shutterstock;
© NeoLeo / Shutterstock

Printed in the United States of America

To the people who dream of a better world.
And then fight to make their dreams come true.

Our hopes have always shaped the world. The whispers of our hearts are candles set afloat on the rivers of eternity, all flowing inexorably toward the Everlasting Dream. The Dream surrounds us. We are born from it. When we die, we return to it. And when we reach out in fear and longing, the Dream provides.

When time was new and the world barely formed, the Sheltered Lands cried out for a protector. So the Dragon appeared from the flames, and the Siren rose from the depths of the seas. A handful of others followed, gods who could hear the whispers of the world itself.

They were the Dreamers, and where they walked, the world thrived.

When they Dreamt, the world changed.

Then they fought, and the world broke. And, in darkness and fear, our nightmares formed the Endless Void.

The War of the Gods
Author unknown

Chapter One
BETRAYER'S MOON

Week Five, Day Eight
Year 2999

Sachielle dreamt of fire.

The flames licked at her limbs, undeterred by the spray dashing up over the barge's bow. Carved wood dug into her palms as she gripped the railing and watched the blaze crawl slowly up her arms, obliterating the thick velvet of her ice-blue sleeves, leaving only crumbling char in its wake.

Such destruction. It tugged at something low in her belly. Plucked at the tight knot of her self-control, teasing. Taunting. This fire could burn her through, hollow her out and blacken her bones.

What would happen if she embraced it?

An attendant stepped closer and brushed surreptitiously at the flowing skirt of Sachi's gown. Heedless of the roiling sheet of flame that had enveloped the fabric, she blotted at the droplets of river water that had soaked the velvet.

Sachi blinked, and the fire dissipated. Her waking dreams had been growing more vivid, but they'd never seemed this *real*. Even now, she was shocked to look down at pristine clothing and unmarred skin, without a blister in sight.

The attendant cleared her throat softly, and Sachi stepped back with a tight smile of apology. If they'd been alone on deck, she might have said the words aloud. But it wasn't appropriate for a noblewoman to apologize to a servant, no matter how necessary or well-deserved it was.

"Oh, *blast*." The light, musical curse heralded Naia's arrival on deck.

Sachielle had met the newborn godling who'd been tasked with ensuring their smooth passage upriver, but they hadn't really spoken. Unlike the blue- and green-skinned water sprites of legend, Naia looked human—rich brown hair and black eyes, with skin the color of sand at dusk, just a few shades darker than Sachi's.

Right now, she stood, her fists planted on her hips, staring in consternation at Sachi's wet dress. "I should have thought of it," she murmured. "The river can get turbulent this close to the Falls."

"What?"

"Your dress." Naia held out her hand. Slowly, silver droplets of water began to pull free of the wet velvet, drawn by her hovering fingers. They danced delicately in the air, joining and separating as they rose.

It was beautiful, and Sachi watched, spellbound, as Naia turned her hand in a beckoning gesture. The water, shimmering in the sunlight, coalesced in her upturned palm. She bent closer, whispering to the rippling ball of water, then blew gently. The drops dispersed, floating over the railing to fall once more into the river.

"Thank you. That was—" Sachi's voice cracked, and she took a steadying breath. "Lovely."

Naia dropped into a deep curtsy. "My lady."

It was a form of address that no god, even a young one, would typically offer a human, regardless of royal lineage. But Sachi was something more than that now: promised to their god king, fated to be his bound bride.

The Dragon's consort.

She could scarcely acknowledge the reality of it, even in the quiet privacy of her own mind.

Finally, Sachi spoke. "I must thank you for the ease and speed of our journey. A trip like this should have taken two weeks or more, and yet here it's barely been one. Just eleven days to travel all the way from the capital."

Naia blushed. "It was the least I could do. A simple matter, really." Her gaze turned dreamy and soft as she looked out over the water. "I merely . . . asked for help. She's quite eager to please, you know. This river."

It shouldn't have been such a jarring thought, the concept that the river could be a living thing with feelings and intentions. Sachi was, after all, standing next to a living piece of the Dream. But no one spoke this way in the city. Sometimes it seemed as though they'd all moved away from the notion of an interconnected world, one created and ruled by emotion. There were people, and then there was the world around them, a dead world of sticks and grass and water—things that existed only as resources to be exploited.

Naia edged closer. "Are you eager? To meet the Dragon, I mean?"

The previous consort had died after three incredibly well-documented years of fear and misery. The letters he'd written to his parents, begging them to end his marriage and bring him home, sat in the royal archives. And his body, repaired and preserved by magic, still lay in state nearly a century later.

Prince Tislaine, his epitaph read. *Duty, honor, and ultimate sacrifice.*

The flames surged again, burning Sachi's palms this time, and she clenched her fists tight to hide them as she waited for the fire to subside. All descendants of the mortal kings possessed a measure of magic. It was their claim, the divine right of royal birth. The reason they, and they alone, were fit to rule the people.

But never like Sachi—never this much, this hot. This close to the surface. The magic of the mortal kings was a whisper compared to Sachi's, a glowing ember eclipsed by a wildfire. And if anyone on their voyage might notice, it was the lovely Naia—newly born, so fresh from the Dream that its tattoo likely lingered in her mind as an echo rather than a memory.

But the spirit made flesh only smiled. "We're nearly there."

The barge cleared the last bend in the river, and a huge waterfall came into view. Water cascaded wildly off the ridge, falling to swirl in a turbulent pool at the base of the cliff. The Midnight Forest grew thickly on either side of the river, the trees' big branches strong even in the shadow of the mountain.

To Sachi's right, the broad, solid walls of a castle peeked through the forest. Blade's Rest, seat of the Huntress. Their river journey would end here. They'd be met by the Dragon's delegation, feast and rest at the Huntress's home, then travel on come daybreak.

Sachielle looked up. She caught a glimpse of the spires of Dragon's Keep, nestled between the snowcapped peaks above.

"Come," Naia murmured. "They're waiting."

A single sharp clap behind them made all the attendants flinch. "Don't stand around gawking like day-old hatchlings," a husky, impatient voice snapped. "The princess's things must be packed and prepared for the journey."

The young women clustered around her dropped a series of deep, abrupt curtsies punctuated by murmurs of *my lady* before they scrambled to obey. Zanya watched them go, her arms folded across her chest, looking more like a military commander than chief handmaid.

Sachi held out her arm. "Please accompany us, Zanya."

Zanya tore her gaze from the attendants and managed to smooth her features. The boat rocked beneath them on gentle waves, but

Zanya crossed the deck with effortless grace and silently extended a steadying hand.

The crew had already laid out the gangplank, a wide board hewn from a single piece of wood, painted royal red and gold. Sachi's toes curled in her slippers as she crossed it as quickly and gracefully as she could in her heavy skirts.

She was immensely jealous of Zanya's wardrobe, which mostly consisted of shorter split skirts meant to be worn over tight trousers. No one chose to wear four cumbersome layers for the comfort or convenience of it. Even Naia's robe would be preferable, though Sachi blushed at the thought of being clad in nothing but the sheer, diaphanous fabric.

She breathed a sigh of relief when they reached the solid safety of the dock, though the feeling was short lived as she faced the crowd gathered at the end of it.

There were guards, of course. Merchants, sailors, and people in court attire. Two horses, one with an empty saddle and another carrying a smiling blonde. A huge cloaked man beside her.

No sign of their dragon god. Unless . . .

Sachielle stopped in front of the cloaked man and curtsied. "My lord."

The hood shadowed his face. She caught a glimpse of a beard and firm lips curving into a slight smile. Then *he* was bowing to *her*, a low rumble edged with wildness rattling out of his chest. "Princess."

When he straightened, his hood fell back, revealing a hard face made of sharp angles, disheveled brown hair—and eyes the color of pure molten gold.

"Don't be a boor." The blonde dismounted her horse with enviable grace—no doubt due in part to the fact that she wore trousers as well. "Introduce yourself, and correct the dear lady's misapprehensions."

It was odd, how that small smile failed to soften his features even a little. "Ulric," he offered in that same rumbling voice. "The Wolf."

Sachi's cheeks heated. "Of course."

The woman shook her head with a low laugh, stripped off one glove, and held out her hand. "I'm Elevia."

The Huntress. Sachi had heard the whispered prayers all her life, seen the sacrifices on pyres in the countryside and offerings on the mountain altars. This wasn't a woman at all, but the god of the hunt, patron of those who stalked their prey in the forest, stared down the shafts of arrows, and prayed for a good kill.

Sachi wasn't sure if it was madness or inevitability that led the Wolf to stand at her side. Even in the absence of malice, they were mortal enemies. Their natures would allow nothing else. Then again, without the one, could the other exist?

Perhaps they were only two sides of the same coin.

"Welcome to my home, my lady." Elevia bowed. "It is a sincere pleasure to celebrate your arrival."

"Sachielle, of House Roquebarre." Sachi mirrored her movements. "And the pleasure is mine."

"I daresay there is enough to go around. And you." Elevia smiled at Naia, opening her arms. "You must be the new little one Dianthe spoke of. There are too few of you these days. You are welcome, cousin."

Naia beamed as Elevia folded her into an embrace, and Sachi shifted her weight from one foot to the other and back again as she surreptitiously surveyed the crowd.

A cold knot sank through her middle like a weighted net, only to settle low in her gut.

He wasn't here.

The Dragon hadn't come to greet her.

The Wolf's knowing gaze landed on her. "There was an incursion at the border," he said quietly. "My brother sent me in his stead."

Relief and irritation clashed within her. Quickly, Sachi schooled her features into a mask of vaguely expectant cheer. She'd have to be more careful here than she had been in the capital.

"I appreciate your efforts on my behalf." Sincerity was her best remaining line of defense, and she deployed it ruthlessly. "More than you can ever know."

"Do you ride, my lady?" Elevia led over the riderless horse, a beautiful blue roan with a mottled gray coat. "Blade's Rest isn't far, but you must be exhausted from your journey."

Zanya had already drifted closer to the horse, her gaze skimming the saddle. As if the Huntress would have to resort to covert tricks if she wanted to remove an enemy. The threats facing Sachi here weren't physical, but that wouldn't stop Zanya from expecting treachery.

Apparently satisfied by her examination, she turned and held out a hand. "My lady."

Zanya helped her into the saddle, then lingered to properly arrange her skirts as Sachi gripped the pommel.

Elevia mounted her horse in one smooth movement and clicked her tongue. The animal responded immediately, turning away from the dock toward the road. "To Blade's Rest," she announced.

To my destiny, Sachi corrected silently.

She would meet the Dragon, would smile and blush and bat her eyes at him. They would be bound, and she would live with him, attend his court. Share his bed. And then, when the time came, she would kill him.

Her very life depended on it.

Chapter Two
BETRAYER'S MOON

Week Five, Day Eight
Year 2999

If dinner in a minor keep like Blade's Rest lasted half the night, Zanya wasn't sure how she'd survive once they reached the High Court at Dragon's Keep.

A harsh judgment, perhaps. The seat of a living god like the Huntress could hardly be considered *minor*. But even the tedious state banquets in the capital hadn't prepared Zanya for the unending revelry of the Huntress's welcome feast.

They'd endured a string of courses already—a delicate seafood soup, a crisp salad of greens that should have been impossible to find this deep in winter, three types of freshly baked bread, two vintages of wine Zanya was not remotely sophisticated enough to appreciate, and venison marinated in something so spicy her tongue still tingled. There was also a dizzying array of rolls and pies with paper-thin pastry wrapped around shredded vegetables and delicate slices of meat, as well as seafood, rice, and some things she couldn't begin to identify.

She might have enjoyed it, if only she'd been able to eat in peace with the rest of the servants. Not that the common folk back in the capital had ever been offered the same delicacies that graced the noble boards. The grand hall at Blade's Rest, however, held dozens of long tables crammed full of stablemen and maids, gardeners and crafters. They dined on the same food being served at the high table, and with considerably more ease.

Zanya envied them their comfortable anonymity.

Sachielle sat on her left, watching the festivities with the same faint smile she'd worn since their arrival. Zanya could see that smile fraying around the edges, but no one else would. Sachi had been trained for this, to sit at the center of attention. Gracious and beautiful. Serene. Not just a princess, but the promised consort of a living god.

"My lady?"

She belonged at the high table. Zanya belonged in the shadows.

"Excuse me, my lady."

Belatedly, she realized the young serving man at her shoulder was speaking to *her*. She leaned back, reluctantly letting her fingers slide from the table knife she'd been absently caressing. He removed her plate and replaced it with yet another, this one boasting five bite-size desserts arrayed in a circle.

Her fingers trembled in her lap as she stared at the delicate confections. One looked like a tiny cake. Another layered nuts with thick, rich honey. A third looked as if it had been dipped in precious chocolate. She could taste the bittersweetness of it on her tongue.

She could feel the strap across her back.

Twenty lashes, with the full strength of a grown man's arm—pain enough to fell most twelve-year-olds. That had been her punishment for slipping into the royal larder and picking the lock meant to protect such treasures. The bean that produced the rare delicacy grew only in the sheltered depths of the Witchwood, after all, and chocolate was seldom seen outside holy days during the Witch's Moon.

The cook's stash had been meant for the king's own table. Sachielle had never confessed what her father had said or done to make her weep like her heart had been shattered, but depriving the great Dalvish II, Lord of House Roquebarre, Mortal King of the Sheltered Lands, of his carefully hoarded sweets had been worth the beating all on its own.

Not that Zanya had done it because of him. She'd done it to see the brief, bright pleasure in Sachi's tear-reddened eyes. Sachi *adored* chocolate.

She still did. As soon as the dessert touched her lips, her eyelashes fluttered with delight and her smile returned in full force. When Sachielle truly smiled, she *shone*. Candlelight shimmered off the honey-colored braids wrapped around her head, and her golden skin seemed to glow. Across the room, gazes lingered on her as she savored the bittersweet kiss of chocolate, her pleasure worth every interminable moment of this dinner.

They were falling in love with her already. Most people did, sooner or later.

And she was as oblivious as always. Sachi finished the chocolate, then cleaned her fingers in the tiny basin of floral-scented water beside her plate. "May I ask you a question?"

Elevia, who had been watching the revelers over the rim of her golden goblet, straightened immediately. "Anything you wish."

"It was something you mentioned earlier." Sachi dried her hands on her napkin. "When you greeted Naia. You said that newborn godlings are rare."

"Because they are." Elevia held up her goblet, and a server stepped forward to refill it. "It takes an amazing amount of belief to pull part of the Everlasting Dream into our world. To give it form, breath. *Life.*"

When time was new and the world barely formed, the Sheltered Lands cried out for a protector. So the Dragon appeared from the flames, and the Siren rose from the depths of the sea, summoned by the dreams of the people.

How many times had Zanya heard High Priest Nikkon chant those words to open a ceremony? Every child in the Sheltered Lands learned to recite the story as soon as they could speak. No one ever questioned it. No one *could*, not with the capital perched on Siren's Bay, with the sea god's distant, forbidding keep just visible on the island that guarded the harbor.

"That's why only Dianthe has any young ones," Elevia explained, as if Zanya's thoughts had prompted her. "If you ask, she'll mutter sage words about the lure of the Siren's call, but the truth is much simpler." She smiled. "She has all those damned fishermen and sailors. Never met a more superstitious bunch. They dream hard, and they *believe* even harder."

Sailors must have softer dreams than Zanya's to pull forth something as sweet as the young god seated at the end of the table. Her laughter rang out like chimes, but Zanya resisted the urge to look. The Wolf sat between them, a solid wall of lean warrior muscle and power that prickled a warning over her skin.

Those golden eyes saw too much. And he might be the ruler of the wild places, his very essence the manifestation of basest survival instinct, but there was a darkness in him that Zanya could almost taste in the air—ash and salt and the metallic tang of blood. The same darkness wreathed the Huntress, for all her golden looks and easy smile.

Death.

They were both predators, each in their own way. Dangerous even without the power to bend the Everlasting Dream to their will—and with it? Fatal. Zanya felt the truth in her bones, like recognizing like.

Because she was a predator, too.

Sachi's lashes fluttered again, and her jaw clenched. Surefire signs she was suppressing a yawn. "My apologies. The journey must have been more taxing than I realized."

Elevia rose and beckoned to the servants and guards that lined the stone wall behind them. "You should rest. Please, let me show you to your chambers."

Finally.

Zanya left the tempting chocolate on its plate and slipped from her seat, doing her best to melt into the shadows as she trailed behind Sachi and the Huntress. Not that there were many shadows to be found. The hallways glowed with candlelight cleverly reflected by brass that had been polished to a mirror shine.

The light fell on the tapestries lining the halls, scenes depicting woodland hunts as well as epic battles. Sachi gazed at them as she drifted past, drinking in the details. "Do you view war as sport, the same as hunting?"

The Huntress laughed softly. "You're asking the wrong question, my dear. I would never hunt for sport, only necessity. The only reason I would ever ride into battle, as well."

"I see."

What Zanya had seen of the keep was sensible—modest, comfortable furnishings and simple decor. Nothing too ostentatious. That changed when the Huntress led them into the guest suite.

A wide bed dominated the space, big enough to sleep five and covered with silken sheets and a fluffy quilt that mimicked the colors of dusk fading to twilight. Bedposts polished to reflect the candlelight held heavy curtains that could be pulled for privacy, and the stone floor was covered with thick rugs to insulate from the cold.

The mirror over the vanity reflected another open doorway, and through it a bathing pool cut into the floor. Natural rock veined with crystal surrounded it, and the water steamed in the cool air, its promised warmth enough to make Zanya's stress-taut muscles ache with longing.

A pair of servants knelt to stoke the fire in the massive hearth, and a third nodded politely to Zanya. "We've left your lady's belongings for you to unpack," she whispered, indicating the trunks stacked beside the vanity. "The rest of her attendants have rooms at the end of the corridor. If you have need of anything, there will be a guard posted outside your door."

To protect them? Or to protect *against* them? It mattered little either way. The important thing to remember was that their every move would be watched. "Thank you."

"We'll break our fast," the Huntress was saying, "and then make for Dragon's Keep. I'm sorry we can't tarry longer, but the journey up the mountain will take the better part of a day."

"It's fine," Sachi assured her. "Thank you for your hospitality."

They both bowed their heads, and the Huntress departed, leaving behind the two servants.

Sachi plucked at the first tie on her sleeve, the ribbon binding it at the wrist. "You may go as well. Zanya will help me."

Zanya waited until the door was shut behind the servants before striding across the thick rug. "Let me. These are impossible to untie on your own."

"I'd pry them loose with my teeth for a chance to be"—Sachi jerked harder, and the delicate ribbon tore—"alone. Damn it all."

Sympathy flooded Zanya. Sachi had been the object of fascination for the entire journey and on display like a prize mare during the endless feast. Zanya made quick work of the ribbons on the other sleeve. "Let me help you with this, and you can explore the bath. Did you see the bathing pool? There must be a hot spring."

"Or magic. This isn't the capital, Zanya. Anyone here could have it."

The reminder was a hard enough kick to make her hands tremble. But Zanya shook her head as she started on the ribbon just below Sachi's elbow. The Wolf's and the Huntress's mere presences had seethed with power enough to set her nerves on edge, but now that they were gone, there was no lingering prickle of magic. Only Sachi's soothing, familiar warmth. "I don't think so. But even if it is magic, it still looks wonderful, doesn't it?"

A stormy frown wrinkled Sachi's brow, clouding her face. "He didn't come. What if he means to avoid me as much as possible?"

If only they could be so fortunate. The Dragon was a monster of legend, with the power to rend the very earth and burn armies on a whim. His voracious cruelty had spelled doom for dozens of sacrificial consorts. The idea of Sachi being forced to spend so much as a moment alone with him kindled rage in Zanya's heart and fear in her belly.

The idea of Sachi being forced to *bed* him . . .

The delicate ribbon snapped under her fingers. Zanya ignored the loss of control and turned Sachi around with gentle hands at her shoulders so she could tend to the row of tiny buttons that marched up her spine. "You'll make the best of whatever situation arises," she assured Sachi in her most soothing voice. "And so will I."

"Of course," Sachi answered immediately. "It just . . . makes things more difficult, that's all."

Zanya wished she could reassure her, but she had no way of knowing what a god could hear in her own home. Perhaps even whispered words of comfort would make their way to the Huntress's ears. Besides, Sachi wouldn't want to hear anything she had to say. They both knew that the Dragon must die, and Sachi remained convinced the task should fall to her. That he would be most vulnerable in her bed.

Perhaps he would be. But Sachi would be vulnerable, too.

Far better if the Dragon ignored Sachi entirely, leaving Zanya free to do what she did best. After all, she was the one who'd spent nearly two decades learning how to kill with lethal efficiency.

Zanya slipped the next button free, her knuckles grazing the vulnerable curve of Sachi's spine above the filmy fabric of her shift. Her smooth, golden skin was unblemished. No beatings for the precious princess, though Zanya felt certain she had come out ahead in that regard. The physical punishment Zanya had endured as part of her training had been unpleasant, but there was something neat and clean about the scars it left behind.

The scars King Dalvish II and his damned high priest had left on Sachi's heart might be invisible, but they were jagged and numerous and still bled. Perhaps the king and Nikkon had imagined they were toughening her up for the task ahead—to lure a god to her bed and slay him there.

An error on their part. Toughness had never been Sachi's problem. With her generous and loving heart, Sachi quite simply wasn't built for cold-blooded murder.

But she didn't need to be. Zanya *was*. And she had no qualms about murdering anyone who laid a finger on Sachi. Even a god.

Especially a god.

The final button gave way, and the dress sagged off Sachi's shoulders. "Sit," Zanya urged. "I'll need to take your hair down if you're to enjoy that bath."

Sachi draped the heavy velvet dress over a chair and stretched her shoulders. "It will take forever to dry."

"I'll brush it out in front of the fire," Zanya promised. "It won't take long."

Sachi sank onto the stool at the vanity. The attached mirror was ornate, the glass edged with delicately carved vines and flowers. She stared into it, her gaze roving over her own features. "What if he finds me displeasing?"

Zanya deftly plucked the pins from Sachi's hair, letting the sleek golden braids cascade around her shoulders. As she began to unravel them, she studied Sachi in the mirror, trying to see her as if for the first time.

Golden skin, just kissed by the sun. Strong, elegant cheekbones. A petite nose made oddly adorable by the slight upward turn at the tip. Her lips were pursed now, her nervousness clear, but she had a brilliant smile that lit up wide blue eyes framed by thick lashes and arched brows. Her smile brought dimples, too—and Zanya had lost many an argument when Sachi peered at her from beneath the fall of her hair, those dimples flashing.

"No one could find you displeasing," she said honestly, combing her fingers through hair crimped by long confinement in braids. "You may borrow trouble if you must, but do not worry about *that.*"

Sachi exhaled sharply—and seized Zanya's hand.

Their eyes met in the mirror. Zanya cursed her loose and reckless tongue, but nothing could stop her from curling her fingers tight around Sachi's trembling hand.

Her name came in a rough whisper, low enough to elude prying ears. "Zanya . . ."

Zanya strained closer, hungry to hear what whispered confession might escape Sachi's lips even though she knew it was dangerous. *Too* dangerous.

Instead, she heard a pounding on the door.

Sachi broke away. "Enter."

The door cracked open, and the Huntress poked her head inside. "Forgive the intrusion, but your intended has arrived and wishes to see you." Her eyes flashed. "I told him you had already retired for the night, but he insists."

"Does he?" Sachi asked mildly.

The Huntress's grin bared her teeth. "One word from you, and I'll send him on his way."

But Sachi only rose and smoothed her unbound hair. "Of course I'll receive him."

Dread flooded Zanya's gut, but she could hardly contradict her mistress in front of the Huntress. She turned for the bed to pick up the robe she'd laid out, but Sachi waved her away.

"Thank you, but no." She squared her shoulders. "It *is* late, and the Dragon must take me as he finds me."

The Huntress pushed open the door, an almost approving smile on her lips. "This way."

Sachi swept out into the hallway, her noble persona wrapped around her like armor. Zanya was left to hurry in her wake, wondering how the young woman who'd peered at her own reflection with such naked doubt only moments before could transform into this ethereal princess. Her spine was steel, and she made a nearly transparent shift seem like appropriate court attire, as if everyone else was hopelessly overdressed.

All too soon, they reached the vaulted entrance to the castle. The doors stood open, revealing a courtyard lit by torches and the thin silver light of the new moons. An imposing man stood a dozen paces from the entrance, clad in blood-spattered armor that left little doubt what task he'd so recently been about.

This was the Dragon. His presence sizzled across Zanya's skin like fire, his power a heavy weight that seemed to pull everything toward him. She could barely see through the storm of magic to mark his features—skin as golden as Sachi's but hair as black as Zanya's own and eyes that hovered between deep brown and molten flame. He was tall and broad, with a warrior's bulk, but his face appeared to be carved from the earth he was said to control.

Hard planes. Hard eyes. No emotion flickered over his face as Sachi stopped before him and dropped to one knee. "My lord."

His gaze raked over her, and Zanya found herself clenching her hands so hard her nails bit into her palms. Sachielle knelt before him, her unbound hair wild, in a shift so thin the cold night air had to be slicing through it, chilling her to the bone. She was as good as naked before him, the picture of obedient submission . . . but her spine was still straight, her eyes bold and curious.

Even on her knee, *she* was challenging *him*.

Zanya held her breath as the silence drew tighter than a bowstring. The entire courtyard was caught on the edge of snapping as time ticked on with only the night wind stirring the trees as proof that movement still existed at all.

The illusion shattered when the Dragon pivoted on his heel and strode away without a word. Flames erupted around him as he walked, burning higher and brighter until his figure was obscured by an inferno that grew into wings trailing fire.

A dragon erupted from the center of the blaze, half the height of Blade's Rest. The downward sweep of his wings stirred a wind so strong that Sachi's hair blew out behind her, and she swayed under the force of it. Zanya hurried forward to steady her, but her gaze followed the dragon—the *Dragon*—as he swept higher in dizzying spirals until the midnight sky swallowed him.

Fear beat a frantic rhythm through Zanya, but she controlled her voice as she helped Sachi to her feet. "Are you all right, my lady?"

"Fine," she murmured, but the pulse in her wrist galloped beneath Zanya's fingers.

She didn't speak again until they were back in the guest chamber, with Sachi submerged in a steaming bath topped with perfumed oil and dried flowers. She leaned her head against the stone edge of the bathing pool and closed her eyes, her fingers drifting through the slick water.

"He may be a god," she whispered, "but he's also a man." A soft smile curved her lips. "I can work with that."

Chapter Three
BETRAYER'S MOON

Week Five, Day Nine
Year 2999

Dragon's Keep was, by any objective measure, both tactically and visually imposing. Sheer cliffs of a thousand spans or more guarded the approach from the west. The pass leading up on the east was only marginally more inviting, consisting of narrow switchbacks cut into the side of the mountain. The harrowing trip to the summit took hours and was enough to leave most visitors weak kneed and humbled before they ever reached the ridge of the caldera.

Only a fool would attempt to bring an army up the main road, where they'd be visible long before they approached the gates, easy pickings for an irritated dragon lord who had not issued an invitation. But as Ash stood on the lookout tower atop the north barracks and watched the Huntress's party make its way up the second-to-last switchback, he couldn't shake his deep sense of foreboding.

Invaders were coming.

The warning tickled up the back of his neck like a whisper. He flexed his toes in his boots, irritated that he couldn't feel the earth beneath his feet. His steward had turned herself into a polite brick wall this morning, determined to ensure that he would not impugn the dignity of *her* castle by greeting his consort shoeless, in well-worn armor. So here he was, trussed up in crimson silk, a tailored black tunic embroidered with metallic flames, and black boots so shiny he could see his reflection in them.

Ash could have reminded Camlia that Dragon's Keep was *his* castle, and that he would wear what he wanted within its confines. He could have reminded her that fine clothing and polished boots were unlikely to mitigate the naked fear he'd faced in the eyes of his last half dozen consorts. He could have confessed that he'd already greeted this girl, and that he'd done so in his bloodstained armor and bare feet.

He could even have roared her into submission. Maybe.

Instead, he'd suffered the silent rebuke and let Camlia's grandson play valet and dress him. Now, especially, having retainers around who didn't fear him was more precious than the rarest jewels.

He'd face fear enough when the princess and her entourage arrived.

A low, fascinated whistle sounded behind him. "Well, now. Don't you cut an impressive figure?"

Ash glanced back to find the Lover leaning against the stone doorway, his full lips curved into an amused smile. Aleksi was dressed in his usual finery—a billowy linen shirt with an open collar, a velvet jerkin he rarely bothered to fasten above his sternum, and black leather pants. It was all tailored to show off his sleek, muscular figure and flatter his light-brown skin and dark-brown hair and eyes.

He was a vision of lazy seduction, as usual. And he was supposed to be on his way home. "I thought you were leaving this morning to prepare for the progress."

"And miss this? Madness." Aleksi strolled to the edge of the tower and leaned over the parapet wall. "Hmm."

Ash followed his gaze. The party was making good time, considering the path was barely wide enough for two horses to ride abreast before the surface gave way to a neck-breaking plunge onto jagged rocks. He could make out the individual riders now, but he doubted that it was Elevia or Ulric who had caught Aleksi's attention.

The princess rode at the head of a string of brightly dressed attendants, and she *glowed*.

"It's not uncommon for the children of the mortal lords to have some magic," Ash pointed out, trying to shake his own discomfort. While a connection to the Everlasting Dream had nothing to do with bloodlines and inheritance, children raised to believe they could shape the world often manifested some small power to do so.

"This is true," Aleksi allowed. "But that? Is not *some*."

No, it certainly wasn't. Ash let his gaze drift back to Elevia. If he focused on the Huntress, he could still see the glow of power around her, as strong and vivid as it had been over three thousand years ago when they'd first found each other. But she had walked in this world for millennia. This realm knew her and the touch of her power, the punishment of her vengeance and the justice of her mercy.

The Wolf was the same. Where Elevia blazed brilliant white, edged with gold, like an unrelenting sun, Ulric's aura was the dappled light and shadows of the wild woods he'd claimed as his own, kissed by the green of the pines that grew in the Midnight Forest. He'd walked this world for as long as Elevia had, and it knew him. Accepted him.

When Ash let his concentration fade, the bright light around them faded with it. But the others . . .

The Siren's young protégée, he'd expected. Naia was freshly born from the Dream, only a few months old. It would take centuries for her to settle into her power, so he was unsurprised to see sunlight sparkle off her like candlelight reflected through many-faceted sapphires and aquamarines.

But the girl. The princess. She simply *glowed*.

He'd never seen anything quite like it. There was no color to it—or perhaps there was *every* color, a translucent rainbow that exploded from her in every direction. He'd almost convinced himself that he'd imagined it the previous night. That the starshine and the stress of the battle and his desperation to see the end of this string of terrified consorts had manifested in a very real hallucination.

Except here she was, even more radiant by sunlight than she had been under the cool light of the stars. "Have you ever seen an aura like that before?"

"Never." His friend's expression didn't change, but the barest hint of a sly smile crept into Aleksi's voice. "Does it intrigue you?"

Ash gritted his teeth to hold back a snarl. Denying it would be pointless—that was the problem with having friends who had known you for thousands of years. Deception swiftly became impossible, leaving you to suffer endless years of torment under the supposed wit of the tolerably clever.

And the truth of it was . . . Ash *was* intrigued, for all the good it would do him. The girl hadn't seemed particularly frightened last night, but the last boy hadn't at first, either. It had taken weeks for the fear to eat through the veneer of haughty distance that had been ground into the young man from infancy.

Even a century later, the pain of it settled in Ash's gut like a stone. Most of the time, he cared little for how the humans of the Sheltered Lands regarded him. Their fear and terror made him every bit as strong as the awe and adoration of the past had done, and strength was what he needed to guard the border. They could curse him in their homes if they wished. He'd protect their lands either way.

But it was a different matter, having that fear live in your own castle. Having it stare at you in accusation across a dinner table no matter how mildly or gently you spoke. Ash had never laid a finger on the last prince, but his trepidation had shivered through the castle from dawn until dusk, until finally the boy's nightmares had grown fangs that endangered the whole castle.

That was what had killed his last consort, in the end. Not his terror, but *a Terror*—the manifestation of a nightmare pulled straight from the Endless Void. Ash rubbed a thumb over the cloth covering the ugly scar on his left arm, wishing he could forget the sight of poor Prince Tislaine, his face pale with death and his eyes unseeing.

Ash had managed to dispatch the Terror before it had consumed the boy's body, though he'd almost lost his sword arm in the process. And unlike normal injuries, wounds inflicted by Void creatures healed badly, even with magic. Even for gods.

Would Princess Sachielle's sweet curiosity give way to that same life-ending dread? At this point, hoping for anything else seemed reckless. It had been a thousand years since a consort had come eagerly to his court, and six hundred since he'd last taken one to his bed. There had been a time when meeting him and coming to see that he wasn't the monster they'd been told had been enough to vanquish their fear.

No more. He'd been a monster in the eyes of his consorts for so long, he was starting to believe they'd made it true after all.

Inconvenient, when his first glimpse of the princess had awoken raw longing in him. Ash had long since mastered his body and its vulnerabilities. Desire, hunger, craving—these were the lot of men, not monsters. But they would make him weak if he could not control them.

Harder to control were the urges of the dragon. To conquer. To possess. To protect. All three had roared within him with the strength of an inferno at the sight of Princess Sachielle kneeling before him in a shift so thin he could trace the lines of her body and see the way her flesh pebbled and her nipples tightened at the touch of the cool night breeze.

With the heat of battle still sizzling through his veins, there had been no thought in his head except to touch her. To wrap himself around her and soothe those shivers with the fire of his own body. To sweep her away from that courtyard full of watching eyes and bring her to his tower, where he could tear away that insufficient fabric and replace it with the blazing heat of his hands and mouth.

He wanted to taste the glow of her skin. He wanted to drown in it. He wanted *her*.

Turning away from her had required every scrap of his formidable self-control. He'd taken to the sky, trusting strong wings to carry him safely and swiftly away from her. It was either that or fall upon her in the cold stone courtyard and slake this madness in the sweetness of her body.

Hardly the welcome a princess deserved.

Down below, Elevia guided the party onto the final switchback. Soon they'd reach the top and the bridge that spanned the lake. He needed to be waiting, polished and composed, or his steward—the *real* monster of Dragon's Keep—would never let him hear the end of it.

Pivoting on one perfect, glossy boot, Ash jerked his head toward the door. "Come along, then. I assume you mean to join me for the official greeting."

"Of course. For moral support, you understand."

"Of course," he repeated dryly. Aleksi didn't even have the grace to look ashamed as they started down the tower stairs.

They heard the excited bustle of activity long before they reached the ground floor and stepped out into the courtyard. Somewhere far above them, the giant bell that rang to warn of raids or bad weather had begun the steady, easy chime that announced guests on the bridge.

"At least you're making all the necessary arrangements for the princess's arrival." Aleksi dodged two men rolling a wooden cart of food-stuffs toward the market square. "Brood all you please, but don't shirk your duties as lord and host." He paused. "Or consort."

Since *consort* was a word that raised too many painful memories, Ash sidestepped it. "I thought you'd guested here often enough to know who the real lord of this castle is."

"Oh, Camlia is harmless," Aleksi purred. "And you're changing the subject."

"How clever of you to notice," Ash bit out. "I never shirk my duties, Aleksi. You of all people know that."

"I do." Aleksi stopped suddenly, halting Ash as well with a hand on his elbow. "Which is why I'm asking—seriously, this time." His expression was somber, almost grave. "If you're not ready for this, say the word. I'll whisk the lovely Sachielle of House Roquebarre off to my Villa, and you'll not have to think of her again."

A kind offer, sincerely meant. The people of the Sheltered Lands had grown to view the terrifying Dragon with more fear than awe, but the Lover was still worshipped with unreserved fervor from the Midnight Forest to Siren's Bay, and from the Witchwood to his own home in the Lover's Lakes—helped along, no doubt, by the generations of storytellers, artists, and musicians who had made his Villa their home and Aleksi their muse.

No doubt Princess Sachielle would find the Lover's company far preferable to his. But when Ash tried to imagine releasing her to his friend's care . . .

No no no no no no.

Thick leather separated his feet from the packed earth of the outer bailey, but the air around him trembled in warning. The unlit torches that framed the doorway to the tower ignited in unison, and the entire keep rumbled in protest, provoking startled cries from those who had gathered for the official welcome. Ash reached and braced his hand against the wall, his fingers splayed wide.

The stone heated beneath his palm. Power raced through him, down through the earth to the magma that seethed at the heart of this dormant volcano he'd made his home. He touched the heart of the earth, the pulsing beat of their very world, and whispered soothing reassurances.

The world responded with fire.

It spilled over from the torches, a waterfall of light and heat that crawled down his arm and wreathed him in flames. He didn't jerk away—the kiss of fire could not harm him. It was as familiar as the blood that rushed through his veins.

So was the voice that throbbed through him, a voice he'd only ever heard in his Dreams. The whisper he'd first heard nearly three thousand years ago, when this castle had been newly raised and the mortal lords had staked their first claims on power.

A promise.

A prophecy.

The Dragon's consort will break the Builder's chains, and the people will dream again.

Flames tickled across his skin, up his arms, around his neck. They whispered over him, as teasing as a lover, their pledge heating his blood and reminding him of how it felt to hope.

How it felt to *crave*.

He met Aleksi's wide stare through the fire.

After a moment, the man rolled his eyes and snorted. "So that's a *no*, I take it? Fine. Keep your princess."

With effort, Ash lifted his hand from the wall. A brief thought extinguished the fire that wreathed him, though the flames on the torches continued to dance wildly. Eagerly. It had been centuries since the world had responded like this to the arrival of a consort, as if the very elements could barely contain their collective anticipation.

And she glowed.

"I do my duty." He shook away the lingering tingle in his fingertips. "And right now, my duty is to greet the princess with enough ceremony to please my tyrannical steward. You may assist in this effort, or you may go home and plan for our visit."

"Have it your way, you touchy bastard." Aleksi grinned and looped an arm around Ash's shoulders. "Come on, then."

They started toward the wide gate, in charity with one another. But with every step, Ash swore he could feel the ground beneath his feet pushing back against his boots, urging him to hurry his pace.

Maybe, after centuries upon centuries of waiting, the Everlasting Dream was about to keep the first promise it had ever whispered to him.

The Dragon's consort will break the Builder's chains, and the people will dream.

And you will never be alone again.

Chapter Four
BETRAYER'S MOON

Week Five, Day Nine
Year 2999

As the sun blazed overhead, Sachi stared at Dragon's Keep.

It was an imposing structure, more because of its surroundings than its construction. It sat on a small island in the middle of a lake. The water bubbled and steamed, because the mountain wasn't a mountain at all but a volcano that had erupted and then collapsed into a deep, sheltered caldera.

A long causeway stretched before her, wide enough for perhaps a dozen people to walk abreast. It was the only thing connecting the keep to the outside world, this strip of black-flecked gray stone.

The blasted man intended to make her work for a proper greeting, that much was clear.

She had risen before dawn, while both moons still hung in the darkened sky, to prepare for the interminable trip up the mountain's many winding switchbacks. Her ass was still numb from sitting so long in the saddle without a break, and it was only through sheer iron will that she managed not to fidget as she waited.

And waited.

And *waited.*

Elevia cleared her throat. "It's tradition. He is meant to meet you halfway across the bridge, then you'll return to the gates as one."

"How charming." Sachi kept her voice light, though her hands shook—not with fear, but with indignation. It wasn't enough that she had to journey upriver, then crawl up the precarious side of the mountain, she also had to walk across this vast expanse to complete her subjugation.

Behind her and slightly to her left, Zanya moved. She eased closer, the back of her hand brushing Sachi's elbow in a soothing gesture.

At the other end of the endless causeway, the wide iron gates of the keep began to swing open.

Sachi took one step forward, then another.

The Dragon appeared, flanked by two figures. At this distance, Sachi couldn't see any of them clearly, but she recognized the way the lord of the keep moved. With purpose *and* dread, as if duty alone pulled him toward her.

She bit her tongue to keep a rueful smile from curving her lips. She understood purpose, and she understood dread. They had these things, at least, in common. Perhaps that would be enough.

More figures spilled out of the vast castle, trailing in their lord's wake until the path to the keep was lined with warriors in stark leather battle harnesses and servants dressed in trousers and tunics and skirts made of fabrics that seemed to capture all the colors of flames in movement.

As the Dragon stalked closer, she could see the colors repeated in the silk shirt beneath his black tunic. The cut emphasized the sheer power of his frame, his wide shoulders and broad chest and arms that strained the seams of his shirt as he moved.

He had seemed more comfortable the night before, clad in battle-worn, bloodstained armor. Had he chosen this finery for her benefit, or had an exasperated attendant pressed the issue?

The latter. *Definitely* the latter.

He kept pace with her approach, but his long strides devoured the stone path. She was still only a third of the way across when he and his entourage stopped precisely at the halfway point.

And then he just *watched her.*

It was everything she hated about the pomp and ritual of formal events. Actions without reason—or, even worse, things that went fully against sense. There was no point in him stopping where he did simply to stare at her just because her legs were shorter than his.

Her temper sparked again, burning away the worst of her agitation. She took shallow, regimented breaths—an old, familiar habit that allowed her to slowly release all emotion, clearing her mind.

The pleasant, vague blankness lasted until she stood in front of him. Irritation flared again, along with something even more primal—awareness. Both emotions prickled up the back of her neck, and she let them, welcoming the heat they brought to her cheeks. It would be a pretty blush, the kind that men enjoyed seeing.

And she was right. Whatever else the Dragon was, he *was* a man. His gaze drifted over her face, lingering on her lips before sweeping down her body in an almost tangible caress. He took his time working his way back up to her face, his appraisal so frank that behind her, Zanya inhaled in sharp indignation.

"Princess Sachielle of House Roquebarre." His voice was a low rumble, like the first crash of thunder on a hot summer night. "Have you come to fulfill your family's promise?"

"I have come to offer myself as consort, my lord." She bent her head as she dropped into a curtsy. "If you will have me."

His silence stretched on just long enough to spark unease in her gut before he replied in that same deep, dangerous voice. "I will have you."

Next, he would offer his arm. She would take it, then use the opportunity to find out what sorts of innocent touches made him think not-so-innocent thoughts. Before they reached the gates of the keep, Sachi would know if he desired a consort with sharp, knowing appetites or one whose naive obliviousness would require more dedicated instruction.

Except . . . he didn't. He stood there, glancing at her and then away, over and over, as if he was . . .

Nervous. Interesting. She'd expected as much the night before—she'd practically been naked before him, her nipples taut from the cold and clearly visible through her gown. Even the most self-assured of men tended to get a little anxious under those circumstances, whether from apprehension or anticipation.

But this was something different altogether.

The man on his left smiled, and Sachi's breath caught. It was a brilliant smile, the kind that poets and artists essayed in vain to capture, and when he turned the full force of it on her, she could only marvel that she hadn't quite noticed him before. He was perfection, both in feature and in expression, a creature so lovely she knew exactly who he was even before he opened his lush mouth in introduction.

"Aleksi," he murmured, holding one hand out to receive hers. "I am at your service, Princess Sachielle."

The Lover, without a doubt. "Likewise. But please—call me Sachi."

"Sachi." He echoed her name with a pleased grin that almost disguised the sharp, prodding look he sent his companion.

The Dragon's flinch was barely perceptible, and he seemed to steel himself before offering his arm. Sachi accepted, sliding her arm through the firm cradle of his. Hard muscle rippled beneath his tunic, and she bit her lip as they turned back toward the gate of the keep.

He didn't speak. Neither did she.

Aleksi was the one who broke the blaring silence. "How was your journey up the mountain?"

Caught off guard by the Dragon's taciturn welcome, Sachi answered honestly. "Long and exhausting."

Another awkward silence. This time it was the woman who had accompanied the Dragon who spoke, an older woman with steel-gray hair and a massive ring of keys jingling at her belt. "Your rooms have been prepared, Your Highness. There will be time for you to rest and recover in comfort before the feast."

"Thank you. I'm sure it will be fine." The rigid arm locked with Sachi's was growing hot. *Very* hot, as if the Dragon was only moments from bursting into flame. She would have to select her next words strategically, decide whether to retreat or strike.

She chose to strike. "I have to say, my lord, I thought you might come down and fly me up."

He stared straight ahead, but she felt the flex of muscle beneath her fingertips. "Did you?"

"My apologies. I thought your visit last night was meant to demonstrate your abilities." Flames licked at the silken cloth beneath her fingers, so Sachi affected innocence, complete with wide eyes and a breathy voice. "Is it considered bad form to ride a dragon?"

Aleksi snorted. Behind them, Elevia choked on a laugh.

The Dragon stopped abruptly and turned with lethal grace. A mere handspan separated their bodies, and the *size* of him struck her as she found herself staring at his broad chest. Strong fingers kissed by very real flames gripped her chin, forcing her head back until her eyes met his.

"It is considered bad form to *taunt* a dragon," he rumbled.

Have you been alone so long you can't tell a taunt from a promise? It was the right thing to say, the next move in this game they were playing . . . but not in front of her entourage or his. They were quiet words, intimate ones, meant for wine and firelight and all the things that came after.

So she told him the truth instead. "I am not afraid of you."

"That's what they all say . . . in the beginning." His thumb slid along her jaw and grazed her throat, leaving a trail of shivering heat in its wake. "Don't spend your courage too recklessly, Princess. You may find you need it when you are locked in the Dragon's tower, bound to him by magic."

"We shall see," she whispered.

His thumb came to rest over her pounding pulse. Without looking away, he raised his voice. "Camlia?"

The older woman stepped forward. "Yes, my lord?"

"See the princess and her people settled. Give them anything they need."

"At once."

He stepped back, still wreathed in fire. Then the flickers of flame *ignited*, and the Dragon unfurled his wings and shot up out of the inferno, straight into the sky.

So much for tradition.

"Well," Aleksi breathed. "That was devious, love."

Sachi blinked innocently up at him. "I don't know what you mean."

His lips twisted with wry amusement. "Of course not."

"Enough out of you, troublemaker." Camlia stepped forward and offered a precise bow. "Princess Sachielle. I'm the steward of Dragon's Keep. If you will follow me?"

Sachi did, staring at the woman's stiff, straight back as she led the group of attendants through the open gates of the keep, leaving the other gods behind.

Inside the massive stone walls, a veritable village stretched out before her. Sachi had expected an influx of pilgrims, of course, people who would travel many days, as she had, in order to witness this momentous event. The Dragon took a royal consort only once every one hundred years; stories of attending these events tended to filter down through generations, shared with awe and pride in equal measure.

33

But this bustle seemed . . . customary. Permanent. Some of it was to be expected, and necessary to the smooth functioning of a remote castle. A smithy sat off to her right, near the stables. A long building that likely served as a soldiers' barracks lay to her left. But at the center of the keep, surrounding a large stone well, stood a number of small shops, their vendors busily selling foods and soaps and crafted goods.

Everyone stopped and bowed their heads as Sachi walked past.

The castle proper stretched up behind all this, as imposing but unembellished as the well. It was smaller than Castle Roquebarre and composed of weathered gray stone. Two identical towers rose from the structure, one on each side, connected by a stone walkway near their pinnacles. The height of it was such that it made Sachi dizzy just to contemplate walking across it. The unsupported stone bridge flared to a wide oval in the center, but she couldn't see what occupied the space.

She hoped it was a garden, then caught herself. After the feast and the bonding, she and the Dragon would be leaving this place on a weekslong traditional progress that would take them to all the major seats of his court.

And she, at least, would never return.

The steward continued her brisk march toward the castle's huge doors. They were also plain, though heavy and reinforced with iron strips and rivets, and whisper-quiet as two attendants hauled them open.

"Welcome home," Camlia told her as she gestured Sachi inside.

The main hall was bright, with plenty of light streaming through the windows. It had been decorated in shades of blue—the royal standards, along with Sachi's lighter personal blue—as well as the deep reds the Dragon seemed to favor. The effect was surprisingly festive.

Sachi smiled. "The castle is lovely."

Camlia merely nodded, though a pleased smile teased at the corners of her mouth. "The Ravens await, Your Highness."

"Ravens?"

"The Dragon's personal guard. Now *your* personal guard as well."

Zanya tensed. Sachi wasn't looking at her, but she could *feel* the emotions, fear and protectiveness and frustration mingling until they threatened to overwhelm her.

So Sachi smiled, taking care to keep her expression serene and mild. "I look forward to meeting them."

As they turned and headed down a corridor, Sachi caught movement out of the corner of her eye. She turned just in time to see a statue of an armored knight slowly lower itself to one knee. A little way down the hall, a roaring lion settled down on its belly and gazed up at them.

Some of the attendants who had accompanied Sachi from the capital gasped. She turned to calm them, but her gaze locked with Zanya's. She wasn't shocked, not like the others, but the borrowed discomfort twisting in Sachi's gut intensified.

Camlia clapped her hands and spoke before Sachi could manage. "Off with you. My assistant will give you a tour of the castle and its grounds. He'll also show you to the attendants' lodgings."

Most of the nobles' young daughters who had traveled from the capital were only too happy to flee the display of magic before them. Only Zanya lingered, and even that she managed to disguise as a wish to have her mistress's explicit dismissal.

But Sachi could read the real question in her eyes. *Will you be all right on your own?*

"You may go," she murmured. "And be sure to pay attention."

Wordlessly, Zanya curtsied, then followed the others.

That left Sachi alone with Camlia and Naia, the new godling. Naia had already wandered farther down the hall and was gazing in wonder at an exquisite carving of a wood nymph. She drew in a sharp breath and held out her hand, then released it on a laugh when the stone nymph did the same.

Then she turned those dark, joyous eyes on Sachi. "The castle knows you've arrived. It *feels* you."

The nymph tilted her head and extended her other hand to Sachi. In it lay a delicate bloom whose stone petals rippled as if stirred by a breeze.

Camlia cleared her throat. "An offering, my lady."

Sachi closed her fingers around the flower, which came away easily in her hand. "Thank you."

The nymph resumed her original pose and fell still.

"This way," Camlia urged.

At the end of the hall, they stepped out into an open courtyard that stretched between the two towers. As Sachi raised her face to the slanting afternoon light, she caught sight of an unkindness of ravens swooping across the sky like a slash of black ink. The birds landed on the stone and, in a flash of magic so swift she barely saw it, coalesced into five people.

The Raven Guard.

In unison, they knelt before her.

Camlia gestured to the first in line, a lovely brunette dressed in rough leather and fur. "This is Malindra."

The woman bowed her head, and Sachi spotted two short swords strapped to her back. "My lady."

Camlia continued. "Kardox."

The man in question had a rough, scarred face. But when he lifted his eyes to meet hers, they were the clearest, truest green Sachi had ever seen.

"And the twins, Remi and Isolde."

Remi was a giant bear of a man, so huge that even though he knelt at her feet, Sachi barely had to look down at him. He wore a grave expression—and two small axes, designed to be suitable either for swinging or throwing.

His sister, on the other hand, smiled up at Sachi, her gray eyes twinkling. Isolde was beautiful, with lush brown hair and fine features. She carried only one axe, a large, double-headed monstrosity etched with runes Sachi vaguely recognized as belonging to one of the tribes of the South Sea.

"It is an honor, my lady," Isolde purred.

Camlia stopped in front of the last kneeling figure, a tiny, delicate-looking blonde dressed in silver mail. "And this is Ambrial. Though all of the Raven Guard are yours to command, Ambrial traditionally serves as the consort's personal guard."

Ambrial slowly drew her sword, a lovely blade of folded steel, and held it, tip down, in front of Sachi. "I am at your service, my lady."

The Guard rose, again in unison, their stiff postures relaxing just a little.

"The Raven Guard is responsible for securing your tower and your safety, Princess Sachielle," Camlia informed her. "When you travel outside the castle, such as for the bonding ceremony, they will accompany you. And they will guard you with their very souls."

Guard her . . . or watch her? "I thank them for their vigilance."

"For now, Isolde will show Naia to her quarters in your tower. The rest will remain here while I show you to yours."

Camlia turned and marched into the tower, leaving Sachi scrambling to catch up without sacrificing her dignity with a jog.

They climbed flight after flight of stairs, with Camlia pointing out which floor held which chambers and offices. After the first few, Sachi smiled and nodded but didn't bother to heed the words. She didn't actually need to know, and her head was starting to throb.

Finally, at the top floor, Camlia threw open a door and waved Sachi through into a spacious room. A fireplace blazed merrily. The walls were hung with tapestries in the same reds and blues that had graced the hall. Through one open door, Sachi spied a large bed. Through another, a bath and dressing area.

A set of double doors stood open to the balcony. Outside, she could see the stone bridge that connected her tower to the other identical one.

"The Dragon's tower," Camlia offered, casting a sidelong look at her as if to judge her reaction.

"Ah." So the bridge connecting it directly to hers was there to facilitate visitation. "I see. Is there anything else I should know?"

Camlia gestured to the door that led out to her balcony. "The outside stairs here lead down to the consort's gardens. Several past consorts have had a particular interest in gardening, so they're quite lovely. Even in winter." Camlia gave her another of those quietly assessing looks. "Do you enjoy gardening?"

"I do, very much." Sachi appreciated when she could give honest, forthright answers. They were easier than careful lies. "I've always wished I had more time for it."

"Once the bonding ritual and the progress are over, your time will be much your own." The older woman tilted her head. "There are traditional duties, of course, but the Dragon prefers that his consorts pursue their own interests."

Now that they were alone, Camlia seemed torn between rabid curiosity and equally rabid maternal protectiveness. It should have been laughable, a middle-aged human zealously guarding the well-being of an ancient god.

Instead, it made Sachi's chest ache with envy.

She unfastened her cloak and draped it over a chair. "Is there anything I should do to prepare, either for the feast or the bonding?"

"It's all taken care of," the steward assured her. "Your trip up the mountain was long. Tonight you'll have dinner in your rooms, with time to settle in before the welcome feast tomorrow night. And then . . ." She hesitated. "How much do you know about the bonding?"

"I've read the scrolls."

The tight set of her lips made it clear exactly how little she trusted anything Sachi might have learned in the capital. "It's a simple enough ceremony. The senior priest will bind your blood to the land, and then bind your heart to the Dragon. Everyone who still holds faith with the

Dragon has been traveling for weeks already. They will celebrate your union and the renewal of the vows made between the mortal kings and the High Court."

It was a lot of words that meant nothing of substance, in their own way no more honest or illuminating than the writings in the archives back at Castle Roquebarre. "Thank you. Before you go, if I may?"

"I am here to answer any questions you have. In fact, my quarters and office are at the base of your tower, both available to you at any hour."

I won't be here to avail myself of your services. Their progress through the lands would last for weeks, and at the end of it . . .

Well, by then, Sachi would either be reviled at Dragon's Keep, branded a murderer, or she'd be dead. Either way, none of this would matter in the slightest.

"My question is of a personal nature," she said instead. "I would like to present my intended with a gift commemorating the occasion of our bonding. I figure you know better than anyone what he might like."

One elegant eyebrow swooped upward. "The Dragon is a man of . . . simple tastes. If you want to give him a gift, give him yourself."

Would that I could, but he keeps fleeing my presence. Sachi still held the stone flower, her offering from the nymph downstairs. She gripped it tightly, so tightly the carved edges bit into her flesh.

Likewise, Sachi bit the inside of her cheek. "That's very helpful," she lied. "Thank you."

Camlia nodded. "I'll show your handmaid where to unpack your things and arrange for the evening meal to be served in your sitting room. Will your attendants dine with you?"

"No. I'd like to be alone, thank you." She'd speak to Zanya later, when it was safe. "This is a night for quiet reflection, I think."

"As you will." The steward strode toward the door but stopped in the doorway with a gentle smile. "If it's quiet reflection you're after, I do recommend your gardens. Now that you are in residence, only the gardeners have access, and only with your permission. I think you will find the grounds peaceful."

"I'll bear that in mind."

The woman slipped through the door, leaving Sachi alone in the sky.

She waited until the quick, efficient steps faded down the stone stairs, then hurried to the spot near the door where her trunks had been neatly stacked. She hauled the smallest one from the top of the pile and lugged it to the closest surface, a plush chair situated near the fireplace.

She opened it with shaking fingers and flipped up the lid so hastily she almost upset the entire thing. Then she dug through carefully packed layers of silks and satins until she found it.

The case.

It was a small chest, solidly constructed of dark, polished wood. Its lid had been decorated with carved flowers, the loops and whorls inlaid with iridescent nacre. Deceptively simple in its construction . . . save for the fact that it had no latch, just a flat gold seal.

These sorts of chests were popular in the capital. Locked with magical keys, they were used to store everything from love letters to secrets to blackmail material. Sachi had locked this one herself, drawing on every bit of her connection to the Dream to call the magic and give it form. It could only be opened with a kiss from someone who truly loved her—which effectively rendered it inaccessible to anyone who wasn't her or Zanya.

But Sachi's sealed chest didn't hold secrets or love letters.

It held her doom.

She raised the chest and pressed her dry lips to the seal. It yielded with a click, and she lifted the lid. In it, nestled on a bed of black silk, lay an hourglass. It was exquisitely crafted in the shape of two silver dragons wrapped around twin globes of glass. Inside, a blood-red grain of sand dropped into the lower globe, as if the contraption was standing upright instead of lying in a box.

It always did that, Sachi had discovered, even if you held it upside down. Because the sand had been given a purpose just as bloody as its color: to remind her of the curse flowing through her veins. To count down to her demise.

It was a deft bit of strategy on Nikkon's part. They couldn't simply send Sachi and Zanya off with orders to kill a god. What if the job proved too difficult, or their wills flagged due to cowardice? What if they simply decided they *didn't want to do* King Dalvish II's dirty work?

No. If she and Zanya failed to kill the Dragon by the time the last grain fell, the curse in Sachi's blood would explode, not only killing her, but sundering her soul from the Everlasting Dream. She would cease to exist, erased from the cosmos as surely as if she'd never been born.

The king's high priest had an unseemly flair for the dramatic.

Sachi shoved it back into the chest, shut the lid with a sharp snap, and left it on a small table. She didn't care to look at it, but Zanya insisted on checking it periodically. She would glare at the offending sand, as if the intensity of her gaze alone was enough to reverse its flow.

If only, my love.

Sachi put it out of her mind as she walked back to the window, absently stroking the stone petals of her gifted rose. She had to focus on the reason she was here.

She had to focus on the Dragon.

Chapter Five
BETRAYER'S MOON

Week Five, Day Nine
Year 2999

Dragon's Keep *ached* with magic.

Zanya had barely drawn a full breath from the moment those imposing gates had swung wide. The massive walls of the castle pressed down on her even as the floor beneath her feet vibrated with the soft reminder of power.

It was everywhere. In the stone, in the air. In the people who moved so casually through these halls, as if years of existing in proximity to the High Court had soaked them in reflected magic.

Perhaps it had. Some legends claimed the entire keep was trapped under a timeless curse, its inhabitants bound to serve at the Dragon's whim for all their endless lives. Others claimed he consumed the souls of those he lured here, fueling his own power with their very essences.

Zanya wasn't sure which would be worse. Forbidden by a curse to return to the Everlasting Dream? No rest or renewal for your soul?

No chance to be born again? Cut off from the gentle rhythms of their world. Cast out. Alone.

But alive. A soul that had been consumed couldn't return anywhere. They were simply gone. Forever.

Bright spots of pain shivered over Zanya's skin. She glanced down and found her fingers curled tightly around one of Sachi's tiaras. The gleaming silver had bent under the force of her grip. The sharp points had cut into her fingers, and when she opened her fist, blood glistened on the diamonds.

To the Void with it all.

Hastily, she wiped her fingers clean on her skirts and lifted the fabric to wipe off the jewels. The mangled silver was another matter. She gripped the delicate edge, and the metal bent for her like warm taffy. With her strength, it would be easy to snap it off entirely. Instead, she did her best to gently pull it back into some semblance of its original shape. The results would suffice from a distance, but they would not hold up to close scrutiny. She was no jeweler, meant for elegant work.

Sachi was the one with the delicate touch. Zanya was a blunt weapon. Too strong, too hard. Thoughtless, even, when her temper got the better of her.

Hard to hurt.

She set the slightly misshapen tiara on its velvet stand and checked her fingers. The wounds had already closed, leaving behind only faint smears of blood. She scrubbed those away with her skirt, relieved that she'd worn her usual black.

It was always good for hiding blood.

Zanya made swift work of unpacking the rest of the jewelry. She nestled earrings that dripped with sparkling crystal next to necklaces of delicate hammered silver that framed twinkling sapphires and perfect emeralds. A dizzying display of wealth and skill, and yet when Zanya rose and stepped back, the shelves designed to display the consort's jewelry were not even a third full.

Previous consorts must have come to this castle positively weighed down with the wealth of the mortal kings. Was that where the legends of the Dragon brooding high on his mountain over a secret cache of treasure came from? Had the succession of consorts been little more than human bribes carrying gold and jewels to stave off a monster's wrath?

If so, the great Lord of House Roquebarre had been stingy with his bribery this time. Zanya supposed he didn't want to risk any more of his own wealth than he had to if Zanya and Sachielle failed.

With the last of Sachi's belongings tucked away, Zanya slipped through the door at the back of the dressing room. A narrow, claustrophobic staircase led down a floor to her rooms, which were surprisingly well-appointed for those of a handmaid.

Fully half of this level of the tower was devoted to her chambers. She had a comfortable bedroom, a private bathroom with hot water running from a tap straight into a tub deep enough to soak her whole body, a cozy sitting room with a fireplace, and even a tiny office from which Zanya imagined she was supposed to handle the day-to-day minutiae of keeping a princess groomed and clothed and effortlessly elegant.

The rest of this floor held smaller rooms for Sachi's other attendants, as well as a hearth where they could keep her meals warm or mix teas and mull wine. Below that was a gracefully appointed private sitting room and library, and beneath that an even more elaborate public receiving room. Then there was a floor the steward's assistant had claimed was devoted to storage. Zanya fully intended to break into it tonight, just to be sure. Then, finally, the ground floor held the quarters and offices of the steward herself.

Camlia was a formidable woman, but not a threat. Not when she'd looked at Sachi and seen nothing more than that gentle fragility she wore like spun-glass armor. She'd watched the soon-to-be consort as if she might collapse into hysterics at any moment. Zanya knew better.

The courage contained in that delicate frame kept Zanya awake at night sometimes.

It was her job to keep Sachi safe. But how could you protect someone who would so willingly walk right into a monster's clutches?

An impossible task on the surface, but Zanya had endured a brutal education in accomplishing the impossible. So she stretched out on her too-comfortable bed and let the soft slide of the too-fine silken sheets lure her toward sleep. Stealing a bit of rest now would leave her alert and ready to prowl the castle tonight.

Sachi, apparently, had other ideas.

It felt as if Zanya had only just closed her eyes when she jerked awake to the sensation of falling. When her eyes flew open, she wasn't sprawled on her bed, but in a cave. In *the* cave, the secluded one on the seashore just outside the capital, where she and Sachi used to sneak away to meet.

It looked the same—colorful paper lanterns and furs that Sachi had smuggled out of the palace, with the high tide blocking the entrance and lapping against the borders of their sanctuary.

"*Finally.*" Sachi surged out of the shadows and grasped Zanya's shoulders. "I thought you'd never go to sleep."

Zanya exhaled slowly and let her arms steal around Sachi. Even here, in the dreamworld Sachi controlled, it felt forbidden and furtive. For more than a decade, Zanya had made do with the constrained intimacies allowed between a princess and her handmaid. The moments they snatched, alone in their retreat, were laced with the fear of discovery. With the agony of knowing their time together would be brief.

This was the only place where it felt safe to simply *hold* her. So Zanya did, cradling Sachi to her chest and burying her face in that sunshine hair that somehow smelled of Witchwood roses even in a dream. "Are you all right?"

"Of course I am." Sachi pulled back and studied Zanya's face. "Everyone was kind to you?"

Concern furrowed her brow. Sachi had always hated that their respective positions made her a princess while Zanya was relegated to the role of servant. But Zanya wouldn't trade places with her for every jewel in the Dragon's hoard. "They're kinder than I would wish. Everyone is curious about us, and overly friendly. There will be eyes watching us at all times."

"I know. That's why I brought you here. It's the only place we can speak freely."

Or so they hoped. No one truly understood the powers of the Dreamers. For all they knew, the Dragon could invade this space at any moment. Rationally, they should confer as swiftly as possible and minimize the risk.

But Zanya could rarely hold on to strategic pragmatism when Sachi gazed up at her with those big, warm eyes. Zanya stroked a gentle finger over that crinkle between Sachi's eyebrows, smoothing it away. Sensation was a funny thing in dreams. The warmth of Sachi's skin shivered over her, almost as if she could sense the pleasure Sachi felt at her touch.

A dangerous temptation. Zanya forced her drifting thoughts back to the point. "I plan to explore the castle tonight. But I don't imagine our best opportunity will be here. The steward's assistant said that only a limited guard will accompany us on this progress."

"Then take care and stay in," Sachi urged. "I know we don't have much time, but we must exercise caution. So far, almost everything is going according to plan. We need to keep it that way."

Zanya couldn't help the eyebrow that swept up. *She* didn't mind the fact that the Dragon refused to spend more than the span of a brief greeting in her lover's company, but Sachi had seemed bothered by it last night. "We still don't agree about the plan," Zanya warned her. "I don't want you trying anything."

"And I'm not having this conversation again," Sachi retorted. "The plan is sound. I've studied all the consorts' letters, Zanya. All the diaries.

He's a monster, but a romantic one. He *wants* to believe. All I have to do is let him."

"The consorts all ended up dead," Zanya said flatly. When Sachi started to shake her head, Zanya gripped her chin. "*Dead*, Sachielle. Whatever twisted definition of romance he lives by, no one in a millennium has survived it. He is not some hapless man at court that you can wrap around your little finger by flashing your dimples. He's a god who slaughters armies."

"And yet, his hands also tremble when he grabs my chin to admonish me. Just like yours." Sachi wrapped her fingers around Zanya's wrist. "You have to trust me, love. I know what I'm doing."

Trust wasn't the problem. Zanya trusted Sachi with her own life. She'd trust Sachi with *anyone's* life, from the closest friend to a chance-met stranger. Even with the life of a terrifying monster.

The only life Zanya couldn't trust Sachi to protect was her own.

She rubbed her thumb along the delicate curve of Sachi's jaw and shaped love and truth into a weapon. "I know you were trained for this. But if something happens to you—"

"You will carry on," Sachi retorted firmly.

Zanya's laugh felt like broken glass in her throat. "You don't usually lie to yourself."

"It isn't belief, it's an order," Sachi whispered. "From your ruler."

Zanya bit back the retort bubbling up in her. Sachi might have been the acknowledged heir of House Roquebarre, but Zanya had never had any use for the mortal king and his vaunted lineage. She respected power to the precise degree it had the ability to hurt her, and not one scrap further.

And that was why she backed down. It didn't matter if Sachi ruled as the princess and consort to the Dragon, or over nothing more substantial than a leaky hut in the woods. She held Zanya's heart in her hands, and had for as long as either could remember.

"I will carry on," she promised, knowing it for a lie. In a world without Sachi, there would be nothing left for her but vengeance and blood. "I would prefer it if I did not have to, however."

Sachi laughed softly, the sound torn between rue and genuine mirth. "Then let me do my job. It shouldn't take long. He is not indifferent to me."

"Why does that not comfort me?" Zanya pulled away and turned, her agitation necessitating the relief of movement. But their dream cave was the same size as the real one, and no more than five paces brought her to the far side. Not nearly enough space to pace out her anxiety. "I don't like it, Sachi. They're *powerful*."

"Of course they are. They're *gods*, Zan."

So the priests often claimed. But the idea of them had always been distant and blurry. It wasn't as if she hadn't faced monsters before. But being here, *seeing* them? "There's knowing, and there's *knowing*. I'm not sure I'm strong enough."

Sachi's arms slid around her midsection, and she pressed her cheek to Zanya's shoulder. "All the more reason for you to trust me. This is the fight *I* trained for."

A training ground Zanya could hardly imagine. Her own brutal schooling in violence and death seemed like a blessing compared to whatever Sachi must have gone through. How did you train a girl to lure a god into her bed? The possibilities had haunted Zanya's nightmares—and Sachi would never tell her.

Shuddering, she slid her hand over Sachi's. "I hate that I can't do it for you. You shouldn't have to . . ." The words wouldn't come. She simply could not form them.

"But I must, and so I will." Another laugh, this one full of awareness. "Don't fret, my love. Unless my betrothed is possessed of some truly terrifying inclinations, I shall manage just fine."

A different sort of unease twisted through Zanya. Not jealousy—that could not exist between them while their fates were not their own.

No, *dread* was what raised the hair at the back of her neck. "You find him attractive."

Sachi pulled back in surprise. "Do you not?"

Zanya tried to conjure the Dragon in her mind. Memory provided the details all too readily. Tall enough to be intimidating, but with a corresponding bulk that would slow him down. She'd fought plenty like him, all muscle and brash arrogance, so sure of their physical dominance and inevitably easier to defeat because of it.

He'd worn battered armor that first night—armor in the ancient style, the kind that bared muscular arms and thighs. She could visualize the long scar on his left arm. His sword arm, most likely, as he'd worn his blade on the right. It might slow him in a fight.

If the Dragon fought his true battles with silly things like swords.

Sachi sighed, as if she'd heard every thought. "Next time, try to look at him with the eyes of a potential lover instead of an opponent, and you'll see."

No, Sachi. One of us has to remember why we're here.

She bit back the words. Sachi didn't need the reminder. She had more at stake than anyone in this terrible game, and that was the source of Zanya's mounting dread. It was hard enough to imagine Sachi killing the man in cold blood even if she hated him.

But if she began to *care* for him?

"It's a dangerous game," Zanya whispered. "Don't let yourself get caught up in it."

"I have to. Don't you see?" Sachi turned her by her shoulders and smiled up at her, sad and soft. "The less I'm obliged to lie, the better. Because we don't have much time."

Zanya could feel the drip of it in her bones, like that elaborate water clock the king had commissioned. Outside the castle where her sleeping body lay, only stars lit the endless night. Both moons would rise just before dawn, mere slivers in the sky for the final day of the Betrayer's

Moon. The last day of the year. The last day before the countdown truly began.

Fifty days in the Dragon's Moon. They had fifty days to figure out how to kill him, or else . . .

"No." Zanya framed Sachi's face with her hands. "We *will* find a way. You will, or I will. But this Dragon's Moon will not be your last, I promise you that. And if you don't think I'd chase you into the Everlasting Dream or the Endless Void itself if you tried to leave me . . ."

"Never." Sachi whispered the word against Zanya's lips with the fervency of a prayer . . . or a vow. "I will never leave you."

It was reckless, and Zanya didn't care. She stole a kiss. Here, in a dream, where she could pretend it was only that. Sachi's lips parted, so sweet and giving, overlapping with memory. Zanya tasted the salt of seawater and tears. Her fingers trembled with the need to *hurry, hurry, hurry*, because their stolen moments had always been just that. A theft from the people who thought to own them. Too brief, too dangerous. Passion shrouded in danger.

But the threat of discovery had never dimmed the joy she felt when Sachi gasped against her lips. Or the hot anticipation of sliding her hands down until silk gave way to skin, and she could stroke those gasps into throaty groans.

The sea roared around them, and Zanya fell back. The bed beneath her wasn't the lush one from Dragon's Keep, nor was it her simple cot from the training barracks, nor even the pile of furs in their shared cave. This expanse was endless, with black sheets that gleamed in the candlelight. A perfect setting for Sachi's golden beauty, a private place.

"I promise I'll stay away from him," Sachi whispered, and Zanya knew she'd fallen into a more mundane dream, the kind that promised her things that could never be. And she still let it sweep her away.

She tumbled Sachi onto sheets improbably strewn with Witchwood roses the same shade of pink as her lips. "I'll protect you," she vowed between kisses, reveling in every cry. She rolled over, pulling Sachi atop her, and all that golden hair tumbled around them like a cloud as Sachi reached down to touch her lips.

"I'll miss you."

Ice slashed through her. She reached for Sachi, but the darkness grew claws that dug into her, jerking her from Zanya's grip. In a heartbeat, she was gone, lost to a swirling nothingness as vast as the Endless Void. Zanya lunged from the silken sheets only to come face to face with a small wooden table illuminated by an impossible beam of light.

That damned hourglass sat on it, silver dragons curled around glass globes, red sand falling one steady grain at a time. Zanya reached for it, but when her fingers brushed the edge, the sand began to fall faster. A river of red as bright as blood streamed into the lower glass, and even when Zanya snatched up the hourglass and tilted it upside down, the sand continued to rush upward into the lower glass, defying reason and natural law.

Screaming, she flung the hourglass at the floor. It shattered, and the sand turned to blood—a river, an *ocean* of blood—and Sachi floated past, face pale, dead eyes staring up into nothingness . . .

In her dark bedroom in Dragon's Keep, Zanya shot upright in bed, a scream trapped in her throat.

Fifty days weren't enough, but somehow, she would find a way to slay the Dragon.

She *had* to.

Chapter Six
BETRAYER'S MOON

Week Five, Day Ten
Year 2999

The feast meant to welcome Sachi to her new home at Dragon's Keep was an odd affair. It was more formal than the dinner at Blade's Rest, with careful seating arrangements, marked by quiet conversations rather than boisterous laughter. The food, on the other hand, was far simpler, consisting of rustic dishes like roasted game, stews, and hearth-baked breads.

It made her wonder about the man sitting stiffly beside her. Would he have preferred a quieter, more private dinner? Perhaps he didn't do well in crowds, and that accounted for his awkward—and quite literal—flight during each of their meetings thus far. It might have less to do with her provoking his nerves and more with general shyness.

She leaned closer. Her gown, a blue brocade studded with silk embroidery and beadwork, was cut in a deep vee that clung to her skin while baring her nearly to the waist. The Dragon glanced over, his gaze lingering on the curves of her breasts. He swallowed hard, his throat working as he averted his eyes once again.

She certainly provoked something in him. Sachi found herself flattered by it, this obviously grudging attention he couldn't seem to stop himself from bestowing.

"Do I make you nervous?" she asked softly.

"Yes," he answered without hesitation. He drained his goblet, but no servant leapt forward to refill it. Instead, he lifted the fine crystal pitcher of wine with one large hand and did it himself. "Do *I* make *you* nervous?"

"No." He evoked a tangle of emotions, from sadness to lust, anticipation to exhilaration, but the pulse fluttering wildly at the base of her throat had little to do with nerves. "But saying so hardly means you'll believe me. Words are just words, after all."

"Words are just words," he agreed. He raised his goblet but did not take another sip. "How do you find your quarters? Are they satisfactory?"

"They are as beautiful as they are empty."

"Empty? What do you mean?"

Sachi sipped her wine and met his gaze. "I'm to occupy them alone, am I not?"

His lips twitched—the first sign of humor she'd seen from him. "That is what makes them your quarters."

"Is it?" She smiled over the rim of her goblet. "In that case, I don't like them at all."

"Am I to take from this that you'd prefer to inspect mine?"

She reached for the carafe of wine, stopping to brush her fingers over his as she did. "Is that an offer, or merely a vague possibility?"

His entire body tensed, flaring with heat. She could feel the flames already, delicious magic dancing just beneath the surface of his skin, eager to break free and scorch everything in its path.

An answering magic, something that could easily be called a *hunger*, sparked within her, and she drew in a sharp, trembling breath. It dragged his eyes back to the skin bared by her plunging neckline, and this time his gaze felt like a shivering caress.

"By this time tomorrow, you will be my consort," he said finally, gently setting her hand back on the table. Then he lifted the wine and refilled her goblet. "My quarters will be open to you at your convenience."

"I won't be barred from them, perhaps. But I'd much rather be enthusiastically invited."

"Mmm." He settled back in his chair, every bit the king at ease for all that he did not sit a throne. "Perhaps it is time we had this discussion, then. What did they tell you about what will happen tomorrow?"

The bonding was a complex magical ritual that not only linked the Dragon with his consort, but also linked the fortunes of the royal family—and the land—to those of the Dragon. There was a level of empathic exchange involved in the process, though none of Sachi's trainers had ever been able to define the exact nature of it—or its full extent. As such, they'd focused on teaching her how to compartmentalize and shield her emotions as much as possible against any sort of attempted invasion into her thoughts.

She'd grown quite adept at shielding herself, adept enough to answer his question easily. Casually. "I was told that it's basically a handfasting. But I assume magic is involved?"

"A good assumption." He gestured with his glass to the far side of the table, where an older woman with gray hair and robes that draped around her like living flames sat in quiet conversation with Elevia. "My high priest, Danika. She'll perform the ceremony as well as the binding. When it's over, we'll have a connection. I'll be able to sense where you are, or if you are in pain or need. And I'll know how you feel, to some extent." He lifted his cup. "Words will no longer be just words."

She'd have to tread carefully, so carefully. It would be more important than ever that she not only believe her lies, but *live* them deeply enough to make them true. She hadn't been exaggerating when she'd told Zanya that the best way for her to accomplish her goals was to fall in love with this man, this Dragon. She'd slip into the emotion, let it envelop and surround her like a warm bath, until it became her entire existence, if only for a little while.

Next to that, slipping a dagger between someone's ribs was child's play.

Her voice was husky when she spoke. "And this . . . connection. It goes both ways?"

"Not usually," he admitted. "Though, in the far past, one of my consorts with particularly strong ties to the Dream said they sometimes felt echoes." A beat. "Do you have particularly strong ties to the Dream, Princess Sachielle?"

One of her hands still rested on the table, and she folded it into a fist to hide the flames that threatened to burst forth. "I suppose we'll see, won't we?"

Though his posture was still that of an idle king, Sachi could sense tension in his body. "I hold back for your sake, Princess. My last consort also spoke quite confidently about how little he feared me. For his sake, I wish I had not believed him so readily."

"Tislaine was foolhardy, so convinced of his own regal superiority that he couldn't see the truth, much less understand it."

That earned her a raised brow and a curious look. "Is that your assessment, or is that how your family speaks of their dead? He would have been . . . your grandfather's eldest brother?"

"Great-grandfather's," she corrected. "And no. At House Roquebarre, Tislaine is revered for his sacrifice." She paused. "'Tis a pity, truly. You see, Tislaine thought of you as a foreign king, and of your marriage as an alliance of nations. Here, he figured out the truth—that his family had offered him to a monster as appeasement. If he'd understood from the outset that that was what he was meant to be, he might have led a long, full life. Instead, he found himself in his own personal hell, and his fear overtook him."

"So you know what happened to him?"

"I've inferred that his fear turned into Terror." Her intonation made the capital *T* clear. "Am I incorrect?"

The Dragon lifted his left arm. Today, his shirt was a deep crimson that turned black in the shadows. He unfastened the golden cuff link at his wrist and folded the fabric up to reveal his strong forearm. A thick, jagged scar traced from just inside his wrist nearly to his elbow, silvered with age but still conspicuous. "Whatever your family believes, I did my best to save him. I bear the scar of my failure."

She reached out automatically, drawn by the physical reminder of his pain, but instinct stilled her hand. *Not yet.* If she touched him now . . .

Instead, she nodded solemnly. "I believe you. And I promise you—I am not Tislaine. Being here, with you and your court, will not drive me to the madness of fright. You will not become my hell."

"Because you already know that you are a sacrifice sent to appease a monster?"

"Because I have already experienced hell." Honesty was sweet on her tongue, like honey, and she finally closed the distance between them, laying her hand on his wrist. "I left it thirteen days ago."

The candles on their table flickered, the flames rising to twice their normal height. All around the open courtyard, torches affixed to the castle walls flared so high that the shadows vanished entirely. Conversation stuttered to a halt. All eyes swung to the high table, where Ash sat beside her, rigid with tension, his gaze fixed on her fingers. As if her gentle touch was the Betrayer's army knocking at their very door.

Abruptly, he shoved back his chair and rose, dislodging her hand. He inclined his head to her—not quite a bow, but a rare mark of respect coming from a god—and descended from the dais in two swift steps.

The entire courtyard watched in silence as their lord strode through the main gate. Fire roared upward just beyond it, and a dragon exploded into the sky, its broad wings sweeping down with a fierceness that extinguished the candles on half the tables.

Every gaze swung toward the high table, toward Sachi, where she sat alone. She smiled, sweet and vague, her expression deliberately empty of concern or hurt.

Well. At least they'd managed a conversation this time.

Chapter Seven
BETRAYER'S MOON

Week Five, Day Ten
Year 2999

This was growing ridiculous.

Ash glowered down at his castle. This western peak towered over the caldera where he'd made his home, and its sheer slopes and deadly crevasses made it unwelcoming to anyone without wings. The thick layer of snow and freezing temperatures did the same for anyone who couldn't generate their own kind of fire.

When Ash needed to brood, he found comfort in the ice-blasted rocks and frigid silence.

If only the cold could truly seep into him, deep enough to bank the heat that flooded his veins every time Sachielle touched him.

The wind shifted, bringing the sound of music up to his perch. The water that surrounded his keep usually lay smooth as glass, but the rising breeze danced over the surface, breaking up the reflections of strong walls and flickering torchlight. There were precious few trees clinging to the bare cliffs, just a few scraggly and determined pines at the edge of the tree line below, but he heard the whisper of shaking leaves and groaning branches, of summer squalls and restless storms.

Fingers of salty air teased at his hair, stirring it across his brow. It caught at his clothing, tugging insistently, and stole the resigned sigh that fell from his lips.

A summons—one not even a fool would ignore.

Not even the Dragon.

Ash closed his eyes and breathed in, dragging the scent of the world deep into his lungs. It always felt simpler up here. Clean air and stone and those stubborn pine trees, the bright smell of the lake, the hint of flames from the bonfires they'd lit in welcome and celebration of the Dragon's consort.

Stone, air, water, flame, life. This world he loved with every beat of his heart. He drew it into him, let it fill him . . .

And then he exhaled and stepped beyond it. Through it. *Into* it.

Into the Everlasting Dream.

The world's heart formed around him, lush and welcoming. A twilight sky stretched above him, shot through with soft pinks and deep violets, with a blanket of bright, twinkling stars scattered across the heavens. The flowers climbing a dozen stone archways bloomed in as many vivid colors, their petals still open to the last rays of the sun.

Stone boulders smoothed into perfect seats circled a tumble of stones shaped into a natural fountain. Water surged up from beneath them and danced down their moss-covered surfaces, splashing into the pond with a lyrical tinkling that sounded like music tonight.

It didn't, usually. But water did like to show off for the Siren.

She sat with her back to him, tight black curls spilling down her back. Blue silk crossed her shoulders and draped down her sides before tucking into the loose pants she preferred. It left her back bare, showing off deep-brown skin and tattoos that glittered on her spine like golden treasures glistening at the bottom of a crystal-blue ocean.

"The sea is restless," she told him without turning around. "The earth vibrates beneath her like an eager puppy who has not yet been taught the patience of the hunt."

Ash winced. "A harsh assessment, Dianthe."

"I almost lost three ships on a calm day." She turned and gave him a slashing look, and he froze in place. Most of the time, her eyes were a warm and welcoming brown. Now, they glowed an almost electric blue—a warning to anyone wise enough to heed it.

Not his old friend waiting for him, then, but the Siren in all her glorious fury.

Cautious of that power—and her mood—Ash circled her and sank to another smooth boulder. "Are your people well?"

Wind whipped around him, tugging at his fancy banquet tunic, but in the next heartbeat, the Siren sighed. The blue faded from her gaze, leaving brown eyes that studied him with the exasperation of a fond sister. "My people are well, Ash. But they won't be if you persist in whatever you are doing." A brief hesitation. "What *are* you doing? Shouldn't you be welcoming your new consort?"

The memory rose too swiftly. Princess Sachielle, sitting sweet and serene at the high table while a veritable rainbow of light glittered around her. The torchlight had suited her, gilding her skin and deepening the color of her hair. Her attendants must have spent hours twisting it into those intricate braids—ropes of gold he could already feel wrapped around his fist.

Beneath his feet, the earth trembled.

"Oh," Dianthe said. "I see."

He slashed a look at her, but Dianthe wasn't watching him. Her gaze was fixed on the tumble of rocks. Fire spilled down them now, twisting with the water until the fountain was tangled in writhing tendrils of flame.

Ash forced his fist to unclench, but the fire continued its dance, teasing and gleeful. An eager puppy, just like she'd said.

"It's not me," he said finally. When Dianthe opened her mouth, he cut her off hastily. "It is not *just* me. The world is . . ."

"Holding its breath?"

"You would know. The world exhales at your pleasure."

Dianthe tilted her head and studied the dancing flames. "Tell me about her."

What could he even say? That her mere presence shivered over him like a cool breeze on feverish flesh? That the innocent touch of her fingers against his had cracked open a craving in him that ran so deep, he might never find the bottom? That he'd fled her presence for a third time now because the mere sight of her stirred in him a ravenous hunger? A *dangerous* hunger.

He wanted to inhale the scent of her until there was no room in his lungs for air. He wanted to shred those prim, endless layers of fabric and spread her out before him. She would be his banquet, and he'd welcome her with his fingers pushing her thighs wide and his tongue buried deep, dragging pleasure from her until her body could take no more.

He wanted the whole court to watch as she sobbed and shuddered with release.

"Tell me about her, Ash." Not a request this time. A command.

"She glows," he said hoarsely. "In three thousand years, I've never seen anything like it. I don't know what she is, but there's power there."

"All the more reason to bind her to you tomorrow." Dianthe rose. "King Dalvish's court is restless. I can taste their discontent on the wind."

Thinking of the grasping lords who made their homes along Siren's Bay sparked a more familiar fire inside him. Carnal hunger might be unfamiliar to him now, after centuries of abstinence, but rage was his constant companion. "What could possibly fuel their discontent?" he snarled. "They have soft lives in grand palaces, with servants to care for them and nothing asked in return."

"They want more. They always want more." Dianthe paced to the fountain and reached out. The water leapt eagerly to her fingertips, and tiny droplets danced around her arm like sparkling diamonds. "Bind their bloodline to the High Court. Bind their fortunes to the health of the land and its people. It is the only thing that will hold them in check."

It had for thousands of years. Ash had to believe it would again. "I know my duty."

"Yes, duty." Dianthe's sudden laughter rolled over him, warm and wicked. The Siren was back, her eyes glowing a mischievous blue. Her voice was the husky whisper that lured sailors to their doom. "Bind the girl to you, Ash. Bed her well. Tell me if she glows brighter when she comes."

Yes yes yes

The image formed, so vivid it was as if the Everlasting Dream was trying to make it real. Sachi, silken braids wrapped tight around his fist, golden skin bared to the torchlight, her sweet lips parted on a cry of ecstasy as he worked into the slick heat of her again and again until that translucent rainbow exploded outward to swallow them both.

"Fuck." He shoved away the fantasy and spun to find Dianthe, but nothing lingered in the heart of the Dream except a waterfall of flames and her teasing laughter—and this impossible, overwhelming *hunger* . . .

The Everlasting Dream shattered. Darkness surrounded him. He clenched his fists around sharp rock and locked every muscle in his body against the urge to fling himself from this jagged peak. Flames licked over his skin. He could already feel the start of the change.

It would take the space of three heartbeats to spiral down on wings of fire. He'd be on her by the fourth. Tasting her by the fifth.

Probably terrorizing her before he even touched the stones of the courtyard.

Harshly, deliberately, he summoned the face of his last consort. Prince Tislaine had faced every day with bold smiles and princely hauteur in the beginning. There'd been nothing weak in him. Nothing fragile. He'd been educated in scholarship and swordplay, brilliant at horsemanship, and clever with a bow. Ash might have liked the boy if soul-numbing terror hadn't slowly hollowed the prince out from the inside.

Ash was the monster of their nightmares. The vicious dragon who demanded fealty from their rulers and burned entire armies with his flames. He ravaged and destroyed and, if you asked the small children of the capital, gained his powers by feeding those who misbehaved to the volcano beneath his castle.

Sachi was right. Words were just words. She might lie as skillfully as Tislaine had in those first few days. But once they were bound together, there would be no lies. Her heart would stand open to him. He'd be able to taste her emotions. He'd know if that reckless courage was a deception she wrapped around herself like all the others had.

He'd know the depth of her fear.

Ash had waited three thousand years for the consort he'd been promised in Dreams. If Sachi was the one, he would not risk losing her to her own nightmares.

Chapter Eight
DRAGON'S MOON

Week One, Day One
Year 3000

The day of the bonding dawned clear and bright, as if the earth and sky were both eager for this blessed event to occur.

Sachi rose early and stared out her chamber window at the grounds below. The land outside the castle was covered with tents, all pitched by pilgrims who'd journeyed to Dragon's Keep to witness their god's latest bonding. It was a once-in-a-lifetime opportunity for most of these followers, a chance for them to bear living witness to history.

It felt . . . *odd* to be part of that.

She ate a late breakfast, then slipped into a steaming bath redolent with oils and flowers. After soaking for so long that her fingers and toes were beginning to prune, Sachi dried off and sat while Zanya silently twisted her hair into intricate braids, then wound them around her head.

"My lady?" One of the maids who'd traveled with them from Castle Roquebarre waited, the first piece of Sachi's wedding dress draped across her arms. "Shall we begin?"

Sachi rose and shook her head. "Zanya will assist me. The rest of you may go."

"But . . ." Uncertainty darkened the girl's eyes. "That will take so long. Let us—"

"We have time," Sachi said firmly. "Thank you, that will be all."

The girl relented with a curtsy. She laid down the swath of fabric and left, the other attendants filing out after her, and Sachi sagged against the wall.

Zanya picked up a length of fabric and scowled at it. "I suppose it's too late to pick a different dress."

The dress was as intricate as the braids that wrapped around her head and would be just as tight when she'd finally donned it. It was comprised of dozens of bits of nearly transparent gauzy white fabric, one for every consort who had come before her. Each piece would be tied onto her body, overlapping until they formed a full garment.

The final piece, a length of fine crimson-red velvet spread across the bed, represented her. The current consort.

This part of the garment, which would be affixed last, would be the first the Dragon would remove.

Sachi shuddered.

Abruptly, Zanya stood in front of her, her eyes feverish and intent. "Say the word," she breathed, the words barely more than a whisper. "I'll take you away."

Sachi smiled and took Zanya's hand in hers, squeezing lightly. "Peace. He has no wish to hurt me, Zan. I believe that with all my heart."

Zanya's chest heaved, her fingers tightening painfully for a heartbeat before she released Sachi's hand and turned. "I trust you." She retrieved the first flimsy strip of fabric. "But I'll be here. Believe that, too."

"I do." She dropped her robe and raised her arms so that Zanya could tie on the first piece of the dress.

After each bit of fabric, she turned. Some were tied with golden cords around her arms, others under her breasts or around her middle. Slowly, the garment began to take shape—flowing and loose, except where it had been bound to her body.

"Will it do?" she asked softly, then winked at Zanya.

Exasperated fondness filled those familiar dark eyes as she settled the final piece into place. The velvet draped across Sachi's shoulder before crossing her body, over her heart, and knotting at her opposite hip—a slash of red across pristine white, a symbol of her innocent sacrifice on the altar of the Dragon's lust.

Zanya fixed it into place and stepped back, her gaze taking Sachi in from her bare toes to the crown of braids around her head. "You're stunning," she said as she turned Sachi toward the mirror, her voice rough with strained emotion. "Hold still, and I'll fetch the jewelry."

Gold cords peeked out from beneath the crimson sash, crisscrossing the white gauze beneath, giving the illusion of a gown that had already been accessorized. Between that and the seemingly unending blush in her cheeks, she couldn't bear to add one more ornament.

"No, wait." Sachi shook her head. "No jewels."

"No?"

"I'll go as I am." It would satisfy her betrothed's simpler tastes and distance her from the mortal kings on their gilded thrones.

It would bring her one step closer to piercing the Dragon's defenses.

Sachi glanced in the mirror. The afternoon light slanted harshly through the windows, casting everything in a red glow, and the glint of sunlight on glass caught her eye. Zanya had unpacked the hourglass. It sat in a small alcove in the wall next to the dressing table, partially hidden from view.

How many times a day had Zanya walked past it and stopped to glare at the inexorably falling sand? Too many times, Sachi knew that much. No wonder she was so upset.

Sachi opened her mouth to tell her to put it away, but the words wouldn't come. They would land like reprimands, and Zanya felt bad enough already. So she smiled instead as Zanya turned back to her and met her gaze in the mirror.

Gentle hands gripped Sachi's shoulders again. "Are you ready?"

"Yes. It's time."

They descended the winding stone stairs to Sachi's garden. The Raven Guard's full complement waited at the back gate, their spines stiff and straight and their eyes locked on her. As she and Zanya approached, they melted into step with them, with three of the guards marching in front of them and two behind.

The gate opened to cheers. Onlookers called her name, and Sachi smiled and waved at the gathered crowd as she passed. She couldn't feel her lips, and her toes were numb. Everything seemed like it was far away, happening to someone else, and she was simply being carried along by it.

She kept it up as she stepped onto the flower-laden ferry that would carry her to the far side of the caldera. The smile only faltered when she turned and caught sight of Zanya, still standing on the shore.

Of course she couldn't come. Why would she? But the realization that she'd be leaving her behind twisted painfully in Sachi's gut. She covered her stricken expression by bowing her head against the harsh sunlight.

And then they were moving. Skimming smoothly across the still waters toward the temple carved into the rock at the edge of the caldera. The sun hung directly over the rock face, partially eclipsed by the Destroyer's Moon. The effect was dizzying, a ring of fire blazing over the temple.

Over her destiny.

Across the water, the Dragon waited, surrounded by the rest of his court. She was about to be standing among *gods*, binding herself to one with very real magic. For the first time, it occurred to her how odd this must be for *him*, to take a new consort so often. A hundred years was the span of a lifetime for her, but for him? It must seem like a dizzying whirl of men and women, all passing through his life with tragic speed.

What must it be like, to lose them so quickly? Painful, even if he only cared for them a little. And if he truly loved them . . .

Sachi's hands shook, but the emotion that tightened her throat wasn't fear or dismay. It was softer and sharper, curling through her like the hint of warmth that accompanied a hot drink on a cold night.

As the endless ride drew to a close, and Sachi could finally make out the Dragon's features, she saw it reflected on his face.

Anticipation.

The ferry slowed to an effortless stop, and Sachi's knees felt weak as she disembarked and ascended the rough-hewn stone steps to an equally rough platform. When she reached the top, the Dragon extended a hand to her. She rested her fingers lightly on his, taking advantage of the steadying contact more than the help as they moved toward the priest.

Danika stood two steps up from them on a dais. Behind her, the sun seemed to balance on the pillar that marked the center of the temple. The Destroyer's Moon formed a perfect circle of darkness within, giving late afternoon a false feeling of twilight as the priest raised a hammered goblet above her head.

"In the time before time, division shattered our land," she intoned, her voice carrying across the water to where the watching throng had fallen silent. "The Betrayer sought to take more than the world could give, and in his greed, he poisoned the very earth. The gods fought the final battle where we now stand. In the violence and chaos, the continents were torn asunder, separating us from the Empire forever."

Her voice lowered, but every word still floated on the breeze to the worshipful ears of the onlookers. "Because the conflict between gods had shaken the world, the High Court in its wisdom knew it was time to withdraw to their keeps and let mortals rule themselves. On the slopes of this newborn mountain, as the sun rose on the first day, the Dragon struck a deal with those who would lead. In exchange for their continued protection by the High Court, the mortal lords must follow three rules."

Behind Sachi, a soft whisper of voices rose, reciting the next lines with her until they swelled over the mountain like a chant. "Respect the land, and do not take more than it can easily give. Shelter the people, for the people are the land's heart."

Danika held up a hand to silence the crowd, then returned it to the goblet as she spoke the last words alone. "And every one hundred years, the mortal king must send an heir to the High Court of Dreamers, binding the ruling family to the Dragon by marriage."

Danika lowered the goblet and extended her hands toward Sachi, the gold cup cradled between them. A liquid the color of blood shimmered within. "Princess Sachielle of House Roquebarre, you have come in accordance with the agreement set down on the first day. You have come to offer yourself as a living bridge between the stewards of this land and its protector. Do you accept this charge?"

"I do."

"Then drink of the blood of the Dragon, and become one with the land he protects."

She started to reach for the goblet, then drew her hands back. No one had said anything about drinking blood. Her first assumption was that the priest must be speaking metaphorically, but did she really *know* that for certain?

The Dragon cleared his throat softly and murmured, "It's not really blood."

Sachi's cheeks burned. "You must think me hopelessly provincial."

"No. Just not accustomed to the old ways."

She accepted the goblet and sipped the cool liquid. As she swallowed, she almost choked as the chilly sensation vanished, replaced by a burning fire that wound its way from her throat to her stomach. Then it began to unfurl like a flower, spreading an inexorable, inescapable *heat* through her entire body.

She wanted to gasp. She wanted to pant. She wanted to throw her head back and *moan*—in protest, in exultation. In invitation.

Danika retrieved the goblet and extended it to the Dragon, whose gaze never left Sachi's as he drained the remaining liquid. Then he extended his hand, and the priest took away the empty cup.

Was that it? Sachi couldn't tell. The moment seemed strangely slow, suspended like an insect in amber. She floated in it for what felt like forever . . . and then the Dragon reached for her.

Yes.

His lips parted, and she had the dizzy impression of fangs as he cradled her head in one hand, tilting her back. "It won't hurt," he promised in a rasping whisper, his breath feathering over the bare expanse of her throat. "Trust me."

His teeth pierced her skin, and time didn't just shudder to a halt. It ceased to exist. Sachi was alone in the world, with only this rising, throbbing pleasure to separate her from the dust or the dew or the dying sunlight that streamed down around her.

Around *them*. He was there, too, her dragon, slipping inside her in ways she hadn't thought to consider, much less fear or crave. The tenuous thread that already connected them stretched taut and spun, whipping apart into thousands of gossamer filaments that enveloped Sachi.

And then he started slipping away.

No. She reached out, not with her hands but with her heart, desperate not to lose this sense of closeness, of *oneness*. To pull it deeper, until he remained inside her, a missing piece of her soul.

And she didn't even know his name.

Fire flared around them, and even though she could feel one arm hard around her and the fingers of his other hand splayed at the back of her head, she had the impossible sensation of wings wrapped around her, sheltering and strong. Then they flared wide, and his lips lingered at her throat as the heat and pleasure began to subside, leaving only the gentle ache of the bite as the world snapped back into focus once more.

A short-acting drug, then—either botanical or magical—meant to dull the sting of being bitten. Sachi stiffened, flutters of panic rising in her belly as memories of her trainers' methods flooded her, and she pushed against the Dragon's chest.

She *hated* being drugged.

A cool breeze washed through her as his grip eased just enough to allow her a step back. Large hands hovered over her shoulders, ready to catch her if she fell, and the Dragon watched her with wary eyes. "Princess?"

She couldn't directly meet his gaze, not with the metallic taste of fear still clawing its way up her throat. "My lord."

He looked like he wanted to say something more, but the priest stood before them with a length of black and red braided cord draped across her hands. A low sound escaped him, a growl like distant thunder, but in the next moment he'd clasped Sachi's hand in his and extended both.

The priest wrapped the cord around their joined hands, securing it with a loose knot that left the ends dangling toward the rock at their feet. "You are bound, Princess Sachielle," she intoned loudly enough for the words to echo from the cliffs above. "Bound to the Dragon. Bound to the High Court. Let the House of Roquebarre walk warily, and serve as fit stewards to the Sheltered Lands, for any harm they do the land will be visited upon the blood of the consort a hundred times over."

It would have been a serious threat, indeed—if Sachi had shared any blood with King Dalvish and his kin. But this priest had no way of knowing the truth: that an orphaned Sachi had been delivered to the capital at the tender age of seven, ready to assume the role of heir and assassin, freeing Dalvish from the constraints of this vow.

And, in time, from the Dragon himself.

Chapter Nine
DRAGON'S MOON

During the festivities at Blade's Rest, Zanya had imagined she would prefer sitting with the servants and common folk, enjoying relative anonymity.

How wrong she had been. For the thousandth time that evening, Zanya peered at the high table over her hammered bronze goblet and tried to map the swiftest path to Sachi's side.

The table was situated on a dais at the south end of the castle's courtyard. Zanya knew from her meandering explorations of the massive keep that the kitchen garden lay beyond the vine-wrapped trellis arch that sheltered the Dragon and his consort. A logical place for the gardens, close to the kitchens that dominated part of the fortress's southern wing. The head cook herself oversaw delivery of each course to the high table, and she ruled over her domain with a steely discipline any of the mortal king's generals would envy, as well as a precision most drill sergeants would find punishing.

There was no path to Sachi through the kitchens.

There was no path from the shadows, either. Torches blazed from the walls, their flames *too* bright, as if the fire was showing off for its lord. Zanya felt exposed under the harsh light, even tucked as she was into a niche behind a towering stack of casks filled with mead.

Approaching the high table by stealth would be impossible. The only path to Sachi's aid was directly through the chaotic throng of dancers and up the three broad steps to where she sat serenely at the Dragon's side, glowing under the loving caress of the eager firelight. If someone threatened her . . .

Zanya choked on a pained laugh. No one would mount an assault on a god in his own fortress. The only danger to Sachi was the one sitting next to her. And Zanya would never be fast enough to reach her before the Dragon did his worst.

Zanya wrapped herself deeper into the scant shadows, soothing herself with their familiar caress. Fire might dance and preen for the Dragon, but darkness had always been her most devoted suitor. When she settled into its sheltering embrace, people tended to overlook her. They did now, swinging past her in joyous dance and calling to each other. Some passed by so closely that she could feel the air stir with their laughter, but no one spared her a second glance.

It was a useful trick for an assassin.

She took another sip of her wine. The flavor of it tingled across her tongue. Bright, fruity, and sweet enough to be deceptive. No hard bite and fire like the liquor the guards in the capital preferred. This wine seduced, its warmth a gentle glide beneath her skin.

She'd seen the distinctive purple glass bottles from which it had been poured—glass that reflected amethyst fire in every direction when it caught the light. Even House Roquebarre's gold couldn't buy the Villa's prized vintage, supposedly grown from grapes planted by the

Lover and tended with his own hands. His acolytes saved it for holy days during the Lover's Moon, or to gift to those who chose to speak their vows in one of his temples.

Something to spice up the night, she'd heard one of her trainers say once, elbowing a friend who'd been considering taking his partner to have their vows witnessed. *They say it puts the Lover's own heat in a man's belly, if you know what I mean.*

Zanya hadn't known what he'd meant. She'd been fifteen at the time, all awkward legs and elbows and regular beatings for not having perfect control of her changing body. She'd had no time for whatever normal girls daydreamed about. She'd dreamt of blood and darkness and the shrill way people screamed when they couldn't outrun their nightmares.

And Sachi. They'd been separated for two years by that point, allowed only the occasional afternoon visit when Zanya managed to please her tutors. She'd hoarded those stolen moments like sparks of light in the endless night, and it wasn't until she was nearly twenty that those sparks ignited into something else.

Zanya sipped the wine again, letting the promised heat kindle in her belly as her gaze traced Sachi's golden hair. The soft, exposed skin at the base of her throat. The graceful way she tilted her head as she listened to the music, and the light that seemed to shine from within her. Oh, she knew now what her trainer had meant. And the Lover's own vintage was everything it was promised to be.

She *had* to stop drinking it.

The shadows stirred around her, a quiet warning. She glanced to her right and caught sight of a massive warrior wearing an impressive dark leather cuirass embossed with stylized birds. High quality, well-fitted, and well cared for, but not ceremonial. That armor had seen battle and so had its owner. He was grizzled, with short brown hair going silver at the temples, and sported two prominent scars—one slashed across his left cheekbone, while the other bisected the right side of his face from just beneath his hairline to the corner of his mouth.

The eyes he must have come close to losing glinted at her in the firelight, a startling green framed by thick lashes. Surprisingly pretty eyes for such a harsh face, and he clearly knew it. He was throwing the entire force of that lovely gaze at her as he strolled up with the supreme confidence of someone who usually got his way. "I can't believe no one has asked you to dance yet."

Plenty of them likely would have, if she hadn't hidden herself in shadow. Zanya had already learned that her position close to the new consort would attract those hungry for a brush with power.

The only thing she needed less than more of the Lover's wine was a string of suitors inspired by said wine to try their best lines on her.

Zanya gave him one cutting look and wrapped her voice in the chill of nightmares. "No."

"No one has asked you to dance, or no one—?"

"No."

At least the man wasn't boorish—or vindictive—when faced with rejection. He certainly looked put out, but he raised both hands in defeat and backed away without another word.

A chuckle rose just behind her.

Zanya started, her heart leaping into her throat as she whipped around. No one should have been able to creep up behind her, not when she stood in her shadows. No one except . . .

A god.

The Wolf stood only a few paces away, dressed in the same battered hunting leathers and homespun fabric he'd worn to the welcome feast the night before. Humble, especially when compared to much of the finery on display, but she supposed a man whose eyes glowed a subtle gold while magic fairly screamed off him didn't need to rely on artificial displays of power.

His voice drifted to her, low and amused, with the rough edge of a rumbling growl. "I haven't seen Kardox look that disappointed since he arrived late to the battle at Betrayer's Cove."

Zanya's brain stuttered. Her gaze swung back to the large man with the scarred face. She'd been so focused on Sachi before the bonding ceremony that she'd barely glanced at their escort guard, but the man and his fancy embossed armor had certainly been among them.

Embossed . . . with *ravens*. Of course.

"He's one of the Raven Guard." She hated the uncertain catch in her voice, but the Raven Guard was almost as legendary as the Dragon himself, warriors so fierce they were said to bring attempted invasions to a grinding halt just by walking onto the battlefield. No one wanted to face them. No one *dared*. The priests swore that the Raven Guard was cursed to fly into every battle in the Sheltered Lands as a swarm of death, and any enemy they touched would be carried directly to the Endless Void, severing them forever from the Everlasting Dream.

Void-touched, the high priest at the mortal king's court had called them. The worst insult known to their world, because Void creatures had no heart, no soul. They spawned from nightmares and returned to them once death had taken them. High Priest Nikkon had not thought highly of the Dragon and his devoted warriors.

Then again, Nikkon had never cared much for Zanya, either.

"Yes," the Wolf confirmed, seemingly oblivious to Zanya's inner turmoil. "Kardox is a member of Ash's Raven Guard. And he doesn't seem happy that I look to be succeeding where he failed."

"Succeeding?" Zanya repeated blankly. *Ash*. That must be the name the Dragon's friends used for him. She'd never heard it before. Perhaps because he had so few friends.

The Wolf held out a hand to her. "Dance with me?"

An invitation that might as well have been a command. How did one deny a living god? Zanya had been trained in a hundred possible ways to slay one, but Sachi was the one who'd been given lessons on polite refusals and courtly manners.

Zanya was a simple servant. And if she declined an honor like this, she'd be a servant to whom everyone paid far too much attention.

She set her fingers in the Wolf's, barely hiding a flinch at the dark spark of his magic. No wonder Sachi felt herself drawn to the Dragon in spite of the reckless danger he represented. They lived in a world where the very earth they walked upon and the air they breathed answered to the whims of the High Court. *Power* was an insufficient word for what they held in their hands.

Zanya could feel the same awareness in her chest as the Wolf closed strong fingers around her hand and guided her to where the dancers circled the fire. Not attraction or desire, nothing as simple as that.

It was primal. Dread, or perhaps awe. Both, braided together into something that frightened her, even as the Wolf smiled and tilted his head toward where Kardox was watching them. *He* didn't seem awe-struck. He glowered at the Wolf, as if Zanya was a prize he was irritated to have lost, and *that* sparked a blessed irritation that drowned out any other feeling.

"Is this a game you two play?" she asked, reclaiming some of her chilly disapproval. "It's not very flattering to feel like a bone being fought over by two mangy dogs."

The Wolf let out another of those dark chuckles and pulled her close as they began to spin with the music. "Whatever Elevia may have told you, I do not have mange."

"That doesn't answer my question."

Deep golden eyes stared down into hers, and the firelight seemed to twirl as he lowered his voice. "What makes you think we'd fight over a bone? It's so much more fun to share."

Heat flooded her cheeks. Innocence, she'd lost that in a night of terror and death before the age of eight. But desire was a weakness no weapon could afford, so she'd done her best to ruthlessly cut it out of herself every time it tried to take root. Only Sachi was safe to love. Everyone else was an enemy, could only ever *be* an enemy. And she did not long to bed her enemies.

How unfair, then, that this . . . man, this *god*, could destroy all her careful work. That he could conjure dark promises of tangled limbs and bare skin gilded by firelight and easy pleasure. That he could make her *want*.

"Don't toy with me," she rasped. "I don't know why you're doing this . . ."

"Because you're beautiful." The Wolf tilted his head, studying her sharply. "Is this false modesty? I've heard that's popular among some of the mortal court, though I have little patience for it. Surely this is not the first time multiple people have vied for a dance with you."

He might be surprised. Zanya knew she had certain qualities that many valued. Symmetrical features. Long, dark hair that grew with a speed the ladies at court coveted. She'd received enough catty compliments about the dark brown of her eyes and the way they were framed by bold eyebrows and dark lashes to know they provoked envy in some. So did the burnished gold of her skin.

But beauty was not such a simple thing to measure. Features arranged in a desirable configuration did little if the soul they housed didn't shine.

Shining had never been among Zanya's skills.

Perhaps she *had* sampled too much of the Lover's wine, because the truth fell from her lips with uncharacteristic honesty. "I make people uneasy."

The words lay between them for a beat, and Zanya wished she could claw them back. Those golden eyes saw too much, and if she were to have any hope at success, she needed to be invisible. This dance had been a mistake.

The Wolf broke the silence with a nod. "I make people uneasy, too."

She wasn't surprised. He was making *her* uneasy, even as he smiled and continued. "However, Kardox may have had an ulterior motive. He likely wants to take your measure, as the Raven Guard will be accompanying us on progress."

"Us?"

"Mmm. Elevia and myself. Perhaps Aleksi, if the whim strikes him. And you, I assume. Whatever other attendants the consort insists on bringing with her, though I suspect Ash will strongly discourage that."

This was the first Zanya had heard about Sachi's attendants not being welcome on their ceremonial tour of the High Court's various seats, and she didn't much care for it. "Is there a reason he wouldn't want them in attendance?"

"Will you take offense if I speak bluntly?"

"You're a god. Are you in the habit of caring whether or not a servant takes offense?"

Golden eyes locked with hers again. "Yes."

Zanya wasn't sure how to reply to that, especially since it seemed sincere. But that searching look was back in his eyes again, dark and predatory. Verbal sparring was hardly Zanya's specialty, but maybe the truth could be an asset here. "I'm not a courtier," she told him honestly. "And I never have been. I prefer bluntness."

The massive man inclined his head. "Ash tends not to travel in the sort of style gently reared noblewomen from the capital might expect. He will make allowances for his consort's comfort, of course, but he will have no patience for nattering girls who will only slow us down."

Zanya could barely tolerate half of Sachi's attendants, and tended to intimidate the rest on her best days. She trusted none of them and expected most had been pressed into service as spies by one or another of the many people pulling Sachi's and Zanya's strings. But she was still affronted on their behalf. "How do you know *I'm* not a nattering girl who will slow you down?"

The Wolf smiled, and there was something uncomfortably seductive in the confidence with which he said, "You're not."

"You're so sure?"

"Are you asking the Wolf if he can tell the difference between a fellow predator and hapless prey?"

Alarm zipped up her spine. The *last* thing she wanted was to be identified as a threat. She started to pull back, but the hand at the small of her back tightened just a little. She weighed the pressure of each finger against long familiarity with her own strength and knew with certainty that she could break his grip. The challenge glinting in his eyes all but dared her to do so.

By fifteen, there hadn't been a single trained fighter in the king's employ who could best her in a fight. By twenty, she'd been cutting her way through a dozen experienced soldiers at a time—and still holding back so they wouldn't understand her true potential.

She wanted to test herself against an opponent where the outcome wasn't inevitable. She wanted to answer that challenge. Something wild rose in her, an eagerness that nearly stole her breath. Her fingertips tingled. Her breath came faster. Thanks to stolen moments with Sachi, she knew the way desire felt when it unspooled low in her belly.

This was nothing so sweet as that. No, this was dark and violent, edged with a hunger to dominate that she thought she'd finally tamed.

Frantic to hide it, she locked her body in place, hoping that her sudden stillness would be mistaken for fear, and dropped her gaze to his chest, where the open vee of his shirt revealed coarse dark hair against tanned skin. "You mistake me, my lord. I'm a simple handmaid. Nothing more."

He spun her abruptly, and it took all her willpower to let her body follow the path he set. Her back crashed against his chest when he pulled her against him, and he chuckled against her ear. "You no longer walk among oblivious mortals, handmaid. You would do well to remember that."

She could feel the muscles in her neck tightening. Her fingers flexed. He'd been kind enough to put his nose in such a convenient position as to be broken by a collision with the back of her head. His hand was already at her waist. One tug and she would—

Cheers erupted, and the music died. The Wolf's grip on her eased, and she tore free and spun in the direction of the high table.

The Dragon towered there, imposing in the firelight that seemed to lovingly caress every unforgiving plane of his face. He extended one massive hand, and panic seized Zanya in a brutal grasp as she watched Sachi slip her fingers over his and rise gracefully to stand at his side.

The roars of the gathered crowd fell abruptly silent when the Dragon raised his other hand. His expression was indecipherable, and had been from the moment his acolyte had tied the final knot in the ceremonial handfasting. Zanya could not read his face, but his eyes were like fire. Feral. *Powerful.*

Predators and prey.

"I hope you'll forgive us if we retire early," he rumbled, the words setting off a fresh wave of laughing cheers. "Please enjoy the celebration."

No. *No.*

Panic seized Zanya, and she had taken two steps before she realized it. She had to reach Sachi's side. She had to . . .

What? Prevent the Dragon from taking his consort to bed? Reveal their entire purpose here and get them both killed? Hopelessly, *pointlessly* killed?

Across the distance separating them, Sachi's bright blue gaze caught hers. Her lips curved up in a gentle, sweet little smile—the one she only gave to Zanya—and she shook her head the tiniest bit. She might look tiny and fragile and so very, very breakable next to the monstrous god about to steal her away to his tower, but her eyes held a steely, unyielding command.

Sachi was the only person Zanya had ever willingly obeyed.

She planted her feet and watched as the Dragon led his consort toward the grand entrance to his castle. Sachi floated gracefully, her dress fluttering around her in dozens of gauzy strips that would serve as little protection when it came time for the Dragon to claim his mate.

Delicate silk around a will of iron. Any man who mistook Sachi for prey would regret it. But that was the point, wasn't it? The Wolf's voice wove through Zanya's memory, haunting and damning.

You no longer walk among oblivious mortals, handmaid.

Now more than ever, Zanya understood the impossibility of her task. These weren't *people* she'd been sent to deceive and destroy. They were the embodiments of elemental forces. They were gods, walking the earth, cloaked in the forms of mere mortals.

If the Dragon recognized a fellow predator in Sachi, he would no doubt move to eliminate her with the swiftness for which he was known.

And Zanya would not be there to help her.

Chapter Ten
DRAGON'S MOON

Week One, Day One
Year 3000

Princess Sachielle's fear was eating him alive from the inside out.

Ash had forgotten that there were so many different flavors of fear. Perhaps his last few consorts had been simpler, driven only by instinct. He was a monster, therefore they feared him. A basic human impulse.

But this princess was a complex creature. The bond should have revealed her heart to him in its entirety, but reaching for her was like the first moments of free fall—a dizzying spin that upended the world before adrenaline washed everything away. Every touch brought an avalanche behind it.

Desire.

Pain.

Anger.

Exhaustion.

Hate.

Anticipation.

Loss.

Determination.

Rage.

Love.

She felt so much, all the time, as if her heart contained the full breadth of human emotion. But the constant drumbeats beneath it all were variations on one note, over and over, so steady and constant that it rattled his bones.

Terror. Apprehension. Dread. Regret. Worry. Doubt. Despair. Anguish. Hopelessness.

Even in those last terrible days before Prince Tislaine's nightmares had manifested as a Terror, he hadn't felt like this. If this was what lived in Princess Sachielle's heart, it was a wonder a full army of nightmares given form didn't dog her every step.

And none of it showed on her face. She was serene as he escorted her up the steps to her tower quarters, golden hair gleaming in the torchlight and a small smile playing over her lips. Her fear had chilled his ardor, but it was that gentle smile and those guileless eyes that truly made him wary.

Prince Tislaine had not been a very good liar. Princess Sachielle, it appeared, was a superb one.

They reached the top of the stairs, and a solid wooden door opened to reveal the consort's redecorated quarters. Ash had not set foot in them in nearly one hundred years, not since the night he'd risen from a restless sleep with the prince's agony tearing through his chest.

Camlia's grandfather had been his steward at the time. He had emptied the rooms after the prince's death, and Camlia had been the one to prepare them again for their anticipated use. Her thoughtful touch was everywhere, and if he cataloged each piece of furniture and every tapestry, perhaps he could find his equilibrium before his new consort wrecked it again.

Sachi walked through the next open door—and into her bedroom, stopping to stand beside the bed.

The bed. There was no way the staff could have brought the monstrosity through the door, so they must have built it here within the room. Ash could have shared it with the entire Raven Guard. Sachi must have seemed small and defenseless within the endless silken sheets when she slept.

No, that was not the path to calming his thoughts.

He paced past her, his restless energy too intense to let him stand still. The room already bore indications of her presence—brushes and mysterious vials spread out across the vanity, a book lying on the table next to the bed. A small alcove held an intricate hourglass, with silver dragons curling around crystal-clear glass orbs. It seemed mainly decorative, for most of the sand still sat in the upper globe, falling one agonizingly slow grain at a time.

"What is your name?"

Startled, he turned to look down at Sachielle. "You do not know it?"

Her smile came just as easily as the ones before. "You are the Dragon, Lord of Earth and Fire. But I assume you don't make your bedmates say all that."

"Plenty of my bedmates have preferred to say all that."

She took a single step closer. "Their mouths weren't otherwise occupied?"

His gaze dropped to her lips. They were sweet, full and curved and stained a tempting pink. He could imagine all manner of ways to keep them occupied, and perhaps he was a monster after all. Because even with her fear rattling through him like thunder, he found himself lifting one hand.

Her cheek was soft under his fingertips, her mouth as lush as he'd imagined. He traced her lower lip with the pad of his thumb before urging them to part. There was no hesitation in her gaze. If he edged his thumb between her willingly parted lips, he knew what would happen next. A teasing brush of her tongue. A knowing look. Open invitation to put her on her knees and let his consort slake this sudden, unbearable lust by wrapping her lips around the cock he hadn't let another person touch in a century.

She'd do it. He could feel the determination gathering through her fear, and there was real anticipation threaded through it, slick and hot. She wanted it, wanted *him*. That much, at least, wasn't a lie.

"Ash," he said in a low voice, his gaze still fixed on her mouth. "My name is Ash."

Her tongue darted out to wet her lower lip, teasing across the pad of his thumb and shooting fire through his veins. "Sachi."

The urge to claim her rose in a sudden, savage wave. He wanted to shred the golden ropes holding her gown in place and tear those gauzy strips of fabric from her body. Or perhaps he'd keep the ropes. The golden silk would look glorious against her skin, binding her in place for him to feast upon at his leisure. An hour or two between her thighs, learning her taste, and she'd be too exhausted to fear him. Too tired to do anything but climax again and again and *again*, until she begged him for respite.

Moving with aching slowness, he edged his thumb between her parted lips, thrusting it into her waiting mouth.

Sachi's eyes fluttered shut, and she moaned, the sound stifled by the pressure on her tongue.

Desire filtered through their bond, tentative but *real*, and the warm glow of it should have been a balm to his aggrieved conscience. He had walked this world for thousands of years, and had known almost as many lovers. With their bond to guide him, he could stoke her need to an inferno. He could build a prison out of her pleasure, trap her with her own senses until her perfect mask shattered and the truth of her lay before him.

She'd offered herself to him, after all. She was his by custom and treaty. By every law of their land. His to bed, his to ravish . . .

His to *protect*.

Her fear still screamed.

He eased his thumb from her mouth and gripped her chin, tilting her head back. "Look at me, Sachi."

She obeyed slowly, her gaze locking on his as one hand drifted up to rest on his chest.

He covered that hand with his, gently confining her before asking, "Why are you so terrified?"

After a moment, she blinked, and those bottomless blue pools sharpened and filled with soft reproach. "You should have warned me, Ash. About the elixir."

The Dragon's Blood. Prepared exclusively in his temples, it was used for ceremonies that involved the giving of blood or the laying of ink. For most, it transposed pain into an oblivious euphoria. For others—particularly those who sometimes enjoyed the skillfully applied kiss of pain—it delivered a rush of pleasure.

The moment the first drop of Sachi's blood had spilled across his tongue, Ash had known she was one of those. Her pleasure had rioted through him, drowning out everything else for that first, glorious instant.

But she'd been given such a small dose. The effect had faded, and in its wake had come a panic that chilled him. The echoes of it swam through her now, and this fear had a new flavor, one it took him a moment to chase down.

When he did, rage filled him.

Memory.

"Who hurt you?" he asked, and though he tried for an even tone, he could hear death in his own voice.

Sachi sighed and shook her head. "I don't like being drugged without my permission. It isn't right. Promise me."

Not an answer to his question, but a promise he could make readily enough. "It will not happen again. My apologies, Princess."

"Sachi," she reminded him in a whisper. "And thank you." With that, she stretched up on her toes, her face tilted to his.

"Sachi." Perhaps with that promise between them, her fear would fade. So he put an arm around her, hauled her up against his body, and claimed her mouth.

He tried for a gentle kiss. A cautious taste, one that would prove he was no monster set on ravaging her. But her fingers found his hair, tangling in it with flattering desperation, and her lips parted beneath his in naked invitation.

No, not invitation. *Challenge.* Her tongue swept over his lips, demanding entry, and his instinctive capitulation was the end of his resistance. The taste of her flooded him with the first brush of her sweet, eager tongue. Berries and wine—not just any wine, either, but the Lover's own vintage, which sparked in his blood like fire.

Ash growled and dragged her closer. Higher. Her feet were barely brushing the floor now, but that didn't matter. Not when a thigh edged between hers gave her a place to rest—and enough friction to make her moan. The gauzy fabric that formed her gown was slim protection. His seeking hand found skin. Her throat. Her collarbone. One almost bare shoulder.

He deepened the kiss and swept lower as a needy whimper rose in her throat. Beneath his hand, her pebbled nipple pressed against his palm through the scant protection of her dress. Her fingers pulled at his hair, tugging as if to beg him to replace his hand with his mouth, to ease that ache and stoke a sharper one with the heat of his lips.

And *still*, fear screamed beneath it all, growing apace with her need, as if one spurred the other along. Growling his frustration, Ash tore away from her and strode across the room to brace both hands against the stone walls of the castle. Deep beneath them, the bedrock trembled in response to his agitation. The entire castle shivered. On Sachi's dressing table, fancy bottles clinked together, and the fear surging across their bond spiked higher.

He could not do this. Not to her. Not to himself.

Not again.

Fabric rustled behind him. "Ash?"

He closed his eyes and sent reassurance down into the earth. The castle stilled its rumbling. One more legend added to his myth. No doubt by tomorrow the story would be that he made the castle shake when he bedded his consort.

No one need know he had not done so.

He turned to face her. Worry creased her brow, but she still looked temptingly disheveled, her braids dislodged by his fingers, her gown dragged low on one side with a clear reddened path where he'd kissed his way down her throat. She looked ravished, and they'd barely done more than kiss.

"I will not bed you while I can sense terror in your heart," he told her as he eased her dress back into place. There was little he could do about the braids, but he smoothed stray strands of hair from her forehead. "You have been raised to fear me. I know that your father resents the duties he owes the High Court, and would just as soon see me dead. Perhaps you feel the same way. But it does not matter. You are mine now, and we have all the time in the world for you to learn the truth of me." With the final strand of hair tucked away, he let his hand drop. "On the day you no longer fear me, I will take you to my bed."

"But—"

"Get some rest," he told her gently, turning for the balcony. "We leave tomorrow to start our progress."

He'd almost made it to the heavy glass-paned doors when Sachi spoke. "What is it like?"

"What? The progress?"

"Not being afraid."

Ash stilled, his hand braced on the stone doorway. The last time he'd felt fear had been on this very spot. If he closed his eyes, he could still conjure the image—Tislaine, sprawled on the floor not far from where Sachi was standing, those beautiful eyes staring up, unseeing. The Terror towering over him, the shadowy claws of one hand already deep in the boy's chest, feeding off the soul that had been encased in flesh.

Terrors had no set form. They were born of nightmares, so they took the shape of them. Skeletal arms, monstrous heads, vines growing where organs should be, spikes and claws and fangs, humanoid figures mixed with all manner of beasts. But Prince Tislaine hadn't feared beasts or vines or spikes or fangs.

He'd feared Ash. And the massive form that had risen on dark legs to turn empty, glowing eyes on Ash had been his own—the Dragon, as one terrified boy had seen him in feverish nightmares. Like looking at a version of himself stripped of anything good, anything warm, anything capable of kindness.

The shock of it had given the creature an advantage, and left Ash with a scar that would not allow him to forget.

Now he had a new fear—seeing it happen again. "You'll find out," he promised her. "You are safe with me, Sachi. Nothing will harm you ever again. And you will not have to fear."

She opened her mouth, closed it again, then nodded and turned away. "Good night, my lord."

"Good night, Princess."

He left her then, escaping out onto the balcony. It was tempting to call his wings and flee to higher ground, to find some place to roar his anger and frustration and need to the empty skies.

But familiar voices teased at him from the fortress wall, so he formed wings only long enough to glide over the consort's garden and alight on the shadowed walkway above the western wall.

Unsurprisingly, the other members of the High Court had gathered there. As Ash approached, he heard the thud of a blade sinking deep into wood, followed by a triumphant cheer and Aleksi's deep laugh. "That's it. Best of five. Ulric, tell me again why I thought it a good idea to challenge the Huntress in this manner?"

"Because you drank enough wine to drown Dianthe," Ulric grumbled, and Ash turned the corner to see him working a knife out of the target. "I can't imagine how you're still throwing in a straight line, Elevia. I'm not."

"Because this is what I do." Elevia finished what was left of her wine in one gulp. "I strike true."

"You mean you—" Aleksi broke off as he spotted Ash. "Huh. You're out and about . . . quickly."

Elevia tilted her head. "Did you forget how these things work, Ash? It *has* been a while for you."

Ash could still taste Sachi on his tongue. The sweetness of her skin . . . and the salt and ashes of her fear. "She's terrified of me. If I'd taken anyone in that state to bed, Aleksi would have cursed me for a thousand years."

"Terrified of you?" Aleksi wrinkled his nose. "That is *not* what I was sensing from your sweet little bride earlier."

"Then you could not sense deeply enough. But our bond is unmistakable." Ash leaned against the parapet and tried to shake free of the lingering ache in his bones. A gentle wind carried laughter up from the courtyard—the celebration carried on and would until dawn. "I gather her life has been an unpleasant one. She has been hurt, and badly."

But Elevia only shrugged. "There are few who cannot claim that distinction."

Aleksi tapped his chin. "What do you know of her?"

"Little enough." Elevia tossed her dagger into the air and caught it by its blade. "She was mostly kept from court until around eight or nine. Not surprising, considering she was born just after the first child, the original heir, died. She's highly regarded, though no one really knows her well. Apparently, she's shy."

Ulric snorted. "Shy? Are they fools?"

No, terror might plague Princess Sachielle, but shyness certainly did not. From their first encounter, she'd met Ash's eyes with bold challenge and issued the most provocative statements imaginable. "The mortal lords are rarely fools. But they may have convinced themselves that I am one."

Ulric and Elevia exchanged a knowing look, and Ash felt every muscle tense. "What?"

"There is something . . ." The Wolf planted a hand on the parapet and used it to boost himself effortlessly up to sit upon it, as if a dizzying fall to earth didn't loom behind him. "Have you noticed her girl? Zanya?"

"Zanya?" he echoed, uncomprehending. "You mean the one who braids Sachi's hair and helps with her dresses?"

"Mmm. That's what I thought."

The incoherence of the statement stoked Ash's temper. "What is that supposed to mean?"

Instead of answering, Ulric drummed his fingers on the stone next to him. "Aleksi didn't notice her, either. Not until he forced himself to concentrate."

Aleksi sighed. "Yes, normally I'm the very first to spot such beauty."

Ash tried to visualize the woman. He could see their arrival in his memory easily enough. Sachi, striding down the bridge to his castle alone, the glow around her an impossible rainbow of light that made it hard to care about anything else. But Ash didn't lightly let strangers breach his domain. He'd at least *looked* at the rest of them, a half dozen brightly garbed attendants and one who'd been dressed dully by comparison. But when he tried to conjure her features, nothing came. Just a vague memory of dark hair and shadows.

That was . . . odd.

It must have shown on his face, because Ulric nodded. "There's something strange about the way shadows move around her. Elevia felt it, too. But once you make yourself see her . . . Well, when you watch her move, you'll understand."

Ash's temper finally snapped. "Understand *what*?"

Elevia launched her dagger at the target, sinking it deep into the heart of the wood. "That they've sent you an assassin along with your consort."

"A hot assassin," Aleksi added.

"An unusually dangerous assassin," Ulric concluded. "If she can sneak into your castle, under your nose, with you utterly oblivious to her existence."

Ash rubbed at the bridge of his nose and groaned. "Not again."

Ulric grinned. "Cheer up. At least this one won't trip over his own shadow and break a leg while trying to stab you."

The disastrous debacle of the consort of 1700 had mostly faded from history, though a few comical ballads lingered, each detailing the boy's escalating—and calamitous—attempts to slay the Dragon. Ash had spent the better part of ten years torn between exasperation and embarrassment. "I do not have the patience for this."

"The presence of an assassin doesn't strictly mean the king wants you dead," Aleksi pointed out. "Who better to protect their princess? An assassin can make for an effective bodyguard."

"That would be a welcome change," Ash grumbled. "It would be nice to think they *care* about the children they sacrifice to a monster." But somehow it did not match the way Sachi spoke of her life in the capital.

I left my personal hell thirteen days ago.

Something was clearly rotten in the court of House Roquebarre.

"Unfortunately for them—and fortunately for you, my friend—they've squandered their perfectly good opportunity to murder you." Grinning, Aleksi threw his arm around Ash's shoulders and shook him lightly. "You and the lovely Princess Sachielle are bonded, which means the fortunes of House Roquebarre are now inextricably tied to yours. They can't harm you without harming themselves."

"Indeed," Elevia concurred. "If they wanted you dead, they should have done it yesterday."

True enough. Slaughtering him now would bring ruin on Sachi's entire bloodline. Of course, in 1700 that had been the point. His plotted death had been incidental, part of a convoluted plan by a scheming king-consort to steal his wife's throne by cursing her entire bloodline and reaping the presumed rewards. He'd been no more successful than his hapless stepson had been, and Ash had let the family drama play out without his interference.

The affairs of the mortal lords were not his concern. He protected the land and held the border against the Betrayer's return. He didn't interfere when men fought and nobles schemed. He didn't take sides in their petty fights as long as they honored the land and continued to send consorts. In three thousand years, he had never been tempted to set foot in their capital and concern himself with their intrigues.

Not until Sachi had arrived with fear burning in her gut and pain twisting through her memories.

If Ash found out who had hurt her, he would make them pay.

Chapter Eleven
DRAGON'S MOON

Week One, Day Two
Year 3000

They made camp in the Midnight Forest, still half a day's ride from the Wolf's Den. This gave Sachi pause, since she'd anticipated spending the night in the rustic lodge Ulric called home.

She needn't have worried. A short walk from the main campsite revealed a grouping of small stone cabins. They were old—centuries old, perhaps—but had been sturdily built and meticulously maintained.

"They were built for the consort's progress," Elevia explained. "The rest of the time, they're used by hunters and travelers. A small group has traveled ahead to prepare each stop for your arrival."

It seemed odd, this dedicated set of structures for an event that happened so rarely. But maybe that was simply too *human* a way to view it. Her experience of time was short compared to theirs and would be far more limited. Perhaps, to the High Court, one hundred years was but a brief pause.

The interior of the consort's cabin was plain. The only decorations involved items of comfort—oils and perfumes laid out on a small vanity, folded bathing sheets stacked beside a small metal tub in one corner. The bedding was freshly laundered and had even been pressed, a discovery that made Sachi have to stifle a laugh.

No wonder the servants bustling around the campsite had been eyeing her with such confused curiosity. They had prepared for a princess. Instead, they got *Sachi*, in her leather and linen riding clothes that were just as plain and sturdy as this cabin.

She left without changing. There would be plenty of time for that after dinner, when Zanya had heated the water for her bath. Sachi wandered back outside instead. The Dragon—Ash, she reminded herself—stood across the shadowed little clearing, talking with the few members of his Raven Guard that weren't helping to set up the camp. He seemed comfortable in their presence, relaxed in a way that he wasn't with her, and it pricked at Sachi's pride.

No, not her pride. This was something lower, darker. Jealousy, lashing through her as her bondmate smiled and clapped a casual hand to someone's shoulder.

She held his interest, as well as the desire that burned in the pit of his belly. She held his *bond*, bore his mark. But she didn't have this easy companionship.

The tall man next to him—Remi, she remembered—murmured something, and Ash threw back his head with a laugh. Sachi's jealousy dissipated, replaced by a twist of longing so intense it stole her breath.

Across the clearing, Ash stilled. His head turned, his gaze finding hers. They stared at each other across the expanse for an endless moment before he said something to his companion. After receiving a nod in return, the Dragon strode toward her.

Sachi's heart pounded. There was nowhere to hide. Not that she wanted to avoid his attentions—she was, after all, on a schedule. But there was an eagerness that gripped her as he crossed the clearing, nerves mixed with sheer, exhilarated anticipation. A maelstrom of emotions that could prove more dangerous than her mission.

"Princess." Before she could speak, he smiled slightly and corrected himself. "Sachi. Is this your first time visiting the Midnight Forest?"

"It is." Her voice came out sounding almost hoarse, and she cleared her throat. "The barge made stops on the journey upriver, but I never disembarked."

"And you've never been in the west before?"

"After the death of their first heir, my parents weren't exactly eager for me to travel. Too dangerous, you understand."

"Ah, then you've never seen one of the Midnight groves at twilight." He extended a hand. "Would you like to?"

"Yes, please." She touched his hand, unsure of what he meant to do. Hold her hand? Tuck it into the crook of his arm?

He did the latter, tugging her close to his side. Several people cast sidelong glances at them as he led her across the clearing. Only Zanya started to her feet, an anxious question in her eyes.

I'll be fine. A silent reassurance and promise before Sachi turned her full attention to Ash. "What's so special about the groves?"

"It's easier to show you than to explain." He glanced up, where twilight had painted the sky in vivid violets and deep blues. A handful of the brightest stars twinkled alongside the bold crescent of the Creator's Moon. "It's best experienced at the new moon, but Ayslin never looks away from us for long."

He spoke the name with familiarity, as if referring to an old, treasured friend. "Ayslin?"

"Ayslin is the old name for this moon." A sad little smile quirked his lips. "So they've finally erased the story in the capital, have they? A pity."

Sachi had been taught many things—how to beguile with a look, how to disarm an opponent by targeting the bundle of nerves that innervated their sword arm. How to lie with the truth. She'd learned many others by chance—how to compartmentalize paralyzing fear.

How difficult it was to clean blood from beneath your fingernails if you let it dry. How to *survive*.

And she couldn't tell him any of that.

"I've never heard a story about either moon." She wanted to smooth away the furrow between his brows. "Tell me?"

He guided her toward a path into the towering trees. Within three steps, their massive branches had blocked out most of the remaining twilight. It left the two of them shrouded in the intimacy of darkness. "My grandmother always told me that the moons were Ayslin and Isere, the lovers who created our world."

That startled her. "Your grandmother?"

A warm chuckle slid over her. "I know the priests say that I stepped from the flames fully formed, wings afire. But people like that—like Naia, souls who are born fresh from the Dream? They are rare. Most of the High Court was born in the usual way. I had a mother who scolded me, and a grandmother who swatted my fingers when I stole berry pudding before dinner."

He had been human once. A child with a child's hopes and dreams, and then a man with a man's worries and despair. It shouldn't have shocked her so much. There was plenty of academic work detailing—or, more accurately, speculating about—the once-mortal lives of some of the gods.

But she'd never suspected that *Ash* might be one of them.

"I haven't been mortal in a long time," he said gently. "Whatever you're thinking about me . . . I am not that. Not any longer. My grandmother returned to the Everlasting Dream over four thousand years ago."

Customs changed, and societies evolved, but people were people. Always and forever. "The story?"

"Of course." His face was shadowed, but she could hear a hint of a smile in his voice. "Ayslin served the Everlasting Dream, and so wielded the power of creation. Isere, on the other hand, answered to the Endless

Void. She was tasked with destruction. Their natures were naturally opposed, for one must always tear down what the other builds."

His low voice shivered up Sachi's spine. Her nipples tightened, and goose bumps rose on her arms.

"One night, however, their paths crossed in the sky, and they fell in love. Stories say they spent an entire year together, their passion grinding the very stars to dust and creating a new world in their place. Our world, one with a special connection to the Endless Void and the Everlasting Dream, because it was formed from the loving union of their two strongest servants."

"But they couldn't stay together," Sachi breathed. "In stories like these, the lovers never do."

"No, they couldn't," he agreed. "Isere's nature was such that any place she stayed too long would inevitably be destroyed, for that was her necessary task—to clear away the old and make way for the new. So she left Ayslin and crossed the sky to resume her duties of unmaking stars, all so that Ayslin could make them anew."

"So Ayslin has to chase her across the heavens for all eternity?"

"She might have done. But Ayslin found herself too fond of this world they'd created together to abandon it. She watches over us, which is why we see the full face of the Creator's Moon every ten days. Isere travels far afield to protect us from her full powers, but once every moon she returns to visit her lover. And on the nights when both moons shine down upon us, we thank them for the love that made our world by celebrating love in all its forms."

Sachi gripped his arm tighter. "And how do we do that?"

"Surely they still celebrate the Union Days in the capital."

In the capital, those days were popular times for betrothals and weddings. People who wished to become pregnant would receive blessings under the two moons, and children conceived on those days were considered lucky.

But.

"I know how Union Days are celebrated in the capital." Sachi stopped walking and turned to face him. His features were still in shadow, but his eyes gleamed. "I asked you how *we* are to celebrate them."

Silence stretched between them, and when he finally broke it, his voice was a low rumble. "It is no coincidence that we'll be at Aleksi's Villa when the moons are full. He tends to celebrate in a very specific way. And when there's a new consort on progress . . ." Ash trailed off. Cleared his throat. "Everyone participates as much or as little as they wish, of course."

So many euphemisms and vague allusions. Sachi blinked up at him. "Everyone participates in what, Ash?" *I want to hear you say it.*

"Fucking, Princess Sachielle." He stroked her cheek, the sword calluses on his fingers rough against her skin despite the gentleness of his touch. "Joyous, unbridled, glorious, messy sex of any flavor you could want, with as many partners as you desire. From moonrise to moonset, there are no rules. Only pleasure, however you choose to claim it."

She had to swallow—hard—just to be able to speak. "And what would I know of any of that? My bondmate left me last night. Alone and bereft."

His fingers traced down to her chin and tilted her face up. "I thought we were past lies, Sachi. Perhaps your family was cruel enough to send you to me untouched, but I will not believe you are untutored." The pad of his thumb brushed her lower lip. "You know exactly what you want."

So many impossible things, but only one throbbed through her veins at that moment. "I want to kiss you."

A soft sigh escaped him. "I know you do. And yet . . . you still fear, Sachi. Terror beats inside you like a second heart. How do you stand it?"

"It's all I know." She reached up, mirroring his movements by tracing the curve of his lower lip. "*Almost* all I know."

His teeth grazed her thumb, and a low sound escaped him. As if he'd made some sort of decision, his hands suddenly found her hips, gripping her tightly through the leather. "Close your eyes."

She slid her hand into his hair as she complied, clenching and pulling, a sharp counterpoint to the flutter of her lashes. "Don't leave me this time."

"I won't."

His fingers tightened, gentle but strong, and her feet left the ground. She clung to him as the world seemed to waver and then steady as she wrapped her legs around him. Ash groaned, his breath mingling with hers, and a moment later her back thumped against a solid surface as he pressed her against a tree.

Then he kissed her.

He hadn't been wrong about her education. She'd been trained not only as an assassin, but as a courtesan as well. She'd been taught all sorts of ways to give and even receive pleasure, to coax and tempt and seduce her way into the Dragon's most intimate confidences. How else was she to get close enough to slay him? In a way, learning to be sexually desirable to him had been her sole occupation.

But no one, not a single priest or tutor or trainer, had thought to warn her about *Ash's* skill or desirability. Sachi had been well-educated, but she was young, not having yet seen her thirtieth year. The Dragon, on the other hand, was ancient. He had thousands of years of experience that she lacked, and he brought the full weight of all that expertise to bear with his kiss.

He coaxed and tempted, enticed and seduced. Sachi whimpered as he teased her tongue with his, stroking and retreating until her entire body burned. She arched off the tree and tried to take control of the kiss, but Ash only grasped her wrists, lifted them above her head, and pinned them to the rough bark.

The position thrust the hard lines of his body closer to hers. Sachi couldn't breathe, but she wasn't sure she cared. Dragging in a breath would have meant breaking the kiss, and she couldn't do that. She *wouldn't*.

But he did. His burning lips blazed a path across her cheek to her ear, and his voice rasped over her in a shivering caress. "Look up, Sachi."

The bark snagged her braids as she tilted her head back. A gentle, warm glow warmed the grove, coming from everywhere and nowhere, all at once. Then, as she watched, tiny sparkles of golden light formed on the leaves above her head, dancing across the lush green edges. She stared at the lights, spellbound, as they began to drift down around them.

She gasped, both at the beauty of the display and the pleasure of Ash's lips on her throat, parting where her pulse pounded beneath the skin. She tensed in anticipation and rocked her hips against his, seeking . . .

Seeking.

His teeth grazed her skin. He didn't use his fangs this time, but somehow the light scrape hit her even harder. Longing twisted low in her belly, and she breathed his name.

His groan seemed to rattle the very earth. But in the next moment he pulled away, pressing his forehead to the tree above her head as his broad chest heaved with every pant. "Tell me," he whispered roughly. "Tell me what terrifies you so much that I can feel it even while you tremble in my arms. Tell me, Princess, so I can fix it."

What would he do if she *did* tell him? If she opened her mouth to confess, if the truth poured from her like a rushing fall after torrential rains?

Don't call me Princess. I am no one—an orphan and an impostor and an assassin. I have lied to you, and I will lie again, because it's all I know how to do. I was cursed by the royal family, then sent to marry you under false pretenses and kill you in your bed. If I fail to do this by the end of the month, I will die. Not by the hand of the king's guard, but by magic, right where I stand.

If you don't kill me first.

I cannot fail.

But you make me want to.

She opened her mouth, but what came out instead was a soft whisper. "I have a private cabin here at the campsite. The bed is small, but big enough for two. Will you come to me tonight?"

Warm fingers stroked her cheek. Her throat. Then he eased away and gently lowered her to the ground. "When you trust me enough to tell me the truth, I will come to you. Until then, your handmaid can guard your rest."

Sachi closed her eyes tightly. Forget all her regrets and soft wishes. She *was* failing, and if she didn't figure out how to stop . . .

She didn't fear death. There were far worse fates, and she'd stared down most of them during her years of torture and training. But she worried what would happen to Zanya when she was gone.

"Sachielle . . ."

She turned away. "I'll see you at dinner, my lord."

Sachi headed down the path without a backward glance. Ash's preoccupation with her fear was a stumbling block, one with the potential to destroy her mission.

Because he was *right*. She *was* scared, but only because she didn't know how not to be. It was the one emotion that had always been a part of her, that colored every memory she could draw forth, no matter how happy or sad.

Zanya often mistakenly claimed that Sachi was fearless. Now, she somehow had to learn how to turn those words into truth.

The alternative was death.

Chapter Twelve
DRAGON'S MOON

Sometimes, after a long day of brutal training, Zanya would fall onto her rigid cot with half-formed dreams of a nebulous future where the Dragon's death was behind her, and she and Sachi could live in peace.

In those hazy, wistful dreams, the home she conjured for them had always looked something like the Wolf's Den.

Den was a misleading title for Ulric's seat, she supposed. Far from a little cave in the forest, the Den was a respectable hunting lodge nestled in a wide clearing. It boasted a tidy kitchen garden, nearly a dozen cozy cabins for guests, a firepit surrounded by long wooden tables and benches, and a fenced-off practice yard, where several of the Raven Guard were currently exchanging taunts as lazily as they exchanged teasing blows.

But it was simple and unpretentious. Comfortable. No fancy high tables, no endless corridors full of nobles and courtiers. Everyone here wore homespun or leather or fur, warm and well-constructed but clearly designed for comfort and ease of movement. Her own preferred outfit of wide-leg trousers and a wrapped tunic, both in unrelieved black, didn't stand out at all.

Zanya wrapped her hands more snugly around a wooden mug of mulled cider and inhaled, savoring the scents of sharp spice and sweet apple as they mixed with smoke from the fire and the inescapable, clean scent of pine that dominated the forest. Even here, in the largest clearing she'd seen yet, the massive trees surrounded them like towering shadows. Though twilight still painted the skies in lighter shades, torches had already been lit in a vain attempt to drive back the darkness.

The Midnight Forest had been well-named. Zanya wished she could disappear into its shadows with Sachi and never return.

The thought of her drew Zanya's gaze back to the table nearest the firepit. Sachi, clad in leather trousers and a homespun blouse with a heavy fur cloak flung around her shoulders, looked happier than she had in years. Zanya had left most of her hair down today, and the wavy golden locks cascaded wildly over her shoulders in tangles it would take ages to tease out in front of the fire tonight. But Zanya didn't mind. The joy in Sachi's eyes at being unbound and imperfect was worth it.

The little old man at her side said something, and Sachi's delighted laughter rang across the clearing. The steward of the Den had charmed Sachi from the first moment he'd greeted them, standing proudly with his weight supported by a cane gripped in his only hand. A painful limp and a missing arm hadn't stopped Justav from herding Sachi out of her saddle while chiding the Dragon for making her ride all day without a rest. The god had actually seemed momentarily chagrined, trailing behind them as the steward ushered Zanya and Sachi up the steps to the Den. His wife, Andra, awaited them in the entryway with spiced wine and platters of fruits and pastries, muttering all the while that she was sure the Dragon had not fed either of them more than crumbs and trail rations. Justav and Andra had both hovered with all the affectionate protectiveness of grandparents delighted by their visit and determined to spoil them both rotten.

At least, Zanya assumed that was what grandparents were like. If she'd ever had any, they'd been gone long before she was born. The same was true for Sachi, but whereas the fond attention heaped upon them by the steward and his wife made Zanya feel smothered, Sachi delighted in it.

Across the clearing, Justav used his cane to gesture toward one of the Raven Guard in emphasis, and Sachi lifted her fingers to her mouth, as if to hold back another laugh. Grandfatherly or not, the powerful members of the High Court clearly held him in great esteem. Perhaps Zanya should be over there, too, listening to whatever stories he had to tell. He might drop a tidbit, some idle bit of gossip she could use strategically . . .

To kill the man he so clearly adores.

Zanya had long thought herself beyond guilt. But sometimes the uneasiness churning in her gut could be nothing else. She took a deep sip of her cider and nearly spat it out again when something nudged her side.

She started off the bench, choking back a yelp of surprise as she spun. Then she froze. An equally startled wolf stared back at her, its head tilted quizzically. It was almost entirely white, except for a spattering of gold fur across its back and down its nose. Liquid gold eyes the same color as the Wolf's stared up at her, and her heart galloped.

"Are you—?"

"That's not me."

Humiliation heated Zanya's cheeks as the Wolf appeared out of the shadows, a lazy grin curving his lips. The wolf bounded to meet him, butting at his hand and receiving a scratch between the ears as a reward.

"I didn't think . . ." She trailed off, knowing the lie to be futile. The Wolf stopped in front of her, the animal at his side all but trembling in excitement as it looked between them.

"I promise, I'm unmistakable in my other form." His grin turned positively suggestive. "And much bigger."

Zanya said nothing. It seemed wisest.

Amusement filled the Wolf's voice. "This is Skonar. He's sorry he startled you. And he would like to meet you, if you will allow it."

"You can—" She bit off the words again. What a foolish question. To hide her uncertainty, she went to one knee and held out a hand in silent offering. Skonar inched forward, approaching like *she* was the skittish wild animal that *he* was trying not to startle. That made her smile in spite of herself. As if recognizing this human expression as permission, Skonar shoved his head beneath her hand in obvious invitation.

So she echoed what the Wolf had done, scratching him behind the ears before running her fingers over his smooth fur. A pleased rumble vibrated beneath her hands, and Skonar shuffled closer, butting her chin with his nose before licking her jaw. Laughter escaped her, rusty with disuse, and the wolf stared at her with his tongue lolling out, clearly overjoyed.

"He likes you," the Wolf murmured.

Zanya continued to scratch behind the animal's ears, reluctant to let the moment end. "I think he probably likes anyone who'll pet him."

"You'd be surprised." She glanced up at the suddenly serious tone only to meet a pair of glowing gold eyes. "Skonar guards the Den when I'm away. If he judged you a threat to Justav or Andra, he'd have torn out your throat before you ever knew he was there."

The momentary pleasure popped like a bubble. Zanya may not pose a threat to a kindly old steward, but she *was* an enemy. Giving the wolf one final pat, she rose. "I'm glad your home has such formidable protections, my lord."

"Ulric," he corrected firmly. "Ash may put up with all the lording and sirs, but I do not."

Zanya hesitated again. Calling him *Ulric* in her head might make it too easy to forget what he was. A god, clad in mortal flesh. An elemental force of magic. *Dangerous.*

On the other hand, perhaps forgetting that was exactly what she needed to do if she wanted to believe she could defeat them.

"Ulric," she said.

"Nice to see you showing the new girl some hospitality, Ric." Elevia strolled over, casually swinging a wickedly sharp blade in one hand. It was larger than a dagger but smaller than a short sword, slightly curved, with a wide, solid spine. The Huntress wielded it with an ease that was almost seductive. "Your manners continue to improve."

"Elevia." Another wicked grin. "Don't get your hopes up too high. Skonar wanted to meet her."

The wolf leapt toward Elevia, his tail wagging in enthusiastic greeting.

"Hello, my sweet boy." Elevia knelt and drove the tip of her knife into the ground, then cupped the wolf's muzzle the way one might cradle an infant's cheek. "Are they taking care of you?"

If there was some sort of communication happening, Zanya couldn't perceive it. But Elevia suddenly laughed, and Skonar's tail swung wildly as he nuzzled her cheek.

"Does he—?" Zanya cut off her question, but curiosity got the better of her. "Can he speak?"

"All things are connected to the Dream," Ulric said. "So everything speaks, if only you know how to listen. Unfortunately, most humans forgot how to hear the world's whispers a long time ago."

"Oh."

"We're going to spar." Elevia rubbed Skonar's ears and laughed again. "Would you like to join us, Zanya?"

Yes. The violent yearning caught her off guard, and she stumbled a little over her denial. "N-no, thank you. I wouldn't know what to do."

A heartbeat of silence followed as they both stared at her in polite disbelief. Then Ulric cleared his throat. "You'll still be able to see her from the training yard, you know."

Her gaze stole to Sachi before she could stop herself. Andra had joined Sachi and Justav and was telling a new story that had Sachi hanging on every word in utter enchantment.

If anything, Zanya would be closer to Sachi in the practice ring. But she could not do it. They might suspect her, but they didn't *know*. Not yet.

Elevia sighed. "This is tiresome." In one smooth, quick motion, she pulled the blade from the earth, spun, and flung the weapon at Zanya.

Instinct overrode everything else. Before the blade had even fully left Elevia's fingers, Zanya had pivoted out of the way. Her mind caught up then, screaming a warning, but these weren't the mortal king's pathetic soldiers who could never be a true threat to her. These were *gods*, and her body reacted to the danger without her brain's permission, exposing her utterly as her hand flashed out to catch the hilt of the blade.

It was over in a heartbeat. Time resumed its normal march, except that the clearing had gone utterly silent. And Zanya stood with the blade she'd plucked from the air gripped expertly in one hand.

"I'll ask one more time," Elevia purred. "Would you like to join us, Zanya?"

Zanya sought Sachi's gaze again. This time, her lover stared back with a mild, unbothered expression.

Fine. So she couldn't hide what she was. Zanya tightened her grip on the blade's hilt and rolled her wrist once, getting a feel for the weight of it. It sliced through the air smoothly and seemed to weigh almost nothing. A finer blade than she'd ever touched, no doubt the work of the Blacksmith herself.

Sparring might expose Zanya's strengths, but it would also expose their vulnerabilities. Surely they had some. If not, all of this would be for nothing anyway.

"All right." Zanya reversed her grip and offered the blade back to the Huntress. "Let's spar."

"Wonderful." The blonde smiled and nodded to the knife as she stretched her arms. "Why don't you keep it?"

She shouldn't. But the handle fit her fingers like it had been made for her, and when she slid her fingertips along the perfectly formed blade, a sensual shiver claimed her. Covetousness rose, and she found herself unable to deny the gift. "Thank you."

"So is that what it's to be, Elevia?" Ulric clapped Zanya on the shoulder, then gave her a little nudge in the direction of the training yard. "Naked blades? Or do you intend to start with something a little less dangerous?"

"It's a bit of friendly sparring," Elevia replied lightly. "There is no danger here. Is there?"

"Of course not," Zanya replied automatically. A lie, and not a very good one. They all understood that this was a test. Zanya didn't know the precise rules, but the stakes were the same as they'd always been—a simple death for her, and something much, much worse for Sachi.

Failure was not an option.

The Raven Guard melted aside as she entered the ring. Kardox watched her with special intensity from beneath furrowed brows, the angry scars on his face thrown into sharp relief by the torchlight. She'd expected the sort of disdain that the mortal king's soldiers had thrown at her, but the Dragon's fiercest guards looked . . .

Curious. *Intrigued.*

"You've met Kardox," Ulric rumbled from beside her. "Have the rest introduced themselves?"

They hadn't, but Zanya had spent the past few days piecing together bits of legend with casually overheard conversations until she had a fairly good idea who was who. The tall brunette in formfitting leather that revealed an impressive amount of deeply bronzed skin—and even more impressive muscles—was Isolde, instantly recognizable by the long-handled axe that stood almost as tall as Sachi. Her gorgeous smoke-gray eyes and seductive, full-lipped smile were as devastating as the priests had always warned—according to the darkest whispers, she used both to lure unwitting warriors into battles where she consumed their life force.

The man beside her was her twin brother, Remi—though, aside from their coloring, they didn't look much alike. He was even larger than Kardox, a burly warrior the size of a bear. The legends about him were the most confusing. Some swore he *was* a bear, or even *the* Bear, able to turn into the creature as readily as the Wolf and Dragon assumed their other forms. Though Zanya had seen no evidence of shapechanging, she *had* seen the way he moved—with silken grace and deceptive swiftness. If she sparred with him, she wouldn't count on his size to slow him down. She suspected that was how most people lost to him.

The woman next to them could only be Malindra. She had dark hair, too, long and braided on one side and shaved short against her scalp on the other, but her skin was pale as snow and her eyes were a piercing blue. They said she hailed from the barbarian clans that eked out a desperate existence on the haunted islands that made up Dead Man Shoals, and her unusual fur armor seemed to confirm it. If the rumors were true, those clans were descendants of the Betrayer's army, abandoned and left for dead after his failed invasion. But Zanya harbored no illusions about Malindra's loyalty—she watched the Dragon with the fervor of a true believer.

The final member of the Raven Guard stuck her sword into the ground as Zanya approached, her gaze raking over her in overt assessment. The tiny blonde might have shared Sachi's scant height and golden coloring, but that was where the resemblance ended. There was no softness in her—neither in the shining chain mail she wore even to practice nor in the painfully tight braids that wreathed her head. And certainly not in her eyes.

Ambrial. Best known for acting as the consort's personal body-guard. Was that why she stared at Zanya with such intensity? Had Zanya usurped her position?

Or maybe they were all simply waiting for her to answer the question. "Your reputations precede you," she said softly. "It is an honor to be invited to spar with legends."

Remi chuckled. "Is that what we are?"

"She's being polite, brother," Isolde replied with a wide grin. "Don't worry, handmaid. I know exactly what the lazy priests who lounge in the king's palace think of me."

"What they said wasn't always complimentary," Zanya admitted. It was easy to smile, because Sachi was right. This was so much simpler when you could tell the truth. "But the priests were never all that fond of me, either."

"I imagine not." Malindra walked around Zanya in a slow circle, and the firelight glinted off the hilts of the twin short swords she wore across her back. "That was quite a trick you pulled, catching Elevia's blade like that."

"Thank you." It took all of Zanya's self-control to let the woman pace behind her, and the back of her neck prickled in anticipation of an attack. But Malindra simply reappeared on her other side, a thoughtful look on her face.

"Ambrial, you're the fastest." Malindra tilted her head at the short blonde. "If the Huntress approves, of course."

"I absolutely do," Elevia confirmed.

The Raven Guard formed a loose circle around the perimeter of the training yard, leaving Zanya to face Ambrial in the center. Heavy torch-light drove back most of the shadows, eliminating Zanya's best advantage, so she assessed her opponent as they both paced and stretched to warm up muscles grown stiff from the long days of riding.

Small was the first word that came to mind. Ambrial might even be a few thumbs shorter than Sachi, who only came to Zanya's chin. She knew how easy it was to subconsciously underestimate a smaller opponent—as a teenage girl often fighting grown men, Zanya had exploited that flaw ruthlessly.

Then the Huntress called the time, and Zanya added another word to her mental description as she wrenched her body desperately out of the way of a lightning-swift attack.

Fast.

Ambrial didn't fight. She *danced*, a blur of silver chain mail and shining steel alive in the torchlight. Zanya barely avoided another graceful swing that would have taken off her sword arm at the elbow if she'd been a fraction slower. She was far too accustomed to being the fastest person in any fight, to having all the time in the world to plan her responses and calculate the best show of force.

It was time to learn how to battle a god.

Zanya eased her grip on her instincts and let her body take over. It knew the rhythm of a fight, the thousands of variations on advance and parry, block and retreat. Ambrial spun into a powerful downward slice meant to disable her sword arm again, but this time Zanya brought up her borrowed weapon in time to block. The force of the blow rebounded through her. Ambrial was stronger than any human soldier she'd ever fought . . .

But not stronger than she could be.

A dangerous fire kindled in her belly—the excitement of a true challenge. The watching crowd faded. Even her ever-present awareness of Sachi dimmed. All that existed was the elegant dance of the blades, the blissful burn in her muscles as she used them to their fullest potential. There was no time to assess each blow or to check her speed. Again and again, she met Ambrial's powerful swings, learning the fluid rhythms of the other woman's style until . . .

There.

A vulnerability. Ambrial overcommitted to that devastating downward slice, leaving her off balance for a fraction of a moment. A slower opponent wouldn't have had the opportunity to take advantage of it, and Zanya doubted Ambrial ever saw anything but slower opponents, even among the gods.

Zanya's wrist was already moving, every joyous impulse screaming for her to exploit her enemy's weakness. At the very last moment, she wrenched her instincts back under brutal control. Their swords clashed with a fearsome noise, and Zanya loosened her grip enough to let the force take the blade from her stinging fingers.

Ignoring the thwarted fury that raged through her, Zanya held up both hands in surrender before the blade had even clattered to the ground. Ambrial checked her next swing easily and pivoted, her blue eyes intense with suspicion.

She didn't voice her qualms. Ulric, on the other hand, did. "Disappointing show, handmaid."

Zanya hated how easily he'd pricked her pride. "I held my own," she said stiffly. "Against a legendary warrior, no less."

"And then you let her disarm you."

There was nothing Zanya could say to that. She *had*. Because the time might come when Ambrial's off-balance overcommitment was the only thing standing between Zanya and saving Sachi's life. She couldn't take the risk that the woman would learn from having her vulnerability revealed.

And she couldn't trust herself not to exploit it.

"Peace, Ulric. Let her be." Ambrial bent to pick up Zanya's blade and held it out to her. "She's testing us. It is her right."

"I suppose," Ulric rumbled, his golden gaze still sharp. For a heartbeat, Zanya was afraid he intended to go next, but instead Malindra was the one who stepped up. She'd shrugged off her heavy fur cloak and stood in a tight leather halter that revealed well-muscled arms decorated with swirling tattoos.

"Test me next," she offered with a fearsome smile.

Yes, whispered that eager, feral part of Zanya. So she gave in and lifted her blade.

Where Ambrial's style was elegant and graceful, Malindra's was abrupt and vicious. From the first clash of steel, Zanya knew this would be no courtly dance where they tested each other's training.

Malindra fought to dominate.

She drove Zanya back across the practice circle, her twin blades a dizzying whirl. Zanya felt the fence at her back and timed her dodge so one sword sank into the wooden fence post. Malindra growled her frustration, but the scant moment she spent freeing it gave Zanya time to whip around with every intention of scoring a stinging slap to the other woman's back with the flat of her blade—a triumphant move that would injure only Malindra's pride.

Instead, the air around Zanya erupted in a hurricane of black feathers and flapping wings as her long knife soared through suddenly empty space, throwing her off balance. Zanya staggered, then let the momentum carry her into a forward roll that brought her back to her feet, out of reach of . . .

Of *what?*

As Zanya stared, a dozen ravens spun in a tight spiral, their dark bodies wreathed in shadow. Cries of protest rose from around the ring.

"Cheating!"

"No powers, Mal!"

The shadows flared, exploding outward in hundreds of tendrils that thinned and became as translucent as smoke. Malindra appeared from their midst, a chagrined smile curving her lips. "Sorry," she said, not sounding sorry at all. "Some things are instinct."

"It's still not sporting," Kardox drawled from the sidelines. His usually dour expression broke into a grin as he caught Zanya's stunned expression. "Did you truly not know why they call us the Raven Guard, handmaid?"

She'd heard the outlandish stories of battlefield ravens devouring souls, of course, but *this* . . . She waved the tip of her sword at Malindra. "Can you all do that?"

"When the situation calls for it." Kardox gave Malindra another stern look. "Which, at the moment, it does not. Play nice, Malindra."

"I never do," Malindra retorted. One heave of muscle pulled her sword from the fence post, and she raised an eyebrow at Zanya. "Though I don't think she wants me to, in any case."

Oh, the challenge in those eyes. It prickled over Zanya's skin, unleashing something reckless. Her fingers tightened on the hilt of her weapon, and she let that challenge sing to her. "I'd rather you play hard," she murmured.

"Good," Malindra said just as softly.

And then she pounced.

Instead of pivoting out of the way, Zanya met her advance. Some final whisper of sanity begged her to hold back, to prevaricate, to *hide* . . .

But she was so tired of hiding. And fighting felt so *good*. She'd never pushed her body so hard for so long before, never fully tested her limits. She was drunk on the feeling of not holding back, reeling from how good it felt to not make herself small for the satisfaction of petty men and petty kings.

This was what she had been born to do. Fight. Dominate. Win.

Malindra's harsh breathing filled her ears. The first sign her opponent was weakening. Her blows came a little more slowly, were a little less steady. It was so easy to feign the same, to trick Malindra with a hesitant feint that made it easy to tangle their blades and send Malindra's first sword flying. Malindra was a heartbeat late in recovering, and a heartbeat was too long. In one of the first moves she'd ever perfected, Zanya grabbed Malindra's wrist and executed a swift and brutal wrist-lock that forced Malindra's fingers open. The other sword clattered to the dirt, but Malindra was already airborne, flying over Zanya's shoulder in a throw that left the woman flat on her back in the dirt. Zanya strad-dled her chest, her knife at Malindra's throat.

The flush of victory was visceral. Zanya sucked in an unsteady breath, floating on adrenaline until the silence of the training yard pen-etrated her giddy high. She *felt* the weight of a dozen different stares. Everyone was watching her.

Everyone was *seeing* her.

Kardox broke the silence with a sudden grunt. "Arman taught you that move, didn't he?"

The name ripped through her, shredding her lingering joy and plunging her into the darkness of her childhood. Retired Captain Arman Melwin had been in his sixties when she'd been given into his care—a warrior past his prime, made of whipcord muscle, scars, and scowls. His job had been to accelerate Zanya's early training by any means necessary. To do whatever it took to turn her into a weapon.

She'd been ten years old and terrified of him.

His fierce exterior had hidden a gruff sort of kindness. Arman had been rough and demanding, to be sure. But he'd been patient with her at times, too, especially when a growth spurt brought ungainly teenage limbs and awkward new height. And he'd been the one to whisper the warning that had likely kept her alive. *Don't show them all that you are. Always hold something back. And if the day comes when they don't believe they can use you . . . make sure they don't know how to kill you.*

Tough love. That was all Arman had been able to offer her, but it was the only love Zanya had ever known, other than Sachi's. And it had gotten him killed in the end, when he'd balked at the increasingly brutal training regimen demanded by King Dalvish. Arman's final assignment had been a stark lesson to Zanya—they'd tested on him the curse that they would go on to perfect with Sachi. Watching his slow, draining death had been agonizing.

And motivational.

Zanya wet her suddenly dry lips and tried to make her reply to Kardox sound simply curious. "How did you know?"

"Because that was *my* move. I taught it to him when he was about twenty years old." Kardox grinned and pushed off the fence, gesturing for her to stand. "Come, handmaid. Let us see what else he's taught you."

Zanya realized she still had the knife to Malindra's throat. Flushing, she scrambled to her feet, offering a hand to help the other woman up. Malindra took it with good-natured humor, groaning her way to her feet and declaring that the hot springs in the Burning Hills could not come soon enough. Zanya barely heard her.

The Dragon was watching her.

Adrenaline surged, her fingers tightening around the blade before she could stop herself. But there was nowhere to retreat, no shadows she could wrap around her body to help her fade into nothingness. She stood in the center of the sparring ring, her knife gripped in one hand, exposed as a killer to the man she was meant to kill.

And he was smiling at her.

A shiver worked its way down her spine. She tried to move, but for a terrifying moment, her limbs wouldn't obey her, as if the stories were true, and the Dragon could turn his victims to stone with one steely look. Her chest heaved with her unsteady breaths, and heat prickled over her skin as his gaze drifted down her body. Not in a lecherous way, like the creeps who lurked in alleys in the worst parts of the city, but the way a warrior assessed a potential foe.

Serious. Attentive. *Intrigued.*

Lifetimes passed before his gaze reached hers again. And for the first time, those flame-wreathed eyes were locked on *her*. Everything felt odd, the dirt beneath her feet shifting, *pushing*, as if the very earth that answered to his call had taken note of her as well. Being the center of his focus was like feeling the world hold its breath. Elemental power in its purest form.

Something inside her stirred in response. The darkness, that part of her that gravitated toward shadow and hungered for violence. If the Wolf had been a seductive challenge, the Dragon was an inferno of temptation. Her fingers flexed on the hilt of her blade, feeling its heft.

She wanted to fling herself at him. She wanted to fight with everything inside her. Not holding back, not pretending she was less. She wanted to feel her blade at his throat, wanted him to stare up at her with that *look* he was giving her now, that look that promised he saw her in all her monstrous, violent darkness and still . . .

And still . . .

The desire was unexpected. A tiny flutter in her middle. A tightening. It crawled up her spine, raising goose bumps as it went, and the image flashed into her mind, blurry and half-formed because she had no practice with fantasies that weren't about Sachi.

Ash, on his knees, grinning up at her over the edge of her blade as his fingers drifted up her thighs . . .

She crushed the image before it could fully form, and panic broke whatever spell Ash had laid upon her. She ignored Kardox's rumbled question and spun on her heel, striding away from the practice ring before anyone could speak to her. Her heart echoed the quick pace of her steps, and she didn't know if it was desire or terror.

No wonder Sachi felt pulled to him. Zanya had borne the full weight of his attention for the space of ten heartbeats and had almost fallen to her knees. He was magic given form. For thousands of years, those who had looked upon his face had erected temples in which to worship him.

She wanted to charge into the forest, but even now the protective instinct forged in their youth pulled her around, her gaze seeking Sachi where she sat safely by the fire.

Zanya's very first memory was using the darkness inside her to keep Sachi safe. Her entire life had been spent training to do so again. Perhaps it would have been better to arrive at the High Court and find

119

the monsters she'd been raised to hate. If he'd mistreated Sachi or terrorized her the way the stories claimed, Zanya could have found endless satisfaction in digging her dagger deep into the Dragon's heart.

This would be no clean assassination. No righteous murder. Zanya wasn't even sure she *wanted* to kill him anymore.

But she had to. Because Zanya had been forced to watch the curse take Arman. She would not allow it to take Sachi, too.

Chapter Thirteen
DRAGON'S MOON

Week One, Day Six
Year 3000

For two days, Ash watched Zanya constantly.

It had gotten easier. She still moved like a shadow and had a tendency to fade into the background the moment he stopped concentrating, as if his own mind conspired to make her forgettable. But Ash had cultivated *some* patience over the past four thousand years. He trained himself to notice her. To *see* her.

And then he wondered how he had ever *not* seen her.

She was mesmerizing. Not because she was beautiful, though Ash supposed she was. In thousands of years, he'd seen standards of beauty change, but some things rarely did, thanks to the generations of artists who had painted Aleksi as the epitome of desirability. Dark hair and eyes were always popular, as was sun-kissed skin in various shades of golden brown. Zanya's coloring was much like the Lover's, which would find favor with many. And she had an interesting face, with bold brows, thick lashes, strong bones, and a generous mouth.

But any beauty in her features was cut to ribbons by the *sharpness* of her. The harsh slash of her frown. The unforgiving lines of her cheekbones. The path her eyebrows made when she glared disapproval, which seemed to be what she spent most of her time doing. She *felt* sharp, too. Like an unsheathed blade held in an unsteady hand.

Ash had seen people like her before. Warriors honed to a killing edge, zealots who had no time for anything but their private war. The Kraken was one of them. Einar's fervent hatred of the Betrayer had consumed anything human in him long ago. There was only the monster now, the beast who lurked off their western coast, sometimes going a century or more without setting foot off his ship. War lived in Einar's heart, filling it until there was no room for anything else.

Zanya hated, too. Ash knew the look of it. The stiff shoulders grown hard from the weight of carrying that burden, the eyes gone old before their time. But the target of her enmity was not here. Hate was too personal to hide, and it wasn't in her eyes when she looked at the High Court. No, what lurked in those dark, beautiful eyes was . . .

Fear, again. That blasted fear.

Elevia and Ulric had cleared enough space beyond their campfire for their nightly weapons practice. The Wolf was currently fending off two of the Raven Guard with lazy ease. Isolde spun with deadly grace, swinging her massive double-bladed axe as if it weighed no more than a feather. Her speed did little to help her against Ulric, though, who melted out of the way of her swing. Her brother Remi was next, his lighter hand axes even faster. But not fast enough. The Wolf's hand flashed out, his claws drawing sparks from armor in warning. Ash knew what was coming, because he'd fallen prey to it half a dozen times over the last century. Ulric executed the same move Zanya had in her match against Malindra—a lightning-fast wristlock, a clever hip throw, and Remi was soaring through the air.

Directly at Isolde.

She tried to get out of the way, but the twins went down in a tangle of limbs and weapons. It was over within moments. Remi laughed and held up both hands in surrender, while Isolde briefly looked like she was pondering another attack. But when Ulric raised an eyebrow and flexed his fingers in warning, she gave a throaty laugh. "Fine. You win. This time. Someday, we're going to figure out how to avoid that damned throw."

Ulric smiled and held out a hand, pulling Isolde easily to her feet. "I look forward to it."

She might grumble about losing to Ulric, but satisfaction shone in her eyes as she slung an arm around Remi's shoulders and hauled him off for a drink. As well it should. The Raven Guard might have become legends over the past thousand years, but they were still young compared to the High Court. Even holding their own against Ulric was an achievement few others in this world could claim. Four thousand years was a lot of time to refine your skill in battle, and Elevia and Ulric rarely missed an opportunity to practice.

Elevia was proving it now. She murmured something to Zanya, who shook her head at first, as if in refusal. Whatever the Huntress said next must have held the sting of challenge though, because Zanya's shoulders stiffened, and her dark eyes blazed. In the next moment, she was on her feet, stalking toward the practice circle.

Near the fire, Sachi leaned forward, watching. Ash tried to sort through the tangled mixture of emotions he could sense from her, though it was getting harder to do so. For the last several days, his consort had seemed distant, not only in behavior but through their bond, as well. It felt like listening to a conversation from another room or being touched through thick, padded armor. Everything about her felt far away, leaving Ash to interpret her moods across a new chasm. Right now, she didn't seem particularly concerned about the outcome of the sparring match, but there was an uncertain anticipation that sparked Ash's curiosity.

If he didn't know better, he'd suspect Sachi wasn't sure who would win this bout.

Drawn by that emotion, Ash approached the tumble of smooth stones around the firepit. "May I join you, Princess?"

She barely glanced up at him. "As you wish, my lord."

Still chilly. He'd wounded her by refusing to go to her bed, but he didn't think it was anything so simple as an injury to her pride. Despair had been the emotion that screamed loudest before she pulled into herself and all the screaming stopped.

Another thing that didn't make sense. Little about her seemed to, perhaps because he'd let lust and frustration guide him. He may not have had Elevia's patience for stalking prey and chasing down secrets, but he could at least make an attempt.

So he settled on a rock beside her, so close that their knees almost touched, and watched as Zanya and Elevia faced off across the rough circle. "Your handmaid has many unexpected skills."

"Yes." Her gaze tracked Zanya as she faced her opponent and began to circle slowly. "I'm glad that your court has encouraged this pastime. She's had precious few opportunities to test herself."

Even muffled by her withdrawal, the warmth of affection that filled her as she watched Zanya would have been enough to make a lesser man jealous. It only heightened Ash's curiosity. "Your family did not encourage this?"

She didn't answer. Instead, she murmured, "Everyone here is so free."

"We are the High Court," he replied simply. "Who could bind us?"

"Who, indeed?"

She'd turned the question aside so deftly. Ash watched the first clash of blades. Elevia was still moving slowly—for her—but most mortals would already be struggling to keep up. Zanya flowed easily from block to parry to attack, every move effortless grace and trembling anticipation. Like a hunting dog still held on a tight leash—one shaking with the need to *run*. "Clearly, she is more than a simple handmaid. Is she your bodyguard?"

Sachi hesitated. "Zanya protects me. She always has."

Another not-quite answer. "Then she has been with you a long time?"

"Since we were children." Sachi's eyes locked with his. "What do you want to know, my lord? If I love her?"

Was that what she was attempting to hide? Some illicit romance, no doubt forbidden by her parents and frowned upon by their court? The mortal lords had grown tediously obsessed with bloodlines in recent centuries, as if their claim on power could be diluted by those of a lower class. It had given them a dim view of sharing pleasure outside the marriage bed as well, with more and more of their children raised to believe their sole purpose was to wed and breed the next generation.

Their lives were so short, and they wasted them so recklessly by making love so small. "Is that what you fear? That I would force you to give her up?"

She shook her head. "You couldn't. But . . . I don't think you would try, either."

He watched Zanya pivot on one foot, her body flowing with a grace that usually took centuries to master. She blocked Elevia's attack with plenty of time to riposte, driving the Huntress back a step with the fierceness of her attack. Ash recognized the focused look in Elevia's gaze from his own bouts with her.

She'd stopped analyzing, stopped playing. This had become a true test of skill.

And Ash had never been more perplexed.

Sachi throbbed with fear she claimed to have lived with her entire life, even though Zanya had protected her from childhood. She had grown up in the palace but knew the horror of being drugged against her will. She had arrived with an entourage of high-born girls to whom she barely spoke . . . and a well-trained assassin she clearly loved.

An assassin who suddenly pivoted with a speed that left Ash breathless, a triumphant gleam in her dark eyes as her blade sliced toward Elevia's unprotected throat. Horror twisted her expression a moment later, and she pulled the blow. Elevia turned and took the blade across the shoulder instead.

The soft hiss that escaped Elevia might as well have been a bellow of pain. Everyone watching fell silent as the long knife slipped from Zanya's nerveless fingers to land in the dirt.

Next to Ash, Sachi rose, her spine stiff and straight. Determined.

"I'm sorry." Zanya's stricken voice broke the silence. "I didn't mean to—"

"Stop." Elevia dropped her blade into the earth and pressed a testing hand to her shoulder. "At its very core, a fight is nothing but truth. Don't insult the moment with a lie."

Sachi swept forward. "It's all right, Zanya. It was an accident."

At the sound of Sachi's voice, Zanya flinched as if she'd been struck. Suddenly, she sank to her knees in the dirt in front of Elevia. "It was me. My mistake. Don't—don't hold the princess responsible. I will accept any punishment."

Before Elevia could speak, Sachi knelt next to Zanya and wrapped her arms around the woman's shaking frame. "Shh. It's all right." She pressed her lips to Zanya's cheek. "Come, let's get you cleaned up."

Elevia watched, baffled, as Sachi lifted Zanya to her feet and led her away toward the small stone hut traditionally occupied by the consort.

She finally spoke. "Well, then. It looks like your consort has a lover. A lover who just *cut me*." She heaved a deep, heavy sigh. "You'd best watch yourself, brother."

Ash grasped Elevia's arm, turning it over gently. The cut had been deep enough to do real damage to a human, but was already beginning to knit closed. Even if the girl had managed to strike Elevia's throat, she likely would not have had the strength to kill her. Not without a Void-touched blade.

But the fact that she'd landed the blow at all was not to be discounted.

"At least now I know why Sachi is scared." Ash released Elevia's arm. A forbidden lover would explain many things . . . and perhaps give Ash an opportunity. "If you'll excuse me, Huntress?"

Elevia barked out a laugh. "Go. See to your women, Ash. You need the practice."

The snug little stone cabin was set far enough away from the campsite to feel private, and its stout wooden door was firmly shut. Ash considered knocking, but his patience for manners had worn thin. This was his building. That was his door.

Behind it sat *his* consort.

He shoved through it with no further warning and endured the spike of wary protectiveness that swept over their bond as Sachi regarded him stiffly from her spot on the bed. But any thought of roaring a demand for answers stuttered to a halt when Zanya flung herself to her feet, putting herself between them in a feverish attempt to bar his path.

"Don't touch her," Zanya snarled, her fingers curled as if she'd launch herself at him armed with nothing but her fingernails. "She had nothing to do with it. If you want to hurt someone, you hurt me. Not her. *Not her.*"

The words fell like stones in his gut. Because Sachi's fear had that flavor again, the one that made him want to spread wings of fire and launch himself at Siren's Bay to raze her family's seat to the ground.

Memory.

Sachi had been punished for Zanya's mistakes before. Out of pettiness or cruelty or simply because someone was looking for an excuse to hurt her. She wasn't the first consort who had come to him wounded in spirit, neglected—or worse—by family that couldn't bring themselves to love the child they meant to sacrifice to a monster.

But she was the first to arrive with such a passionate defender. At last, Ash understood the game he was playing. Dangerous or not, Zanya was the key to unlocking Sachi.

And Ash knew the key to unlocking *her*.

He took a step forward. Just one, a calculated advance to see if he could make her retreat. She trembled but held her ground, and he liked her more for her reckless courage. "I will say this only once," he rumbled. "Princess Sachielle is the Dragon's consort now. Anyone who touches her in violence will die. Anyone who speaks a cruel word to her will be lucky to keep their tongue. Anyone who so much as wishes harm upon her will find their dreams turned to dust and their nightmares made real. She is mine, and I protect what is mine."

Zanya stared back at him, her dark eyes blazing, and an unexpected shiver prickled over him at the naked challenge in her gaze. The years had grown tedious in their sameness, and danger had become a delicacy. Not knowing whether or not she could hurt him elicited an unexpected thrill. So did the boldness of her response. "And who protects her from you?"

Ash smiled. Not a gentle smile, not even the one he showed to his friends. This was the Dragon's smile, all fangs and promise, and he thrilled again when she didn't shrink from it. "You do, Zanya. Isn't that why you're here?"

She didn't disappoint him. "Yes."

"Good." Ash leaned forward, lowering his voice to a whisper as his lips almost grazed her ear. "I am not some insecure human boy, to feel threatened by my consort having another lover. If you want each other, then take her. Pleasure her well for me, Zanya. I'll enjoy feeling her come."

Zanya inhaled sharply and stumbled back a step. A retreat, finally— not in the face of potential violence, but at the permission to give in to pleasure. Ash made note of the vulnerability before inclining his head to Sachi. "Sleep well, Princess."

His consort stared at him, her lips pressed tightly together, as if to hold back whatever words she might speak. She felt like that inside him, too, her tightly coiled emotions such a closely held jumble that he could not tease apart the individual feelings.

Not even the fear.

Anticipation kindled in his belly, and he let it as he strode out of the little stone hut and into the welcoming darkness of the Midnight Forest. Every step felt light, as if the earth trembled along with him, pushing up to meet each step, carrying him deeper into the silence of the towering pine trees.

Fire burned through him and settled in his cock as an insistent ache he could not afford to indulge. Not yet.

His consort and her lover still held too many secrets close, but Ash had not lived for thousands of years by being a fool. Dianthe had warned of discontent in the mortal court, and now a princess arrived with magic dripping from her fingertips and an assassin so skilled she might as well be death itself.

King Dalvish II, Mortal King of the Sheltered Lands, was truly trying to kill him.

It wasn't the first time his line had toyed with defiance. Every few hundred years, the mortal lords tested the boundaries of their agreement with the High Court, though few had been foolish enough to think a human assassin could do what the Betrayer could not. The tragic consort whose attempts to murder the Dragon had become the stuff of bawdy tavern comedy had humiliated them and provided motivation to find subtler means of rebellion.

Then again, Zanya was no Prince Robard, whom Ash had repeatedly had to rescue from his own disastrous and half-formed assassination plans. Keeping the boy alive while he attempted to murder Ash had kept the decade interesting, at least, if frequently absurd.

Zanya wouldn't fumble. Memory summoned the lethal grace of her body, the effortless way she held a blade. A predator in human skin, who had been stalking Ash from the beginning. Knowing he was her intended prey only stoked the fire in his loins.

He'd been the only monster in his castle for too long.

But she wasn't *his* monster. Not yet. And Sachi wasn't his, either, for all the magic that bound her to him with unbreakable ties. Whatever terrible secrets lurked in their shared past had committed them to this task. Two weapons bent on his destruction.

Two weapons he would claim for his own.

Sweet Sachi would be easy. Her body was already weak for his touch. He could take her now, and she'd be willing. But if he was patient, if he played out the game . . .

The handmaid was skittish. There was no frank sensuality in her movements, no knowing glint in her eyes. Ash would wager his entire castle that the only pleasurable touches she'd ever known had come at Sachi's hands. She'd be slow to warm to him, slow to trust. He'd need to let her grow accustomed to his presence . . . and teach her to associate said presence with Sachi's rapturous pleasure.

With her lover and protector openly acknowledged and close at hand, perhaps the fear that ate away at Sachi's heart would fade. And then . . .

And then.

Beneath him, the earth seemed to shiver in anticipation. He closed his eyes, and the Everlasting Dream whispered to him the promise he'd heard in his heart from the first days after the world had shattered.

You will never be alone again.

Chapter Fourteen
DRAGON'S MOON

Week One, Day Six
Year 3000

Sachi trembled, torn between horror and elation.

Her mind churned, turning over the cascade of events she'd set off with her careless words. She'd whispered of love, and Ash had listened a little too closely and too well. He'd taken her momentary lapse of control, tasted its honesty, and jumped to a conclusion that was both wildly incorrect . . . and the only true thing in her life.

He thought it was all about her and Zanya. That the fear that lived in Sachi's gut, growing and pulsing like a sentient thing, was over the prospect of their affair being discovered. And, with his self-assured words about security and desire, he'd done it.

He'd flipped their entire situation upside down and given Sachi the perfect opening, and he didn't even realize it.

So far, he wouldn't fuck her because of the fear that permeated her being. He still thought she was scared of him—or, at the very least, that her dread was something from which he could rescue her.

She would still be afraid. But her feelings for Zanya were strong enough to disguise that fear. And when Ash reached across their bond, perhaps he'd only be able to taste Sachi's desire.

They stretched out before her, the lines demarcating all the paths available to her.

She could deny her feelings, say she felt nothing for Zanya. Ash would not believe her, but he wouldn't push her, either. He would let it go, and her mission would proceed much as it had been.

She would fail.

She could acknowledge her love for Zanya but turn it away from his gaze. Keep it private, in effect denying him access to the furthest reaches of her heart. He would respect her secret feelings but, despite his confident words, the loss would wound him.

She would fail.

She could tell him that Zanya had no interest in him or in any other man. Ash would likely apologize, and they would carry on as before.

She would probably fail.

Part of her wanted to choose any of these paths, because the last one was . . . messy. It involved more duplicitousness, a web of hidden lies wreathed in lust, and Zanya would be dragged into it. Zanya may have had blood on her hands, but at least the rest of her was clean. If they did this . . .

Sachi's heart would break.

She would probably succeed.

Sachi surged off the bed, crossed the room, and grasped Zanya by her shoulders. "We have to talk. I have to make sure you understand."

Zanya shuddered, every breath still coming fast and unsteady. "Did you hear what he said to me?"

"I did. He thinks he's figured everything out."

"Hasn't he?" Zanya closed her eyes. "I cut the Huntress, Sachi. They *know*. They know I'm not . . . normal."

Sachi snorted indelicately. "Didn't you see his face? He was thinking all *sorts* of things about the two of you making me scream. You're dangerous, but he likes it, Zanya. He *wants* it."

For all the brutality of her training, Zanya could be heartbreakingly innocent sometimes. It took another moment for her to understand, and then a flush washed over her golden skin. "You think he wants both of us? Together?"

"Yes, I do." But she wouldn't force this, no matter how great an opportunity it presented. Not even to save their lives. "The choice is yours, Zanya. I trained for this, but you didn't. It isn't the same as combat—it's darker, and you can't wash it off at the end of the day. Isn't that why you worry about me so much?"

Zanya cupped her cheeks and pressed her forehead to Sachi's. "I worry about you being alone with him. I worry about something happening when I'm not there to protect you. This would be so much better. It's just . . ." Her voice hitched.

Sachi's heart twisted. "You don't have to do anything you don't want to do, Zan. I swear it."

Zanya shook her head. "It's not what you think. I'm scared, but . . ." She pulled away suddenly, pivoting to pace the confines of their cabin. It took only five of her long strides to reach the far side, where she turned again, her eyes fever bright. "I cut the Huntress. Do you know why?"

Sachi blinked. "It was an inadvertent slip, surely."

Another shake of her head, and Zanya twisted her fingers together. "I forgot," she whispered. "In the capital, they never let me forget. They feared me, and they hated me. Every person I crossed blades with looked at me and saw a monster on a leash. The more powerful I grew, the more they loathed me. But here . . ."

"They don't fear you," Sachi finished.

"No." Zanya stared at her across the cabin. "They treat me like I could belong. Like I could be one of them. And I know that it's a lie. I know why I'm here. But facing the Huntress and seeing respect instead of hatred . . . I forgot that they're the enemy." Guilt shredded her voice as she covered her face. "I forgot that your life and soul hang in the balance."

"Oh, Zan." Sachi touched Zanya's wrists, then slid her hands into her lover's dark hair, loosening its ties. "Sweetheart, look at me. Please." When she finally did, Sachi kissed her softly. "I forget sometimes, too. But it doesn't mean what you think. It only means that it's impossible to do this, to live this way, without getting wrapped up in the fantasy, at least a little."

A small, hoarse laugh escaped Zanya's lips. "I thought my price would be higher. A pat or two on the head, and they've seduced me into wanting to believe in their fairy tale. I don't have your training. What if I can't play the game? What if *he* makes me forget?"

Then Sachi would be in good company. "Let that worry claim its own day." She kissed Zanya again, lingering this time, coaxing instead of comforting. "The choice is yours, my love. There are a thousand things I can tell him to end this fascination of his right now. And I will. But you have to be honest with me."

Zanya's fingers settled on her hips and flexed slightly, tugging her closer. "You said you find him attractive."

A weak word for the molten fire that burned in Sachi when Ash whispered her name. "Because I do."

Zanya's lips feathered across her cheek, tracing a sweet path to her ear. "And you like the way he touches you?"

"I wish he'd do it more. But he thinks I'm *fragile*." Sachi shivered. "You could show him how mistaken he is."

"Not fragile," Zanya agreed, pressing forward until Sachi's back hit the wall. The contrast between the cool stone and the blazing heat of Zanya's body made her shiver again as Zanya's teeth grazed her ear.

"But precious. And sweet. I could show him how sweet you are. Is that what *you* want?"

"Yes. But then, I always want you." Sachi touched Zanya's jaw. "And I want you to see. I love you, and they will, too. You're so beautiful, Zanya. So honest. Of course he wants you."

Zanya's fingers curled around Sachi's throat, stroking with possessive hunger. "But it won't be honest. Even if I go to bed with him, even if I *like* it . . ." Zanya pulled back, and the look in her eyes was beyond love. Devotion, determination . . . Sachi could never doubt she was the center of Zanya's world.

Zanya forged ahead. "I don't care if he fucks us both weak-limbed from dusk until dawn every night. He might make me forget for a while, but all I have to do is look at you, and I'll remember why he has to die."

"We'll both remember."

It was more than a vow. It was *the way*, the path straight through Ash's defenses. And now that Sachi knew it, she had no excuse. While her attempts at seducing the Dragon had been falling short, she'd been able to ignore the obvious—and the inevitable. It didn't matter if she planned to kill him at some point in the nebulous, unformed future, because nothing about that future was yet within her grasp.

But now, she knew how they could do it. She could even guess when, within a certain degree of probability. Which meant she had to move forward.

She already didn't want to kill Ash. But she would.

And Sachi's heart would break.

Chapter Fifteen
DRAGON'S MOON

Week One, Day Eight
Year 3000

The problem with agreeing to help Sachi seduce the Dragon was that Zanya didn't have the slightest idea how to do that.

For several nights, he'd joined them at their campfire, telling stories of ancient history and fierce battles, obviously doing his best to set them at ease.

No, to set *Zanya* at ease. With her undaunted courage, Sachi needed no such coddling. She drank in the Dragon's words like a scholar who had uncovered a rare manuscript, her eyes bright and delighted.

Zanya mostly felt like she was being hunted.

Still, the stories weren't bad. She'd always hungered for tales of the battles against the Empire. Her trainers had denied her lessons in strategy, scoffing at the very idea that she might need to know the ways of armies and battlefields. She was an assassin, not a warrior. A single blade sharpened for a single purpose.

Somehow, she had to forget that purpose enough to relax around the Dragon . . . and yet still remember it enough to do what must be done.

An impossible balance.

She brooded over it as she washed with water heated over the fire in their tiny cabin. Sachi was already tucked into the bed, her long braid thrown over one shoulder and a hand curled beneath her chin. Until Sachi's confession about their relationship, whoever had ridden ahead to prepare the cabins for them had always set up a tiny cot for Zanya to sleep on.

Now there was simply the bed and her lover. Her acknowledged lover.

At least Zanya didn't have to pretend about that anymore.

She braided her hair and changed quickly before sliding into the bed. Sachi snuggled up next to her and murmured a few incoherent words before drifting back into slumber. The softness of her cheek against Zanya's shoulder and the slow, steady sound of her breathing should have been enough to bring sweet dreams.

Instead, dark thoughts chased one another through her mind.

Could she lie to the Dragon? Could she make him believe she welcomed him to Sachi's bed? It had seemed so simple when Sachi proposed it. And it wasn't as if Zanya didn't feel drawn to him. There was something seductive in all of these gods, something lush and dangerous that she wanted to wallow in.

Her twisted fascination with them was one thing. Sharing Sachi with them? That was another thing entirely.

From the time Zanya had first understood the king's plan, the Dragon had loomed large in her darkest dreams. Not because High Priest Nikkon had done everything he could to make Zanya loathe him, to make her *fear* him—though he certainly had—but because the Dragon had been the monster who would one day take Sachi from her. Every possessive part of her rioted at the idea of letting him touch her.

But Sachi wanted him.

At least, Zanya *thought* she did. The Dragon's blasted magic curled around Sachi's mind and soul like a cage. Her thoughts and feelings could never be her own. She had to convince herself she loved him, or he would feel the emotions through their bond and recognize the threat she represented. She'd told Zanya as much before the bonding ceremony—a warning Zanya hadn't fully appreciated at the time.

She shuddered. She'd take every beating she'd ever endured a dozen times over rather than know that there was no privacy or safety, even in the darkest corners of her own heart.

No, a hundred times.

A *thousand* times. High Priest Nikkon could have had her beaten from dawn until dusk and still—

The violent sting of the lash exploded across her back, and she jerked. Her teeth instinctively dug into her lip to hold back a shout of pain, because she never gave them the satisfaction. She never—

Chains rattled with her movements as she spun in the darkness. The heavy metal cuff around her ankle dug into her flesh, jerking her to a stop as the chain pulled taut. Shadows swirled around her, revealing a windowless room she knew all too well. A mere six paces across, it contained a stack of flimsy blankets in one corner and a massive ring driven into the cold stone floor to hold the single chain trapping her ankle.

It felt so real that the chill beneath her bare feet raised goose bumps, even though she knew this was a nightmare. This room existed only in her memories, after all. At nineteen, she'd torn the ring from the floor, battered down the thick wooden door, and used the chain to strangle the first guard who'd arrived to subdue her. With his sword in hand, she could have held off half the guards in the castle.

But High Priest Nikkon hadn't needed the castle guards, only a good grip on Sachi's hair and a knife to her throat. Zanya had walked into a new cell on her own, lesson learned.

Her defiance could get Sachi killed.

Zanya's heart beat faster. Panic made her hands tremble as she reached for the chain. One violent heave should have ripped it easily from the floor—she was much stronger now than she had been at nineteen—but it didn't budge.

"It seemed best to limit your range of movement, all things considered."

She whipped around at the familiar voice, and rage battled with the fear to fill her heart. Rage won. It always did. She lunged at him, but the cuff around her ankle snapped her back, her curled fingers slicing through the air just a pace shy of his face.

"I've never believed the superstition that dying in a nightmare will tear your soul from the Everlasting Dream." A cruel smile twisted his lips. "But that doesn't mean I intend to let you put your dirty hands on me."

Zanya stared at him, her entire body shaking with the need to claw his smug blue eyes from his pretty face. Though she'd heard whispers at court that he was old enough to have attended King Dalvish II's birth, his face was unlined, his body still strong. No gray marred the gold of his hair. As the king's personal advisor, it was Nikkon's job to lead the court in celebration on all the various feast days and to remind the mortal lords of their duty to the High Court of Dreamers.

If you listened to the oldest servants who warmed their bones by the fires at night, there had been a time under King Dalvish I when *duty* had been a joyous word instead of a curse. But resentment had curdled in his grandson, and his priest now preached fear and condemnation, each god the terrifying epitome of some excess he abhorred. Nikkon often railed against the mindless hedonism of the Lover, the poisonous duplicity of the Witch, the merciless judgment of the Huntress, the feral inhumanity of the Wolf, and the deadly seduction of the Siren. Of the Phoenix, he spoke as little as possible, but of the Dragon . . .

There had the bulk of Nikkon's wrath been centered. In the Dragon, Nikkon had taught, lived the worst flaws and dangers of all the other gods combined. Greedy hedonism, poisonous wrath, merciless rage, feral seduction. The story of the fierce warrior who guarded their borders had turned into tales of a vicious monster who served as their jailer.

Zanya had known the priest was untrustworthy. Oh, how she had known. Still, she'd let herself believe what he said about the Dragon because it was convenient. It made her job easier.

But she'd known something else, too. The darkness in her had recognized the same in him from the very beginning. The king's high priest might wear the robes of one dedicated to the High Court, he might curse the Void-touched as if they were vile creatures worthy only of banishment, but the Everlasting Dream was most certainly *not* the power he worshipped.

No. High Priest Nikkon whispered his fervent desires to the Endless Void.

And he'd pulled her into a nightmare with him.

He sneered at her. "Nothing to say, girl?"

Since she couldn't reach him, Zanya took a step back. With enough give in the chain, at least she would have a chance to react to anything he might do. "I assume you brought me here for a purpose. You'll come around to it, once you've finished entertaining yourself."

That made him laugh. "Do you think I long for your presence? You will tell me of the bonding ceremony."

Warning raced up her spine. "The what?"

"The *bonding* between Sachielle and the Dragon. Was it accomplished?"

Zanya's thoughts raced. She couldn't imagine why he would ask. He certainly wasn't motivated by concern over Sachi's well-being. Had they known beforehand how completely her soul would be laid bare to the Dragon? They must have at least suspected, or else they wouldn't have trained her to suppress her feelings.

They'd purposefully, *deliberately* sent her to have her heart violated.

"Answer me, girl."

She glared at him and ground her teeth together. Fury at her defiance filled his eyes, and he flung out a hand. Shadows rose from the floor, grabbed her, and dragged her back toward the wall. Pain spasmed through her body as she crashed into the stone, her instinctive struggles stilled by the phantom chains that bound her.

Nikkon strolled up to her, his head tilted. Assessing. "Yes, I believe it was done. Excellent."

"Why does it matter?" Zanya snarled.

"Can you truly be this ignorant? The king never wanted to waste your time with tutors, but perhaps that was a mistake. Come now, Zanya. Think about it. I'm sure Sachi has already worked it out." One elegant golden eyebrow arched, and his sudden smile made a mockery of pity. "I can see why she wouldn't confide in you, though. Your conversation must be stultifying."

When Zanya didn't reply, his hand shot out to grab her face. His fingers dug painfully into her cheeks, his thumb pressing so hard into her skin that if this had been the waking world, she might have been left with bruises bearing the whorls of his thumbprint.

"The point, you idiot child, is that we have something the Empire needs." He all but crooned the words, his eyes bright with fervent glee. "Thousands of leagues of untouched land and the precious minerals that lie beneath. The High Court has chained the royal family for centuries, preventing them from claiming their due. But now the Dragon's wretched curse has entangled Sachi, along with whatever common ancestry she can claim. Who cares? All that matters is that it isn't House Roquebarre. Now the king can take what he wants from the land without fear of reprisal."

She stared at him. On some level, she'd always known there had to be a reason they'd "adopted" Sachi and claimed her as their own. But she'd never truly believed that whatever harm came to the land would be visited upon the consort's family many times over. Surely it was pure fabrication, or an exaggeration at best. There were so many other reasons to steal Sachi to be their princess. Easier to send a changeling to be the Dragon's captive in place of your own beloved child. Easier to torment and train and break and hurt an orphan who did not share your blood.

Easier to pillage the land and raze the forests if the High Court's magic would rebound on someone else?

Apparently, the king believed so. "So it was never really about killing the Dragon?"

He released her face with a harsh laugh. "Of course it is. But this way, *that* won't rebound on the royal family, either. And whether you succeed or fail, your attempts will provide a delightful distraction." He smiled. "A rather elegant plan, don't you think? No matter the outcome, I get what I want."

Hot rage turned to ice. The shadows pinning Zanya to the wall trembled, and she *felt* the uncertainty in the dream.

He dared to call *her* a fool? He was the one who had brought her into a nightmare. He was the one trying to bind her with shadows. And a lifetime of fear, of feeling small and helpless before him, had almost made her forget the truth.

Nightmares obeyed her whims. Shadows danced for her pleasure.

Zanya flexed her fingers and called to the shadows, opening herself to her own darkness. Something cool slid around her fingers, a curious tasting. She felt their delight, their *recognition*, and her bonds shifted from a terrifying cage to a loving embrace.

"I will kill the Dragon," she whispered. "But if anything happens to Sachi . . ."

Nikkon realized the danger a moment too late. Zanya bared her teeth and *shoved* through the shadows, and the priest slammed back against the opposite side of the room with enough force to crack the wall.

Chains sprung up to imprison him. The cracks in the wall widened, and hunks of stone began to fall away, revealing a swirling darkness all around them that whispered to Zanya with the eagerness of a dozen excited puppies.

The metal cuff encircling her ankle turned to dust. She held out one hand, and the shadows coalesced into a long, viciously sharp knife.

Nikkon struggled against his bonds, his arrogance a thin shell over true panic. She reveled in it, in the slowly mounting fear in his eyes.

How many times had he hurt her? Had her beaten? Ordered her locked away? Punished, just because she hadn't bent to his will with sufficiently supple obedience?

How many nights had he come to her and woven dark tales of what the Dragon would do to Sachi if Zanya didn't stop him? He'd given her nightmares that had taken root in her soul and grown poisonous fruit. But the Dragon had not hurt Sachi. He'd never lifted a hand to her, never made her cry.

Nikkon *had*.

The knife felt sweet in her hands. She lifted it, and the high priest finally found his voice. "Take one more step, and I'll kill her tonight."

Zanya froze.

"Do you think I can't?" Nikkon snarled, fear rendering his voice harsh. "I set the curse. I can accelerate it, too. If you cross me, dear Sachi will simply go to bed one night and never wake."

It was another knife held to Sachi's throat, so much more powerful than any direct threat against Zanya could ever be. And Nikkon knew it. She saw his triumph as her blade vanished. And she saw something else—his rage. She'd witnessed fear in him tonight, and he would never forgive her for that.

She could only pray that Sachi wouldn't be the one who suffered for it.

The chains holding him vanished. The shadows receded, wrapping around Zanya in apology. In comfort. Nikkon stood, straightening his robes, cloaked in his disdainful superiority again like armor. He knew who held the power here.

"Slay the Dragon, Zanya. It's the only way you can protect her."

On those words, the nightmare shattered. Nikkon was swept away in a swirl of darkness. His path glittered through the endless night surrounding her, but Zanya didn't dare follow. She didn't dare move. She barely breathed.

Curled up in the darkness, she shivered until the shadows soothed her back into a restless sleep. But she still woke before dawn and slipped silently to the trunk where the hourglass was packed away.

The metal seal was cold against her lips. She shuddered as the lock disengaged at her kiss, then lifted the hated thing from its bed.

In the dim light from the fire, she reassured herself that the bulk of the sand still resided in the upper chamber. Then she held it and watched helplessly as Sachi's life slipped away, grain by grain.

Chapter Sixteen
DRAGON'S MOON

Week One, Day Ten
Year 3000

If the Midnight Forest had felt like Zanya's natural habitat, the Witchwood felt just the opposite.

Since they'd crossed the subtle border, the towering pines had grown sparser and smaller, interspersed increasingly with the peculiar Witchwood maples that only grew here. Black bark covered the thick trunks that shot up to the height of two grown men before splitting into hundreds of sprawling branches. And from each of those branches . . .

Nowhere else in the Sheltered Lands did leaves come in so many colors. Bold teals, wild violets, deep blues, shining golds, pinks so vivid they practically glowed. At night, they *did* glow. The Dragon's party slept in clearings ringed by glittering vines that sprouted bold flowers as bright as torches. When Sachi expressed wonder on the second day, Isolde had only laughed.

"Wait until you see Witchwood Castle," she'd promised, and Zanya had wondered what could possibly top that living rainbow.

Now she knew.

Witchwood Castle lay ahead of them on the edge of a rise, an improbable collection of soaring towers carved from delicate white stone that flowed with the surrounding woods as if it had been grown instead of built. Several massive Witchwood maples seemed to be part of the architecture, boasting pathways to platforms high in their branches from which vines dripped like waterfalls. Flowers bloomed everywhere in every color imaginable—and a few Zanya would forget, if possible.

Two waterfalls tumbled over rockfalls on either side of the path to the main gate, the mist sparking rainbows in the air that added to the cacophony of color. There were no shadows here to retreat to, and dressed in her usual black, Zanya felt painfully obvious.

Riding beside her, Naia gasped in awe and wonder. "Oh, Zanya. Isn't it gorgeous?"

"It's beautiful," Zanya agreed, trying to sound half as enthused as Naia. The newborn god had attached herself to Zanya's side this morning with open enthusiasm and curiosity and had proceeded to pepper her with cheerful questions, none of which were out of line or pushy but all of which made Zanya defensive.

Naia had been oblivious to her for the entire trip upriver to Blade's Rest. But she wasn't oblivious to Zanya now. No one was. Because they all *knew.*

Zanya was the consort's lover.

The secret Zanya had held closest to her heart for her entire life now stared back at her from the eyes of everyone in their party. She felt naked and exposed, her greatest vulnerability laid bare. And she felt . . . giddy. Even if it was only for a week or two, she could love Sachi openly.

What an unexpected gift at the likely end of a wretched life.

Up ahead, the gates swung open. A single pale woman stood dramatically framed by them, clad in a deeply cut bodice as black as anything in Zanya's closet. A black skirt fell from her hips in layers that whispered of feathers, and when she took a step forward, the skirt split at the front to reveal a riot of dark pinks as vivid as her forest. The color was echoed on her lips, in the flowers woven into her dark braids—and in her eyes.

That was what gave her away. Her violet eyes glowed a magnetic pink around the irises, as inhuman as the liquid gold of the Wolf or the flames that lurked in the gaze of the Dragon.

Zanya was staring at the Witch.

The woman spread her arms expectantly, and Ulric strode forward in silence to accept an embrace. "My wolf," she murmured fondly. Dark fingernails dragged through the Wolf's unkempt hair, and she shook her head with a throaty laugh. "Elevia, you've allowed him to grow shaggy again."

"Come, Inga. If I told Ric the sky was blue, he'd proclaim it green just to spite me." She looked up and grinned. "Though, here, in your domain? I suppose it could be true." She stepped forward and kissed the Witch's cheek. "It's good to see you again."

"The Huntress is always welcome here." The Witch stepped past them, her gaze locking on the Dragon, who was helping Sachi from her horse. "And here is the creature who has set the world to whispering. Introduce me, Ash."

"Let her get her feet on the ground first, Inga." He sounded grumpy, but there was a thread of warmth beneath the chiding, and when he took Sachi's hand and led her forward, Zanya was shocked to see the Dragon actually smiling. "Princess Sachielle, this nagging, impatient witch is *the* Witch."

"Inga," the woman added absently as she reached out to lift Sachi's chin. "He's very disrespectful, isn't he? It can be annoying, but we tolerate him because he has a good heart. And so do you, child. Dianthe was right. You glow."

"I'm honored to meet you," Sachi murmured, her expression serene.

"What lovely manners." Another warm chuckle, and the Witch stroked Sachi's cheek before letting her hand fall away. "She's perfect, Ash. Don't ruin this for the rest of us by scaring her off."

"Of course not," he replied dryly. "I wouldn't want to disappoint you."

"I have another introduction to make." Sachi turned, met Zanya's gaze, and beckoned.

Every muscle in Zanya's body felt made of stone. All eyes swung to her in unison, and she felt the tangible weight of them as Naia quietly urged her out of the saddle. She walked stiffly past the Raven Guard, fixing her gaze on Sachi as if she were a lifeline.

If she thought about this as simply walking to Sachi's side, she could do it.

When she had closed the distance between them, Sachi took her hand. "This is Zanya, my lover and protector."

And there it was. Spoken for the first time, words given to the world that could never be snatched back. Zanya expected some sort of shock, but the Witch only raised her eyebrows and turned to Ash. "I admit, it has been some years since I visited the capital. Have they become less rigid, then?"

"Not particularly." Ash ran a possessive hand over Sachi's golden braids, and there was nothing but proud affection in his voice. "But her heart is bigger than theirs. And she has chosen well."

"Has she?"

Zanya had barely parsed the words before the Witch was *there*, standing so close that her breathtakingly beautiful face seemed to fill Zanya's entire field of vision. She clung to Sachi's hand as the Witch reached out. A dark-tinted nail traced a shivering path from her temple to her chin, and Zanya didn't understand the odd tug deep in her belly, as if this woman held the answer to some question she didn't even know how to ask.

But that same pull was there, even stronger than she'd felt with the Wolf. The darkness in her rising, stretching, *yearning* to test itself against the woman who ran a soft thumb along her jaw and smiled at her. "Oh, aren't you delicious? Wherever did you find such a prize, Princess?"

"She saved my life," Sachi answered lightly—the truth, though most who knew the story were long dead. "And she's *mine*."

"I can see that." The Witch finally released Zanya and turned, her skirts flaring. "Oh, the seamstresses will have fun with the two of you. Come along. Dinner will be served in your suite tonight, but there's plenty to be done before tomorrow."

"Tomorrow?" Sachi asked.

"The ball, my darlings. Come, let me show you to your quarters."

Zanya followed behind Sachi and the Dragon, hoping her face didn't reveal her dread. As the consort's handmaid, she might have had a chance of fading into the shadows and avoiding the scrutiny of the Witch's court. As the consort's *lover* . . .

"It won't be as bad as you think," a voice murmured at her side. Malindra fell into step beside her, her saddlebags thrown easily over one shoulder.

"I wouldn't presume—" Zanya started, but the other woman laughed.

"You don't need to lie." Malindra jerked her head at the Dragon, who had offered his arm to Sachi as they started up the steps. "You can't possibly hate the progress more than Ash does."

"Then why does he do them?"

A shrug. "The people love it. A whole generation will spend years planning their lives around being there, just so they can say they were part of it. Just so they can say they saw or talked to or danced with *him*. He takes his responsibilities to the people seriously."

Zanya didn't want to hear that. She didn't want to think about how he'd continued to seek out their company at night in order to tell Sachi more stories about ancient history and the time before the gods, just because he'd noticed how much those tales enchanted her. She didn't want to think about the other small courtesies, either—how the foods

Sachi enjoyed had appeared more and more often, how someone was sent ahead every evening to make sure a fire was laid in her cabin, how her favorite spiced wine would be warmed and waiting whenever they made camp.

Zanya especially didn't want to think about the sudden appearance of *her* favorite dark cinnamon tea waiting for them when they rose each morning, a blend so rare because the spices only grew in the Witchwood. Or the fact that the Dragon insisted on tempting her with the stories of great battles that fascinated Zanya in spite of her stubborn desire *not* to care.

She didn't want to know that she didn't *have* to seduce the Dragon, because he was clearly more than capable of seducing her.

And she *absolutely* didn't want to think about the fact that she might like it.

Chapter Seventeen
DRAGON'S MOON

Week One, Day Ten
Year 3000

Ash's strategic assault on Zanya's defensive walls hit an improbable road-block a few minutes into his evening foray, and it was not one he could have anticipated.

His gambit had started out well enough. He'd joined them around the campfire for the past few nights, letting Zanya grow accustomed to his presence as they shared dinner and he told them stories. Sachi had a particular passion for history and eagerly drank in the authoritative first-person accounts of events she'd only ever read about in books. Zanya had been harder to entice, but Ash had figured out quickly enough that tales of legendary battles entranced her. Her joy didn't shine on her face like Sachi's did, but she would lean closer, her full lips parted in fascination, holding her breath through the most dangerous bits.

Coming to them in the private intimacy of Sachi's guest suite at Witchwood Castle was a gamble, but he'd saved a good story for tonight. He'd raided Inga's kitchen for the finest chocolates in her stock-pile, precious delicacies even a king could not hope to find outside of the Witchwood.

And that was where it all went sideways—when Zanya opened the door at his knock and caught sight of the chocolate.

Ash stood in the doorway of the sitting area, the tray in his hand, and watched all life leach from the handmaid's face. For one heart-rending moment, pain stood naked in her eyes—and Ash had known too many soldiers with war wounds on their souls not to know that look. A memory had seized Zanya, the kind so vivid and raw it was like reliving the past, and he could do nothing but watch her swallow hard and regather her composure.

Sachi's voice drifted in to break the silence. "Who is it, Zanya?"

She flinched. Her gaze shot to Ash's, filled with clear resentment. She hated that he'd seen her moment of vulnerability, and her glare warned him to say nothing of it to Sachi. She snatched the tray from him and turned, though there was no hint of pain in her voice as she replied. "The Dragon has come to visit, and he's brought you a gift."

Sachi appeared from the adjacent bedroom, a book in one hand. She still wore her clothes from dinner, a simple gown of emerald velvet embellished with gold brocade, and she smiled at him. "This is certainly . . ."

The words trailed off as she spied the tray. Ash tensed, but her smile only grew wider. "You brought us chocolates. How sweet."

"Sachi loves chocolate," Zanya said, throwing him another warning glance over her shoulder. She was far easier to read than Sachi was. Zanya's eyes promised a world of pain if he said or did anything that might spoil Sachi's pleasure in the gift.

Ash acknowledged both the spoken and unspoken comments with a single nod. "Inga has a cook here whose entire job is working with chocolate. You'll never taste finer."

"Well, then. We shouldn't delay." Sachi set her book on a small table and regarded the tray with sincere gravity, finally choosing a small caramel topped with ribbons of rich ganache. She held Ash's gaze as she popped it into her mouth.

A moment later, her eyes fluttered shut with a soft moan.

Her enjoyment bordered on erotic, and it wasn't an act. The sensual pleasure of it throbbed across their bond, sweet and decadent, and the fact that it wasn't artifice made it all the more irresistible.

There were a dozen more confections scattered across the tray. Ash selected one with a distinctive deep-red glaze and held it just shy of Sachi's lips. "This is my favorite, but it's only for those who like the kiss of fire."

"I'm not afraid of a little heat." Her teeth nipped his fingers as she took the chocolate.

No, she wasn't. Her hot anticipation zipped along his nerves, but when he glanced at Zanya, she still stood somewhat stiffly, the tray held in front of her. He plucked it from her hands and carried it to a table before a vine-edged window. "I thought I might share another story with you tonight, if you were interested."

"It's late," Zanya said immediately, "and we've had a long day of travel. The princess is tired."

"A pity." Ash let his words fall casually as he carefully baited his trap. "I thought I could tell you the truth behind the legends of the Western Wall."

Sachi chuckled softly.

Zanya's fingers flexed at her sides, her interior battle playing itself out across her face. Reluctance, burning curiosity . . . The words seemed dragged from her against her will. "Is he real? The Kraken?"

"Oh yes. As real as any of us."

Zanya glanced helplessly at Sachi, who smiled indulgently.

"It sounds fascinating, but Zanya is right. I was about to get ready for bed." She paused, her slight smile full of mystery and unmistakable invitation. "Perhaps you'd be so kind as to join us in my bedchamber?

Zanya has started a fire, and you can regale us with your tale while she helps me undress."

Then she turned and walked through the open doorway. After a tense moment, Zanya followed, glancing back over her shoulder just once with a curt, "Well, come along, then."

Such naked, snarling challenge in those beautiful eyes. It was tragically easy to imagine how she must have scraped at the egos of the withered mortal lords. How they must have hungered to put her in her place and raged when they could not. Abuse at their hands would have been inevitable.

Purging the whole lot of them sounded increasingly appealing.

But rage had no place in the game tonight. So Ash followed them into Sachi's bedroom and made himself comfortable on the colorful woven rug laid before the hearth.

Sachi pulled the small stool away from her dressing table until she could settle onto it, facing Ash. She tugged a single decorative pin from her corona of braids and arched an expectant eyebrow. "What story did you bring us tonight, my lord?"

Flower-shaped candles floated in water-filled globes on Sachi's dressing table, accenting the firelight. Ash watched the golden braids tumble to her shoulders before smiling. "How much do you know about the last time the Betrayer invaded the Sheltered Lands?"

"There are scrolls in the archives, and my tutors made sure I glanced at them, at the very least." Sachi tilted her head, a movement that bared the vulnerable line of her throat. "More than two thousand years ago. 975?"

"Close. 980." As he spoke, Zanya's graceful fingers began to unravel Sachi's first braid, combing swiftly through the strands. She kept her gaze on her work, but she was clearly listening. "The Betrayer knew the approach was impossible from the west and south. But the Blasted Plains are flat as far as the eye can see, and mostly deserted. And there's a deep-water bay large enough to land an army in secret."

"Betrayer's Cove," Zanya murmured.

"That's what it's called now," Ash agreed. "So you've heard something of the story, Zanya?"

She finished smoothing out the first braid, her fingernails ghosting over Sachi's scalp. Warm, sleepy pleasure twisted through his bond with Sachi, so tangible he swore he could feel Zanya's fingernails dragging through his own hair. "I heard that the Betrayer built a thousand ships and brought them to our shores to conquer us."

"Very nearly a thousand. More ships than any of us had ever seen." He could still remember his first glimpse of them as he soared high above the ocean. The ships had gone on forever, spilling out to the horizon. How tempted he had been to end that foolish war before it could begin. To set fire to their ships and let Dianthe drag them down into the depths.

Fear had held him back. Fear that his former brother was lurking among them, and that the resulting clash would finish what they'd almost started. That it would unmake the world.

"If there were so many, what happened?" With her hair nearly undone, Sachi dropped her hands to the laces at the front of her velvet gown and began to untie them. "The Sheltered Lands had no fleets of their own to turn them back. And I know you didn't intervene. I would remember that."

His gaze followed her fingers, and each lace loosened felt like a victory. "I did not. In those days, we feared another war between the gods more than we feared invasion. Perhaps, if they had reached our shores in large enough numbers, I would have risked it. But in the end, I did not have to."

"Because of the Kraken?" Zanya asked, her fingers still combing delicious tingles through Sachi's hair.

Those tingles were impacting him more than he'd anticipated. Ash had to clear his throat and shift his position—though hiding his current state of arousal was impossible. "He was just a man then. Einar, one of the few captains brave or mad enough to hunt the great swordfish that live off Dead Man Shoals. His ship was named the *Kraken*, and he was the first to bring warning to Elevia's people."

The lush green velvet of Sachi's bodice fell open, baring the gauzy cream-colored chemise beneath. Zanya's fingers stroked over Sachi's shoulders, and Ash nearly forgot what part of the story he was rattling off as he watched the handmaid ease the velvet from Sachi's body. When she rose to make it easier, the candlelight behind her shone through her thin chemise, outlining the curves of her body.

Sachi reached for the ribbons tying the front of it together. She rubbed the silk ribbon between her fingers, toying with it as she met and held his gaze.

Then she tugged the first ribbon free.

Fire leapt from the candles, filling the globes and spilling down into the water. The hearth roared behind him, flames licking at his back with eager encouragement.

Oh, she was dangerous. That spark in her eyes all but dared him to let the chains on his self-control shatter, to swoop across the room and take her. He had imagined a dozen ways already—on the floor on her knees, on the floor on her back. Bent over the chair while he sank both hands into the golden hair Zanya had so thoughtfully unbraided for him.

He could sit in the chair and pull her into his lap, onto his cock. He could spend the whole night watching her whimper and writhe, impaled and needy but unable to get the leverage to *move* while he stroked and nipped and etched his claim on her into her very bones.

Or maybe he couldn't. Zanya would never stand idly by and leave her wanting. She didn't now, bending instead so her lips grazed Sachi's ear. But her dark-brown eyes blazed with that same dangerous awareness, and her words were no whisper. They were sheer challenge. "Your bath is ready."

His consort stepped through the archway that led into the bathing room. Though the walls were stone, the archway had been edged with a carved wooden jamb. The rich, warm tones of the polished wood set off the color of the huge copper tub, and Sachi slipped into the space like she didn't just belong there, it had been *made* for her.

She was facing away from him when she dropped the gauzy chemise and stood naked, wreathed in steam, next to the tub. Instinct drove him to his feet. Hunger drove him across the room. The tattered shreds of his self-control were all that stopped him at the threshold. He gripped the top of the doorframe, tethering himself to the spot.

He had gone a century without release. One hundred years without giving in to the occasional demands of his body. Surely, she could not break him in one evening.

He would not cross this line.

With Zanya's help, Sachi climbed into the tub. She slid completely under the surface, then emerged a moment later. The floral-scented water darkened her hair to honey and clung to her lashes as she blinked up at him.

Then she laughed, low and musical. "I do believe you've forgotten why you're here, my lord."

Zanya's lips quirked into a smile—not quite smug but certainly amused. Proud that Sachi had so thoroughly distracted him, perhaps. When her gaze found his, it was fond commiseration he saw, and the distance between them collapsed into nothing as Zanya shook her head as if to say, *No one can resist her.*

Ash imagined very few could.

Zanya selected a bottle from the shelf and poured something into her hands, then smoothed it into Sachi's hair. "You were telling us about Einar. He was the first to bring news to the Huntress."

"Ahh, yes. And he sailed through a gale that sank the scouts pursuing him to do it." Though all sailors pledged their first allegiance to the Siren, many of the fiercest served the Huntress, too, carrying news for her across the continent and warning her of danger. Einar had been one of those. But with his message delivered, he hadn't sat back to let the war play out. "Most would have considered their task complete. But Einar and his people traded their fishing gear for weapons and turned right back around. The Betrayer planned an invasion. Einar started a war."

He had Zanya now. Her hands moved dreamily through Sachi's hair, massaging the cleansing oil into it, but her gaze was riveted to him. "A war at sea? How?"

"However he could." The ghosts of her fingertips seemed to roam his own scalp. Ash tightened his grip on the wooden doorframe and tried to let the memories of war chill some of his ardor. "No one had ever done it before, so no one was prepared for him. He set fire to their sails with burning arrows, and punctured the hulls of their ships with harpoons. He sank dozens by chasing them into Dead Man Shoals—that's how they got their name, in fact. No one could catch the wind like Einar, and people began to whisper that he was not human."

"But you said he was," Sachi reminded him.

"At the start of the war, yes." Ash tilted his head, curious. "What have the priests told you about how a Dreamer comes to be?"

"Frankly, I'm not sure they believe it happens." She shifted position, sitting up straighter, until her nipples peeked out of the water. "They mouth all the right words about the miracle of belief, but they're just that to them. Words."

Rivulets of water slid down her throat as Zanya rinsed her hair, and Ash could almost feel his fingers following that path. It took real effort to focus on his words. "You know that some, like Naia, are born directly of the Dream, but that is rare. Most of us manifest as I did. It happens when the desires of a heart and the needs of the world collide. Einar needed to be powerful, and the world needed a powerful defender. So he became a weapon, and his legend grew. The more the Empire feared him, the more formidable he became. And the more formidable he became, the more the Empire feared him."

Water splashed as Sachi lifted one leg onto the edge of the tub. "Like you?"

Every candle in the bathroom flared until the room was as bright as midday. The floor beneath his feet actually shuddered. Inga would be furious with him if his barely contained lust rattled the castle and broke so much as a single glass. But he was the one who'd decided to play out this game.

"Like me," he rasped. "The more people fear me, the stronger I become."

"And many people fear you," Zanya said softly. Her fingers stroked down Sachi's throat and disappeared beneath the water. "You must be very strong."

The muscles in Zanya's arm flexed. His bond with Sachi trembled, pleasure blazing so bright it outshone the dancing candles. If any fear lingered there, it was buried beneath waves of satisfied desire and hunger and the safety she felt when Zanya touched her.

"I *am*." He didn't tear his gaze from Zanya's, even as another spike of reflected pleasure danced down his spine. "But there are many kinds of power. Sachi knows that. She's the most powerful person in this room right now. We all dance to her pleasure, don't we, Zanya?"

That fond, proud little smile curled Zanya's lips again as she turned her face into Sachi's cheek, her lips grazing her skin in a soft kiss. "I do."

And she loved doing it. Loved pleasing Sachi, loved making her feel safe, loved all of it so much that some long-neglected part of Ash ached with envy. Friendship, he'd had for centuries, and pleasure was easy enough to find. But this inferno of passion, the kind of love that was personal and deep and knew no limits?

No one had ever felt that protective, possessive burn for the Dragon.

"So dance for me." Sachi held Zanya's lips to her skin and took her arm, guiding it lower in the water. All the while staring at Ash, daring him to look away.

His hands felt melded to the doorframe. If he let go, he couldn't be sure his self-control would hold. "What is the princess's pleasure?"

"Watch." It was a command and a plea, all tangled up in one breathless syllable. "I can feel how much you want this, even more than your own pleasure. So *watch*."

She turned her head, meeting Zanya's ready mouth with a fierce kiss, tongues and teeth flashing. And that was all there *was* to watch, that dizzying kiss and the gentle movement of the water as Zanya's fingers shifted below the surface.

The handmaid clearly knew how to use her hand. Aleksi would have been impressed by the speed with which she coaxed Sachi to helpless moans. Taut, excruciating pleasure washed over their bond, climbing Ash's spine and tightening every muscle in his body as Zanya skillfully lured Sachi to the trembling edge.

At the last moment, Zanya turned to look at Ash. Her fingers sank into the wet strands of Sachi's honey-gold hair, twisting tight enough to provoke a gasp as she craned Sachi's head back, baring her throat. "Tell him who you belong to," she whispered against Sachi's ear, her dark gaze holding Ash's.

"*You.*"

"Me," Zanya agreed, and Ash didn't know if it was something she did beneath the water, or the fact that she closed her teeth over Sachi's pounding pulse in a primal claim, but release roared down their bond. Sachi's back arched with ecstasy, and she muffled a shuddering scream between clenched teeth.

The doorframe cracked under his grip, and it wasn't from the sheer pleasure of watching her come, as piercing as that was. It was the *glow*, like dizzy sunlight reflected through a thousand crystals, and the way the world seemed to hold its breath as Ash's heart pounded and his body ached with need.

Ours, whispered that voice inside him, the voice of Dreams, the voice of the earth, the voice of the very world that he cherished and loved.

Yes, he replied.

Soon.

Chapter Eighteen
DRAGON'S MOON

Week Two, Day One
Year 3000

Many hundreds of years before Tislaine's ill-fated turn as consort, there had been a princess named Alysaia who wrote letters to her younger sister, Megaine—the eventual queen—detailing the progress. She wrote in minute, brutal detail about everything from the colors and temperaments of her horses to the crowds that had gathered at each stop. She left out nothing, a fact that had led to her being dubbed, somewhat sarcastically, the Secretive Consort.

Of the Witchwood, she had written only, "There was a ball at the castle, which I greatly enjoyed."

Alysaia, it seemed, had kept some secrets after all.

Calling the spectacle before Sachi a *ball* was accurate only in that the Witch's guests were, indeed, dancing. But instead of the formal, choreographed dance sets popular in the capital, people were . . .

Touching. A lot.

It might not have been so very scandalous were it not for the attire. The point of a dance *was* surreptitious contact, that much was true everywhere. But those clandestine caresses on waists and strong, broad shoulders were usually dulled by several layers of fabric.

Sachi barely wore one. Jeweled silver adorned her throat, shoulders, and waist in fine webs of exquisitely wrought metal fitted close to her body. The collar, epaulets, and belt were all connected by gossamer-thin chains, and beneath them . . .

Sachi hadn't understood the seamstress's seemingly singular focus on shaping the adornments. Now it made sense, for she wore nothing beneath the delicate silver but a few lengths of strategically draped diaphanous cloth. It was a lovely ice blue several shades lighter than her eyes, and it barely covered anything when she stood still. When she moved, the gauzy cloth shifted to expose a truly shocking amount of bare flesh.

If they'd dressed Alysaia like this, it was no wonder she hadn't breathed a word of it to Queen Megaine.

But now Sachi understood the rumors about the fae folk who lived in the Witchwood. In addition to the ethereal attire, the place more than looked magical. It *was* magical. Lights floated above the revelers, illuminating a vast stone courtyard surrounded by trees that seemed to grow as one with the rest of the castle.

Vines wound around the trees and stone, laden with night-blooming flowers that looked white at first. But when the petals caught the light, Sachi realized they were shimmering with iridescent color. Birds flitted between them, their trilling songs melding with the music.

The main part of the floor had been reserved for dancing, but white-draped tables ringed the space. There were trays of food and metal fountains that bubbled with colorful liquid. It poured into crystal glasses, somehow never spilling a single drop.

Taking it all in made Sachi feel slightly dizzy, as if she'd drunk too many of those bubbly drinks already. Everything felt surreal, turning the entire experience into something dreamlike and heady.

She turned to Inga, who stood by her side, watching the dancers as they whirled across the stone courtyard. "You have a lovely home."

"Thank you." Inga's costume for the night was a slinkier version of the gown she'd worn to greet them. Thin black silk clung to her body, eventually giving way to an elaborate feathered hem. She cradled a delicate crystal goblet in one hand with a satisfied smile. "It's made brighter by your presence, Sachielle."

She said it as if she meant the words, wholly and without reservation. "You're too kind, Inga."

"Not usually. If anything, I'm quite often considered the opposite." One elegant eyebrow lifted. "What are they saying about me in the capital these days? Do I still lure children into my castle and devour them?"

Embarrassment warmed Sachi's cheeks. There were people who spoke of the Witch as if she were a demon, bent on devouring not only those children but their souls as well. "The healers revere you. Others are, perhaps, not so enlightened."

Judging by Inga's warm chuckle, the thought didn't bother her. "I've always unsettled those who do not understand that life and death are not enemies at all, but fond lovers. I delight in their unenlightened stories."

"Not everyone can shrug them off so easily." Ash, in particular, seemed to suffer under the weight of the tales whispered about him in the capital. Though maybe that was because he kept having to bind himself to its terrified royals.

Inga's gaze bored into her, like she could see through to the very fabric of Sachi's soul. "You're right, of course, though Ash would never admit that it bothers him. But then, in the earliest days, they revered him. All he has ever done is bleed for their lands and their soft, comfortable lives. In a way, I think your family has come to resent him for it."

She couldn't see everything, then, not if she still thought of the royal family as belonging to Sachi. And she certainly wouldn't be standing here, making pleasant conversation with the orphaned bastard who'd been sent to kill one of her fellow gods.

Luckily, the truth was on Sachi's side. "Then they're wrong," she answered simply.

"Naturally." Another piercing look. "Don't forget that."

"I am in no danger of forgetting." How could she, when all she had to do was recall her childhood and the cruelty Dalvish and Carlania had visited on her and Zanya? "I know who they are. Better than most."

Inga considered her as she took a sip, her eerie violet eyes flaring to pink around the rims from the power gathering within her. "Perhaps you do, at that," she said finally.

Ash appeared out of the crowd, approaching them with purpose. He was clad in red linen, a short skirtlike garment covered with strips of leather studded with iron. Sandals wrapped around his lower legs, and bracers encircled his muscled forearms.

He wore nothing else, and the amount of bare skin on display made it hard for Sachi to breathe. She had to drag her gaze away from the granite-carved lines of his shoulders, chest, and stomach to keep from reaching out.

She resorted to decorum instead, dropping a low curtsy. "My lord."

"My princess." Warmth caressed the title, and his fingers brushed beneath her chin, guiding her gently to stand. "It is customary for the Dragon to share a dance with his consort. Will you join me?"

"Of course."

Inga released her goblet, which remained floating in the air where she'd left it as she clapped her hands twice. The lights above the dance floor flared then dimmed, and the other dancers cleared the floor as the music melted into something slower. Deeper.

Sachi grasped Ash's hand, and he led her out into the middle of the courtyard. The stone warmed beneath her slippers as he spun her gently and tugged her close. Bare skin met bare skin as his strong arms curled around her, and Sachi swallowed a whimper as desire twisted through her. If she was already responding to his nearness, he'd truly been teasing her for far too long.

Then he began to move, and the friction started.

"I see Inga's seamstresses had their way with you," he murmured, his fingertips tracing one of the chains that crossed her shoulder blades. "You look lovely."

"Thank you." They turned, and for a moment, the inside of her thigh brushed the outside of his. "I'm almost as naked as I was last night. You, on the other hand, are much *more* naked. I approve."

She couldn't hear his low chuckle as he spun her, but she felt it in the vibration of his chest as he pulled her back against him. His skin blazed against her bare back, hotter than any human could ever be. His fingertips burned, streaking fire over her hip. The chains securing her skirt heated, and the draping fabric caught.

The flames consumed her skirt and licked up to her stomach, trailing Ash's touch. She closed her eyes against the searing light. Everything was heat and a hunger that felt like him, and Sachi was reminded of her journey up the river to Blade's Rest. She'd dreamt of fire then, a fire that had scorched her entire being not with blistering pain, but with warm anticipation.

She'd dreamt of *Ash*.

Sachi dropped her head back to his shoulder with a moan. She wanted to keep her eyes shut, to close out the rest of creation until this fire had been quenched. So she opened them instead and caught sight of the creeping vines with their lush flowers, only they had changed.

"The flowers," she whispered. "They were white before."

"Inga has cultivated these for centuries," Ash murmured against her ear. "They respond to the emotions of the dancers." His lips grazed her ear, and the blush pink creeping across the petals darkened to a lush reddish violet. "Desire."

"So what—" Her voice broke, and she had to clear her throat. "What did the white represent?"

"Everything." Ash's hand splayed across her midsection, holding her against him as they rocked in a slow circle. "When everyone is dancing and feeling so many different things, they . . ." His voice trailed off.

He was hard behind her. In response, liquid heat pooled in her belly.

"They glow," he rasped, his thumb stroking her abdomen. "As if a rainbow was to become light."

It was a lovely thought, as intoxicating as the drinks and the dancing and the fire of his touch. Then they turned again, and there was Zanya, standing at the edge of the dance floor. The seamstresses had dressed her in sheer midnight blue. Tiny black beads were sewn onto the dress, each one reflecting a dazzling array of light.

A rainbow, just like Ash had said, but made of shadows instead of light. And she was watching them.

The flowers darkened to deep purple. Suddenly, even the heat of the flames dancing between Sachi and Ash wasn't *enough*. She grasped his hands and pulled them up until he was cupping her breasts. His fingers slid over her taut nipples, then closed suddenly, pinching them.

Ash nuzzled her temple. "Do you want her to join us?"

Oh gods above and below.

"You mean Zanya?" Sachi inhaled and swallowed the pleading answer that sprang to her lips—*yes*. "No, she'd be miserable out here. She hates being the center of attention."

Ash spun her again, dragging her up until her toes barely brushed the floor. His knee parted her thighs, giving *friction* a whole new meaning as the music seemed to swell to something dark and primal. "I can feel how much you want her here," he murmured, his fingernails tracing her bare spine.

"I always want her."

"And I can feel how much you want to be trapped between us."

The words *resonated*, reflected back at her across their bond—and doubled because of it. "Spoken like someone who understands. I always think fantasies are best when they're shared. Don't you agree?"

He laughed softly. "Are you asking if I covet your lover, Princess?"

"I don't have to." She rocked down on his thigh and stifled a moan against his shoulder. "I see the way you look at her. I can tell that you *understand*."

Zanya had left much of Sachi's hair loose tonight, with tiny ropes of braids holding the rest back. Ash's fingers sank deep into it, twining the strands around his fist until her scalp tingled. One gentle tug forced her head back, and she met his blazing eyes. "She's magnificent. Fierce and deadly and beautiful. Most of the Raven Guard would fight wars to earn a smile from her. I think Ulric is smitten. But she only has eyes for you."

And Ash, though he didn't realize it yet. "Don't be so hasty to count yourself out, my lord. You intrigue her, but Zanya moves . . . slowly. Carefully. It is her way."

"She's wounded." The arm around Sachi's waist tightened protectively. "I don't know what happened to the two of you at your family's hands, but I will not let anyone hurt her again. Whether I intrigue her or not, it does not matter. She is yours. So I will see her protected. You have my promise."

His words elicited another ache, this one high in her chest, somewhere between her heart and her throat. He had no idea what that promise meant to her, but he'd made it anyway. What was more, he *meant* it, clear to the bottom of his eternal soul.

She managed a nod, then stretched up to kiss his cheek. "You speak as though you're accustomed to this, Ash. Have your consorts often arrived with lovers?"

"Once or twice." The flowers above them bled from deep violet into indigo with blue at the tips of the petals, and she swore she could taste an echo of loneliness from him as the flames engulfing them slowly died. "Those were the easiest to deal with, once they understood that I had no intention of devouring their loves and picking my teeth with their bones. The ones who wanted to flee from me, on the other hand . . ."

Like Tislaine. Still, they'd been able to make a martyr of him in the capital for one reason: he was an outlier, an oddity. Most of the Dragon's consorts lived long, boring—if isolated—lives of relative safety.

"What about the others? The ones who came ready and eager to bind themselves to you?" she asked softly. "Did you love them, Ash?"

He didn't answer right away. The song ended, and applause broke out around them, a brief tribute as the music swelled into a new melody and people returned to the dance floor. Somehow, lost in the sea of bodies, the moment seemed even more intimate when he rested his chin on the top of her head and sighed. "I loved them all, in the beginning. They came to me with open hearts and deserved nothing less. But losing them hurt. And perhaps I began to guard myself against grief."

She'd considered it briefly on the day of their bonding, what it must be like for him, this endless string of fragile humans. How they must have swept in and out of his immortal life like the tides, here and gone in far too short a time. "How do you stand it?"

"I made a promise to the Everlasting Dream," he replied. "And it made me one in return. So I do my part, even when it hurts."

His pain prickled over her skin like ground glass. "I didn't ask why you still take consorts. I asked how you stand it."

"Because I must, Princess." His tiny smile seemed to mock his own words. "Perhaps it grows easier, the more they hate me. They imagine me to be a heartless monster, so I become one for them. That's how our world works, you know. If the people dream something for long enough, it becomes real."

Only a few short weeks before, she would have agreed with him readily. But now, she wanted to deny it, if only to refute those sorrowful words.

For his sake.

She touched his cheek and stared at him until his mocking smile faded. "You deserve to be loved."

"We all deserve to be loved." This time, his smile was warmer. "And I am. The High Court is my family. We sometimes squabble, but you will learn that there is always love there. And they will love you and Zanya, too."

No, they wouldn't. But now Sachi understood Alysaia's letters. The woman had lied to protect Ash, and possibly the rest of the High Court. How many others had done the same? Sachi would never know.

So all of the information she'd gleaned from the consorts' writings was compromised. Either the journals and letters had been written by simpletons who feared Ash out of prejudice, or they'd been altered to reveal nothing that might hurt him.

Sachi understood. If Dalvish and his advisor priests had cared to have her report back to the capital on the status of her mission, she would have lied for him, too.

But they didn't give a damn. All they wanted was Ash dead . . . and Sachi and Zanya out of the way.

She took a deep breath, inhaling his scent. "I'm glad you have them, then. Your friends, and the rest of the Court."

He smiled, and Sachi glanced up, hoping to see that the forlorn blue had vanished from the flowers' petals. But it lingered, and she knew—*she knew*—it wasn't coming from Ash this time.

This sorrow was all hers.

Chapter Nineteen
DRAGON'S MOON

Week Two, Day One
Year 3000

Sachi was the heart of the party.

Ash leaned back against a tree and watched, amused, as Inga's court fell in love with his consort. Whether it was artifice, strategy, or simply who she was, she held them all effortlessly in the palm of her hand. They vied for her attention and hung on her every word, and Ash felt his smug pride reflected back to him from the very world itself.

The Everlasting Dream had made him a promise. More and more, he suspected Sachi was the long-awaited fulfillment of that promise.

But not Sachi alone. Zanya sat at her side, a glittering midnight rainbow with her own admirers. He wasn't surprised to see Kardox and Isolde deep in conversation with her, but the third member of their quiet group would have chilled the blood of a wiser man.

Three of the younger Dreamers made their home at Inga's court. The eldest was a serious young man who could heal injuries even Inga might have struggled with. His lover, the youngest of the trio, could have been Naia's twin—except that instead of water dancing to her will, the wild things of the woods answered her call. Both of them sat with Sachi, bright-eyed and laughing as the nymph made a vine weave itself into a flower crown.

But it was the third Dreamer who gave Ash serious pause. Livia was a fresh-faced blonde with a tumble of curly hair and clear blue eyes that could look as guileless as Sachi's when she wanted. Behind her easy smile lay a familiarity with poisons so comprehensive that there were already whispers of her beyond the Witchwood. Not all Dreamers ended up with the notoriety and title that turned them into living gods, but those mortals who dared the Witchwood and sought Livia's knowledge and patronage had already given her a name. It was taken from a delicate, deadly creature of the Blasted Plains, one whose near-painless sting brought inevitable death.

The Scorpion.

She and Zanya seemed to be getting on tremendously. Ash would have to remember not to eat or drink anything that passed through Zanya's hands for the next few weeks.

Just to be safe.

A cloud of glowing blue butterflies fluttered into view, blocking his clear sight of Sachi and Zanya. He stepped to one side, only to have them follow, dancing and spinning wildly through the air in front of him. He waved a gentle hand at them, but they only drifted out of the way before coming back to form a stubborn, ethereal wall.

Fine. He could take a hint.

Retrieving his drink, he pushed off from the trees. Half the butterflies immediately broke away to helpfully spin a glittering path around the shadows of the open courtyard for him to follow. The rest ghosted through the air as if herding him, an assault on his dignity that he allowed only out of affection.

The Dragon was being driven like a stubborn goat by a cloud of glittering butterflies. Inga's sense of humor truly was perverse.

The trail led him to a semiprivate bower protected by a fall of soft vines and flowers. Within, Ulric lounged against a moss-covered rock with Elevia sprawled lazily across his lap and Inga leaning against his shoulder.

"Sweet, obedient boy." Inga patted the ground next to her. "Make yourself useful. I need a pillow. Elevia has stolen mine."

"I got to him first." Elevia was dressed in a finer version of her usual clothing—draped panels of hunter-green velvet and butter-soft leather leggings. She held a goblet loosely in one hand, the liquid sloshing dangerously close to the rim. "Besides, look at Ash's face. Someone has to hold him down, or he'll float away."

Ash obediently took his place against another rock, cocking one knee to give Inga a backrest. "What did you put in that punch concoction this year, Inga? I think you've actually gotten Elevia drunk. Aleksi will be furious he missed it."

"A little something special I've been cultivating." Inga leaned against him and patted his thigh. "And don't change the subject. Elevia is violently jealous, so of course I have been demanding every last detail."

Ash quirked an eyebrow at the Huntress. "You're jealous, are you?"

"How could I not be?" She reached up to tangle her fingers in Ulric's hair. "Every night, you can retire to your consort's sweet embraces. My bedroll, on the other hand, is lonely and cold."

"You *are* drunk." Ulric gently gripped Elevia's chin and turned her face toward Ash. "Does that look like a man who has been retiring to *anyone's* sweet embraces? Even his own?"

"No, no, no." Elevia shook her head. "I said he *can* retire to Sachi's bed. I didn't say he *has been*. The fact that he's not having any orgasms is his own wretched fault."

"Really?" Inga tilted her head back to study him. "You rattled my castle's walls last night. Do you mean to tell me that *wasn't* the culmination of a passionate consummation?"

Ash gritted his teeth. "I missed whatever rule was passed that made my orgasms official High Court business."

"Poor Ash." Elevia clucked her tongue, then shrugged, giving lie to her sympathetic tone. "When they make the very ground beneath us tremble, they become our business, whether we want them to be or not."

Ash let his head fall back against the moss-covered rock. "It's complicated."

She waved that away. "Don't care. Have you managed to answer Dianthe's question yet?"

"Which question?"

It was Ulric's turn to grin at him, and he cursed the Wolf as a traitor at the amusement in those golden eyes. "Does the lovely Sachielle glow even brighter when she comes?"

Oh. *That* question.

Even his irritation at the fact that they'd all clearly been talking about him couldn't survive the pure dark pleasure of the memory—Sachi in her bathtub, her wet skin glistening by candlelight and flushed with desire. The admittedly impressive glow of magic had been transcended by the extremely physical—and extremely carnal—bliss of watching her shatter apart under Zanya's knowing touch.

"Well?" Inga poked him with her elbow.

"Can you see the glow from the heart of the sun?" he countered.

"Oh, that's definitely a *yes*." All hint of teasing fled from Elevia's expression, and she smiled warmly. "It's good to see you like this again, Ash. Alive."

Inga hummed in agreement, and even Ulric grunted a vague assent. Had Ash's discontent in recent years been so obvious? Or had it been the dread he felt as he endured an endless march toward another consort who would arrive, bringing fear and pain and eventual loss? Had he hardened his heart so much after Tislaine?

Apparently so.

He reached out to catch Elevia's hand and squeezed it in quiet gratitude. "This could all still end up a Void-cursed disaster, you know. The situation *is* complicated. The handmaid is . . ."

"Possessive," Inga noted.

"Protective," Ulric added.

"No, it's worse." Elevia narrowed her eyes and leaned forward. "She's a cat with her leg caught in a trap."

"She's wary," Ash agreed. "I don't think either of them has known much kindness in life. And Sachi might be eager enough for the pleasures of the bed, but Zanya seems more . . . sheltered."

"She would almost have to be, to be so well-trained at such an age," Ulric said softly. "Because she's talented, but it's more than that. Her entire life must have been lessons in violence."

A tragedy, if true. Ash reveled in his skills as a warrior. So did Elevia and Ulric and the entirety of the Raven Guard. But violence was a tool, one you kept sharp in case you needed it to protect those under your care. But that was all it should ever be. A tool. Not your entire life.

"It isn't sport for her. She fights like a warrior." Elevia held up her arm, displaying the scar where Zanya had cut her. "Like her life depends on it—because it always has."

A cut with a simple steel blade should have healed without a mark long since. Ash nodded to Elevia's arm. "You decided to keep it?"

"I did. It's a good reminder."

"Of?"

"Of things I shouldn't forget." She finished her drink and held it out to Inga, who snapped her fingers and refilled it. "How do *you* remember?"

Inga answered for him. "Brooding. Haven't you ever seen him up there on the cliffs above his castle? He perches like a gargoyle in the freezing cold and stares down at the world thinking tragic thoughts."

Ulric, the traitor, grinned. "Yes, he did it in the middle of his consort's welcome dinner. Every time she touched him, he turned into a dragon and flew away."

Inga's throaty laugh filled their little bower. "And they call *me* melodramatic."

Ash jostled the Witch with his leg, earning him a sour look. "You could all sit around teasing me, or you could help me figure out what to do to *fix* this. Do I tell them I know they were sent to kill me?"

Inga's elegant brows drew together tightly above her eyes. "What purpose could that serve? You would only force them to lie to you."

Ulric scoffed. "They're already lying to him. This would give them the option to tell the truth."

"But *are* they lying?" Inga insisted. "Have they told you that they're *not* here to kill you?"

"It isn't traditionally something one has to say to their betrothed." But when Ash thought back over the many conversations he'd had with Sachi, he frowned. He would sense deception, and Sachi knew it. Everything she said to him held the clarion ring of truth. And he knew all too well how she could turn a conversation when she didn't wish to answer a question.

"Sachi doesn't lie," he admitted. "I think she shrouds herself in truth when she can, and does her best to divert me when she cannot. But she is a master at hiding what she's thinking. Zanya, on the other hand, hardly speaks to me at all. And I suspect she's a terrible liar."

"Then don't give her a reason to become a good one. You have the time to play this out and gain their trust, do you not? It's not as if they can *actually* kill you." Inga frowned suddenly. "Can they?"

Every gaze turned to Elevia, who laughed ruefully. "I suspect Sachi could kill him anytime she pleased. Ash would hand her the knife, then hold still and smile pretty while she used it."

Ash glared at her. "You're not amusing."

"All right, in all seriousness . . ." She considered the question. "It depends. If Zanya had Void-steel? Her chances would be excellent."

Ulric gripped Elevia's arm, his thumb sliding over the scar she'd decided to keep. "There's not much of it out there anymore. And while I don't often approve of some of the more extreme opinions of the city priests, they *have* chased most of the Void priests underground. So unless the mortal lords have been dabbling in darker magics than usual . . ."

The Endless Void had not been considered evil in Ash's childhood, simply a natural counterpoint to the unchecked creation of the Everlasting Dream. Ash supposed those who lived hundreds or thousands of years could afford to take a more thoughtful stance on the inevitability of death, though. Mortals, with their quick, short lives, tended to fear and hate the end that rushed at them before they were truly ready to move on, and priests who worshipped the chaos of destruction found scant welcome in mortal enclaves.

The fact that creatures and objects tied to the Void were among the only threats to the lives of the High Court made those priests unpopular outside of mortal enclaves, as well.

"Aleksi would have sensed it if she'd brought Void-steel within my castle," Ash said firmly. "So unless someone slips it to her along the progress, I think we can rule that out."

"Zanya is only human. Without Void-steel in the picture, you'd have to be extremely careless." Elevia sipped her bubbling liquor. "Or terminally distracted by thinking about fucking."

Inga laughed again. "Is that how she got you?"

A sly grin curved Elevia's lips. She leaned over, whispered something into Ulric's ear, then nipped his earlobe. *"Absolutely."*

Inga groaned. "Ulric, *do* something about that, would you?"

Ulric only laughed, tugging Elevia more solidly into his lap. "There's no doing anything about Elevia. She's feeling frisky. We'll find her a playmate to tumble into her cold, lonely bedroll as soon as we've sorted out Ash's problem."

"Fine. On to business." Inga frowned at her empty goblet and snapped her fingers again. Something deep indigo sloshed into it, bubbling gently. A wave of her hand paired with a gentle whistle summoned the butterflies back. They swarmed into a chaotic cloud before a murmured command from Inga turned them into a glowing white wall. Colors began to swirl across the canvas they made as their wings shifted until a picture came into hazy view.

It was Sachi, smiling as Naia wove a flower crown into her braids. Next to her, Zanya still sat close to Livia, both of them intent on their conversation.

"Oh, that's not good," Inga murmured. "I wouldn't eat anything Zanya gives you after tonight. I don't *think* Livia knows of any poisons that could kill you, but she does often surprise me."

"I'll do my best not to let her poison me," Ash replied dryly.

"Good. So all you have to do is convince the handmaid that you can be trusted, and promise to pry her leg from its trap."

Oh, just that. As if he hadn't been *trying* to present the least threatening front possible. "It isn't easy, Inga. Children have been raised to fear me for a thousand years."

"Your consort doesn't fear you," Elevia told him confidently. "And neither does her lover."

"Sachi fears *something*," Ash countered. "And badly."

"Yes," she replied just as confidently. "I assume you've offered to kill it, this thing she fears?"

Anger stirred in him. "I *will* kill it."

"And what if that isn't helpful?"

"Why wouldn't it be?" Confusion joined his anger. "If anything or anyone threatens her, I will destroy it."

Elevia groaned. Inga rubbed at the bridge of her nose with a sigh. "Oh, Ash."

Ulric was the one who took pity on him. "The mortal lords have spent thousands of years sending you prey. You've forgotten how to court a fellow predator."

"I don't know. He's been doing a fine job of courting Sachi." Elevia paused and frowned down into her drink. "Though perhaps I have that backward."

She definitely had that backward. Sachi had been courting him with a devastating skill even Aleksi might envy. But she had likely been trained to do just that—to make herself appealing to a terrifying dragon god.

Ash had never enjoyed similar tutelage. "How *do* you court a predator?"

Ulric chuckled and tugged at Elevia's free-flowing hair. "Respectfully."

"And if all else fails . . ." She bared her teeth at Ulric. "You get down on your knees."

She'd planted the mental image on purpose, and it worked. His mind conjured the fantasy all too readily—Zanya leaning back against the wall, those graceful, clever fingers buried deep in his hair. Her nails digging into his scalp as she writhed on his tongue. The tremble of her thighs, the groans she would struggle to hold in check. Zanya wouldn't be open like Sachi, gifting every gasp and sigh. She'd hold them back, prizes he'd have to earn by driving her beyond the edges of her endurance.

The first full-throated scream would be the sweetest sound he'd ever heard.

As if she could sense his thoughts, Inga shook her head. "Not that. Not yet. You say she's sheltered." Inga tilted her head, studying Zanya's reflection on her ethereal living wall. "If she's caught in a trap, they've taken away her power. You have to gift it back to her. Let her feel she is in control of this, if nothing else."

He could do that. A negotiation that respected Zanya's prior claim and made it clear he had no desire to usurp it. He could let her set the ground rules, then abide by them, no matter how hard desire rode him.

That might appease her, but it wouldn't *woo* her. The stories he told in the evenings were helping on that front—she might not have had any choice about her training, but she *loved* tales of great battles and daring victories. She anticipated his presence now instead of dreading it, and she enjoyed listening to him. But the fantasies burning Sachi up from the inside demanded something far more intimate than placid enjoyment.

He would have to test the spark between them. He felt it sometimes, an ember Zanya banked ruthlessly every time it threatened to flare. She was drawn to him—and not just as a man. She was drawn to the violence and darkness in him. The monster.

Just as he was drawn to her.

There was only one way to coax that spark into a flame. Just the thought of it heated his blood. The fact that desire held the wary edge of danger made it all the sweeter.

He would step into the sparring ring with her and let her test herself against him. If he was right, if she *wanted*, there would be no hiding it in the honesty of a fight.

If he was wrong, she might actually kill him.

Not knowing which it would be should not have been so arousing.

Chapter Twenty
DRAGON'S MOON

Week Two, Day Three
Year 3000

The pace of the progress was getting to Sachi.

Zanya knew that Sachi would die before she complained. Though her lessons in history, guile, charisma, and comportment might have prepared her well for being the center of attention at each of their stops, she simply wasn't accustomed to long days in the saddle, and no number of soft beds or warm baths could make up for it.

The second day out from Witchwood Castle, Zanya drew a hard line.

The little stone cabin that was tonight's stop didn't even have a bath, just a pump connected to a little outdoor well that poured out frigid water and a small hearth on which to heat it. Zanya heated enough water to help Sachi clean up, then convinced her to take her evening meal in bed.

Halfway through her bowl of stew, she was already nodding off. Zanya set her food aside and brought out her toothbrush, then coaxed her down into the blankets to sleep off her exhaustion. But though sleep came swiftly, there was little peace in it. Sachi shifted restlessly, her lips moving soundlessly. When her confused whispers turned to distressed murmurs, Zanya hurried to the bedside.

Soothing nightmares was simple enough for her. She stroked Sachi's cheek softly and let the shadows inside her rise to the surface. The shadows in Sachi did the same, as if drawn to Zanya's power. Sachi twisted on the bed, kicking at the blanket, and Zanya murmured and stroked until something sparked gently at her fingertips.

Zanya with a knife. Screaming. The Dragon, his gaze like flames, fingers tipped in claws, coming after her.

Zanya let the nightmare sink into her and dissipate. Beneath her gentle touch, Sachi quieted. A faint smile curved her lips as more pleasant dreams came, and she sank deeper into sleep. The one gift Zanya had that seemed *good*—the ability to grant a sweet night of rest.

If only a similar magic could drag Zanya into the bliss of unconsciousness.

Unfortunately, nothing about long days in the saddle was sufficient to burn through Zanya's excess energy. From the time she'd been separated from Sachi as a child and pressed into training, her life had been movement from dawn until dusk, and sometimes far into the night. She'd been athletic as an adolescent, but puberty had brought its own changes—strength and stamina beyond anything a mortal human should possess, along with a restlessness in her very bones that made finding sleep a struggle.

Zanya needed the cleansing exhaustion of a good fight. Luckily, in this group, someone was always sparring after dinner.

Tonight, it was Isolde and Kardox exchanging lightning-fast blows as they practiced some sort of unarmed fighting under Ulric's critical eye. Zanya crouched on the sidelines and watched with interest as

Isolde followed Ulric's instructions to perfect a throw that sent Kardox skidding through the dirt, even though he was easily half again her size.

Zanya could almost feel the throw in her body already. She watched Kardox dust himself off for a second attempt and flexed each muscle in turn with Isolde, trying to commit the movement to memory. Not that she could be sure to replicate it without practice, but maybe she could—

Fingers brushed her shoulder, and she started to her feet, barely checking the instinct to fling an elbow back and break the nose of the person stupid enough to sneak up behind her.

"Sorry," the Dragon murmured. "You were so focused, you didn't hear me speak your name."

Zanya stiffened instinctively. The Dragon lifted his hand, his fingers spread wide in the kind of placating gesture you'd use with a skittish wild creature. Inside her, wariness fought a nasty little battle with pride. It was good that he continued to underestimate her. Good that he seemed distracted from any danger she might represent because he was busy trying to . . .

What? Seduce her? Sachi thought he was doing exactly that, but the idea still seemed laughable to Zanya. She knew how powerful men *seduced* servants, and it wasn't with careful touches and a hunter's endless patience and . . . and *bedtime* stories. When she'd first joined Sachi at court to solidify her status as a simple handmaid, she'd endured the amorous advances of wealthy merchants and puffed-up lords, and they'd made it clear that her only role in their seductions was flattered acquiescence.

Not that Zanya had accommodated them. Oh, she'd let them grope her once or twice, but only because her skill with nightmares was so much clumsier than Sachi's power over dreams. She could only take away someone's nightmares if she was touching them—and it was also the only way she could *send* nightmares. Zanya didn't know what their sleeping minds did with the seeds of terror she planted there, but several had fled court entirely in the aftermath, and none had resumed lurking around the servants' quarters in search of easy conquests.

Powerful men seemed to prefer when *other* people suffered for their pleasures.

And yet, here was the Dragon. The most powerful man of all. He could do anything he wanted to either of them with no repercussions, and only a handful of his closest friends even strong enough to attempt to stop him. If the campfire teasing was to be believed, it had been a hundred long years since he'd slaked his lust at all, much less with a partner. A century without an orgasm. And still he held back, waiting for . . .

For what? Had Sachi been right this whole time? Was the monster a romantic, one who yearned for the giddy, eager acceptance of his consort *and* her lover?

"Zanya?"

She had to say something. Dragging her gaze from him, she gestured to the match underway. "I was watching the fight."

"Mmm. Ulric is very good. Very few can beat him in unarmed combat."

Zanya huffed. Ulric might not have weapons, but she'd seen his partial-shifting trick. "Is it really unarmed if you can form claws through magic?"

"I suppose it depends."

"On?"

Ash grinned. "If the people you're fighting can do the same thing."

Curiosity got the better of her, and she told herself it was only logical to ask. She needed to know, after all. "Can you?"

In answer, the Dragon held out his hand. Fire wreathed it, the flames licking over his skin without burning him. As the flames swirled around his fingertips, his hand seemed to blur. When he flexed his fingers again, each one ended in a wickedly sharp claw.

Zanya reached out without thinking, then froze. "I'm sorry."

"Why?" The flames faded, and he extended his hand toward hers. "Touch them, if you'd like."

She wanted to, and she didn't *want* to want to. But it was knowledge, so Zanya took it. His hand was massive but human, with warm flesh and a swordsman's calluses on his palms. She shivered as she skimmed up to find the claws that had replaced his fingernails, and her pulse leapt as she felt them, smooth and hard.

The flames flared again. She started to recoil, dreading the searing agony, but the fire didn't burn her. Flames licked at her skin, twining over her wrist with a playful curiosity that carried a tingling warmth in its wake. Not pain, not quite—but the sort of gentle sting that rode the edge of pleasure, like when Sachi bit her in the midst of—

Heat flooded Zanya's cheeks. She jerked her hand back, but the flames had already faded, taking the claws with them. The Dragon's hand was just a hand, a strong one with broad, thick fingers and—

No. *No.*

"The real ones are bigger, you know."

The teasing words brought another wave of heat. "Real what?" she demanded, hating the fact that he was watching her now with open amusement.

"The real claws." He flexed his fingers again, as if reminding her of how big they were. "When I'm a dragon, just one of them is larger than your hand."

Zanya wasn't sure if he was bragging or trying to terrify her—and she wasn't sure if she was intrigued or horrified. "Then why bother with all of this?" she asked, desperately trying to steer the subject back to safe ground. "Why spar as a human?"

His sudden, slow grin did wicked things to her stomach. "Because it's fun, Zanya."

Her name on his lips did things to her, too. She shifted, trying to dispel the anxious energy and odd restlessness inside her that could have no outlet while Sachi slept. The Dragon's gaze didn't help, especially when he lowered his voice to a coaxing rumble. "Come, handmaid. Spar with me. No weapons. No claws. Just show me what you can do."

He was taunting her, and she knew it.

Just like she knew she was going to give in.

She could shroud it in pretty rationalizations, justify it in a dozen different ways. But in her heart, she knew none of them were real. She was simply a creature of dark desires and darker impulses, and everything inside her *wanted* with a ravenous hunger that she didn't know how to stop.

She wanted to fight him. So she would. "One round."

The Dragon didn't gloat over his victory. He merely smiled and turned to clear the practice ring. Zanya followed behind him more slowly, testing the feel of the earth beneath her boots, the strength of the wind, the depth of the shadows.

The torchlight bent toward the Dragon. He was dressed humbly today, in sturdy trousers and a tightly woven shirt under a worn leather vest. Nothing that would be easy to grab or tangle him in—in fact, his shirt was so tight she could see the formidable flex of his muscles as he stretched like a lazy animal preparing for the hunt.

She waited for his attack, but he simply watched her, a small smile on his lips, one eyebrow quirked. *I dare you . . .* that smile whispered, and she knew it was bait. He was taunting her again, but this time she wouldn't give in to temptation, even if it killed her.

And it might. Her awareness of him increased with each throbbing beat of her heart. His smug smile faltered, melted into fascinated curiosity. His gaze swept over her body in a tangible caress, lazy heat kindling in his eyes as they drifted back to hers. But she refused to falter, refused to cede this battle of wills.

He was the Dragon, a living god. The world itself bowed to him.

Zanya would not.

And the Dragon realized it.

His low, appreciative chuckle fractured the silence, a sound like liquid smoke that was her only warning. Then he was moving, lunging with a speed that left her breathless. She twirled out of the way, feeling a slight brush along her hip as his fingers closed on air instead of the back of her shirt. Momentum carried her in a full circle, and her elbow sailed toward his rib cage.

A massive hand caught her arm just before impact, absorbing the force. But his angle was awkward, and she broke his grip and dove out of the way of his answering swing. This time, his fingers grazed her long braid, and she silently cursed herself for not pinning it up out of the way.

Too late to worry about it now. She used the momentum of her dive to tumble past him, coming up safely out of reach—and barely got her footing before he was on her again, one massive arm looping around her waist to haul her against his chest.

She burned everywhere their bodies touched, and they were touching *everywhere*. His chest against her back, his solid thighs trapping hers, his arm like steel around her stomach as he made a disappointed noise against her ear that vibrated through her like an earthquake. "I don't think you're even trying."

"Of course I am," she countered, hating the revealing rasp of her voice. Could he sense the sudden tremble of need winding its way through her? Self-consciousness twisted with anger, and she surged forward, trying to break his grip.

"Uh-uh." His hand splayed across her stomach and dragged her back so hard she grunted in shock. His breath feathered across the back of her neck, a hot and teasing caress her traitorous body answered with a tightening of her nipples and an ache between her thighs.

Something inside her snapped. A sweet, languid power flooded her limbs, and she raised one hand to the arm trapping her and raked her fingernails over his bare skin in an almost threatening caress. Behind her, where her ass rested against the cradle of his hips, his body stirred.

His lips parted on the back of her neck as she curled her fingers around his biceps. His arm loosened its iron grip just enough, and her body took over as it had done a thousand times before. Grip, pivot, hook the calf—

He was huge, but the dark strength flooding her made it easy. The Dragon went airborne, and she savored the shock on that granite-carved face as he skidded over the dirt and came to rest a dozen paces from her, sprawled on his back.

Silence reigned for one heartbeat. Two. On the third, flames kindled in the Dragon's eyes as he stared up at her. "There you are."

Yes, here she was. Reckless and foolish, not even trying to hide. Tomorrow, she'd probably regret it, but her good sense had fled. Only the giddy relief of being unbound remained. "Here I am."

The Dragon rolled to his feet in an effortless flex of muscle and flicked his fingers at her in imperious command. "Again."

She bared her teeth at him. "No."

He laughed. "So defiant. There's only one problem, handmaid."

"Really? Only one?"

He was there suddenly again, towering over her, breath hot against her ear. "You *want* to beat me."

Zanya swung straight for that smug smile. He responded exactly as she anticipated, catching her fist just before it impacted his face. Her other fist, already moving, drove into his unprotected side with enough force to provoke a startled grunt from him.

His laughter washed over her, a deep sound that scraped at her pride as he shrugged off the hit and bore her down to the dirt, his body pinning hers in place as he grinned. "Unless you *don't* want to beat me," he rumbled, the suggestion unmistakable as his chest grazed her tight nipples.

His face was right there, carelessly within reach of her teeth. Zanya bit his jaw hard enough to draw a hiss of shock, then tangled her legs with his. One violent heave and they rolled, leaving her on top of him.

Instinct told her she didn't have the right leverage to pin him, so she kept rolling, coming to her feet in a crouch just out of reach.

Fire-wreathed eyes met hers. That smug smile was gone. The Dragon stirred, gathering himself to rise, but Zanya was ready this time and lashed out in a lightning-fast kick that swept his legs out from under him at the worst possible moment. He hit the dirt on his back again, spitting curses.

The words escaped before Zanya could stop them. "I don't think you're even trying."

This time he didn't roll to his feet like a lazy cat toying with easy prey. He sprang up and charged her, an avalanche of muscle and determination driving right at her. Anticipation heated her body as she met him in a crash of blows so fast that conscious thought faded as muscle memory took over.

They were too well-matched. Size against speed. Experience against stubbornness. She broke free of his grapples, and he caught her attacks, each fleeting victory giving way too quickly to a rally and momentary defeat. The only constant was the *feel* of him—flexing muscles and hot flesh and their bodies clashing together again and again until she felt the imprint of his touch on every part of her.

And that was the true battle they fought, one the Dragon would win eventually because it was *working*. When he caught her thigh mid-kick, his fingers seemed to brand her even through the fabric of her pants, a taunting promise of how it would feel if he slid his hand up the inside of her thigh with nothing between them. When he grasped her braid to haul her head back, the tingle of her scalp lingered, whispering of how it would feel to have those strong fingers fisted in her unbound hair.

The Dragon *was* seducing her, and the sudden realization staggered her so thoroughly that he caught her off balance and spilled her to the dirt again. His body came down over hers, hot and hard, already *familiar* in a way it couldn't be, shouldn't be, *must not be* . . .

But she wanted it to be. She wanted to give in, just once, to rake her nails down his back until he bled and take her pleasure in his easy acceptance of her violence and rage. She was more like him than she'd ever been like Sachi. She was a monster who would hurt and kill. Why did she keep fighting it?

For Sachi. For Sachi. Fight it for Sachi.

Panic lent her strength. Terrified instinct made her brutal. A swift headbutt left the Dragon with a split lip and Zanya with a throbbing pain in her head, but his startled recoil gave her the space to reclaim the upper hand. Her body moved without her awareness, heaving him off her and scrambling to pin him in place and end this threat.

That was what she had to do. End this threat. End it before she forgot who mattered.

"Handmaid."

End it all.

"Zanya."

Hot fingers flexed on her thighs, his thumbs so high he would only have to sweep them upward to find how deeply her body had betrayed her. Zanya trembled and blinked, her brain struggling to make sense of what she was seeing.

The Dragon stared up at her, gentle tension in his eyes. Silver glinted at his throat. Her boot knife, clutched in a steady hand even as the rest of her trembled. She must have pulled it on him, and now the keenly sharp edge rested so close to his skin that a thin red line appeared when he swallowed.

He squeezed her thighs again. "I yield, handmaid."

Zanya glanced up. The Raven Guard and the rest of the High Court were scattered around, all watching with expressions shrouded by shadows. No longer amused, but not worried or tense . . . yet. No one was preparing to defend the Dragon, because even with a blade kissing his skin, no one truly believed she could hurt him.

But she could.

The Dragon was tense beneath her, though not with fear. The slow circles his thumbs were making on her inner thighs were meant to soothe and placate. He was treating her like a wounded creature again.

Which she was.

But his compassion could be his death. All she had to do was cut fast enough, deep enough . . . Even the Dragon could bleed out, couldn't he? Her task would be complete, and Sachi's soul would be safe.

The temptation to give in would be over.

So would her life. Even if she managed to kill him, one instinctive flex of his claws could shred the large blood vessels in her leg. She'd bleed out with him. Of all the ways to die, it was not the worst she had imagined. It would be swift, at least.

And Sachi, sleeping helpless and unaware, would be left to pay the price of the High Court's vengeance.

Zanya lifted the knife from his throat and returned it to her boot. The Dragon raised one hand and wiped away the blood at his throat. The skin beneath it was already healed, smooth and unblemished.

She shuddered and rose to her feet. With one boot planted in the dirt on either side of his hips, she stared down at him, knowing she had to say *something* to break this awkward tension. "Here I am," she whispered. "Are you sure you wanted to see me?"

Ash's hand touched her ankle. She tensed, bracing for him to yank her off her feet, but he only dragged his fingers up the outside of her calf in another of those soothing, placating caresses. "Absolutely."

It sounded like the truth, and that might have been the most terrifying part of all. Zanya jerked away from his touch as if it burned and pivoted, stalking away from the practice ground. The Raven Guard parted silently before her, but she could feel the weight of their gazes on her back. Quiet. Assessing.

Accepting.

In the cabin, the fire in the small hearth had already burned low. But there was light enough to see, and warmth enough for Zanya to wash up in front of the fire, even if the water she poured into the bowl was frigidly cold.

Probably better that way. Her body was a riot of confused desires, with the ghosts of the Dragon's fingers lingering on her hips and the sensation of him hard between her thighs an impossible temptation.

Wanting him might make this easier, but Zanya had never been placid in her desires. When she wanted, it was with an out-of-control hunger that bordered on madness. It came from that monstrous darkness at the heart of her, greedy and demanding, as if no degree of possession could fill it.

The brightness in Sachi was the only thing that had ever soothed her impossible hunger.

The locked box holding the hourglass sat on top of their trunk. The compulsion to press her lips to it and reassure herself that the sand had not quickened its pace overwhelmed Zanya. She knew Sachi hated to look at it. She knew *she* shouldn't look at it.

But once the thought took root in her head, it could not be banished.

She lifted the box. Her love for Sachi beat so strongly through her veins that she was surprised it didn't fall open in her hands, but the brush of her lips unlocked the small chest.

The hated hourglass lay inside. Zanya lifted it and watched the firelight reflect off the glass as the fine red grains dropped one by one, their rhythm seeming to match the hard thump of her pulse.

Too much sand had fallen. It covered the base of the hourglass now, the red glow of it ominous in the light from the hearth. Time was slipping away.

"Zanya?"

Sachi's sleepy murmur had her packing the hourglass swiftly away and hurrying to the bed. She slid into it next to Sachi, chilled from her bath and still hot from the fight, lost until her seeking hands found warmth and welcome.

"Where were you?" Sachi murmured against her shoulder.

"Sparring." She brushed her lips over the top of Sachi's hair and let the peaceful stillness that seemed to surround her smooth over the sharp edges left inside. "With the Dragon."

Sachi went still, then leaned her head back and peered up at Zanya. "You were sparring with Ash?"

"Yes." Zanya stroked a comforting hand down Sachi's cheek. "He offered, and it seemed like a good idea. Until it seemed like a very bad idea."

"Because you liked it too much."

"Far too much." Which didn't seem like such a terrible thing now. Maybe that was Sachi's own brand of magic, the way just being around her made the world seem brighter, and everything feel *possible*. That had always been the mortal king's plan, hadn't it? Send Sachi to lull the Dragon into sleepy complacency with sex and magic . . .

And Zanya to strike the killing blow.

"Zanya . . ." Sachi sighed softly. "If you feel—"

She was about to offer Zanya an escape, even though it was *Sachi's* life and soul on the line. Suddenly, her own fear enraged Zanya.

She could do this. She *would* do this. For Sachi.

Zanya cut off the words with a swift, desperate kiss, then slipped from the bed.

She told herself it was merely strategy as she padded across the cool cabin floor and opened the door. Night had fully fallen, but the Witchwood still glowed softly outside. She had no trouble finding Ash's familiar figure silhouetted against the fire. "Dragon!"

Everyone around the fire turned in unison. The sheer black pants and sleeveless top in which she preferred to sleep offered little protection from the curious gazes of the gods, but Zanya weathered their attention. The only one who mattered was the one who stared at her with eyes that burned like fire. "Yes, handmaid?"

"Your consort needs you."

Zanya turned and strode away from the open door, letting the teasing laughter of the High Court follow her back to the bed. She'd barely slid a knee onto it when a massive body blocked out the light. The Dragon hovered in the doorway, as if unsure of his welcome.

Strategy. Nothing more.

Zanya moved up the bed, placing her back against the wall before tugging Sachi closer. The bed had not been built for three, but it *had* been built for the Dragon to share with his consort. The soft mattress stretched toward him, open and inviting. "Don't let out all the heat," she told him tartly. "And don't think you can hog the blankets. Sachi will fight you for them."

"I don't think I'll have to." Sachi pulled the covers back and patted the mattress. "I'll be plenty warm."

After another silent moment, the Dragon stepped in and gently shut the door. He removed his boots in silence, then started on the ties of his leather vest. The soft glow of the fire painted him in taunting shadows, revealing a flash of golden skin as he stripped off his shirt. Then he prowled toward the bed, fully human but still so obviously *not*.

The mattress dipped as he slid onto the bed. Sachi flung the blankets over him and settled down with a sleepy smile, and Zanya didn't blame her. Even from the other side of Sachi's body, she could feel his blazing warmth.

It was strategy to run her chilled fingers over Sachi's side and let them graze the inferno of his chest. He hissed in a shocked breath, but before she could pull away, he caught Zanya's hand and pressed it more tightly to his skin.

It was strategy to let him warm her, inside and out. To let him settle a blissful Sachi protectively against his side. To let him into their bed, not just for the carnal distraction of fucking but for *this*—the seductive intimacy of belonging.

It had to be strategy. Because otherwise, Zanya would fail. And Sachi would pay the price.

Chapter Twenty-One
DRAGON'S MOON

Week Two, Day Four
Year 3000

Sachi didn't want to wake up.

She was having the *best* dream, one where she was cradled in warmth. Surrounded by soft curves and hard muscles, and every way she turned, there was nothing but the delicious slide of skin over skin.

A low chuckle tickled her ear. "As tempted as I am to let you keep going, Princess, it doesn't seem entirely sporting."

A strong hand caught her fingers, which had been gliding over firm muscle, and tugged it up. When she opened her eyes, it was to the sight of Ash smiling as he brushed a teasing kiss to the backs of her fingers.

She wasn't dreaming.

In a breathless rush, she remembered—Zanya sparring with Ash and coming back to the cabin practically vibrating with confusion and a need Sachi wasn't sure her lover even recognized.

Then Zanya calling Ash to their bed.

"Good morning," Sachi whispered. She wasn't sure what else to say, what the boundaries were in this situation. If it was a stolen moment of time . . . or the beginning of something she didn't have the words to define.

Behind her, Zanya made a grumpy noise and snuggled her face more deeply against Sachi's shoulder. "Of all the mornings for you to wake up early. It's still dark outside, and it's very warm in this bed."

"My sincerest apologies, Zan. I know you abhor early mornings. But I think my brain realized something beautiful was happening and didn't want to miss it."

Zanya huffed, but her lips traced a soft kiss to the back of Sachi's shoulder. "I should have warned the Dragon about your wandering hands."

"Ash," he corrected in a low rumble. He smiled at Sachi and nipped at her fingertips. "And why am I not surprised she has busy hands?"

"*Intelligent* hands." Sachi pulled free of Ash's grip and resumed her journey over his abdomen. "They know when they have places to be."

It was Zanya who thwarted her this time, chuckling at Sachi's impatient noise as she twined their fingers together and nudged Sachi onto her back, gently but firmly pinning her hand above her head. "Aren't you impatient this morning? Don't either of us get a kiss first?"

Her teasing tone made Sachi's chest ache a little. She hadn't realized just how much she'd felt pulled between the two of them until Zanya had invited Ash into their bed. It felt *right*, warm and comfortable, but with a sharp edge of need that smoldered like a banked fire, ready to be stirred into full flame.

And there, hidden beneath those smoking coals, was joy. She could have this. *They* could have this.

Ash's hand found her chin, tilting her face toward his. His eyes were more molten copper than pure flames this morning, and his expression was one of pure wonder. "You're not afraid today, Princess."

"No, I'm not." With the two of them so close, all around her, there was no room for anything else.

"Good," he murmured, then kissed her.

It wasn't a soft kiss, but Sachi didn't want one. She wanted that fire, instant and all-consuming. She wanted *Ash*, everything he'd promised her with his words and his body, if only she could be patient.

Now, that patience was nothing more than a distant memory. Frustrated, she moaned into his mouth and flexed her hands, trying to break free of Zanya's grip to reach for more. But Zanya held her tight, and Sachi moaned again—not in frustration this time but in eager anticipation.

Ash's lips left hers, trailing down the side of her throat in kisses so gentle they left her trembling with the need for *more*. Zanya gripped Sachi's chin with her free hand and turned her into another blistering kiss. This one held just as much hunger, but it was enveloped in the warm, comforting cloak of familiarity.

Zanya's teeth dug into Sachi's lower lip, a teasing nip just hard enough to zip pleasure through her. "Not so gentle," she murmured to Ash. "Sachi isn't fragile. She knows what she likes. Don't you, my love?"

Sachi leaned up and mirrored the caress, closing her teeth on Zanya's lush bottom lip. "*I* know . . . but he doesn't. You'll have to tell him."

"I know some things," Ash rumbled as he shifted to his knees. The blankets tumbled back, baring Sachi's sheer nightgown and the glorious expanse of his naked chest. He lifted one hand, and the fire in the hearth roared to life, filling the cabin with enough light to admire him properly.

She had to touch him, to trace the way the firelight limned his body. She reached out with her other hand, only for him to catch it.

"Ash," she murmured. *"Please."*

He pressed her hand back to the sheets, holding it there until Zanya obliged him by pinning it in place. "I know you like a kiss of pain," he whispered, rubbing his thumb along her lower lip. "True or false, Zanya?"

"True," Zanya whispered back. "Just the right amount, and at just the right moment."

Ash flexed his hand in the air, and flames erupted from his skin. "I know my fire makes you ache with hunger. I can feel it."

Sachi held her breath. As the flames wreathed his fingers, she glimpsed the sharp curve of a claw emerging from the fire. Her heart stuttered as he lowered his hand to her chest and sliced through her nightgown. The flames did the rest, destroying the delicate silk as she tried not to writhe beneath his touch.

It was exactly like their dance at Witchwood Castle. It was sensation without injury, the precise application of just enough heat to elicit a reaction, even as her nightgown burned to ashes under the force of his magic.

Sachi whimpered.

"True," Zanya whispered again, her fingers skimming up the curve of Sachi's breast. They were chilly compared to the fire of Ash's, the contrast so intense that she arched in shock when Zanya's thumb found her tight nipple.

Ash's hand splayed over her belly, his fingers wide, and fire licked up her body like a dozen tongues made of pure heat. The slightest flex, and she felt the tips of his fingers, his claws exquisitely gentle as they traced over her skin.

Sachi hissed in a breath and arched again, trying to get closer to Zanya's caressing touch and the sharp kiss of Ash's claws. But Zanya pulled away just enough to barely maintain contact, and Ash never allowed those edges to bite into her skin.

"Now I think you want the dragon as much as you want the man," Ash murmured.

"I thought you knew." Her voice came out hoarse and a little slurred, as if she'd already grown drunk off of them. "I want all of you."

Another flex of his hand, and the claws vanished. Human fingers touched her lips, but his skin still burned as he dragged them down her throat and lower, between her breasts and across her abdomen. Then he was gone, the mattress heaving beneath her and the world seeming to tumble. Blazing hands grasped her knees, pulled them wide. Broad shoulders settled between them.

She stared down her body and met Ash's gaze as his thumbs caressed heat up her inner thighs. "How hard can she come, Zanya?"

"You want to know?" Zanya pinched Sachi's nipple just tight enough for the pain to tumble her closer to the edge. "Find out."

"Yes," Ash rasped.

And then his mouth was on her.

There were those thousands of years of experience again. He knew exactly when to lick and when to suck, when to tease her and when to push her higher. Sachi tried to reach for him again, but Zanya held her tight, captive to the rising pleasure.

Pleas fell from Sachi's lips, not quite begging but closer to a prayer. "Zan—*Ash*—"

"Shh." Zanya's free hand found her cheek, turning her face so there was nowhere to look but into Zanya's gentle, loving eyes. "Let go," Zanya whispered, stroking Sachi's lips, and she wondered desperately if Zanya realized the pad of her thumb moved with the same rhythm as Ash's tongue against her clit. "I've got you."

"I know." It was always true, but never more than now. In a way, they'd stepped out of the darkness of secrecy. For the first time, they were *together*. "Tell me what you see."

A low chuckle, and Zanya stared down Sachi's body. "A Dragon who wants to devour you. I don't blame him. I know how sweet you taste. How wet you are."

Ash groaned, the vibrations of it shaking through her. "What does she need?"

Zanya turned back to Sachi, staring into her eyes as she answered. "Your fingers. Two of them."

"They're big," he warned.

"I know." Zanya's thumb pressed against Sachi's lips. "She can take them."

Hot fingertips parted her, and if the heat of his touch had been intense against her skin, it was nothing compared to the way it felt sinking into her body. Just one finger at first, defying Zanya's command. Sachi arched her hips off the bed, both at the sensation . . . and what would come next.

"Two," Zanya said again, her voice hoarse with desire but so confident. So *demanding*. She'd only ever turned this tone of voice on Sachi, and hearing it directed at someone else was dizzying.

Ash obeyed, either because he liked being bossed around by Zanya or because he wanted to fuck Sachi with two fingers anyway. He thrust them inside her, and she had to bite her lip until it bled to keep from crying out.

It had been *so long* since Sachi had been taken like this. She and Zanya had been watched so closely in the capital prior to their departure, and until very recently, the danger had been too great on this journey.

Then, once Ash *knew*, it had felt too much like performing with his permission . . . and at his pleasure. It had all been too muddled up for her and Zanya to come together like this.

But it made perfect sense now. *Here.* Sachi moaned as Ash curled his fingers inside her, and he echoed the sound when Zanya dipped her head and coiled her tongue around Sachi's aching nipple.

The heavy thread of pleasure snapped. It whipped through Sachi, stinging and sharp, before melting into hot waves that crashed over her. It went on and on, drawn out by their fingers and tongues, slipping and gliding over and inside her.

When she stilled, Zanya brushed Sachi's damp hair back from her forehead as she gasped for breath. She couldn't stop trembling, especially when Ash crawled up and seized her mouth in a rough kiss. His body pressed hers down into the feather bed, and she wanted, more than anything, to stay there.

But they had to travel on.

When Sachi found her voice, she asked the only question that mattered. "Will you come to us tonight?"

"Are you getting greedy, love?"

"You owe us another story."

Ash smiled against her lips and brushed his nose over hers. "We'll see."

Chapter Twenty-Two
DRAGON'S MOON

Sachi hated to leave the Witchwood behind. It was a warm, dark place full of heady, sensual magic, the sort that felt not only out of place but out of *time*. Where nothing quite seemed real, and you could be so easily swept away, your senses bewitched.

She hadn't realized how much she needed that bit of respite until she'd recklessly spent it all.

They'd traveled out of the forest by midmorning. The Burning Hills had been visible in the distance, separated from the forest by a flat plain. A dark smudge nestled against the base of the Hills had grown larger and larger during their journey until it had coalesced into a village.

So far, they'd camped in the woods or enjoyed the High Court's hospitality at one of their individual estates. But Willett's Grove was a proper—though small—town, with banners stretched across the streets, children running everywhere, and a mayor who beamed proudly when she greeted them.

And when the sun dipped below the horizon, the town lit up in celebration.

They'd staged a feast that rivaled anything King Dalvish II had ever had on the tables of his great hall. It must have taken them *years* to prepare—to grow and raise and craft what they could, and save to buy what they couldn't. All to fête her, the Dragon's new consort.

Sachi sipped her wine, a vintage imported across the Hills from the capital. She suspected it had been acquired especially for her benefit, since most everyone else had been served local ale.

Every drop fell bitter on her tongue.

They'd probably already carved or cast a plaque to commemorate the occasion. It would be placed in the local tavern, or perhaps in the town square, where people could someday remark on it and hear tales from one of these rambunctious children, by then a stooped old man, about the night the Dragon and Princess Sachielle had come to town.

But those tales would never materialize, would they? What would they do instead? Would they whisper mournfully of their dead Dragon, murdered by his own wife? Or would they spit angry words about the impostor who had tried to kill him, a woman so reviled that her very name had been erased from history?

"Princess?"

She turned to find a cluster of children at her elbow, led by a young girl who must have been about twelve or thirteen. Her dark hair was cut short, framing a heart-shaped face and big brown eyes. In her hands, she cradled a clumsily crafted ceramic pot with a single Witchwood rose growing out of it. When Sachi smiled in encouragement, the girl held it out to her.

"This is for you," she said shyly. "We grew it."

"At school!" a younger boy added excitedly. He couldn't have been more than six or seven, and both he and the girl looked exactly like the mayor. "We made the pot, too!"

"Well, thank you." Sachi gingerly accepted the pot. "You did a lovely job. It's beautiful."

The girl dropped a clumsy curtsy, and her younger brother dissolved into giggles, as did the other children. A warning look from the mayor sent them scurrying away, their excited chatter drifting back on the wind.

"They've been tending it for two years," the mayor told Sachi, a smile curving her lips. "Their teacher is clever. Most aren't very interested in their gardening lessons, but everyone wanted to be able to say they helped grow a gift for Princess Sachielle."

The smile came to Sachi's lips with practiced, hollow ease. "They're precious. And I'll treasure the gift."

"I'd best go make sure they're not about to cause mischief." The mayor rose, executed a respectful bow, and hurried after the group of children.

As she set the pot on the table in front of her, Ash's fingers found her arm. "Are you well, Sachi?"

"Very," she answered brightly, mostly out of habit. "It's a lively party, isn't it?"

"It always is." His gaze lingered on her, because of course he *knew* she wasn't well. But he didn't challenge the lie.

She was slipping, allowing her negative emotions to bleed through their bond. She'd have to be more careful in the future—especially as her time grew short, and they neared the capital. Two things guaranteed to shake her iron will and pierce through her shields if she let them.

So she cast about for an excuse, anything that would be halfway believable . . . and enough of a distraction to turn Ash's attention to other matters.

"It's the children," she confessed finally. "They make me nervous. Most royals are brought up for that very purpose, aren't they? To continue the line. But no one ever spoke to me of such things."

"Ahh." Ash reached for his wine and took a thoughtful sip. "Are children something you want?"

He practically *vibrated* with tension, and Sachi fell back on blunt honesty. "Frankly, I never considered it. I assumed they weren't a possibility."

The answer seemed to release something in him, and he exhaled softly. "I don't know that they are impossible, but . . ." He hesitated, then shook his head. "No one in the High Court has ever had a child, to my knowledge. Simply wanting a child is not always enough to make one possible, but dreading the idea practically always ensures it is not."

"And do you? Dread it?"

He drained his wine before looking away. "It is not the children I dread, but the loss. As I told you, I know something of how it feels to outlive those you love. And what we are, this connection to the Dream? It is not a thing of bloodlines."

Of course. Any babies he fathered—assuming it was possible—would be human. And there were echelons of grief, deaths that hurt more and less than others. Parents were expected, lovers a tragedy, siblings an aching void. Children were the only losses that went so against the usual order of things that the pain was incalculable. Almost unimaginable.

She'd accomplished her short-term goal. Ash was thoroughly distracted from her melancholy, now sinking into his own. The smart play would be to let him.

But she couldn't.

"What you wish can become reality." Sachi took his hand and squeezed it firmly. "Or else what use is it, being a god?"

A wry smile twisted his lips. "Sometimes less use than you might expect."

"*Would* you want them? Children?"

"If I knew that outliving them wasn't a certainty?" He seemed to consider it. "Honestly, I cannot say. The castle is often full of children, so I have never felt their lack. They can be charming. But they are also . . . fragile. Sometimes that makes me nervous."

"All humans are fragile, Ash. *You* were too, once."

"A very, very long time ago." He slanted a look at her. "Is this your way of telling me that you would like to have children? If you wished it, I would try. Sometimes pain is worth it."

The offer hurt because he *meant* it. He would expose himself to that incalculable, unimaginable pain simply because she'd asked him to.

No. She swallowed the denial. She shoved it down to the place where her pain lived and locked it away with all the other sobs and screams she couldn't release.

So her voice was smooth and light when she shook her head and smiled. "It's far too soon to make such plans. We have time, Ash."

He reached for her hand, his fingers gentle as they curled around hers. He lifted it to his lips and pressed a gentle kiss to the backs of her fingers. "We have all the time in the world."

Somehow, she made it through the rest of the feast, through the speeches and the songs and the dedication of that godsdamned plaque. Sachi smiled as she sat, regal and serene, all the while digging her nails into her palms until they threatened to pierce her flesh.

And then, at the first opportunity, she fled. As a small band tuned their instruments in preparation for a boisterous dance, Sachi whispered to Ash that she was tired from their journey, overtaxed by the glare of the sun. She needed to lie down for a while in a dark, still place and rest her head.

"Enjoy at least a few dances for me. And make sure Zanya has some fun, won't you?" The words left her with the same casual ease as always, and Sachi marveled at every syllable.

How could she sound so calm—*be* so calm—when she was scream-ing inside?

A serving girl from the local tavern showed her to her rooms. It was a simple bedroom and small bath above the inn, both plainly furnished but scrupulously clean. Sachi murmured her appreciation, and the girl left with blessedly little fanfare.

Sachi had been biting her tongue so long and so hard that she could taste blood. She sank to the floor, dreaming of escape. By the time her knees hit the rough wood, she was somewhere else.

Her refuge had no form, no color. It was pure light and energy, still and silent, with nothing and no one in it but Sachi. Which was why it still *roared*. With all her pain, her regret. And the fear—dear gods, the *fear*.

She floated in the nothingness, truly alone with her panic for the first time in days. It was nothing like the dread that widened Zanya's eyes when she thought Sachi wasn't watching. That was focused out-ward, on the mission and its dangers. On Nikkon and his damnable curse. On the threats that surrounded them.

Zanya didn't realize yet that the true threat, the one that could destroy them both, was *Sachi*. All of this was coming too easily—the subterfuge, the manipulation. The lies. She opened her mouth, and the most casual inventions poured effortlessly forth, as if she didn't even have to try anymore. The exploitation just *happened*.

She was too good at it. No amount of training could do that unless there was something fundamentally *wrong* with Sachi, some flawed, rotten core that enabled her to take mercenary advantage of heartfelt confessions and moments of vulnerability.

Surely a good person would struggle with even a fraction of what she'd already done to Ash. He'd always treated her kindly, just as he'd always desired her sexually. He respected her mind and her stub-born will. But that indulgent fondness had begun to deepen into something catastrophic. He was falling in love with her, and she was encouraging it. Enjoying it, even knowing how futile, how ill advised, his affections were.

Forget slipping a blade between his ribs—she had already blithely hurt him in ways he might well rank worse than death.

And she would keep doing it. Because she had to, because she was running out of time. It was all she knew, the only way to save Zanya. The sword hanging over both their necks.

And, the quiet, snarling voice inside her whispered, she would keep doing it because it was who she had become.

In her tiny, sequestered corner of the Dream, Sachi threw back her head and screamed.

Chapter Twenty-Three
DRAGON'S MOON

Week Two, Day Eight
Year 3000

The Burning Hills, in spite of their name, were neither barren nor particularly warm. Especially in the depths of winter.

The warmth of the sun had melted the ice coating the river they followed, but it was still cold enough to be bracing when Ash washed off the day's travels after dinner by taking a swift plunge into the crystal-clear water.

Bracing was fine. The Dragon couldn't be banished by a little cold water. Unfortunately, neither could the anticipation that had been growing steadily in him since midday, when Sachi had accepted a wineskin from him with a brilliant smile and told him that she looked forward to whatever bedtime story he would tell them tonight.

A thousand skins of wine couldn't wash the taste of her from his memory. Every time he closed his eyes, he saw her laid out before him in carnal offering, flushed with need and begging for his touch.

She'd been helpless before him, and yet the fear that had plagued their every touch had dwindled to a pinprick, overwhelmed by love and trust so bright they outshone the sun. Zanya made her feel safe. And Zanya . . .

A different sort of anticipation stirred. Ulric was right. It had been too long since Ash had courted a fellow predator. He'd forgotten the thrill of it—and the danger. He'd also forgotten how long it could take. Zanya had not brought him into *her* bed. She'd brought him into Sachi's bed, tolerated him because Zanya wanted to please her lover, and she would use anyone and anything necessary to pursue that goal.

Ash could relate. And if the object was pleasuring Sachi, he was more than willing to be used.

Still, he respected Zanya's domain enough to knock softly at the cabin door, only crossing the threshold when she issued an invitation. The consort's cabins were much the same along the entire progress route, though this one was larger than the last. A copper tub stood in one corner behind a screen, obviously recently put to use. Zanya's damp hair was twisted up off her neck, and she had pulled a chair in front of the fire. Sachi sat before her on a pillow in one of those translucent shifts, her eyes half-closed as Zanya brushed out her hair.

A slow, welcoming smile curved Sachi's lips. "Good evening, my lord."

"Princess." There was already another cushion on the threadbare throw rug next to her, as if laid out in invitation. Ash stretched out on his side facing the two women. "Did you enjoy your bath?"

"Yes and no," Sachi answered. "It's always nice to scrub off a day's worth of travel. But it's so *cold*."

Was it? The cabins were snugly built but old. Ash reached out a hand to the floor beyond the rug and spread his fingers wide. His power sank into stone, and he traced it along the building, feeling the ancient joints and tired foundations, the tiny cracks where cold winds stole away heat and left a chill in their wake.

That wouldn't do at all. Especially since he was so personally invested in Sachi remaining clad in nothing but that slip of a nightgown. Or perhaps not even that. If he burned through enough of them, she'd be naked when he came to her each night.

A pleasing thought.

He sank fire into the cabin, urging it to work with the stone. Words weren't required, but he whispered them in his heart anyway. *Help me protect my consort.*

The cabin shivered. Heat surged, as if fire thrived in the rocks and mortar. Zanya's brows shot up as she reached out a hand, her fingers hovering just shy of the wall. "How useful, to have the lord of fire at our beck and call. Is that better, love?"

Sachi's smile grew as she stretched out her bare legs and tested the stone beyond the rug with her toes. "Much." Then she sank her teeth into her lower lip. "What story have you brought us tonight, Ash?"

"Since we're officially in the Burning Hills, I thought I could tell you a story or two about the Phoenix before you meet them."

Zanya's fingers trailed through Sachi's hair. "I don't know much about the Phoenix. Only that if you can find a temple dedicated to them on one of the holy days, you can walk through the flames and see who you truly are." She hesitated and tilted her head. "Or become who you truly are? I'm not sure which. I've never met anyone who wanted to face their true self, I suppose."

Many didn't, and some who tried were not yet ready to know the truth. But those who faced the flames with an open heart rarely had anything to fear. "It can be both. The flames reflect the truth of your soul. Sometimes that simply means facing the lies you've told yourself. But sometimes . . ." Ash lifted a shoulder. "Sometimes you already know who you are, but you were born into a body that does not match your soul. The Phoenix's flames are rebirth. So when you pass through them, you become who you truly are."

Sachi smiled. "That's lovely. But how are the flames able to do such things?"

"We are all tied to the Everlasting Dream, but no one understands it like the Phoenix. Even though they're the youngest of the High Court, they have walked paths in the Dream that the rest of us would not know how to find. The Siren and I feel the world around us most closely, but the Phoenix feels the Dream. Perhaps that's why."

Sachi tilted her head and regarded him. "Why what? It doesn't sound as though you speak of the cleansing flames."

No, he supposed he hadn't been. "Why they were the first to realize the Betrayer had lost his way."

Zanya leaned forward, her curiosity a living thing. "What *was* his way? The priests talk about him as if he has always been evil, as if he came from the Void itself. But he was one of you, wasn't he? A Dreamer?"

Amazing that even after three thousand years, the sting of betrayal hadn't entirely faded. "He was not of the Void," Ash said softly. "If anything, he hates it more than anyone. The Void is chaos. Destruction. In those early days, he was called the Builder. And he craved order and progress."

Sachi went still. "I've seen his standard in the royal archives. His crest is—*was* a hammer, wasn't it?"

"Yes. Much of the capital was his original construction, including the castle in which you grew up, Sachi." And he'd been so *good* at what he did. Gifted. The fact that the palace still stood when the severing of the continents had destroyed so much was a testament to his skill. Not even three thousand years of weather and wear could bring down the Builder's finest work. "But he wanted more. Faster, always faster. That was why he tried to claim the Burning Hills."

She shook her head. "I don't understand."

Ash put his hand on the floor and spread his fingers wide. It took little thought to sink his awareness into the land. Heat met him, welcomed him, and he smiled. "The Burning Hills got their name because the Phoenix claimed them, but long before that, they were known for their hot springs. You'll see some on our climb to the plateau tomorrow, and still more as we continue. They were considered sacred by many. A place to connect with the world and the Dream."

Zanya's brows drew together. "He found a way to use them?"

"Yes. Because the Hills have something else. A new kind of ore, a dozen times stronger than steel but only a fraction of its weight. He thought to mine it, then harness the power of the springs to process vast quantities. He wanted to build whole cities from it."

"Wouldn't that harm the land?" Sachi leaned forward, her face soft with sympathy, but Ash could only see how the dancing flames on the hearth backlit her now. That flimsy little chemise might as well be transparent, letting his gaze follow the curve of her breast down to the dip of her waist and the flare of her hip.

A much sweeter thought than his ugly memories of war. But he had promised them a story. "The mine he built drove away the wildlife, and though many of the displaced creatures died, he swore they would adapt. Then he drilled into the earth seeking to power his creation, and the hot springs began to die, as well. That was when we told him to stop."

Zanya's fingers drifted up and down Sachi's throat, though Ash couldn't tell which of them she was trying to soothe. Then her gaze sought his, and her lips quirked. Those fingers dove deeper, edging beneath the neckline of Sachi's chemise. Taunting him. "But he did not stop."

"No."

Sachi leaned up even as she pulled Zanya's head down to whisper in her ear.

"Not yet," Zanya whispered, urging Sachi back to her pillow. Her fingers dipped beneath the chemise again, then lower, moving in a circle so slow and blatant that Ash could all but taste the bud of Sachi's nipple against his tongue. Sachi shivered, her head falling back, and Ash started to rise on one elbow.

"Not yet," Zanya repeated, this time for him. Her gaze held him in place as she stroked a whimper from Sachi. "You haven't told us the good part."

Ash heaved in a breath. "It was a war, handmaid. There were precious few good parts."

"The Burning Hills stand unspoiled, so there was at least one." Zanya watched him, her eyes bright, and Ash couldn't tell what she anticipated more—the game they were playing, or the chance to relive the violence of victory long past. "You stopped him."

"The Phoenix stopped him." He lowered his voice, forcing her to lean closer. "The rest of us were arguing about how to talk him out of it. We still thought reason could prevail. But he built a manufactory that poisoned the earth itself. So the Phoenix walked into his compound and warned the Betrayer's people to run. And then the Phoenix burned it all with their own fire."

Zanya frowned. "Burning down what he'd built couldn't have saved the land."

Ash raised a hand and kindled fire at his fingertips. "I am the lord of fire. I can burn something if I want. A building. An army. But my fire is mundane. It leaves behind carnage and destruction. When the Phoenix burns . . ." He tried to find a way to put it into words but couldn't. Dozens of generations of poets had failed to capture it. How could he be expected to?

Zanya and Sachi both were looking at him, enraptured, so he tried. "Their flames are the fire of creation and rebirth. When the Phoenix burns, they don't destroy. They . . . *renew*. The Betrayer's compound burned for three days, and when the Phoenix walked down the hill and the flames had faded, it was as if none of it had ever been. The springs were clear. The poison had been leached from the earth. Not so much as a nail or brick remained to prove anything had ever been built there. In three days, the Phoenix erased three decades of exploitation."

Sachi smiled at him, her eyes shining. "That's amazing. A true miracle."

"It was." He let the fire twine down his arm, the teasing caress of it whetting his arousal. "The Betrayer may hate the rest of us, but he fears only one person. And soon, you will meet them."

"It will come sooner if we go straight to bed," Zanya murmured.

Sachi gasped a wordless protest.

"Though I suppose it *would* be rude not to thank you for the story," Zanya added.

Ash squeezed his fist, and the fire extinguished. "And how do you wish to thank me, handmaid?"

"If you want to find out . . ." She smiled, and there was nothing but sleek challenge in her eyes. "Take off your clothes."

Perhaps she thought arrogance would stop him from obeying. But Ash had never let pride get in the way of achieving his desires, so he reached for the fire that consumed him when he shifted forms. The magic always took his clothing first, which made for a convenient trick when one was in a hurry. Flames roiled down his body, and when they vanished, he was naked.

Naked . . . and very, *very* aroused.

Sachi's gaze traveled over him, lingering on his erection with covetous desire. She licked her lips and moved toward him, only stopping when Zanya caught her by the hair. Zanya wrapped the bulk of it around her fist, her gentleness a sharp contrast to the hot challenge as she locked eyes with Ash. "I've heard them tease you. They say you haven't come in a hundred years."

"They say a lot of things," Ash rumbled. "Foolish things."

"So they lie?"

"No." Though the sensation of Sachi's impatient yearning twisting through him was almost enough to make him spill now. Especially when he closed his fingers around his cock, and her hunger soared as she leaned forward again, tugging against Zanya's grip in her hair. "It has been over a century."

"Why?" Zanya pressed. Her gaze burned into his. "You could have taken yourself in hand at any time. You could take yourself in hand now. Why did you wait?"

Because his grief had turned to apathy, and apathy to doubt. After Tislaine, he had been on the verge of losing faith for the first time in almost three thousand years, and desire and sex had been too tangled up in the idea of consorts for him to face either.

Until her. Until *them*.

"I waited for you," he said truthfully, letting his hand fall away from his cock. "I'll keep waiting, until you're both ready."

The promise lay between them in sudden silence, cut only by the crackle of the fire and Sachi's unsteady breaths. Then Zanya leaned down to kiss her cheek and released her. "Take what you want, Sachi. Take what is yours."

"Take what's mine?" she whispered, untying the ribbons that laced the top of her shift. It fell open, and when she crawled forward, she left it behind at Zanya's feet. "I don't know what that is yet."

She touched Ash's thigh, then ran her hand up to his bare hip. "I'm yours," she continued, her voice musing. Wondering. "That's how they refer to me—*your* consort. *Your* bride."

It took everything in him not to reach for her, not to roll her beneath him and *take*, with his cock thrusting deep and his teeth at the back of her neck, marking his claim. As good as it would be, somehow this agonizing anticipation was even sweeter.

Her fingers skimmed over his stomach and up his chest, then lingered on his cheek. "But what about what *you* are to *me*?" She brushed her lips over his cheek, then began to retrace the path her hand had taken, this time with her mouth.

He would be anything she wanted, as long as she did not stop.

Sachi slid one leg over his—slowly, so slowly—until she was kneeling over his thigh, her hands braced next to his hips. "Are you mine, Ash?"

"Yes." There was nothing to cling to for self-control. His fingernails dug furrows into the stone beneath him as he tried not to reach for her. But he couldn't stop himself from lifting his thigh, grinding up against the slick arousal and savoring her sharply indrawn breath. "Crawl higher," he demanded. "Let me taste you again. Make yourself come on my tongue."

"No." She reached for him, sliding her fingers around his cock. *"Are you mine?"*

Zanya answered for him this time, her voice warm with amusement. "He's been waiting to come for a century, and he's still digging his bare fingers into stone, trying to lie patiently still for you. I would say you've tamed the Dragon."

"But I haven't. Can't you see that he's trying to lure me in to being claimed yet again?" Sachi clucked her tongue.

Then she squeezed her fist tight around him.

Ash's self-control wavered, and he drove his hips up, thrusting into her grip. It wasn't enough, and it was already too much. He could come now, if he pleased—he'd felt that mouth around his thumb, sucking and eager. He'd felt her come around his fingers, squeezing him in tight, impossible heat. He could imagine either enclosing him now in place of her fist, and release would roar through him with the violence of an erupting volcano.

But he was tired of imagining. He wanted the real thing.

Stone shattered under his fingers, and he smiled at her—the Dragon's smile. Hot. Hungry. "I don't need to lure you," he whispered. He lifted his thigh again, grinding up against her. "I feel what you feel, Princess. I know what you want."

She tilted her head, and her unbound hair tumbled over her bare breasts to trail across his naked flesh. "What's that, my lord?"

He sat up abruptly, bringing them face to face, and he caught her chin before she could rear back. "You want to tease the Dragon until he snaps." Ash whispered the words against her lips. "You want my self-control to shatter." He closed his hand over hers, sliding her fingers up his cock. "You want me to throw you on your knees and work this into you until you don't think you can take anymore, and then you *want* to take more. You want the Dragon to fuck you until you can't think or feel or breathe, and when you've screamed yourself hoarse from coming, you want him to do it again."

"Very much." She drew in a shaky breath and touched his face. Licked the corner of his mouth. "What do *you* want?"

"All of that and so much more." He freed his hand and leaned back far enough to brush his thumb over her lips. "But in this moment? I want what you taunted me with that first night. Do you remember?"

"I remember everything." Sachi pushed at his shoulders, slowly easing him back to the rug. Then she slipped down his body, closed her hand around his cock again, and circled the crown with her tongue.

Light exploded behind his eyes, and it wasn't just her lips, as sweet as they were. For one disorienting moment, Ash felt as if he'd *become* fire itself, as if wanting this for so long had burned through what was human in him and left only flames behind.

But he was still a man, made of flesh, and Sachi was the light. She glowed so brightly that it was hard to look at her as she parted her lips and took him deep. An iridescent rainbow exploded outward from her, as if their pleasure had become visible. And that was all he felt from her as she worked at him with her hand and mouth, streaking bliss through his body—*pleasure*.

She savored every twitch of his hips, every groan. When his control shattered and he sank his fingers into the loose locks of her hair, she thrilled at his touch. When he curled his hands tight and guided her strokes, that thrill turned dark and liquid.

Ash looked past her, to where Zanya watched them both with dark eyes. "Now you know the secret," Zanya whispered, sliding to her knees. Her fingertips grazed Sachi's spine, gentle and protective. "The more you try to claim her, the more she claims you."

Sachi lifted her head, reached for Zanya, and dragged her closer, close enough to kiss. As their tongues dueled, she drew Zanya's hand down between her thighs. After a moment, Sachi broke the kiss with a gasp, then bent her head and turned her attentions back to Ash's aching cock.

He hissed out a breath as the cleverness of Zanya's fingers ricocheted through Sachi and into him. A wicked smile curved the handmaid's lips as she did something that made Sachi's lips vibrate in a muffled groan.

"You can feel it, can't you?" Zanya murmured. "Her pleasure."

"Yes," he growled. The cabin floor seemed to shiver beneath him as Sachi's tongue danced over him, too gifted, too hot, too *good* . . .

"So feel it." Zanya's satisfied command was practically a purr. It accompanied a lightning flash of ecstasy as Sachi shattered, her cry of release muffled by his cock as she struggled to take more, to take it all, to take *him*.

Yesyesyes.

It wasn't his own voice, but the whisper of the world, satisfied and elated as the dam within him burst.

And then there was only heat, the magma flooding his veins finding its echoing pulse deep within the earth as he roared and slammed his hands down on the stone floor. Through the flames filling his vision, all he could see was Sachi, her face flushed from her own release, her eyes bright as she stroked him with unsteady hands, not faltering as a hundred years of thwarted need jetted forth to paint her skin.

Ours, the world whispered, and Ash could only lie there, panting in the sudden stillness, and agree.

Sachi blinked as she leaned against Zanya and struggled to catch her breath. "Did the earth . . . *move?*"

The answer came from outside the cabin in Inga's low, throaty voice. "Ash, you've rattled the Burning Hills from one end to the other and also collapsed my tent. Please tell us that was finally an orgasm, or I'm going to become concerned."

"Leave the man be," Ulric called from the other side of the camp. "A hundred years is a lot of pressure to release all at once."

Ash groaned and covered his face with his hand. "I can make them shut up, if you'd prefer."

But Sachi only laughed, the sound full of satisfaction—and joy. "No. I'm too pleased with the world and everything in it right now. Are you not, my lord?"

"Very pleased." He traced his fingertips up Sachi's bare thigh. Higher. His seed painted her breasts and belly, and he was base enough to enjoy the way she looked like this. Flushed and naked, still glowing—metaphorically and literally. Marked by him in a primal way.

His wandering fingers encountered Zanya's, still slick with Sachi's desire and now teasing glistening circles around Sachi's tight nipple. Ash grasped her wrist and gave her a moment to break free, but she just watched him as he tugged her fingers to his lips and dragged his tongue over them.

Zanya's chest heaved. Her hand trembled in his grip. He held it the way he held her gaze as he teased her, savoring Sachi's lingering taste mixed with his own, and the way Zanya's breathing grew less and less steady as he showed her what he would do with his tongue when she gave him the chance.

But not tonight. Not until she wanted it so badly, she demanded it.

He ended his teasing with a gentle nip of her fingertips and raised one eyebrow. "I think the Princess needs another bath."

"Yes," Zanya agreed huskily. "And you should help wash her. It is your mess to clean up, after all."

Sachi rolled her eyes. "And then bed?"

Zanya laughed and kissed Sachi's cheek. "Poor Sachi. Now you will have two of us hovering over you. Bathing you. Soothing you to sleep and waking you up with kisses. Whatever will you do?"

"I suppose I'll have to manage," she murmured dryly. "Luckily, you are both *very* sweet to me."

Zanya laughed and moved toward the bath, her movements brisk and efficient. If any thwarted desire lingered, she gave little evidence of frustration. It was clear that Sachi's pleasure had been her singular goal tonight, and even Ash's had only mattered to her inasmuch as his release pleased Sachi.

The handmaid might have accepted Ash into their bed, but she was far from accepting *him* as a lover. For now, she would allow him to be her coconspirator in protecting and pampering Sachi, a role he would gladly accept.

For now.

Sachi had been worth the wait. Zanya would be, too.

Chapter Twenty-Four
DRAGON'S MOON

Week Three, Day One
Year 3000

They continued their trek through the Burning Hills the only way they could—by climbing them. Unlike the narrow switchbacks that led to Dragon's Keep, the paths to their destination wound gently up, past rolling hills and valleys. The terrain was stark and mottled, stone gray and sand brown, dotted with caves and hot springs instead of abundant vegetation.

By midday, they reached a plateau. Sachi blinked as she drew her mount to a stop and gazed out over the expansive space. Though it bore only one permanent structure, the plateau was positively blanketed with colorful tents. Some were simple, utilitarian shelters, while others were adorned with golden ropes and baubles, fancier than most of the consort's cabins she'd stayed in during the course of the progress.

Elevia drew even with her and hummed. "Pilgrims," she explained. "Second only to the number that will gather at the Lakes."

"I see," Sachi murmured.

The only clear space surrounded the lone structure on the plateau—the Phoenix's Tower. It rose up, silhouetted against the clear blue sky, overlooking the Hills. Leading from the Tower's door, a walkway burned with brilliant blue flame.

The Phoenix's fire, tended by their acolytes. It always burned, except when it died out and was reborn, like the Phoenix themself. There was a prophecy in the old texts, a warning that if the flame ever died out for good, so would the very world.

Sachi shivered.

Elevia nudged her horse into motion once more. "This way."

A handful of robed acolytes streamed out of the Tower and lined up to greet them. Ash stopped at the edge of the walkway, his brow furrowed, as silence fell. His gaze swept the row of acolytes before landing on one whose robe was belted with thick interlocking rings of gold. "Flamekeeper."

They bent their head in deference. "Dragon."

"The Phoenix isn't here?"

"No, my lord." They hesitated, then lowered their gaze once again. "It's been many years since we've been blessed by their presence."

"Well, how long can it have been?" Elevia demanded.

"More than ten years, Huntress."

It was a long time—though perhaps not for an immortal god. Perhaps the Phoenix was prone to disappearing like this, losing track of human time as the years stretched into decades.

But a cold knot of worry twisted in Sachi's stomach, so sudden and foreign that her pulse began to race. Then she glanced at Ash and saw the icy fear reflected in his tight eyes and rigid shoulders. It was *his*, this worry, shared with her through the bond that was growing stronger by the day.

She laid a comforting hand on his arm. "It could be nothing."

He tensed, shooting her a surprised look, and his voice dropped to a low murmur. "It's not like the Phoenix to miss a consort's progress. They believe in the importance of binding the mortal lords to the world more than anyone."

That didn't sound promising. "What can we do?"

"Nothing, for the moment." He glanced at Elevia. "Can you send out riders?"

"Of course," she said immediately, beckoning one of her men closer. "Rest easy, Ash. If there is information to be had, my riders will find it."

That knot of worry still pulsed inside her, but Ash only nodded and swung easily out of the saddle. A youth in a simpler version of the acolyte's robes rushed forward to claim the reins and lead the horse away as Ash reached up to clasp Sachi's waist and lift her easily from her horse.

Once she was steady on her feet, he turned toward Zanya, who gave him a flat warning stare and dismounted herself. Ash put a hand at the small of Sachi's back, and the other on Zanya's shoulder. "Flamekeeper, it is my pleasure to present my consort, Princess Sachielle of House Roquebarre, and her lover and protector, the Lady Zanya."

Sachi bent her head, mirroring the acolyte's gesture. "It is an honor."

"The honor is ours," they answered. "We have been preparing for the ceremony in the Phoenix's absence. I hope you will find the proceedings illuminating."

She'd read about the pilgrimage to the Tower, but the specifics had always been hazy, described in the most vague and flowery of terms. She'd learned more in only a few words from Ash the night before.

Though thinking about the previous night made her blush. She covered by addressing the Flamekeeper. "I look forward to it."

The acolyte's somber mien lightened a bit, and they almost smiled. Then they turned, along with the others, and filed back into the tower.

Ash gestured to a table where almost two dozen pilgrims had already gathered, some looking nervous, some anxious, and some eager. "I don't usually do the flame walk, but you're both welcome to, if you want. It's safe enough." He hesitated. "Though sometimes facing your own truths can be an emotional experience."

Zanya cast a wary look at the flames before shaking her head. "I'd rather not."

"I haven't decided," Sachi admitted. She didn't need to find out who and what she was. She knew already—and that was the problem, wasn't it? What if walking through those vivid blue flames physically revealed her true nature?

What, exactly, did a liar look like?

She shook herself. "I am eager to see the lights, though. Could I meet some of the pilgrims in the meantime? Some of them have traveled so far."

"Of course." Ash held out his arm. "Just tell me if it becomes too much. People will be eager to greet the Dragon's consort."

There were many pilgrims, dozens who approached but hesitated, as if no one knew the precise etiquette for addressing a god. Though Sachi supposed that must be the case, since even the oldest among the supplicants would have been mere babies the last time Ash traveled through the Burning Hills with poor, doomed Tislaine.

Ash greeted them all, repeated their names, and held their hands, even though the set of his shoulders grew more rigid with each passing tick on the candle clock. Sachi could feel his unease, though he was careful never to let it show on his face.

It made her think back to all those times he'd fled from her after their first meeting. She'd briefly wondered if he was, perhaps, simply shy, and now she could see how accurate that assessment had been. Ash was more at ease with these people than he had been with her at first, but he was not truly *at ease* with them.

His slight awkwardness was endearing, almost as sweet as the protective way he hovered when anyone moved to stand too close to her. Sachi's chest ached, and every time he glanced at her, she encouraged him with a smile.

But he had so many tasks to attend to, not the least of which was the ceremonial flame walk, and Sachi missed Zanya. So she left Ash at the Tower, but not before extracting a promise that he would seek them out when his duties allowed.

She found Zanya sitting near the edge of the plateau. The view from this spot was simply breathtaking. The last of the light had almost faded, but just enough remained to glint off the Lover's Lakes in the distance, as well as the North Sea beyond.

"May I join you?"

Zanya looked up and smiled. "Of course. Always."

Sachi settled beside her lover and gazed up at the darkening sky. "How was the sunset?"

"Beautiful." Zanya stretched out an arm behind Sachi, as protective in her own way as Ash always was, if more subtle. "Not that much can compete with sunrise over Siren's Bay."

"No, but the Bay doesn't have these lights." The first glimmers were beginning to lick at the deep gray sky, reflecting off the clouds in strokes of green, purple, and blue. "Will you wish for a vision?"

Zanya shook her head. "Visions have always been your burden," she said softly. "And I have never envied you that. The future is terrifying enough to face without knowing what's coming."

If only it worked that way. "I don't know what's coming, Zanya. I don't see the future. I only catch glimpses, and half the time, they mean nothing until I'm able to interpret them through hindsight."

"Do *you* wish for a vision tonight, then?"

What would the lights show her if she asked? If she begged? A future already set, or a myriad number of options that could only be determined by their choices? Would they show her the answer to their dilemma, one that only the Phoenix, in all their knowledge and mercy, could provide?

Or would they show her oblivion, the fate that awaited her with the arrival of the Witch's Moon?

Zanya leaned closer, her voice dropping to a breathless whisper. "Vision or no, we must have a plan, Sachi. This game . . . It is too dangerous. I cannot play it forever."

"You won't have to." The ache in Sachi's chest solidified into a sharp stab of pain. "It will end soon, one way or another."

The arm resting behind her back turned to stone. Zanya wasn't a good enough liar to keep her turmoil from her face. "No, there is only one way."

There can't be. It wasn't merely that Sachi had fallen in love with Ash—although she had. Their bond, forged by magic and tempered by affection, grew stronger with each passing day. Killing Ash would mean killing part of her soul, *literally*. Not because they had become lovers, or because she cared for him, but because he was a part of her now. Their bonding ceremony had assured that.

It was a complication that hadn't occurred to her or to Zanya, and if King Dalvish or his priests had realized the import of what their mission required, they hadn't cared.

Zanya stared at her, her brows drawn together in confused consternation. Sachi opened her mouth to explain, but a flash of light in the night sky dragged her attention away from the conversation.

She looked up at the swirling lights. She might have stared at them for a moment, for a lifetime. For an eternity. All she knew was that something lurked beyond the mélange of colors, some profound revelation that was hers and hers alone.

Slowly, the lights coalesced into a figure Sachi knew well. It was her own face that beamed down at her, a gentle smile curving her lips. She stared back at the image of herself, taking in the plain white gown, the crown of flowers atop her head.

The figure in the sky held her hands out at her sides, palms facing forward, silently entreating Sachi to come closer. To *listen*. Then, from every direction, Sachi heard a voice. *Her* voice.

There is only one way, it whispered. *One truth.*

Was this the answer Sachi so desperately sought? She waited, dragging in sharp, shallow breaths as the moments stretched on and on.

The figure's beatific expression didn't change as blood began to seep from the center of her chest, soaking the pristine white gown.

Love is all that matters.

"Sachi?"

Everything was quiet, save for the soft murmur of conversation blanketing the plateau. The lights still shone above, but they were muted, nothing like the dazzling ribbons of color that had seared her very existence only moments before.

Love is all that matters.

Had it really happened? Or had she wanted some sliver of hope so badly that she'd imagined it?

No, it had definitely happened. The absolute certainty of it stole over Sachi, along with a strange sort of peace. There were so *many* paths. It didn't make sense for there to be only one way forward.

"Everything will work out," Sachi whispered.

"What?" Zanya's fingers brushed her cheek, turning her face. "Sachi, did you see something?"

Her eyes met Zanya's, and the gentle bewilderment in their dark depths almost made her smile. She knew she wasn't making sense, but she wasn't sure she *could.* "There's a way, Zan. We just have to find it. And you have to *trust me.*"

"Sachi . . ." Reluctance. Worry. "I trust you with my life. But I don't know if I can trust you with your own."

On that count, at least, she could reassure Zanya. "I want to live, desperately. So that I can love you . . . and Ash."

Zanya closed her eyes with a soft groan. "Really?"

"You disapprove?"

Zanya laughed helplessly and fell back into the faded yellow grass, her hands covering her face. "I don't know what I expected, honestly. You told me it was the easiest way to do this. The *only* way."

"I did, but this isn't even that." Sachi dropped back to lie beside her, reaching out to clasp her hand. "He isn't what they said, Zan. None of them are."

"Of course they aren't. Everyone at court is a liar." Zanya's hand tightened around hers. "I'm drawn to the High Court, too, you know I am. No one has ever accepted either of us. But you can't let that blind you to the reason we're here."

"I haven't forgotten. But . . . I think we belong here, Zanya. I *feel* it."

Zanya rolled onto her side to face Sachi, and twilight shadowed her features. "How? We have three weeks left. That's it."

"I haven't forgotten that, either, no matter what—"

Warning tingled over Sachi, silencing her words just as firm footfalls materialized behind them. Zanya rolled effortlessly into a crouch that left her fingers conveniently close to her boot knife, but when Sachi sat up and turned, it was to see Ash approaching them both with a weary smile. "You found a wonderful spot to view the lights."

"Yes, they're beautiful." Sachi reached up to take a stack of folded blankets from him, then patted the ground next to her in welcome. "Please, sit. How long do they last?"

"Oh, the whole night." He swung a bag off his back and set it next to them. "Most everyone spends the night under the stars. I brought blankets and some dinner. It's not much, but the wine is spiced, and the hand pies are warm."

Sachi was so distracted by the food—and his presence—that she almost missed what he said. "We're sleeping out here?"

"If you think you can. There are guest quarters in the Tower, but just between us? The ground is more comfortable."

"I sincerely doubt that."

Ash crouched next to Sachi with a teasing smile, but she had the oddest feeling he was nervous. "If you're worried about the cold, I've been told that spending the night curled against a dragon is very comfortable."

Zanya snorted as she began to unpack the food. "Yes, we know."

"No, you don't." Ash rose and took a step back. Flames licked at his arms as he raised them. "I don't mean the Dragon. I mean *a dragon*. If you want."

No wonder he was nervous. Sachi hadn't seen his other form up close since that first night at Blade's Rest, when he'd demanded she appear before him and then flown off without a word. A glance at his anxious expression confirmed that he, too, remembered that inauspicious beginning.

She stood and stretched up until she could brush a kiss over his chin. "I would be delighted."

Ash glanced at Zanya. "And you, handmaid?"

Zanya looked almost as nervous as Ash, but she hid it behind bluster. "If you can't provide the princess with a decent mattress, it's only fitting you offer yourself as one."

Ash laughed, and the flames around him danced as he backed up a dozen paces. Fire kindled at his feet, then rose around him as a column of flames. Around them, people gasped. The gasps echoed and grew in volume and number when Ash's wings unfolded from the inferno. They stretched out, extinguishing the flames, and he stood there before them.

A dragon. *The* Dragon.

Hers.

Sachi went to him. His head was easily three times her size, with huge teeth. Spikes rose from his wingtips and back. She reached for him, smiling as she touched the warm and surprisingly soft skin of his massive jaw.

"You're lovely," she whispered.

Ash huffed and nudged her back gently. Then he settled on the cold ground, arranging his body so that she and Zanya could nestle in the circle of his limbs. When Zanya hesitated, Sachi murmured and pulled her along. They curled up against him, and Ash folded his wings around them and laid his head on the ground.

The entire night was redolent with magic. It hung in the air above them, rose and fell with rhythmic breaths beneath them. In a world so full of wonder, Sachi couldn't help but wish for a bit of her own.

Love is all that matters.

Help me make that true.

Chapter Twenty-Five
DRAGON'S MOON

Week Three, Day Two
Year 3000

Zanya awoke shivering.

It should have been impossible to feel cold when snuggled against the heat of a dragon, but the chill hadn't merely been a dream. She opened her eyes and stared up into a dark sky scattered with thousands of bright stars, trying to figure out why it felt like ice filled her veins instead of blood.

It wasn't simply the fact that they were outside. This was the second night on progress where no cabin had greeted them as dusk fell, but Zanya understood why. The path down the Burning Hills was steep and treacherous. This sheltered clearing in the midst of a steep valley was the closest thing to flat ground they'd seen all day. Towering trees covered most of it, but they'd made camp in the scant clear space. The Witch had erected her fancy little tent again—Zanya had a hard time imagining Inga sleeping on packed dirt in well-worn armor, though the

Dragon swore she had during the war between the gods—but everyone else was wrapped in bedrolls scattered around their campfire.

Everyone, that was, except for Sachi and Zanya. They were curled up against the pleasant furnace of an enormous dragon, sheltered beneath his protective wing.

Zanya sat up slowly. To her left, Sachi lay trustingly against Ash, her body fitting perfectly in the crook of one leg, her cheek pillowed on his side. Somehow, Zanya had always imagined the dragon would be covered in uncomfortable armored scales, but his hide was surprisingly smooth and warm. Too warm for the chill that still clamped tight around Zanya.

Except now that she was awake, she felt something tugging at her from the woods. Something that resonated with the shadows inside her. Something . . .

Panic brought her to her feet. Had she been having nightmares? Had she accidentally manifested some tangible proof of the nerves that had twisted her in knots? She took two steps, then froze as a dragon's eye larger than both her fists cracked open.

Her heart fluttered. "I'm going to visit the woods," she whispered, hoping he'd take that to mean she had to attend to necessary needs in private. He must have, because his wing shifted slightly, clearing a path, and his huffing sigh blew back her hair as his eye closed again.

Zanya crept across the clearing, reaching out to the shadows to ease her silent passage. The tree line was only a dozen steps away, and she slipped into the deeper shadows, following that tugging sensation. She braced herself, half expecting to find a Terror lurking between the trees, its misshapen bone and wood limbs and horrifying features enough to shake even the strongest of hearts.

What she found was worse. So much worse.

The shadows convulsed around her. Her stomach dropped as if the ground had fallen out from beneath her. When she recovered, High

Priest Nikkon stood before her, his handsome face tight with fury. "Sleeping well cuddled up with the enemy, Zanya?"

"How—"

"Did I get here?" He strolled forward, and the dappled moonlight piercing the trees highlighted his vicious smile. "You would do well to remember that you are never beyond my reach."

Zanya's heart pounded. Her fingers curled, as if she could already feel the hilt of a knife within them. But memory stilled her hand. Attacking him would only result in another threat against Sachi.

"What do you want?" she whispered.

"Only to remind you of the stakes in this game you play."

"Believe me, I never forget the stakes."

"Do you not?" He leaned closer. "Did you think we wouldn't have spies? That no one would tell us how you slept with the Dragon at the Phoenix's Tower? How both of you now fuck him so readily and eagerly?"

Zanya hissed out a breath. "That's why you sent her to him, isn't it?"

"Her, yes. You? Never." His gaze raked over her, disgusted and judgmental. "We should have known better. You've always been twisted inside. Of course you threw yourself at the first monster who would take you."

If only she had. Every day that passed with Zanya holding herself back from the Dragon marked fewer precious grains of sand in the hourglass counting away the rest of Sachi's life. She should have embraced pleasure the way Sachi had. Thrown herself into it and forgotten everything but the moment, the bliss.

But no matter how the darkness within Ash drew her, Zanya could not. Maybe she didn't even know how. Pleasure made you vulnerable—wasn't that the very point of turning it into a weapon they could wield against him? Perhaps Sachi, with her fearsome courage, was brave enough to let go beneath the hands of an enemy.

Zanya was not.

"Will you not even attempt to deny it?"

She could, and it would be truth. But Zanya would be damned to the Void before she explained anything to him. "I'm still waiting to hear why you traveled all this way. Hopefully not just to imply that I'm some sort of deviant."

His hand shot out, strong fingers curling tight around her throat. His nails sank into her skin until it broke beneath them, and the metallic scent of her blood filled the shadows. Air wheezed past his grip when she sucked in a breath—enough to keep her from fighting back in purely instinctive panic.

Enough to scream?

Any hint of a disturbance would summon the Raven Guard, at the very least. Perhaps the High Court as well. It would be one way to end this impossible standoff. And the crunch of Nikkon's bones as the Dragon bit him in half would be so satisfying . . .

"You could," the high priest whispered, his voice low and mocking. "You could scream. You could call for help. You could even kill me yourself, perhaps. You're certainly violent enough. But you won't, will you, Zanya?"

His other hand shot out. Shadows writhed around it, and when he withdrew his hand once more, he was holding an hourglass. Not the one from Sachi's chest—Zanya knew every twist and hollow of the engraving. She practically knew the number of scales on the dragons wrapped around the globes.

This one was smaller, with no decoration. Just red sand, falling one grain at a time from the top to the bottom.

Zanya's heart beat faster.

"Killing me won't help Sachi." Nikkon held up the glass. "That would only lock the curse in place forever. I'm the only one who can change it. I can make it go slower . . ." He swept his thumb up over the glass, and the sand within froze. Zanya watched, hypnotized, but no further grains joined the swirling red on the bottom.

Precious seconds added back to Sachi's life.

But only for a moment. Nikkon's smile was cruel as he swept his thumb in the opposite direction. "Or I can make it move more swiftly."

Red sand spilled from the upper globe in a tiny, continuous stream, and Zanya's heart stopped. "Please," she whispered. "Please, no."

The sand slowed once more. One grain fell. Another. It felt like her heart only resumed beating when the grains continued their slow, stately march.

Shadows swirled again, consuming the hourglass and carrying it away. Nikkon flexed his fingers around Zanya's throat with bruising strength, reminding her of the threat he posed. "You will not forget your mission. You will not seek to betray us. The High Court cannot help you. They were born of the Everlasting Dream and hold no sway over Void magic."

A tiny hope she hadn't even known she possessed fizzled.

"However they attempt to seduce you, the High Court are not your friends, Zanya. What are they?"

The words tasted like bitter lies, but they weren't. The truth could be bitter, too. "My enemies."

"And what happens if you seek comfort from your enemies?"

"Sachi dies."

"Not just dies." He dragged Zanya closer, until all she could see were his pretty eyes, hardened by hate and cruelty. "Her soul is severed from the Everlasting Dream. She will never be reborn. She will never again know comfort. Death would be a blessing compared to the fate that awaits her if you fail to act."

Helplessness surged through Zanya, fueled by rage and grief. "Why her?" she whispered hoarsely. "Why do this to her? She's never hurt anyone. She's kind and good."

"Because she's useful," he told her flatly. "Some doubted it would work, you know. They saw the monster hiding behind your pretty face.

They swore you would abandon her at the first opportunity. But I knew better. I saw what you did to protect her when you were children."

Zanya closed her eyes. It was a mistake. The memory came, soft around the edges because she'd been so young, but still bright with fear and rage. And blood. So much blood. Bodies strewn everywhere. Limbs torn off. Villagers savaged.

A massacre unlike any other. And at its heart, Sachi, her face streaked with tears, her body still bruised from the beating they'd given her.

A normal person would feel regret. Zanya never had.

"The carnage was exquisite," Nikkon whispered. "You were so small, and so vicious. The perfect weapon, with only one vulnerability. Her. I sometimes wondered if you'd realize how weak she made you and find a way to cut yourself free of her . . . but you were never that bright, were you?"

She was smart enough to know that loving Sachi had never made her weaker. Every fierce, dangerous impulse inside her had been honed to killing sharpness against the whetstone of that love. Zanya glared at him, ignoring the bruising grip of his fingers. "You should have cursed me."

Nikkon laughed. "Do you think I didn't try? Of course I did. But there's nothing good inside you, Zanya. You're a creature of shadows and darkness. A creature of the Void. And you can't curse the damned."

The words fell like blows, and she barely noticed him releasing her until her knees gave way and she crumpled to the forest floor. Leaves crunched beneath her fingers as she dug them into the dirt, but the words wouldn't stop.

Nothing good inside you.
Creature of shadows and darkness.
Can't curse the damned.

She was the monster she'd always believed, and it was her fault that Sachi suffered under this nightmare. Her fault for being uncursable. Her fault for being the weapon they so coveted. Her fault the priest had found them to begin with.

All of it, all of it, all of it was her fault.

"Do your job," Nikkon advised in a harsh voice. The shadows already swirled around his legs. She could feel a sick lurch as they gathered tightly. "Kill him soon, Zanya. Because we will be watching."

Nausea gripped her, and she didn't know if it was the unsteady drop in the world as the shadows sucked him away or the import of his words falling into the pit of her stomach like stones that would never leave.

She had no choice. She had to open herself to the Dragon. She had to find the courage to be vulnerable. She had to find a way to lure him into complacency.

And then she had to embrace what she truly was. A creature of darkness. A monster with nothing good inside her.

Damned.

Chapter Twenty-Six
DRAGON'S MOON

Week Three, Day Three
Year 3000

Two days after leaving the plateau, much to Sachi's surprise, they were still making camp in the Burning Hills.

They were traveling as swiftly as ever. But the gently sloping journey up the mountains had been deceptively quick—clear, uncomplicated trails that were easily navigable for both person and animal.

The paths down the other side were treacherous. The elevation dropped precipitously, leaving them on steep, narrow grades littered with evidence of recent rockslides. They had to travel from clearing to clearing, stopping to let the animals rest and graze whenever they could.

At the end of the day's travel, Sachi was pleased to see a set of stone cabins. "You know I'd never besmirch the comfort you offer in your dragon form," she murmured as she clasped Ash's hand to let him help her from her horse. "But I will be happy to sleep in a *bed* tonight."

His chuckle warmed her as much as the gentleness of his hands as he lowered her to the ground. "And this cabin offers more comforts than just a soft bed."

"Oh?" She leaned in, pressing her body closer to his. "Are you flirting with me, my lord?"

"Quite certainly." He leaned down so his whisper tickled her cheek. "Your cabin has a back door. Follow the stone path and wait for me. I'll be along once we've made camp."

"Mysterious." She smiled as she nipped at his earlobe. "Will you tell Zanya where we'll be?"

"Of course." Ash dropped a kiss to her cheek before stepping back. "I'm far too wise to tempt her wrath by stealing you away."

"Liar." She glanced over to where Zanya and Malindra still sat astride their mounts, deep in conversation about something—likely weaponry. "I suspect you often daydream new ways to tempt her wrath, you enjoy it so much."

Another low chuckle, this one laced with dark promise. "I'm not the only one who enjoys it."

He had a point. Sachi turned toward the consort's cabin, calling back over her shoulder. "Don't be long."

She stopped inside the cabin only long enough to leave her riding boots and stockings by the front door. Then she slipped out the back door, bare feet hurrying across the shiveringly cold stones, and followed the path.

It ended at a gorgeous, steaming pool of water, one of the many hot springs that graced the Burning Hills. Elevia had told her about the springs, how some were as chilly as any fresh water that sprang from deep within the earth, while others boiled with a heat that could kill a man in mere moments.

But some relatively rare pools were just *perfect*. Sachi knelt at the edge of the spring and tested the water with her fingertip, then plunged her hand into the pool and sighed with pleasure.

Forget the bed. She'd sleep in the spring if she could figure out a way not to drown.

She hurried out of her riding clothes and draped them across a nearby boulder. The pool was secluded, set away from any potentially prying eyes, but she didn't care if the whole camp could see her. She longed to feel the hot water on her bare skin, to sink to the bottom of the pool and let it close around her like a cocoon.

Sachi slid into the spring with a moan. It was deep—to her chin when she stood in the middle and dug her toes into the sandy bottom—and lined with a carved rock ledge under the water that perplexed her until she sank down to sit on it.

Seats. Of course.

Joy bubbled up within her, and she splashed her arms in the water and laughed.

"Enjoying your surprise?"

Ash leaned against a tree near the path, watching her.

Sachi turned toward him and informed him imperiously, "Enjoy the rest of the progress without me. I live here now."

"Aleksi and Dianthe will be terribly disappointed." He bent to begin unlacing his boots, his gaze never leaving her. "Shall I bring them all here to pay tribute to my consort in her new home?"

"By all means. They can come here and visit me in my watery kingdom."

"Be careful what invitations you issue the Siren. If she wanted, she could dive from her castle into Siren's Bay and surface in your bathtub." One boot hit the ground, and he started in on the other.

"Could she? Well, then." Sachi floated to the other edge of the pool, rested her chin on the edge, and watched Ash. She wanted to keep up the teasing tone of the conversation, but the moment he straightened and reached for his shirt, words nearly left her. "I'd better be very, *very* nice to Dianthe."

"Wise people always are." The words were muffled somewhat by his shirt passing over his head, but soon the fabric fluttered to the ground, leaving her view of the fine muscles of his chest unrestricted. "I rule the High Court only because Dianthe finds the idea too tedious. She is truly the strongest of us all. This world is more sea than stone, and there is nothing the wind does not touch."

"True." But the rest of the Court followed him without complaint, even gladly. Sachi had seen the evidence of that with her own eyes. "But there are different kinds of strength."

"Many kinds." His hands lingered on the front fastening of his pants, and he smiled. "Do I join you now, Princess? Or wait for Zanya?"

"Is that how you think this works?" Sachi drifted away from the edge to float on her back. "I can only touch you when she's here to monitor the situation?"

"Sometimes it seems like *Zanya* thinks it works that way." The soft slide of fabric over skin told her he'd stripped away his pants. "She's yours, and precious to you. I don't want to hurt her."

Sachi's heart ached a little. "That's very sweet. She worries, that's all. That you're going to hurt *me*." She met his gaze. "I know better. You want to do a lot of things to me, but *harm* isn't one of them."

"No," he confirmed, his voice low and raspy. "Never."

He stood there, naked and practically trembling, *waiting*. For an invitation, for her permission. For her to want him.

As if she could ever stop. "Come to me, Ash."

He slipped into the water gracefully. Water that came nearly to her chin lapped playfully across his chest as he lounged back on one of the smooth stone benches, his arms outstretched along the stone rim. "Were you thinking about touching me anywhere in particular?"

Sachi ignored the question and floated closer. "You like to tease me."

"It is an intimacy I'm rarely allowed."

Did he tell himself that? Did he truly believe there weren't those who, god or otherwise, would throw themselves at his feet and at the mercy of his need for companionship as well as his appetite for carnal pleasure?

He couldn't possibly. And yet, Sachi would have sworn that he did. It would not stand.

"No." She reached out, her fingertips grazing his wet shoulder. "An intimacy you rarely seek or indulge, perhaps. But now you have me to tease, and that's fine." Closer, until her legs brushed his under the water. "One way or another, I *will* be satisfied."

"Yes, you will." He stroked a finger along her jaw until his finger rested, crooked, just beneath her chin. With only that gentle pressure, he urged her closer, until her knees bumped the seat on either side of his legs. "But you forget something else, my princess."

Sachi framed his face with her hands as she braced her knees on the stone and stretched up. As attractive and strong as he always was, there was a particular beauty in this—a moment of unguarded vulnerability.

She brushed her lips over his. "What is that, my lord?"

He caught the end of her long braid and slowly wrapped it around his fist. "I can feel just how much you enjoy being teased."

"Fascinating." Delicious anticipation wound through her, and Sachi bit back an eager moan. Instead, she took his other hand, placed it at the hollow of her throat, and began to pull it down her body. "What else can you feel?"

"Probably your impossible impatience." Zanya's amused voice drifted to her, and when Sachi looked up, the handmaid was leaning against the same tree Ash had chosen. "He's not very good at resisting your dimples, is he?"

"Don't you dare encourage him to do that." Sachi's heart pounded a little faster, and she tugged Ash's hand beneath the water. "I may like being teased, but I *adore* being well-fucked."

Ash hissed out a breath, his fingers splaying wide on her abdomen. Then he began to move his hand on his own, stroking upward again, until his thumb found her nipple. "Is that so, Zanya?"

"Oh, yes." She bent down to unbuckle one boot. "Sachi indulges me most of the time. Lets me take it slow and lose myself in how good I can make her feel. But sometimes I see that look in her eyes, and I know she only needs one thing."

Ash's lips brushed Sachi's. His thumb and forefinger caught her nipple with a gentle tug, then a firmer one, testing her responses. When she sucked in a sharp breath, he grasped her chin and turned her face toward Zanya. "Is this the look?"

Zanya kicked free of her second boot and strolled toward the pool, shrugging off her thick jacket as she approached. Underneath, she wore only loose pants and one of her tightly wrapped sleeveless tunics. Leaving the garments in place, she slid into the pool, settled beside Ash, and cupped Sachi's cheek. "Oh, love. You need it badly, don't you?"

"I need . . ." Sachi moved, angling her body so that she was surrounded by heat—Ash, Zanya, and the water. *"This."*

Zanya didn't make her ask again. Strong, familiar fingers held her in place for a searing kiss that felt like coming home. The teasing nip of Zanya's teeth, the commanding swipe of her tongue, the way she kissed Sachi as if there was nothing more she could want or need but *this*. Them, together.

It was bliss. And then Ash's lips found her throat, and *bliss* took on a new, more intense meaning.

Ash and Zanya kept kissing her, kept touching her, redefining the word every time their fingers clashed, pulling at her hair or pinching her nipples.

Between them, Sachi burned.

"Just like that." Zanya trailed kisses along Sachi's shoulder, and the water licked teasingly over her skin as the other woman shifted behind her. Zanya's fingernails dragged gently up Sachi's thighs beneath the water, and her lips hovered over one ear as Ash nipped at the other. "I know you want all of him, but you're not ready. Not yet. He's too big."

He *was*, but that didn't stop Sachi from wanting him so much there was no room for good sense. She shifted her hips, grinding against Ash. "Do you concur, my lord? I hope not."

He groaned against her ear, his fingers clenching on her hips. "But it's so much fun to *make* you ready."

"Mmm." Zanya's teeth closed on her nape, jolting through Sachi like a static shock. Then her fingers circled Sachi's clit, knowing, taunting, with just the right pressure to drive her wild. "Open for us, love."

Us. The import of the word hit Sachi as Ash's fingers joined Zanya's, and she whimpered helplessly. *"Yes."*

Ash worked two broad fingers inside her, pushing and retreating, pumping slowly. She gripped his shoulders and tilted her hips to his touch. There was no pain, exactly, only a primal sense of *invasion* that she embraced, even welcomed, because it meant having him inside her. All the while, Zanya kept stroking her, murmuring against her ear and her temple, words interspersed with the hot, familiar glide of her tongue over Sachi's cheek and mouth.

Another. She wasn't sure if Zanya said it, or if Sachi only wished she would, but Ash thrust a third finger inside her, as if he, too, had heard the command, wordless or otherwise. Sachi moaned into his mouth, her nails scratching over his back as she tried to ride his hand.

Zanya wrapped one arm around Sachi to still her frantic rocking. No matter how much she squirmed, she remained trapped between them until Zanya leaned back, bringing Sachi with her. The shift in angle drove Ash's fingers deeper, and Zanya pressed a soothing kiss to Sachi's temple as she whimpered. "She looks so delicate. So soft. And she'll always try to push you for more and faster. But if you're patient, and you take your time, she can take so much. She *needs* so much."

"Please—" Sachi reached out and wound one hand in the wet fabric of Zanya's tunic. "Help him fuck me."

"Shh." Zanya's fingers ghosted over her clit again, dragging her toward the ragged edge of release. But then they drifted lower. Ash's fingers withdrew, curled around Zanya's. When they pushed back into her . . .

Sachi choked back a cry. Zanya kept talking, but she couldn't hear the words over the blood rushing in her ears. There was pain now, the soft sort that bordered on pleasure, the two so inextricably linked that she couldn't separate them. She wanted *more, now.*

Ash groaned, and she realized she was whispering the words with the fervency of a prayer. She opened her eyes and watched him, her gaze locked on his face as he lifted his free hand to cup her cheek. His thumb pressed against her lips. "Soon," he promised, as their fingers plunged deep and the heel of Zanya's hand ground against Sachi's clit with maddening pressure. "Come for us, and you can have anything you want."

Her need overwhelmed her, making her desperate, and she raked her nails over his cheek. "Promise me."

It was Zanya who answered, her lips hot against Sachi's cheek. "We promise."

She came hard, and *oh, gods.* The sharp, jagged shocks of pleasure that shook her limbs also made her clench around their fingers. Every clench set off another wave that crashed through her, then rebounded into the next, on and on, until all Sachi knew was the feeling of being held in place—Ash's mouth against her forehead, Zanya's cheek against hers—along with the raw sensation of having screamed herself hoarse.

Gentle hands stroked her everywhere—her arms, her back, dragging softly down her legs and soothingly over her cheek. "Here she is," Zanya whispered, kissing her cheek again. "Welcome back, love."

Sachi turned instinctively to steal an open-mouthed kiss, then tangled her fingers in Zanya's hair to hold her still for a second, longer kiss. When she spoke, her voice was low, hoarse. "Do you still think I can't handle fucking my Dragon?"

"Impossible brat." Zanya nipped at her lower lip. But her smile faded as she tenderly stroked several wet strands of Sachi's hair back from her face. "I always know exactly what you can handle."

And now Ash was finding out. Sachi wrapped her arms around his neck with a slow smile. "And you, my lord?"

"I—" His words cut off with a hiss. He arched up against her, and Sachi felt not only the hard, hot length of his cock, but Zanya's fingers wrapped around the shaft as well.

Sachi shuddered and bit his jaw. "A taste of your own torment, my love. Tell me how it feels."

Ash chuckled hoarsely. "I already know how clever her fingers are. I've felt what they do to you."

"Ahh, but I've spent years perfecting my knowledge of how to torment Sachi." Zanya's fingers skated up beneath the water, and Sachi could sense the curiosity in her slow movements. "This is unexplored territory."

"Not to mention . . ." Sachi ground against Ash's cock—and Zanya's fist. "I happen to like filthy words."

"Well, then." Ash caught Sachi's braid and tugged her closer, until their lips were almost touching. "I feel *you*, Princess." His voice was a low rumble. "I felt your helpless pleasure with every finger we worked into you. I felt you take the pain and yearn for more. And now I feel you wondering if anything can be as good as having our fingers buried deep inside you. But it can, Princess. Oh, it can."

"Still teasing me." She bit his lower lip, licked the spot with her tongue, and slipped one hand under the water. "Perhaps I should guide Zan in her . . . explorations." She traced over Zanya's fingers, then thumbed the spot just beneath the crown of Ash's cock.

He hissed, his head falling back. His strong throat worked as he swallowed, but whatever he was going to say disappeared in a growled curse when Zanya followed her lead and stroked the same spot. "I see what you like about this," Zanya murmured.

"Mmm, yes." Watching desire and pleasure overtake Ash sparked a renewed hunger deep in Sachi's belly, and she leaned close enough to whisper in his ear. "Would you like to come like this? Fucking up into our hands? Or do you want something else?"

His response came as a rumble. "There's no part of you I don't want to come while fucking."

"Hmm. Did that sound like an answer, Zan?"

Zanya lifted her free hand to clasp Ash's chin, forcing him to meet her eyes. Beneath the water, her fingers dragged from base to tip, testing his length. "We made her a promise, Dragon."

Flames danced in Ash's eyes. "Yes, we did."

"Lift your hips, Sachi."

Trembling with anticipation, Sachi released Ash, rested her knees on the stone ledge, and pushed up, levering herself above him. Then she held her breath and *waited*.

Something passed between Ash and Zanya, a silent communication where they must have decided *how* this would happen. *How* Ash would take her for the first time. Sachi felt the broad head of his cock pressing against her as his hands locked onto her waist, steadying her. And then he began to guide her hips down.

It took an eternity, both out of necessity and because Ash refused to let Sachi drive down against him in her eagerness. And she would have, even if it meant not being able to sit her horse for a solid week. Anything to have more of him, and faster. Harder.

She made a soft, incoherent noise, a plea that he thoroughly denied by stopping entirely. He held her in an iron grip, suspended above him. Half-impaled on his cock, waiting, *waiting—*

Then he let her go. Sachi slammed her hips down against his in one furious, frantic stroke, taking the rest of him with a rough, wordless cry. It was *fire*, a single blazing moment that swept through her, burning away everything that wasn't them—Ash, trembling beneath her, Zanya's teeth on her shoulder. The flames that were surely licking through the water with what was left of Sachi's self-control.

Instinct guided her to roll her hips. Zanya was right there, moving behind her, *with* her, dropping hot kisses to her cheek and her temple as she whispered encouragement. "Ride him, Sachi. Take all of him."

Every movement elicited another rough pulse of pleasure. It was instinctive, primal, this urge to rock against him, harder and faster, until the hard knot of need unraveled inside her.

Ash grunted as he drove up into her, and it was such a *small* thing, but it tipped Sachi over the edge, that tiny, frantic noise. She came, her rhythm stuttering as she clenched around him.

Zanya reached for Ash, clutching his jaw with fingers as harsh as her command. "Don't you *dare* come. Keep fucking her."

He did, wrapping an arm around Sachi's back. He curled his hand over the top of her shoulder, then used the grip to haul her down into his next thrust. It drove a sharp cry from her throat, and Zanya soothed her with a soft hum and the quick glide of her tongue over Sachi's cheek.

"So sweet," she murmured as she moved with them. Her clever hands stole around Sachi's body again and squeezed her breasts. "Should we tell him, love? How you always come the hardest with my tongue on your nipples?"

Sachi moaned, because she knew what was coming. Ash was too great a warrior to ignore a key piece of intelligence, on the battlefield *or* off. So she saw it in her mind's eye even before it happened—Ash, bending his head, licking pure fire over the stiff peak of her breast where it peeked through Zanya's fingers.

Then it *did* happen, and it was even better than she'd imagined. Her heart pounded, and she couldn't breathe for chanting their names, over and over, begging for mercy. For release.

Ash's teeth scraped her nipple, and Sachi screamed as the rest of the world vanished in the white haze that stole over her vision. Her entire body shook, and she clawed at Ash's shoulders as he pumped into her and groaned her name.

Silence.

Sachi opened her eyes just in time to see Ash and Zanya's mouths fuse in a kiss. The impact of it hit her like the thunder that follows a lightning strike. It was an inevitable clash of forces, primal and undeniable, like the sun and moons rising and setting, or waves returning to crash against the shore.

She sank her hand into Zanya's hair and nuzzled Ash's jaw, drawn in not only by the heat of their kiss but by the frisson of satisfaction that snaked through him.

"Holy *fuck*," Sachi breathed, hoarse and dazed, and their pleased, approving laughter curled around her, even warmer than the water.

Chapter Twenty-Seven
DRAGON'S MOON

Week Three, Day Five
Year 3000

Sparring with Ash again was a reckless decision. Zanya had known it from the moment he smiled at her across the makeshift sparring circle and crooked his fingers, murmuring, *Come play with me, handmaid.*

All Zanya made these days were reckless decisions.

It had gone sideways right from the start. Not because desire twisted through her when their bodies clashed. Not because the unquenchable need to best him made her careless with what she revealed.

It went sideways because Sachi was *watching* them this time, transfixed by their every move, and that turned every Void-cursed moment of it into seething foreplay. Sachi's cheeks turned pinker with each clash. Her sharp inhales when one of them pinned the other to the dirt echoed through the night air like explosions.

At least Zanya's torment was limited to observing Sachi's reactions. Whatever magical bond connected him to Sachi had clearly impacted the Dragon's state of arousal.

Either that, or he *really* liked wrestling Zanya to see who would end up on top.

Zanya called a halt to the whole mess after a particularly fraught scrabble that left her alternately pinned beneath Ash, fighting with every scrap of self-control not to grind up against the formidable bulge rocking between her legs, and straddling his chest while he grinned up at her, somehow managing to conjure lurid fantasies about letting him drag her hips up and tear away her pants.

Yes, Sachi's vivid appreciation of the cleverness of the Dragon's tongue had intrigued her, but not enough to ride said tongue in front of the entire party. And she'd begun to fear exactly that would happen.

So she fled, leaving Ash and Sachi to their post-dinner stroll. She no longer worried that the Dragon would harm her. Sachi had never been safer than she was when surrounded by the Dragon and the Raven Guard and these gods who doted on and adored her.

Until the final day of the Dragon Moon. Tomorrow night, both moons would be full, marking the halfway point. Twenty-five days gone.

Twenty-five left before the curse claimed Sachi.

Days were trickling through Zanya's fingers like sand. Every day bound them more tightly to Ash and his people. Every day made it more likely Zanya would succeed.

Every day made it more certain Sachi would never be able to forgive her.

Or maybe she would. Zanya couldn't tell anymore where Sachi's deception ended and her true adoration for the Dragon began. She said *trust me* and *everything will be all right*, and it was either sublime strategy or desperate delusion. All Zanya knew was that Sachi might be trained for this level of intrigue, but Zanya had no defenses in a heart that had rarely known affection and a body that would have been starved of pleasure without Sachi.

Ash offered her pleasure now. Pleasure on *her* terms, even if he'd never let her forget his obedience was that of a wild creature submitting willingly to a leash but never to be tamed. She wanted it. Wanted his too-broad fingers and his too-clever tongue and maybe even that too-massive cock, though the thought of commanding him to fuck Sachi into boneless ecstasy was somehow even more arousing.

Gods, she wished she had another of those frigid mountain streams to throw herself into.

But there wasn't one. They were out of the Burning Hills now, riding across the farmlands that bordered the Lover's Lakes. Tonight's camping spot was nestled in an orchard with winter-blooming cherry trees. The cabin was one of the grander ones, with a bathing area separated from the large bed and sitting area by a folding screen with cherry blossoms painted across it.

The bathing area consisted of a hand pump that brought in cold water and a large tub. No hearth or stove had been provided to heat the water, probably because Ash could do it with a gesture if he wanted.

Ash wasn't here, and Zanya didn't want the water heated anyway. She stripped naked, stood over the drain, and dumped an entire bucket of icy water over her head.

It barely helped. She still *wanted.*

"There you are." Sachi slid one soft hand over Zanya's wet shoulder, then laughed ruefully. "Oh, the water's freezing. Are you that miserable, love?"

Any good the frigid water had done vanished under the wave of warmth that always followed Sachi's touch. A dozen days' worth of thwarted need roared up, and she dug her teeth into her lower lip to hold back a moan. Her belated "I'm fine" sounded not at all convincing.

"You are *not*," Sachi countered immediately. "Just watching you and Ash roll around on the ground was enough to make me blush, and I've been having frequent orgasms. Unlike you."

Which was her own fault. Sachi would have eagerly and joyously relieved Zanya's simmering frustration. But she hadn't found the courage to make herself vulnerable in Ash's presence. Even with Sachi's life trickling away, one blood-red grain of sand at a time, she was still a coward.

Sachi was the only person she'd ever trusted to watch her fall apart.

An alcove in the wall held a stack of fluffy towels. Someone must have put them there just for this trip, because when she pulled one free and lifted it to wipe her face, it smelled clean and fresh. "Sachi—" she started, but the all-too-recognizable tread of boots behind her froze the words in her mouth.

She clutched the towel to the front of her body, knowing it was futile. Her back was on full display, and any furtive attempt she made to cover it now would only prolong this miserable moment she'd been so carefully avoiding. She knew what he was looking at, and she could *feel* his building rage, as if the very floor shivered beneath her bare feet.

Scars crisscrossed Zanya's back, nearly a decade's worth of abuse painted in ugly lines of remembered pain. Not that they'd stopped beating her at sixteen—no, once they'd realized how swiftly she had begun to heal, the real punishment had started, driven by fear and anger at her resilience. Though her scars had faded to a latticework of thin, pale stripes, the evidence was still damning enough.

And Zanya hated for people to see it.

Zanya pivoted, lifting her chin as she met Ash's implacable gaze. Then Sachi was *there*, a robe already in her hands, wrapping it around Zanya's back to hide the patchwork of scars. Zanya thanked her with a soft touch on her cheek, then belted the robe in place and stalked past the Dragon.

Silence followed her. She sighed. "We might as well get it over with. Pity or horror, whatever you'd like to express, please do it quickly."

"Rage, handmaid." The Dragon turned to watch her, and the flames danced in his eyes. "I'm feeling rage."

Her heart stuttered. She'd seen this look in his eyes before, this towering anger and dizzying protectiveness. But it had been focused where it should be—on Sachi. Zanya had approved of that focus without fully appreciating how it felt to be the center of it. For one wild moment, the world seemed to vibrate around her, as if the Dragon had marked her as *his* and now the very earth beneath her feet would fight to protect her.

A foolish whimsy. But it *felt* real, and Zanya tasted something wild and alien, a dream that had been so out of reach she'd never bothered to wish for it.

Safety.

A seductive promise, and ultimately a lie. She rejected it with a sharp shake of her head. "Any rage you may feel is at events long past. I heal better than most. Most of the scars that linger are from when I was very young."

The ground truly did tremble beneath her feet this time as the Dragon's voice dropped to a dangerous whisper. "If you wished to calm my rage, you have said the wrong thing. What sort of monster beats a *child?*"

"The usual kind," Zanya retorted. "Terrors come from human nightmares, don't they? People have always harbored more cruelty than we care to admit."

"Names." Ash took one step forward, hands fisted at his sides. "You will give me their names."

Zanya huffed and dropped to the edge of the bed. "Do you honestly think they're still alive?"

That stopped him in his tracks. His head tilted, and satisfaction turned his small smile chilling. "You took care of them? Good."

Of course he misunderstood. He was a god of violence and vengeance trapped in human flesh. He saw the same impulses in Zanya and respected the danger they represented, because they were alike. They would always carve a direct path to the object of their rage and dispatch it with brutal finality.

Neither of them would last a day as nobility in the viper pit that was the court of King Dalvish II.

"I didn't say *I* took care of them," she told him, and the blank confusion on his usually confident face was worth giving up this secret. When she judged that he'd suffered long enough, she glanced toward the corner, where Sachi had paused in pouring a cup of wine.

"I wasn't sure you'd noticed," she said finally. "You never asked."

"I didn't, not at first," Zanya admitted with a gentle smile. "But the men who hurt me had a tendency to end up accused of treason, challenged to duels, or otherwise embroiled in life-ruining scandals. Eventually, the coincidences became too much."

The Dragon turned, one eyebrow sweeping up as he assessed Sachi. "Your handiwork?"

"You protect what's yours, my lord." She pressed the cup of wine into his hands, then grasped his chin in the same merciless grip he so often applied to hers. "So do I."

With breathtaking grace, the Dragon folded himself to his knees in front of Sachi. He drained the cup without looking away, then let it clatter to the floor. "So fierce, Princess. I like you this way."

"You like me any way you find me, Ash." She pushed her thumb between his lips and tilted her head to regard him thoughtfully. "Would you like to have him, Zanya? To ride his tongue and teach him the taste of your pleasure?"

She'd hoped the unwelcome vulnerability of having him see her scars would chill her ardor, but his gaze seized hers and she might as well have been back on her knees in the practice circle, his large hands gripping her hips, his gaze promising earth-shattering pleasure if she let him drag her a little bit higher . . .

He was exactly like Sachi. Far more dangerous on his knees, his sweet play at obedience a trap she knew better than to fall into.

Maybe if she did it just once. Maybe she wouldn't be so vulnerable if Sachi was the one making the demands. Maybe if she got this *need* out of her system . . .

It's strategy, that's all. Just strategy.

What a pretty lie.

"Once," she rasped, clutching at the blankets on either side of her hips.

Sachi pulled in a deep breath and bent close to the Dragon's ear. "Crawl to her."

For a moment Zanya wondered if the Dragon's pride would get in the way. She should have known better. The pride of a god encompassed the heavens and could not be humbled so easily. Ash stalked across the floor like one of the lions that supposedly made their home in the heart of the Blasted Plains, every movement graceful and deadly, his flame-colored eyes hot with anticipation.

Zanya tightened her grip on the blankets and held her ground.

When he finally knelt before her, he reached out to touch her shoulder. Sachi halted him with a single word.

"Wait."

Ash froze, the fond frustration in his expression so familiar that Zanya bit her lip, struggling to hold back a smile. Sachi had the Dragon twined around her delicate little finger.

Sachi crossed the room and sank to the bed beside her. "Before you can touch her," she murmured, toying with the edge of Zanya's robe, "you have to learn how."

Zanya couldn't help it this time. She laughed. "Sachi, he's been fucking women since before the first day. Surely he has an idea or two."

Sachi met her gaze, her blue eyes deep and full of untamed affection as she stroked Zanya's throat with the backs of her fingers. "But he hasn't been fucking *you*, my love. If he's to do it at all, he'll do it properly. Or he'll answer to me."

"So fierce," she murmured, echoing the Dragon's words. They were truer than he might ever know. Dipping her head, she nipped at Sachi's fingertips. "Fine. Tease your dragon, Sachi. See how long he can take it before he snaps and gives you what you want."

"This isn't a tease, darling." A quick, soft kiss to Zanya's tingling lips. "It's a lesson."

She went on, her fingers trailing down to part the robe, just baring the tips of Zanya's breasts. "I like to be overwhelmed, it's true. But Zanya is different. She likes a slow build, pleasure dancing at the edges of her senses until the slightest touch can send her reeling. You've had lovers like this before, my lord?"

"Mmm." Ash braced his hands against the bed on either side of Zanya's, so close she could feel the heat of his skin. But the only touch was a gentle graze of his thumbs over the backs of her fingers, so fleeting she might have imagined it, except for the tingling fire left in its wake.

"Good. Then watch."

Sachi caught her mouth again, her fingers easing beneath the edges of the silken robe to slide over Zanya's skin. Nothing so substantial as a caress, just a glancing brush of fingers at her shoulder, her collarbone. Across her nipples.

She shivered, already primed for Sachi's touch. The robe fell away, and Sachi's mouth dropped to her skin, licking over all those same spots. Then she closed her lips around one of Zanya's nipples, teasing her tongue over the taut, aching peak. It was a sharp pulse of bliss that ended abruptly as Sachi threw her head back with a low moan and a muffled curse.

Her blue eyes were glazed, unfocused. "He's so eager," she rasped. "To taste you, to fuck you. To *hear* you come." Her hand fell to Zanya's thigh. "I can feel all that hunger so deep inside."

Ash's thumbs swept out again, this time resting across the back of Zanya's hands. Not enough pressure to pin her in place, but a stark reminder that he was *there*, waiting. As if she couldn't feel him there, heat and muscle and impatience crouched at her feet, dancing to Sachi's every whim.

"My hunger," Ash agreed in a low rumble. "And *yours*." His gaze followed Sachi's fingertips as they stroked a path down Zanya's body. "I've felt you come screaming on my cock, and you loved it. But I think you love making Zanya tremble even more."

"I give myself easily." Sachi breathed the words into Zanya's ear. "But her release is hard-won. When I make her come, I know I've done something right."

Love slashed through her, the purity of it almost pain, and for a stolen heartbeat, it was just the two of them as Zanya turned her face to Sachi's and whispered the truth against her lips. "You're my tether. Without you, I'd be only darkness."

Sachi shook her head, her hand tightening on Zanya's thigh. "You're my light. And you'll be his, too."

No, she'd be something else to the Dragon. Death or betrayal or bitter memory . . . and the reality of their hopeless situation nearly swallowed her lust. But when she turned to meet the Dragon's eyes, there was no blind adoration there. Just recognition, one monster to another—darkness and pain and violence and death. Those were the building blocks that made them both.

Sweet Sachi was the one who saw light in them. Her own reflected light, glowing bright enough to bring two reluctant monsters to this unlikely alliance. He knew exactly what she was, and he didn't care. Her pleasure pleased Sachi, so he'd pursue it with a hunter's zeal, and perhaps that made it acceptable to give in.

Or maybe it was merely another sweet lie. Zanya didn't care anymore. She closed her eyes and sought Sachi's lips in a desperate kiss. Sachi's tongue greeted hers readily, gliding over Zanya's even as she urged her legs apart. Her fingers slid over slick flesh, mimicking the movement of her tongue.

"Now?" A question for Zanya . . . and a command for Ash.

"Yes—" she whispered, and it was the only word she managed because suddenly *he* was there, broad shoulders driving her knees wider, his mouth hot and open, his tongue licking over Sachi's finger, licking over *her*—

A groan tried to escape. Zanya gripped the blankets with all her strength and muffled the sound against Sachi's lips. She'd shut this fantasy down with such furious commitment every time it tried to form, she wasn't ready for the reality of it. Her brain scrambled in a dozen directions at once, grasping to understand the import of so many sensations.

It was the stubble that sent her mind spinning. Sachi's cheeks were so smooth, but Ash's cheeks bore a day or two's growth of beard, and it rasped over sensitive skin and left her shuddering. Then Sachi's fingers shifted, leaving his tongue unfettered access to her clit, and she learned why Sachi squealed when he buried his face between her legs.

Slick, hot, *fire*, but so good. Too good. Her hips tried to buck—away, closer, she couldn't tell—and she didn't realize she was falling until her back hit the bed.

Instead of falling with her, Sachi pressed one more soothing kiss to her swollen lips, then slid down off the bed to join the Dragon.

Zanya struggled to her elbows, only for the view to almost knock her flat on the bed again. Ash, so deadly intent. Sachi, full of gleeful mischief, savoring her moment in charge as much as she'd savor the moment Zanya took over and paid her back for every teasing touch.

Sachi's fingers danced up the inside of Zanya's thigh, and she shuddered and let her head fall back. "The more you help him torment me, the more I'm going to help him torment you."

"I look forward to it." Then Sachi's tongue joined the Dragon's, slipping and searching. *Demanding.*

Her elbows gave out again, but it mattered little. She couldn't keep her eyes open anymore. Couldn't fight the way her body bucked in spite of her. Her grasping hand found Ash's hair, the strands just long enough to tangle in her fingers as she bit back another groan. Then she twisted her fingers tighter in his hair and *he* groaned, a deep vibrating rumble that brought her hips off the bed.

"Fuck," she whispered as her body began to tremble. She tried to writhe back, but Ash's hands curled around her thighs, pinning her in place. Sachi's tongue led Ash's to all the places that stole Zanya's breath, and those clever, elegant fingers stroked lower, pushing into her in a rhythm Sachi knew would drive her wild.

It was Ash who shoved her to the brink, lifting his head just enough for his words to ghost across sensitive skin. "Her love for you burns so bright inside me, handmaid. You and I could take her to the brink and leave her there for hours, and she wouldn't crave her own release as much as she craves yours right now."

Sachi's sweet, eager moan confirmed it, and the tension in Zanya drew tight enough to destroy her.

"Come for her," Ash rasped against her. "Come for Sachi."

She did. The burn inside her ignited, driving everything else before it as it spread through her body like flashfire. No self-control could hold back her desperate groan as it reached the edges of her awareness and rebounded, the bliss agonizing as she shuddered in their grip.

It felt like an eternity before she sprawled limp in the aftermath, limbs shaking in tiny aftershocks. Ash's hands stroked her legs and hips, gentle and soothing, as Sachi dropped kisses to every bit of skin she could reach. When she finally looked up, her blue eyes were bright and gleeful. "Again."

"Sachi—"

"Please." Sachi licked her inner thigh. "For me?"

"Brat," Zanya whispered, threading her fingers through the disheveled blonde hair. But she couldn't say no, not when Sachi pleaded in that sweet voice. Pleasure still thrummed in her veins, and the languid shift of her hips drove Sachi's two fingers deeper. She shuddered and tightened her fist in Sachi's hair. "One more," she commanded. "But I'll make you pay for it."

Sachi's grin told her that was the point—or at least part of it—and Zanya laughed and sprawled back against the bed, savoring the lazy heat in her limbs as Sachi leaned toward Ash and whispered something.

That sweet afterglow shattered when one broad, strong finger worked its way into her.

"Shh," Sachi soothed, dropping more kisses as Zanya shuddered. She'd stared at those fingers far too often, and still it was somehow better than she'd imagined. One was delicious friction. The second was a sweet stretch that turned glorious when Sachi's knowing tongue returned. Heat flared too bright, too fast, driving her hips up, which only drove those fingers deeper.

But that wasn't what shattered her last fragile string of self-control. It was Sachi, whispering *faster* and *deeper* and *harder—no, just a little* and *lick here* and *higher*, gleeful in her bossiness, reveling in her knowledge, using Ash shamelessly to pleasure Zanya within an inch of sanity. And it was Ash, a living *god*, a man who destroyed armies and single-handedly won wars, so obediently following every command as if he had no arrogance, no pride, no desire in this world but to give Sachi joy.

She tugged at Sachi's hair, dragging her lover's mouth toward hers as she clenched around Ash's fingers, release so close her toes were already curling. "I love you," she whispered, and Sachi smiled that brilliant smile and kissed her. Zanya tasted Sachi and herself, and she wanted to weep with the joy of it.

And then Ash did something with his tongue that sparked bright lights behind her eyelids, and she screamed into Sachi's mouth as the Dragon used his fingers and his tongue to fuck her through an orgasm so dizzying and impossible she had no idea how long it lasted, only that it ended with her sprawled bonelessly on the bed, the Dragon and Sachi smiling smugly as she panted for breath and tried to regain her ability to think.

At last, she did. Her legs felt rubbery as she rolled to her hands and knees and crawled up the bed. She collapsed on her side and held a hand out to Sachi. "Come here."

She rose, glowing with satisfaction—and trust. "Should I undress first?"

"Yes. Wait, no." Zanya propped her head on her hand, and smiled at Ash, letting dangerous suggestion fill her voice. "Those riding clothes are unfit for your consort. Rid her of them."

At least the Dragon didn't need a stronger hint. He rose, fire already wreathing his hands. Claws appeared, razor sharp, and Sachi's breathing sped as he *oh so gently* grazed one down her throat to snag in the top of her tunic.

Fabric rent. Fire consumed it, charring it to ash. Sachi flushed, trembling as he traced his claws over the bare skin at her abdomen before performing the same service on her pants.

When she was naked, Ash swept her up and carried her to the bed, dropping her gently in front of Zanya, who nodded her thanks and waved a hand. "Do something about your own, too."

While Ash used his fire trick to vanish his own clothing, Zanya tugged at the tie on the end of Sachi's disheveled braid and began to unravel the strands. "Did you have fun tormenting me?"

Sachi nipped at her arm. "Don't I always?"

"Too much fun." Unbound, the golden strands of Sachi's hair fell around her flushed body. Zanya tugged on it to guide Sachi to the bed on her stomach. Anticipation was a buzz in the air, growing heavier when Zanya stroked her fingers down Sachi's spine. "But I had fun, too. So I'm going to give you what you want. What you *need*."

"Surely we should ask Ash. What if he doesn't want that?"

"You sweet fool." Zanya twisted her fingers in Sachi's hair and turned her head, so she could see Ash looming over the bed, fully aroused and still wreathed in gentle flames. The Dragon himself, his self-control dangling by a thread.

A thread Zanya meant to snap.

Sachi's ear was right there. Zanya let her voice drop to a low purr of command. "On your knees, my love." Sachi started to rise, but Zanya only tightened her grip on her hair. "Uh-uh. Hands out in front of you, flat against the bed. Don't move them."

Slowly, still watching Ash, Sachi stretched out her arms. Then, keeping the top half of her body on the bed, she rose up to her knees.

It was Ash's turn to shudder. Zanya savored it as she stroked an approving hand down Sachi's spine again. The flush of her skin and the rapid, unsteady breaths told her all she needed to know about Sachi's state of arousal, but she still slipped her fingers over her hip and down, driving a moan from Sachi's lips as she sank two fingers deep to test her readiness.

Next to the bed, Ash swayed as the last thread of his self-control visibly frayed. But Zanya knew now that he would stand there until time ran out of days, if he must. Because whatever kind of monster he was, he wasn't the kind who would take what wasn't offered.

Zanya withdrew her fingers, then worked three into the clenching heat of Sachi's body. She whimpered, rocking back against the touch, and a low rumble filled the cabin as Ash actually *growled*.

"What do you think, Sachi?" Zanya eased her fingers free, soothing Sachi with soft touches as she whimpered again at the loss. Once Zanya was stretched out on her side again, she stroked Sachi's hair. "Do you think the Dragon wants to claim his consort?"

"Yes," she gasped. "Zan, *please*. Give me to him."

"All right." Her gaze met Ash's, the warning there as much as the command. But in this, at least, she trusted him. With the bond strung out between them, he would know how to find that delicate line where enough became too much. Because of that, Zanya commanded of him what would thrill Sachi most. "Don't hold back," she ordered softly. "She wants the Dragon to take her."

His chest heaved. He nodded once, in acknowledgment of both her commands, spoken and unspoken.

And then the Dragon pounced.

The mattress heaved under his sudden weight. Sachi drew a sharp breath, but in the next moment he was over her. Zanya watched, entranced, as his knees drove Sachi's wider. One hand gripped her hip, the other steadied his cock. He pushed into her, slow and relentless, as she moaned and arched her back, thrusting her ass higher.

Her fingers curled into fists, crumpling the bedding. But she didn't move them.

Zanya stroked her trembling fists. "Good girl. Good, sweet girl. You can take him, can't you?"

Sachi squirmed in their grip.

Ash stroked her hip and eased back, prompting an immediate moan of protest. But he only returned again, pushing deeper, working himself into her a little more with each roll of his hips. Feeling his length under the water had been one thing, but watching his merciless advance left Zanya torn between thrilling at Sachi's pleasure and aching with envy.

What would it feel like to be so overcome? To *feel* to the extent that your body could? To take, passively, trusting in the pleasure to come? The trust in Sachi's trembling body was a gift that humbled them both. And they would reward her for it.

Zanya slid her free hand down, over Sachi's belly and lower. At the first slick brush against her clit, Sachi jerked in their grip, but Ash soothed her with a gentle hand on the small of her back. "Let it happen," he rasped, working deeper into her again. "Every orgasm will make it easier to take me."

Sachi whimpered again. Her breath came faster and faster as she rocked into Zanya's touch, until finally she squeezed her eyes shut and dropped her head to the bed with a long, low moan.

Zanya reveled in it. She always did—the only proof she'd ever had that she could be built for something other than pain and violence. Every smile, every gasping sigh, every screaming orgasm, she craved them with a hunger that never seemed satisfied. No sooner had Sachi's trembles stilled than that wild compulsion had her stroking Sachi again, savoring the helpless noise of pleasure that followed.

She was boneless now, loose in their grip. Ash made a choked noise as he drove fully into her, one echoed by Sachi's breathless moan. "That's it," Zanya whispered, brushing the hair from Sachi's face and turning her head so she could watch her face. "Can you take more, love? Do you want him to fuck you?"

"Yes." She had moved beyond trembling now. Her entire body shook, and the words began to spill from her. "Please, Zan—please—*tell him*—"

Zanya met Ash's gaze. "You heard her. Take your consort, Dragon Lord."

Flame-wreathed eyes locked on to hers and refused to release her. His hands fell to Sachi's hips, lifting her slowly, positioning her perfectly for that first thrust. He eased back, until only the head of his cock remained inside her, and hesitated there. And in that hesitation, Zanya understood the fear that chased him. That if he gave in and took his pleasure in Sachi's body, he would hurt her somehow, lose this precious trust, and become the monster he saw reflected in the eyes of so many people.

Zanya rose to her knees. Ash watched her warily, but she only curled a hand over his shoulder and leaned in until her lips grazed his ear. "She's stronger than she looks," she whispered, pricking his skin with her nails. "You hurt her more by not believing she knows her own body than you could hurt her with a sound fucking. Do you trust her or not?"

"Yes," he said without hesitation.

"Do you trust yourself?"

He paused again. But in the end, his answer sounded honest. "Yes."

Zanya bit his ear, earning a harsh gasp. "Then fuck her the way she wants to be fucked."

Ash shuddered, flexing his fingers on Sachi's hips. Then he drove into her. A shriek tore free of Sachi that could have been ecstasy or pain, but Zanya could see when the pleasure cascading back across their bond hit him. His head dropped back, and his breath hissed in. Zanya raked her nails down his back and laughed. "I told you so."

He answered her with a growl and another thrust that drove a grateful cry from Sachi's lips. Every pleased outcry only seemed to drive him on, until the bed shook under the force of his thrusts and Sachi's gasping pleas formed a desperate refrain. Stretching back out on the bed, Zanya pressed soothing kisses to her flushed cheek, murmuring filthy nonsense until Sachi seemed strung out on the edge.

Then Zanya trailed her fingers back down Sachi's body and stroked in slippery circles until Sachi shattered with a scream muffled by the pillows.

Nothing muffled the Dragon's answering roar. He slammed into Sachi one final time, flames dancing over his skin, and the cabin rattled around them. She collapsed into a boneless heap, and Zanya wrapped her arms around her and moved them both out of the way before Ash slumped to the bed, his chest heaving.

For several long moments, the only sound was panting breaths. When it became clear no one was moving anytime soon, Zanya reached for the covers.

Before she had even settled the quilts around them, Sachi's breathing had fallen into the easy rhythms of sleep. Amazingly, so had Ash's.

He didn't stir, even when she smoothed the heavy blanket into place over his chest, only murmured softly and nuzzled Sachi's hair.

They'd worn out the Dragon.

The plan coalesced so easily, springing into Zanya's head fully formed. Before she could stop herself, she reached out and stroked Sachi's face from temple to chin. No nightmares leapt to her touch—unsurprising. Given the evening's activities, Sachi's dreams were undoubtedly sweet. But she stroked again, calling secret fears to the surface and coaxing them away.

They jumped to her fingertips like invisible sparks, bringing with them the usual half-formed glimpses.

—Zanya with a knife. Screaming. The Dragon, his gaze like flames, fingers tipped in claws, coming after her—

She let them settle over her, taking the pain and fear with a shiver and then soothing it before it could take root in her heart. With every stroke of Zanya's fingers, with every potential nightmare quieted, Sachi sank deeper into sleep. Only a bucket of cold water or being wrenched bodily from the bed would wake her now.

So Zanya turned to the Dragon.

Trying felt dangerous. The powers that worked so easily on mortal men would likely bounce off a living god. But if he caught her touching his face now . . . Well, she'd never have a more plausible excuse for the stolen tenderness.

She held her breath for the first brush of fingertips over hot skin. Ash turned slightly into her touch but didn't wake. She stroked her fingers from his temple to his chin once without doing anything more, testing to see if he'd awake with a roar to demand an explanation.

He did not.

Slowly, so slowly, she let the darkness in herself spool down her arm to wrap around her fingers, shadows as bait for any dark thoughts. At first, he seemed as peaceful as Sachi, his dreams of smooth skin and lust and fire. But on the next stroke she almost recoiled at the force of the spark.

Digging his hands into sand. Glass cuts his palms. Blood mixes with dirt mixes with glass mixes with ash. The ground shudders.

Tearing. Howling. Stop fighting, stop fighting, STOP FIGHTING.

We broke the world.

Blood.

We broke the world.

Shattered bone.

We broke the world.

NEVER AGAIN!

Pain accompanied the shriek. Zanya tasted blood—*her* blood, sharp and metallic and all too familiar—and the nightmare splintered around her. She'd bitten into her lip to keep from crying out, a purely instinctive response that had saved her. Another person's nightmares had never overpowered her before—but she supposed that was the risk when meddling in the mind of a god.

Her fingertips still tingled with the shock of it, but when she stroked her fingers down the Dragon's cheek again, he didn't stir. Tentatively, she braced a hand on his shoulder and gave him a soft shake.

He responded with a gentle snore. A harder shake provoked only a grumbled sigh.

Head spinning, Zanya swiped the blood from her mouth and settled back against the mattress. Sachi snuggled into her side with a sleepy murmur, and Zanya soothed her by rote. The import of what had just happened was still too vast to contemplate. She'd think about it tomorrow. Tomorrow, as they rode toward the Lover's domain.

Tomorrow, as they rode toward a debauched celebration of Union Day that would leave the entire High Court wrung out and sated, too tired to respond to a crisis.

Tomorrow, as they rode toward a castle where she would share a private room with Ash and Sachi, a room where no one would disturb them once the door had closed behind them.

Zanya shut her eyes, resolving not to think about it at all. But all too soon salt joined the metallic taste on her lips. She swiped away silent, stubborn tears, telling herself there was no reason to cry. She hadn't made any decisions yet.

Liar, whispered the only nightmare she couldn't banish. It wrapped loving arms made of darkness around her and twirled her into sleep, and when she dreamt of steel and blood and the death of the Dragon, she didn't weep because she wasn't sure if she could kill him.

She wept because she *knew* she could.

Chapter Twenty-Eight
DRAGON'S MOON

Week Three, Day Six
Year 3000

After over four thousand years of living, there were few places in the Sheltered Lands that didn't carry the taste of memory for Ash. But nowhere was that taste as bitter as in the glorious bounty of the Lover's Lakes.

Even in winter, with the lush farmlands to the south lying fallow in anticipation of spring, the land around the lakes seethed with life. The road to Aleksi's Villa followed a meandering path through fields blanketed in winter-blooming wildflowers. Dozens of crystal-clear lakes reflected the blue of the sky and served as winter resting places for thousands of brightly colored birds. Their songs filled the air as the party skirted another lake, this one no more than a hundred paces across and barely deserving of the name.

Ash could still feel the way his bones had shattered to create it.

Hoofbeats clattered behind him, and Inga appeared at his side, perched lightly on her massive black mare. "We could have come by boat, you know."

"This was more convenient."

"For the rest of us, maybe."

Ash shot her a quelling look. "It has been three thousand years, Inga. Leave it be."

A gloved hand touched his arm gently. Sachi. "What's wrong, Ash?"

He did his best to moderate his expression before patting Sachi's hand. "Nothing, Princess. Ancient history."

"Mmm," Inga replied. "Quite literally." She eyed Sachi and Zanya, who had ridden up next to her. "What were you taught about how the Lover's Lakes came to be?"

It was Zanya who shrugged one shoulder. "The same thing most children were, I'd wager. Perhaps Sachi learned some deeper truth from her tutors, but I was told this is where the Betrayer and the Dragon first confronted one another." Her lips quirked. "That the force of their bodies slamming into the ground created the lakes, and that you filled them with your tears."

Her tone said she found it ridiculous. Ash didn't blame her. He'd been there, and the destruction still felt unreal.

"I did not fill them with my tears," Inga said, the remembered pain in her voice wiping Zanya's smile away. "By the time I was done putting Ash back together, I was too tired to cry. I didn't think a man could bleed that much and live. Not even a god."

Sachi went still. Pale.

Zanya was watching him with those impossibly dark eyes and that tiny furrow between her brows that meant she was assessing something about him. When her gaze broke and swept over the scattered lakes, he understood. She was imagining the force it would take to crash into the earth hard enough to create craters thousands of spans across.

He hoped she never learned.

"So it's true?" Zanya asked finally, her voice troubled.

"More or less." Ash cleared his throat. "I didn't take the threat seriously, to my peril. I didn't realize how strong he'd grown . . . or what would happen when we fought. None of us ever had before, not truly. Not like this."

"The world panicked," Inga said quietly. "That's what he means."

"The world?" Sachi asked, bewildered. "The earth itself?"

"Have you never wondered why the earth trembles when you please him?" Inga asked with a smile so teasing that Sachi's cheeks flushed. "We all hear the whispers of the Dream. That is what makes us Dreamers. But Ash and Dianthe have always been different. For her, it's the sea and the wind that dance simply to please her. But the world we stand on adores Ash, like a faithful hound with a beloved master."

"Inga," he chided. "The earth has no master."

"See how protective he is? Like a mother hen with one chick." The Witch smiled and shook her head. "Our world adores him in return. And when the Betrayer hurt him, the world—"

"Enough." The abrupt word cut her off midsentence, and he hurried to fill the silence. "We do no honor to Ayslin and Isere to tell old stories of battle and tragedy on a day that is meant to honor their love, and the world they gave us."

Inga said nothing, but her deep violet eyes were rimmed with pink, a dangerous warning to any who knew well enough to heed it. She turned her horse, stepping it off the dusty path into a stand of wildflowers, and let the party sweep past her, falling in behind the Raven Guard.

"You upset her," Sachi murmured.

He had, and he'd have to apologize before this evening. "She worries about me. About the memories. Especially here. I think it was harder on her than it was on me, in some ways. All I had to do was bleed. *She* had to heal me."

Sachi's skin blanched again, and she shook her head. "It doesn't seem real, the kind of carnage the two of you describe. But I know it *was* real, and that . . . hurts." Her wide blue eyes met his. "Does that sound foolish?"

Ash reached out for her hand. The gloves stopped him from enjoying the soft brush of her skin, but somehow, he didn't care. The trusting way she twined her fingers with his was enough. And here, under the bright noonday sun, she glowed like a handful of diamonds. "It sounds as if you care."

She squeezed his hand. "I do, Ash. You must know that."

How could he doubt it? Whatever secrets she still held close, he felt her adoration, her passion, her affection. Not just for Zanya anymore, but for *him*. Sometimes that old persistent fear broke through, but more and more, all he felt from her was the warmth of courage and loyalty.

He rubbed a thumb over her gloved hand. "It's not all bad, you know. Aleksi swears that the blood we shed here is why the earth is so fertile, thousands of years later. The farmlands around the Lover's Lakes feed most of the Sheltered Lands with their bounty. So even in pain, there can be hope."

She smiled and lifted his hand to her lips. "Yes."

Their horses topped a gentle rise, and there ahead of them was the largest lake of all. It was dominated at its heart by an island, accessible by only a single stone bridge crossing the water—not so different from Dragon's Keep.

That was where the similarities ended.

Aleksi's Villa was no defensive fortress of stone. It had been built of cream-colored stone, and its delicate spires reached toward the heavens. The winter gardens and the Villa itself were reflected in the mirror-smooth surface of the crystal-clear lake. Artists had spent their entire careers attempting to capture its glory, making it the most recognizable seat in the entire High Court.

Sachi stopped short, drawing her mount up by the reins with a gasp. "It's beautiful. Isn't it, Zanya? Like something from a dream."

Zanya tilted her head. "The paintings in the palace don't do it justice."

"They never do," Ash said. "Something about the colors, I think. The sun shines a little differently here."

Down below them, Aleksi had just crossed the bridge. He urged his horse up the hill at a canter, then met them with a broad smile and a gesture that somehow managed to look like a full bow, even though he remained in his saddle.

"Princess Sachielle. Ash." Aleksi's smile turned into a grin. "Welcome to my home."

"Well?" Ash asked lightly. "Do the paintings in the palace do *him* justice?"

Zanya's gaze flicked over Aleksi in an assessment that clearly weighed his threat as a potential warrior and just as clearly found him wanting. Ash struggled not to feel smug about that—Zanya still might not *want* to want him, but he no longer doubted she did. It was refreshing to not come in second place to Aleksi for once.

Sachi only laughed. "Pardon her manners. She only has eyes for Ash these days. And me, of course."

Aleksi arched an eyebrow and regarded Ash. "You've been busy."

"Yes," Ash answered, not seeing any point in denying it since Sachi seemed so openly pleased. "We've settled into a suitable arrangement, and if my consort is happy, then I am happy."

Aleksi opened his mouth, then closed it again and gestured toward the Villa. "Ladies."

Sachi slanted a look at Zanya, and the two of them rode ahead, leaving Ash and Aleksi behind.

"Well," Aleksi said, laughter lending the word a lilting tone. "Tell me everything."

Ash huffed and guided his horse into an easy walk next to Aleksi's. "I assumed everyone would have caught you up already. They've clearly been gossiping with Dianthe in the Dream. Were you not invited?"

Aleksi sniffed. "I do not engage in gossip, old friend. Not when it comes to matters of the heart."

"I think their gossip focused on regions a good bit lower than my heart."

Aleksi leaned closer. "Both regions are of utmost interest to me. Tell me, Ash—were they worth the wait?"

Something in his old friend's eyes made it clear that Zanya's and Sachi's relationship had not been a surprise to him. Then again, few entanglements of passion or romance were. Aleksi read love in the hearts of those around him the way Ulric caught a scent on the wind or Ash felt the tremble of the earth. "You could have warned me, you know."

"I don't gossip, remember? Other people's secrets of the heart aren't mine to tell."

"Then I won't, either." Ash stared ahead to where Zanya and Sachi had leaned close to discuss something. "But yes. They were worth the wait. They *are* worth the wait. They may share their bodies, but they're still holding back their hearts."

"Ahh, well then. You'll just have to work harder to secure their affections, won't you?"

"We have time. And it will be easier, once this progress is over." They'd be at Aleksi's through the first day of the fourth week, when he'd host the official banquet in Sachi's honor. After that, it was an afternoon's ride to where they'd board a barge and sail downriver, safely past the capital and through Siren's Bay. This endless string of parties and celebrations would culminate with Dianthe's always-charming ball.

And then they could go home. Maybe safely ensconced in Dragon's Keep, they'd trust him enough to finally tell him their secrets.

Chapter Twenty-Nine
DRAGON'S MOON

Week Three, Day Six
Year 3000

Sachi had heard that Aleksi, as the member of the Court with the most devotees, received more pilgrims in a year than any of the others did, even on a special occasion like the consort's progress. As such, she'd expected the area around the Lover's Lakes to be crowded, the ground heavy with tents and the air full of laughter and smoke from crackling campfires.

So the stillness and quiet of the deserted lakeshores confused her. She asked Ash, and had her answer in the way the tops of his ears reddened as he murmured the words *private party*.

The Lover intended to entertain them all with an orgy.

But it wasn't until she'd entered the courtyard's lush garden that she realized she'd had expectations about *that* as well. If asked, she would have assumed that Aleksi would set a stage even more exotic than the

Witchwood Ball, with glittering lights and bubbling drinks, a scene of lust and surreal excess.

But the only light came from the two full moons above their heads. They shone down on the courtyard as if blessing the proceedings with the light of their love. It illuminated the chairs and tables and cushions, which were all obviously designed and arranged with carnal indulgence in mind.

Sachi took a few more steps, descending closer. Trays of food and decanters of various wines and water were scattered about, with one table holding an assortment of philters and potions in small bottles. Aphrodisiacs, most likely. The Dragon's Blood, of course, though she didn't recognize the others.

"Do you remember this?" Ash lifted a purple bottle from the table. It glittered as the light caught it, as if jewels had been crushed into the glass. The liquid he poured from it into a crystal glass was a pale pink and smelled like the sweetest spring morning. "The Lover's own vintage. He brought some to our bonding celebration, but I'm not sure you had a chance to try it."

Sachi thought of some of the drinks served at the Witchwood Ball. "Is it merely wine, or . . . ?"

"Yes and no." Ash poured a second glass, held it up, and considered the liquid before drinking deeply. "Aleksi tends these grapes with his own hands and oversees the processing and bottling. His power lingers. Nothing too overwhelming, and nothing that can take your will or choice from you. That is not the Lover's way." She could feel the warmth of his gaze as he watched her, the newly awoken hunger. "But it makes the desire you already feel much more . . . potent."

"I see." Her cheeks heated. Inga's party had been a tease, a mere hint of the seduction to come. But this?

This was true uninhibited debauchery.

"Excuse me," he murmured, setting the empty goblet aside.

Ash walked to the edge of the courtyard and touched a low stone wall that curved around its perimeter. Flames erupted from the wall and shot up into the night sky. He repeated the action three times more, until a veritable wall of fire surrounded the courtyard, broken only by small walkways in each of the four cardinal directions.

The space immediately grew warmer and *brighter*, the light of the flames flickering almost lovingly over the coils of silken rope and other toys that had been laid out for their enjoyment.

Zanya stepped up next to Sachi, her gaze sweeping the tables. "So. This is how the gods celebrate Union Day."

"So it would seem." Sachi glanced at her, trying to discern her mood from the sharp angles of her profile. "Are you pleased or displeased? I cannot tell."

Zanya claimed the second goblet of wine that Ash had poured and took a bracing sip. "I have resolved not to think tonight. Don't we deserve this? One night of magic?"

Sachi claimed the glass and finished it. The wine danced over her tongue, sweet and light. A moment later, heat unfurled throughout her, like a full-body flush. "You deserve all that and more, my love."

Aleksi swept down the stairs and into the courtyard. "My friends! Is everyone comfortable? Do you need anything?"

Elevia followed behind him, her pace lazier but somehow still coiled. The stalk of a predator. "Give them a moment to breathe, Aleksi. These things take time to fully process."

"If you plan to sharpen your tongue on me tonight, El, I have a few more pleasurable suggestions."

"Do tell." The Huntress smiled and dropped to one of the large, curving couches. "*After* you've fetched me a drink."

"I've got her." The Wolf prowled from the shadows, a goblet already in hand—and his shirt already discarded. He was barefoot, clad in loose pants alone, and the firelight danced over a well-tanned chest, covered in dark hair and battle scars. His strong muscles flexed effortlessly as he hopped over the back of the couch and slowly sank into the seat next to Elevia. "Your favorite."

"A thousand thanks, my sweet."

Sachi took a seat at the other end of the couch, with Zanya close by her side. "This seems . . . intimate."

The Lover smiled. Of course he understood her meaning. "When you've spent millennia with the same people, you get to know each other very, *very* well. Fucking is the least of it. And while there's a certain comfort to be found in the well-known, sometimes it does get—"

"Boring?" Elevia supplied with feigned innocence.

"Predictable," Aleksi finished.

Sachi quelled a laugh as she passed him her goblet for a refill. "Is that your way of saying that Zanya and I are here to spice up your sex party?"

He gasped in outrage that didn't look feigned at all. "I would never! Not that I don't appreciate you and the myriad charms you offer. I meant only that bodies are easy. Minds, on the other hand? Those are *exciting.*"

"Aleksi . . ." The warning grumble came from behind her, and when she tilted her head back, she found Ash looming there, a chiding expression on his face. "I'm watching you."

"What? I am having a harmless conversation."

"You're seducing his consort," Elevia laughed.

"Point of correction . . ." Aleksi smiled, the expression turning his handsome face into something devilish and alluring. *Come*, it said, *and be naughty with me.* "I'm seducing all of you."

Malindra laughed as she dropped to the soft grass at Elevia's feet and leaned back against the Huntress's legs. "It sounds boastful, doesn't it?" she asked Sachi. "But he's being modest. A couple decades ago, Kardox bet him that he couldn't outlast the Raven Guard. He fucked the lot of us into weak-limbed exhaustion, and then gave Ulric *and* Elevia a hard ride. I didn't walk right for a full moon."

Aleksi raised one eyebrow, and Sachi could read the thoughts dancing behind those mischievous eyes. He was waiting for her to display the hubris of the mortal lords and make a bet of her own.

Perhaps, one day, given the chance, she would. But not tonight. Instead, she reached for Ash's hand and drew it to rest on her shoulder.

Aleksi chuckled. "Point taken, lovely Sachielle. I envy our Dragon."

"Whatever for?"

He finished his drink and set his goblet on the table in front of him with excruciating gentleness. "He has found it. The one thing that surrounds, suffuses, and eludes me."

Elevia groaned. "Dream help us, he's getting maudlin already. Someone please touch his dick."

But Aleksi held up both hands in supplication. "Music," he declared. "And dancing. Zanya, will you join me?"

Zanya hesitated. But somewhere beyond the flames, a drum began to beat, its steady rhythm that of a beating heart. A second drum joined it, and a third. Without looking away from Aleksi, Zanya shoved her glass into Sachi's hands and rose. "Why not? It's a night for foolishness, isn't it?"

"It is, indeed." He kissed the back of her hand, then drew her toward a clear area in the midst of all the furniture.

Ash's thumb swept out from Sachi's shoulder to stroke her throat, trailing tingles in its wake. "Zanya seems determined to enjoy herself."

"Mmm. It *is* a night for pleasure."

Elevia hummed her approval as Isolde came forward and pulled Malindra to her feet and into a soft kiss. They backed away, their bodies joining the growing throng of dancers.

"The consort understands," Elevia whispered, then turned her lips to Ulric's ear. His low chuckle sounded like fur sliding over skin, and he grabbed her hips and dragged her into his lap before pulling her down for a kiss.

Sachi's skin burned. It felt like she wasn't getting enough air into her lungs. She drew in a deep breath, but it brought only the heady scents of the wine and *Ash*.

She looked up, caught his gaze. "Are you going to dance, too?"

"Only if you'll dance with me."

Sachi stepped out onto the stone floor, the heat of Ash's body just behind hers. She'd worn only a simple, thin dress tonight, but even the weight of that fabric seemed too heavy in the midst of the fire and the dancing. A sheen of sweat had already formed at the small of her back, and she gasped as she ground against Ash.

She raised her arm and reached for him, wrapping her hand around the back of his neck. "What do you usually do at Aleksi's parties? I want to know."

"Not much, of late," he admitted softly, his lips against her ear. One large hand slid around her hip to splay across her abdomen, urging her even more tightly against him. He was hard behind her already, arousal turning his voice into a low rasp. "In centuries past, however, there is no one whose companionship I have not shared. Aleksi, especially. His touch is . . ." He paused, dropped his voice to a low growl. *"Potent."*

Even Zanya wasn't immune. Her skin was flushed, sweat dampening the hair at her temples as she danced with Aleksi. She looked *ready*, and the sight made Sachi's nipples ache. "So you're saying Malindra's story was true?"

"Oh, yes." Ash's other hand landed on her hip, and his fingers flexed slowly, gathering the fabric of her dress. "I was there. Sex can't exhaust him. Every scream and moan he coaxed from their bodies invigorated him. Every orgasm made him crave another. They were wrung out when he finished with them, and he was *alive* and ravenous for more." A low chuckle. "Sometimes Zanya reminds me of him. She can be remarkably single-minded about your pleasure."

"Yes. But this is . . ." She turned in his arms, heedless of the tearing fabric, and looked up at him. "It's so different, Ash. It's hard to know what to do. Teasing is one thing, but I don't want to hurt you."

"You can't hurt me. Not tonight." One fluid flex of muscles, and he'd hoisted her off the ground and guided her legs around his hips. It brought them face to face, even as his erection ground tauntingly between her thighs, driving a whimper from her lips.

"I know what's mine, Princess. No one can take that from me. We are bound by blood and magic. If you want me to forbid anyone else from touching you, I will. If you want to see if *you* can exhaust the entire Raven Guard . . ." A wicked smile curved his lips as he brushed them over hers. "Then I'll help you cheat. Take your pleasure in whatever way gives you the most joy. But know that when the night ends, you'll end it in *my* bed."

She touched his face—his beautiful, expressive face—and wondered that she had ever found his features forbidding. In that moment, he was completely open to her, with nothing hidden or held back.

"I will." It was more than a promise. A vow.

So Sachi gave in. To the music, to the whirl of movement, to the heat of the fire and the grinding bodies. She danced with Inga, who melted away into the waiting arms of Kardox and Remi. Elevia and Ulric immediately filled the empty space, though they swayed together with a languor that defied the thrumming beat of the music. Their bodies brushed hers, skin slick with sweat and the promise of something far more carnal than a dance.

Naia's delighted laughter rang out, followed by Aleksi's deeper chuckle. Instinctively, Sachi turned toward the sound—and caught sight of Ash. He sat lazily on one of the couches, arms stretched out across the back of it, his long legs sprawled before him and crossed at the ankles. Debauched revelry whirled around him, but he seemed oblivious to all of it.

His gaze never left her as he smiled his encouragement.

"Would you like to go to him?" Aleksi's low rumble vibrated against her back and tickled her ear.

"I want . . ." Aleksi's fingers skimmed up Sachi's arm, and she shivered. "I want him to feel it, too. All the possibilities."

"Oh, love." He grasped her chin and turned her head, tilted it up so she could meet his eyes. "Ash hasn't felt that in a long time. It's not this party burning him up from the inside out. It's *you*. You want to give him something tonight? Give him that. *Your* discovery."

He brushed his lips over hers, a quick, gentle caress, and turned her head toward Ash again. Her dragon's smile remained in place, but something dark and hungry had kindled in his gaze. Riveted, Sachi tilted her head, baring the vulnerable line of her throat to Aleksi's questing mouth. His tongue slid over her skin, wet and beguiling, and Sachi sucked in a shaky breath as the hunger in Ash's eyes twisted in her belly.

"Say the word, lovely Sachielle. We'll find your pleasure and put it on display for your lover." His teeth grazed her earlobe. "Every flushed, trembling, dripping-wet moment."

Could she yield to this temptation? Abandon herself to the hedonistic promise of bliss that glittered before her?

"Yes," she murmured, as much for herself as for Ash and Aleksi. Because Zanya was right. No matter what happened tomorrow or the next day or the next, they deserved this. One stolen night in which to live out a fantasy that should have been reality.

Aleksi hummed his approval. "Another word from you will stop everything," he swore as he tugged down the strap of her loose, thin dress. Ash had already ripped the delicate fabric, and it slithered down her body to pool at her feet. "Anything you don't want doesn't happen, and no one will touch you out of turn. Do you understand, Sachielle?"

"Yes." They had captured more gazes than just Ash's, and her nipples pebbled under the caressing weight of their stares. "But please, call me Sachi."

"I never use pet names before I've had my tongue inside someone." Aleksi stroked her jaw with a slow smile. "Is this a formal invitation, Princess?"

Before Sachi could answer, nimble fingers tugged lightly at her hair, and Elevia sighed heavily. "You've always been a greedy bastard, Aleksi. But you're getting downright *stingy* in your old age."

"Scandalous falsehoods, Princess, to conceal her jealousy." His hands slid around Sachi's body, where he cupped her breasts and rubbed his palms over her nipples. "And lust. Can't forget the lust."

Elevia had, indeed, stalked over silently—a huntress with her sights set on ready prey. She leaned back against the broad wall of Ulric's chest as she watched Aleksi's hands move, then licked her lips. "Shall we leave you, Sachi?"

"Stay." Sachi reached for Elevia's hands, pulled her closer. Close enough to whisper the next words against her lips. "Touch me. Please."

"So sweet." Elevia's smile turned into a kiss as she closed the last of the distance between them.

It was a heady kiss, open and a little rough, her tongue sliding over Sachi's as her hands clashed with Aleksi's. Even Ulric obeyed the whispered plea, dragging the edge of his teeth over Sachi's bare shoulder. The sensations melted together, boiling through her already heated blood.

Sachi shuddered.

Elevia's mouth left hers, drifting lower. As her tongue circled Sachi's nipple, Aleksi spoke again. "Open your eyes, love."

The first thing she saw was Zanya.

She had joined Ash on the couch. Though several handspans separated them, they were united in mutual purpose—to watch with fixed, rapt focus as Aleksi held her and Ulric bit her and Elevia sucked Sachi's other nipple into her mouth.

"How long will they watch?" he asked softly. "How long *can* they before their need for you overwhelms them? Before they have to be the ones stroking and licking and fucking? Making you come?"

Her head was already swimming, her knees weak. "I don't know."

"Let's find out." Aleksi drove his fingers into Elevia's hair and hauled her head back. "Isn't it time you paid tribute to the Dragon's consort, El?"

She heaved a breath, then stretched up and licked his mouth before turning her lips to Sachi's ear. "May I kneel before you, Princess?"

A quick nod was all Sachi managed before Aleksi squeezed her breasts again, his fingers gliding over her wet nipples. Elevia dropped to her knees, pausing to kiss and lick Sachi's stomach, her hip. Her thigh.

Sachi held her breath.

Aleksi pulled her more tightly against his body and urged her legs apart. "Open, love, and tell me where else you're going to let Ric bite you."

"Where—" A moan choked off the word at the first touch of Elevia's eager tongue. "Wherever he'd like."

Ulric growled against her collarbone, and Aleksi hummed again. "That's a dangerous offer to make to a Wolf, Sachielle. He might eat you alive."

Heavy pleasure pulsed through her, loosening her tongue. "Only if Elevia will share."

Aleksi chuckled, delighted. "Sweet, beautiful Sachielle. You burn with joy, and I want it all over me." He parted his fingers, making room for Ulric to close his teeth on her nipple. "Someday, love."

Everything was swimming now. Her entire body thrummed with desire so strong it felt more like an ache. Sachi bit her lip and rocked her hips, chasing the fleeting, sharp shocks of ecstasy that danced just out of reach.

Then Ulric bit her nipple, a stinging accompaniment to the taut ache, and a low noise tore free of her throat as she came. Fast, hard, harder when Elevia hummed her approval and Ulric licked away the sting of his bite.

By the time Sachi could almost breathe again, Aleksi's iron grip was the only thing holding her up. She sagged against him, one hand wrapped around his forearm and the other buried in Elevia's hair.

"Again." Aleksi's voice held an imperious edge of command as he pushed Ulric to his knees beside Elevia.

Sachi gasped as he pulled her legs wider with his hands under her thighs, holding her open to Ulric's mouth now as well as Elevia's. And then she cried out as they obeyed Aleksi's unmistakable command.

Sachi writhed, her chest heaving. Elevia and Ulric moved almost as one, as if this was something they were *meant* to do, no different than a hunt. Together, they stroked and sucked, curling their tongues around her clit and thrusting their fingers inside her.

"So bright," Aleksi murmured. "Next time we do this, we'll put you on Ash's cock. Zanya and I will lick you both until you come, then start all over again. We'll . . ."

His voice faded, melding with the dull roar in her ears. All she could feel was the pounding of the music, the hardness of Aleksi's body behind hers, the searing heat between her open thighs.

And all she could see was Ash, his clenched fists on fire. Zanya, her tongue lingering at the corner of her mouth.

When Sachi came this time, she didn't stop. One orgasm rolled into another, then another, as she shuddered and shook helplessly in Aleksi's arms. The world receded, everything growing darker and brighter at the same time as she tumbled through every cresting wave.

"Enough, Lover. Let her catch her breath." It was Zanya's voice, and Zanya's face that Sachi saw when her vision cleared.

Sachi whispered her name.

Zanya stroked Sachi's cheek before leaning up, bringing her face even with Aleksi's. "Thank you for pleasing her so well," she whispered, her lips so close it looked like she was about to kiss him. Instead, she dug her teeth into his lower lip with a warning growl. "But I'm done sharing tonight."

Aleksi licked his bitten lip and lowered Sachi to the ground. "You're welcome. And, Zanya?" He grinned wickedly. "Help Ash shake the Villa for me, won't you?"

Zanya only laughed.

Sachi's knees wobbled, so Ash swept her into his arms. Candles sprang to blazing life, lighting their way as they climbed the stairs and moved through the Villa. In Sachi's room, he laid her carefully on the bed.

Her limbs were still liquid, her head still spinning, by the time they disrobed and joined her. Zanya caught both of her arms and urged them above her head, where one of Ash's large hands pinned them in place.

"Sweet, sweet Sachi," Zanya murmured, trailing her fingers down the front of her body. "You looked beautiful tonight. I love watching you come."

Sachi arched off the bed, mindless with hunger despite the orgasms. "Please, Zanya."

Ash's teeth scraped her earlobe. His free hand rested on her abdomen, and she felt the burning tingle that meant he'd conjured flames, along with the softest graze of his claws. "Do you like being naked for us? So sweet and vulnerable, helpless to stop any way we want to claim you?"

Desire twisted into a hard, hungry knot in her belly, and she turned her head and bit his jaw. "Let me go, and I'll show you how *sweet* I feel right now."

Zanya laughed this time, her fingertips circling one of Sachi's nipples. "Oh, you're going to scratch him to ribbons when we let you go, aren't you? I can't wait."

"Neither can I," Ash rumbled. Then his mouth descended onto hers, hot and demanding.

His tongue slicked over Sachi's as fire swept over her, burning away everything but her two lovers. As Ash conquered her mouth, Zanya's hair trailed over her tingling, bare skin. Then the wet heat of her tongue slid over Sachi's nipple. Her fingers found Ash's where his hand rested on her abdomen—a soft, distracting burn and fine, tiny pinpricks.

"Dragon."

Groaning, Ash tore his mouth from Sachi's, his eyes burning. "Handmaid."

Zanya held up her hand with a wicked smile. "Can you conjure your flames around my fingers?"

He tilted his head, clearly considering. A moment later, fire curled up Zanya's wrist in a sensual caress that had her digging her teeth into her lower lip. The flames licked over her hand and wrapped around each finger, and Zanya stared at them for a moment before meeting Sachi's gaze.

Then she lowered her fingertip to circle Sachi's aching nipple.

She gasped at the contact. In Zanya's hands, the flames felt less like heat and more like tiny shocks that tugged at Sachi's core. She arched again, an almost pained moan slipping free as she twisted her wrists in Ash's grasp.

"Shh," he soothed, tightening his grip. His other hand slid lower, and she shuddered as she realized that this time, he hadn't made the claws vanish. His fingers spread wide across the sensitive skin of her inner thigh, the sharp tips of his fingers kissing her so gently her head spun. Then he was pulling her thigh wide, parting her legs to leave her helplessly exposed.

Zanya's fire-kissed fingers circled her other nipple, her hand moving with the desperate wrench of Sachi's body. "Too much?" she whispered against her cheek. "Too much? Or more?"

It took Sachi a moment to find her voice. "More. Please."

"Good girl." Zanya's hand drifted lower, sparking involuntary shivers and bright stabs of tingling pleasure as she found the soft, sensitive spots she already knew. Her leg slid over Sachi's, coaxing it as wide as the one Ash gripped. Anticipation twisted tight, Sachi's entire body tensed for what she knew must be coming.

"Look at me," Ash rasped.

Sachi had to force open her eyes, which had gone heavy with anticipation and lust.

"Do you like this, Princess?" he rumbled, flexing his fingers just enough that she could feel his claws again—a dangerous threat rendered intoxicating by the sure knowledge that Ash would never, *ever* hurt her. "Do you like when I pin you down so Zanya can fuck you with the Dragon's own fire?"

Sachi bit her lip, arched her hips toward Zanya's touch . . . and said nothing.

Tingling shocks danced up the inside of her thigh and stopped as Zanya stroked her. "So stubborn," Zanya said fondly against her temple. "Be good now, love, and I'll help you be *so* bad later."

Yes. "I don't like it, my lord. I love it."

The way his eyes blazed at her words was a sweet reward, almost as sweet as the jolt that zipped up her spine as Zanya slicked her fingers over eager flesh. The sensation nearly overwhelmed Sachi, driving a cry from her lips as her hips bucked. Ash held her in place, his voice a soothing rumble as Zanya parted her and let the flame-kissed tip of one finger circle her clit.

Every nerve sizzled, still affected by the wine and all the orgasms Sachi had enjoyed. "What did you see?" She closed her teeth on Ash's chin. "When they were pleasuring me?"

Claw-tipped fingers skated up her abdomen and across her collarbone. "My consort," he rumbled. "Coming alive. Taking what she wanted."

"Yes." She arched her hips again. "And I'm not finished yet."

Zanya nipped at her ear as her finger made another dizzying circle, little sparks of pleasure radiating out with the kiss of fire. "Neither am I," Zanya whispered as her fingers swept lower. Sachi's entire body drew taut with anticipation, and she shuddered as two flame-wreathed fingers worked into her, the shock of it curling her toes.

Sachi drew in a breath only to have it rasp out of her lungs again as Ash wrapped his hand around her throat. There was no pressure, nothing but the gentle presence of his fingers . . . and his claws.

Then he kissed her. He kissed her as Zanya fucked her fingers deeper, kissed her as Sachi desperately lifted her hips to greet every thrust.

He kissed her as she tipped over the edge into another jaw-clenching orgasm.

Then he turned her face to Zanya's, right into another blistering kiss that somehow turned into the three of them kissing, tongues gliding together as Sachi bucked and trembled.

She collapsed back to the bed, shaking with the aftershocks, and Zanya's soft, dark laughter wrapped around her. "Well, Dragon? She gave us what we wanted. Is it her turn?"

Flames tickled across her cheek, and Ash's fingers were only fingers again, gentle as he traced Sachi's kiss-bruised lips. "Do with me as you will, Princess."

She flipped him onto his back and climbed atop him in a single smooth movement that one trainer had made her practice on every surface—from a bed to cobblestone to a sheer sheet of ice. "You still think I'm harmless," she mused, drawing her fingernails down the center of his chest. "Sweet little Sachielle."

"Not harmless," he murmured, his hands coming to rest on her hips. "No more than I'd call Aleksi harmless. But sweet? Oh yes."

She curled her fingers until her nails pricked his skin.

He hissed softly. On the bed next to them, Zanya propped her head up on her hand. "Oh, harder than that, love. Show him *your* claws."

Sachi pressed harder, until just the tiniest bit more pressure would have meant drawing blood. Ash's eyes flamed, and she kept up the painful caress as she angled her hips over his and took him deep inside her.

A groan escaped him, dropping into a growl as she sank all the way down. His fingers flexed on her hips, but he didn't try to move her.

"Now. Let me tell you what's going to happen." She scratched another set of red streaks down his stomach. "I'm going to fuck you, and Zanya's going to help me. If you want us to stop, say so. But if you want us to go on fucking you, keep telling me how sweet I am. Yes?"

A slow, dangerous smile curled his lips. His thumbs swept out, stroking her skin. "You're the sweetest thing I have ever seen."

Sachi held one hand out to Zanya. "That you've ever tasted, too. Don't forget that part."

"You're both sweet to taste," he rumbled, earning him a warning look from Zanya as she rose to her knees and took Sachi's hand. "So sweet."

Sachi rocked her hips slowly, grinding down against him as she moved. "Are you convinced, Zanya?"

"That he'll say anything to make you keep going? Absolutely." She leaned closer. "He's not being very inventive yet though, is he?"

Ash arched up against her, eyes burning at the challenge. "Do you want to hear how sweet the clasp of your body is, Sachi? How tight and hot and wet from how many times you've already come tonight?"

The words—and the depth of the need behind them—made Sachi clench around him.

"That's it," he murmured, fingers tightening on her hips. "That's when you're sweetest. When someone is whispering dirty words in your ears, and your whole body shudders. What did Aleksi say to you that made you come so hard?"

"He made some delicious promises about your cock and his tongue. Zanya's, too."

Zanya lifted Sachi's hand to her lips, tickling a kiss across the back. "And where do you want my tongue now?"

"Patience, my love." Sachi stopped moving. "Do you see how our darling Ash has tried to reassert control? He can't help himself." She drew Zanya closer, the command forming instantly. Effortlessly. "Give him something better to do with his mouth than tease me."

Zanya's breath caught. She glanced back at Ash, whose smile had only broadened. His hands fell from Sachi's hips, spreading wide in silent invitation.

Zanya ignored him, sliding a leg over his chest so she was straddling it facing Sachi. She framed Sachi's face, thumbs gentle as she stroked her cheeks. "You're beautiful when you're bossy," she whispered.

She was hesitant, so vulnerable it made Sachi's chest hurt. But it was past time she learned about pleasure. "Do you trust me, Zan?"

"With my life."

"Then be a dear and *fuck his face*." She caught Zanya's lower lip between her teeth, then smiled. "You may assist her, my lord."

Zanya started as Ash's hands rose to clasp her hips. Flames tickled her skin, and she groaned, her head falling back. "This is what it feels like?" she rasped.

Sachi leaned forward, covered Ash's burning hands with hers. "Yes."

"How did you stand it?"

She had to laugh. "Who says I did?"

Ash tugged, hauling Zanya's hips up his body until she was straddling his shoulders. Large hands wreathed in teasing flames curled over her thighs, locking her in place against his open mouth. Zanya gasped out a curse, her hands slapping down against his chest, her entire body shaking.

"There you go, love." Sachi steadied her, nuzzling her neck through the thick, dark fall of her hair. "Show him that he doesn't know what sweet is, not yet."

Zanya shuddered again, her breath rasping out in a shaky moan. "Kiss me," she pleaded. "Kiss me."

Sachi did, drinking in Zanya's cries as they both rode Ash. The tension was unbearable, an ever-tightening knot of bliss drawn tighter by Ash's reactions, by the way he groaned beneath Zanya, the way he shook when Sachi scratched him again. By the emotion she could feel, reflected and redoubled, through their bond.

They were all caught in this storm together, and it drove Sachi wild. She fucked Ash faster, scratched him harder. She licked and sucked Zanya's lips and throat and shoulders, then moved on to her nipples.

Zanya came first, her usual restraint shredded as she cried out and clung to Sachi. The victory only seemed to spur Ash on, his determination stark as he hauled Zanya more tightly against him and drove her to a second climax. By the time Sachi came, Zanya was boneless against her. Only Ash's tension remained, but as pleasure swept through her, it must have caught him up, washing along their bond in a heated wave.

He stiffened beneath her, his hips jerking upward once, twice. Then he growled, driving another hoarse whimper from Zanya, and Sachi held her as they rode Ash's climax together.

It was all Sachi could do not to fall over. Shaking, she guided Zanya to the mattress, then dropped next to her. Ash rolled onto his side, throwing a heavy arm over both of them. "It is a good thing Aleksi keeps his home warm, even in winter. I find myself too tired to reach for the blankets."

Sachi snorted. "You brought this on yourself, my lord."

"It is the proper night for it. I am only worshipping the lovers who created our world as they deserve." He kissed her shoulder, and she felt his smile against her skin. "Allow me some time to rest, and I'll do it all again."

Affection swelled, spilling through Sachi along with a warm satisfaction she recognized as belonging to Ash. "Bite your gorgeous tongue." She snuggled closer to Zanya. "I still have to be able to walk tomorrow."

"Yes, you do," Zanya said softly, stroking her fingers through Sachi's hair. "Sleep, love. Morning will come soon enough."

"True." But the word came out slurred, because Sachi was already sliding into a deep, exhausted sleep.

Chapter Thirty
DRAGON'S MOON

Week Three, Day Seven
Year 3000

The Lover's Villa was silent in the deepest part of night, but the drums still beat in Zanya's head.

Or perhaps that was her own heartbeat, rapid and unsteady, growing ever louder as she slowly disentangled her arm from Sachi's possessive grip.

So tempting to linger just a few moments longer. To try to lock in this memory of Sachi clinging to her with fierce devotion. Of Ash's large hand resting on her hip in acceptance and affection. To savor the last time in her life she would be loved and cherished.

But if she gave in to temptation, she might not do it at all.

Reaching out, Zanya touched Sachi first. Shadows danced around her fingertips, but for the longest time, nothing happened. Her princess dreamt of joy and hope, even now. It took forever to coax her fears to the surface, and even then they were only tiny sparks and fleeting glimpses. Losing Zanya. Losing Ash. Grief.

Zanya tasted the salt of tears on her own lips, but forced herself to continue, lulling Sachi into a deep, restful sleep before switching to Ash.

His dreams were as sweet as Sachi's on the surface, leaving behind the vague impression of lust and laughter. But the darkness seethed just beneath the surface, called by her own, and it roiled toward her. She braced herself this time and still wasn't prepared when pain sparked at her fingertips, sharp enough to numb her hand. The nightmare swamped her, plunging her into a dream so vivid, it must have been memory.

The land is bleeding.

The pain of it slices deeper than superficial wounds of the body. The final battle to cast out the Betrayer shattered bodies and flayed skin from bone. Dangerous injuries—quite nearly mortal—and yet trivial in the face of what this fight has done to the land.

The world whispers. Whimpers. Standing with bare feet planted on the fire-blasted dirt. The discomfort of healing is nothing compared to the desperate agonies of the world. The Witch's magic might knit fractured bone and mend rent flesh, but she can't help a land torn asunder by a war between brothers.

A war between gods.

Gods.

The word enrages. They had been born as mortal as any soldier in these armies. They had run to mothers with skinned knees and secret hurts, played in the meadows behind their homes as their parents worked the crops. But the world had whispered to them then, too. In their dreams, at first, and then waking.

The world doesn't whisper now. She weeps.

The Betrayer's army flees across those blasted plains, carrying the body of their fallen god with them. Jagged cracks crisscross the bare rock. Huge chunks are missing on either side of the crossing, as if the earth itself had been scooped up by a giant hand and the sea had rushed in to claim it.

Fingers flex. The ground trembles in response.

The strength of the earth still rises, as if bare feet stand rooted in bedrock. Warmth floods an aching body, a tentative offering. Even wounded, even shattered by godly will and godly war, the world offers itself. Trusting, eager.

Could any of them be worthy of such a gift?

Kneeling. Pressing one hand to the ground. Fingers sink deep into rich loam mixed with pulverized rock and blood, and that is where the power must go. Deep. To the bedrock. They have ravaged the land, split it to the quick. Only the world can make itself whole.

Heal. Heal, and be strong, and show us how to protect you. Because the Betrayer will always find and gather those who want to take more than you can give.

The continent groans, tearing apart as if to open a rift between the enemies. The ground shakes with the force of it, and fearful cries rise as distant waves climb to towering heights and the earth quakes.

"The seabed is cracking," the Siren whispers, her husky voice holding the power of waves crashing, of the wind howling through a storm-swept night. "I can feel it in the depths. She'll tear herself apart if you don't stop her."

Fingers close around the bloodied earth. Power reaches deep. Finds the answer.

A fracture, where none had been before. A chasm growing wider by the second, as if the world believes it can avoid a second war by splitting the continents apart, separating the fallen brother from his siblings forever.

Not like this. Hands clutch into fists. There is no body, no self. Just the aching land, magma pumping through it like blood, the core pulsing like a heart. The world is alive, has always been alive, will always be alive.

And it screams. Protest and denial. A shuddering, alien fear. Not the whisper of a world but a chaotic, protective shriek.

The land isn't tearing apart to protect itself.

It's trying to protect them.

Not like this. This will not save us, it will kill us all.

The wind howls. The ground shudders. Gasps turn to screams as they cling to each other, to the very earth, as they cry out to the gods who broke the world and are breaking it again.

Then there is no wind. No screams. Nothing but the crash of continents and the pulse of lava and the world remaking itself to protect the ones who loved it best . . .

The terrifying vision released her without warning. Zanya swallowed a whimper, shaking her hand as if she could shake the tingles away. The Dragon's nightmares were powerful, and she had the unsteady certainty she'd just witnessed the sundering of the continents that had raised the mountain range that guarded their western border.

Ash looked so unbreakable, made of muscle and bone and the strength of the earth. But she could remember the feel of his body shattering, could remember the impossible pain of it—and how much worse it had hurt him to know he'd harmed the land. You could pummel the Dragon until he was nothing but pebbles and dust, and he'd find a way to go on fighting if it meant protecting the world that gave them life.

This was the man she'd been sent to destroy.

Zanya eased Sachi away from the Dragon so their bodies were no longer entangled and then slipped free of the bed, tears stinging her eyes. This would have been easier if they had given her Void-touched steel, but even a god should die if she cut off his head, and she had the physical strength to do it.

All she needed was the will.

The small, locked chest had been unpacked and placed on Sachi's vanity. Zanya's lips, still tingling from the force of the Dragon's kiss, unlocked it. She lifted the hourglass and touched the glass, and her heart lurched as she saw how much had fallen.

Was the sand moving faster? Or did fear play tricks with her memory? Bright-red sand swirled in the bottom globe like blood, and Zanya shuddered as she packed it away again.

There was no choice. No *time*. This was her mission. Her purpose. The one thing she'd been training to do her whole life.

Save Sachi. That's it. Save Sachi.

The long, viciously sharp knife the Huntress had gifted her with sat on a table. She eased it silently from its sheath and returned to the bed. The blade felt heavy. That was good. It would be easier that way—one swift swing downward with all her strength.

Sachi would be furious. But faced with the assembled wrath of the High Court falling on Zanya, she would accept the reality and flee. What she would never do to protect herself, she'd agree to in order to keep Zanya safe. A bag packed with necessary supplies already rested in Zanya's quarters.

She simply had to strike.

She lifted the knife, staring at Ash. Trying not to see him. Trying not to *remember*. But the memories came regardless, stubbornly clawing their way up from the depths of her scarred heart.

Ash, telling her that Sachi would be safe. Threatening to kill anyone who would hurt her. Threatening to kill anyone who had hurt *Zanya*. His devotion to Sachi's comfort. His laughing pleasure whenever Zanya bested him in a match. His fire and his touches. The scorching heat of his kiss.

His promise to keep them both safe.

Maybe she could wake him up and tell him everything. High Priest Nikkon had claimed the High Court couldn't touch a curse rooted in the Void, but the priest was a liar, was he not? If the Dragon descended on Castle Roquebarre and promised to burn them all to dust, perhaps Nikkon would find a way to break it.

Or perhaps he'd simply make good on his threat and accelerate Sachi's curse, and Sachi would die before anyone had a chance to save her.

Ash had watched dozens of consorts pass, through his life and then away. His possessiveness of Sachi was likely nothing more than that of a child with a new favorite toy. What was a human life to a man who had been old three thousand years ago? They were flickers of amusement in an endless life. He must be numb to the pain of losing the mortals who came and went.

Losing Sachi would make him sad, but it would not end him.

Not like it would end Zanya.

She tightened her fist around the knife and let everything human bleed away. She couldn't trust the Dragon. She couldn't trust *anyone*. That lesson had been hard learned in childhood. No one ever came when she screamed for help. She and Sachi were alone. They'd always been alone.

They would always be alone.

Sachi would never forgive her for this. Might never be able to love her again.

But she'd *live*.

Help. Help. Help me, please.

Only silence answered. Tensing her muscles, Zanya positioned herself carefully and lifted the knife—

And nearly cried out as a thundering bell sounded directly overhead.

More bells joined it, a dire chorus screaming in alarm until it felt as if the walls vibrated with the sound. Zanya pressed her hands to her ears, but it barely helped. On the bed, Sachi murmured a protest, beginning to stir.

Lights flared outside the window. Zanya bolted to it and threw open the delicate glass panes. Madness had descended on the courtyard, with guards running from all directions and torches blaring to life. And beyond the thin, decorative walls—

"Oh, no," Zanya breathed as she watched the first towering, misshapen creature crawl from the water. A nightmare, made of shadows and fear. A Terror.

Oh gods, not again.

Blankets rustled behind her. Zanya spun. Ash was grumbling, still held by her magic, but Sachi had pushed herself upright. Their eyes met, Sachi's sleepy and confused expression giving way to understanding. She knew how it felt when Zanya took her nightmares.

Then her gaze dropped to the knife still clutched in Zanya's hand, and horror filled her features.

Screams of panic drifted up from the courtyard. Betrayal stared back at her from Sachi's face. Zanya let the knife clatter to the floor. "I'm sorry," she whispered.

And then she ran.

Chapter Thirty-One
DRAGON'S MOON

Week Three, Day Seven
Year 3000

The frantic pealing of bells tore Ash from the sweetest, softest dream he could remember straight into a nightmare.

Sleep clung to him in wispy shreds even after he struggled upright in the unfamiliar bed. A frustrated shake of his head ordered his thoughts enough to recognize his usual suite in Aleksi's Villa, but any further deduction seemed trivial compared to the *sound*—

Not light, cheerful bells. Not joy. The deep somber tone of this bell sounded the same at every seat in the High Court, and it rang for only one reason.

Terrors.

Sachi clutched a sheet to her chest and sucked in a ragged breath. "Is it an alarm?"

Ash kicked free of the blankets, battle-readiness shaking away the last cobwebs of sleep. His pants were a few steps from the bed and easily pulled on. No need to find his armor and sword. The best way to fight a Terror was in his other form, though fire wasn't guaranteed to destroy it.

He reached the window, and his heart sank. Not a Terror, but *Terrors*, dozens crawling out of the lake on either side of the stone bridge, their broken, terrible bodies unfolding and rising until they towered at twice the height of a man.

"Ash."

"Terrors," he ground out, turning from the window. She looked so small and fragile, alone in the sea of disheveled blankets, with twin lines of tears tracking down her cheeks. Fear and darker emotions churned across their bond. "The bells mean Terrors have been spotted. You need to stay here, where it's safe."

She scrambled to the end of the bed. "No. I'm going with you."

"You *can't*." He jabbed a finger at the bed. "I mean it, Sachi, it's dangerous. Zanya will—"

The words died on his tongue. Panic clenched his heart.

Sachi, *alone* in the bed.

He spun, his gaze raking the room, his mind scrambling for sense. No one in the bathing room. No one on the chairs or the rug before the hearth.

And the door to the hallway stood ajar.

His curse of rage escaped on a growl. Frenzied panic gave him strength to rip the door from its hinges. Some tiny shred of sanity stopped him from flinging it behind him and possibly hitting Sachi. He tore out into the Villa, his snarl shaking the rafters. *"ZANYA!"*

Zanya didn't respond. Ulric did, his piercing whistle leading Ash to a courtyard chaotic with Aleksi's scant household guard. Ash took the stairs to the top of the palace wall three at a time, his heart racing as he considered the flimsiness of these fragile walls as protections. Aleksi's delicate Villa simply wasn't built for war.

At the top of the tower above the main gate, he found Aleksi, Ulric, and Elevia staring down into the darkness below. Aleksi wore only a dressing gown, while Ulric and Elevia were dressed for battle.

"As usual, the monsters have impeccable timing." Elevia held her bow at her side, loose but ready to raise and draw in moments. "At least we arrived ahead of Aleksi's legion of worshippers. They'd be camped out there, defenseless."

"*We're* defenseless, love." Aleksi said it without any great alarm twisting his voice—yet. "My home is a place of welcome. It's ill-equipped to stand against a siege."

"Good." Elevia smiled. "I prefer to greet my enemy on the battle-field anyway."

"There are too many," Ash muttered, his gaze sweeping the court-yard below. It did no good. Zanya could disappear into shadows on a sunny day if she wanted. On a night like this? He wouldn't find her unless she wanted to be found.

The only thing he could do was turn his focus toward the enemy.

Elevia pulled an arrow from the quiver at her back. "We can slow them with fire, but you'll have to take wing. Or get me more archers."

Ash was already summoning fire when a soft voice spoke from behind him.

"It's all right."

The flames died. He whirled and saw Sachi, shivering in the chilly night air with only a light robe haplessly belted over her thin chemise. His protective instincts roared to life, and he reached for her, pulling her back from the castle wall. "You can't be here, Sachi. Go inside. Bolt the door to your room."

"No." She gripped his forearms, her face pale. "It's all right, Ash."

Her thumb pressed into the scar he'd earned trying to save Prince Tislaine. That had been *one* Terror, just one, and he hadn't been fast enough or strong enough to stop it. A dozen were already crawling across the grass toward the Villa, enough to slay the entire High Court if they weren't careful, then devour the souls of every person inside the Villa.

Fear was a wild thing inside him, a creature of claws and teeth raking furrows through his attempts at composure. It was as if all the fear Sachi had ever felt had taken root in his heart, because *she* had taken root there. The idea of failing to keep her safe was intolerable.

But there was no fear in Sachi. Their bond trembled with the strength of her emotions—love, worry, resignation . . . but no fear.

When she said it would be all right, she believed it.

Ash opened his mouth to ask why, and the torches along the wall flared wildly before snuffing out one by one, as if extinguished by an invisible hand. In the courtyard, a scream of panic sparked a second, upsetting the calm Aleksi's steward had tried so hard to instill.

"Oh, *shit*," Elevia breathed.

Ash spun and lunged for the wall, and discovered a new flavor of panic.

Zanya walked across the grass, a slight figure made of shadows. She wore her usual bedtime attire of loose black pants and a sleeveless tunic, and her long dark hair hung unbound. If it weren't for the two moons hanging full and bright in the sky, she would have faded into the darkness. But moonlight made her an impossibly tempting target as she walked straight toward the monsters massed against the shore.

Ulric's growl lowered in pitch as magic spilled from him. A massive wolf took his place, strong body tensed to leap. Farther down the wall, Kardox and Malindra exploded into a mass of ravens.

Ash summoned flames again, ready to form wings and launch himself from the palace wall. Again, Sachi grabbed him, her fingers digging into his arm, her voice tight and insistent. "Wait—"

"I have to go, Sachi. They'll *kill* her!"

"No," she whispered. "They won't."

The Terrors converged on Zanya from all directions. As tall as she was, they towered over her, some twice or more her height. Multiple limbs sprouted claws sharp enough to slice through bone, and misshapen mouths gaped with fangs as long as Ash's arm. More screams rose in the courtyard, and Ash let the fire consume him, forming wings—

Zanya reached up to brush her fingers over the monstrous face of the nearest Terror, and it bent to her touch like an eager puppy.

Ash's flames sputtered out.

Another creature folded to its knees, bumping against Zanya's hip as if seeking attention. She stroked the moss-covered horns curling back from its forehead with the gentle tenderness of a mother, and it settled onto the earth, preening under the touch.

Ulric's uneasy growl rumbled through the night, the only sound as a third and then a fourth creature bounded forward for Zanya's caress. The wind shifted, carrying her wordless murmurs as she petted them and stroked them until they surrounded her in an anxious circle.

"Are they . . . ?" Inga stepped forward, her hands braced on the balustrade, her eyes glowing. *"Look."*

As if anyone might look away. But then Ash realized what the Witch had already noticed—as Zanya's soft voice soothed the Terrors, they were beginning to break apart. Shadows crept from their hearts, leaving mangled bits of bone and rock and twigs that finally shattered into harmless debris.

"Void-touched," someone in the courtyard whispered, only to be immediately hissed into silence. But more whispers rose, overlapping, wary and awed and most of all *scared*, with one word rising again and again.

Cursed. Cursed. Cursed.

Fear filled Ash's heart, and he didn't know if it was his own or Sachi's. She stood at his side, her face a perfect blank mask, as the last Terror collapsed into a tangle of vines and bone, and Zanya rose to her feet. She turned to face the Villa, standing stiff and wary in a perfect ring of destruction. The wind tugged at her dark hair, and the whispers below them surged.

Sachi nodded slowly, her hair whipping across her face. Inside Ash, their bond trembled with fierce protectiveness.

Aleksi stood like stone. Elevia rubbed her fingers over the arrow's shaft, as if she was still considering nocking it. Magic whipped across the top of the wall, and Ulric appeared again in a defensive crouch, his eyes glowing gold. "What is she?" he demanded hoarsely.

Sachi whirled on him, practically baring her teeth. "She's the person who just saved your life," she hissed. "So leave her alone, or you'll answer to me."

Before anyone could respond, she turned and fled the tower, her bare feet silent on the stones.

"Ash," Ulric rumbled.

Ash held up a hand to stop him. "I don't know."

"You didn't even let me ask the question."

"Because *I don't know*." Sachi's protective rage was an ember in his chest, making it hard to think. "Aleksi, get your people back inside."

One nod from his fellow god had the Villa's steward capably herding people back inside the walls. Another nod and the Raven Guard burst into flight and headed down into the courtyard to provide assistance.

His task complete, Aleksi turned to Ash with a flourish that seemed both delicate and irritated. "Can someone please explain to me what just happened? Because I'm fairly certain I've missed something here."

Ash watched Zanya walk stiffly through the gates. The crowd parted hastily before her in the courtyard, and she ignored terrified looks and damning whispers alike as she followed the path Sachi had taken back into the castle.

"Ash?" Inga prompted softly.

"I don't know," he said for a third time. "I knew Zanya was strong, fast. A good fighter. But something like this? That was . . ." He trailed off, not wanting to say it.

Ulric did. "That was Void magic."

"Well." Elevia slammed the arrow back into its quiver and turned to lean against the cold stone. "I take back everything I said about her probably not being able to kill you. If she's been trained by Void priests, she absolutely *can* and *will* murder you."

Ash huffed. "Then why hasn't she? I've given her plenty of opportunities. And tonight, she *stopped* the Terrors. If she wanted me dead, this was her chance."

"I've never heard of anyone who can unmake a Terror," Inga said. "Not even a Void priest. They can summon nightmares, and the strongest can force a Terror to manifest. But that . . . They seemed *fond* of her. Like pets."

"There *was* a rumor that reached me a few years back . . ." Elevia tilted her head. "Everyone knows about the Slaughter at Travelers' Home."

"A small village in the foothills west of the capital," Aleksi confirmed. "Terrors attacked in the night. No one survived the massacre."

"So they say. But I heard whispers . . ." Elevia glanced over her shoulder, into the darkness where the Terrors had stood. "They say a captain of the King's Guard was searching a building—an orphanage—for survivors." She met Ash's gaze. "And he found two."

As if from a great distance, he heard the memory of Sachi's voice lightly answering Inga's query regarding where she'd found Zanya.

She saved my life.

"Two girls?"

"I believe so." Elevia shrugged. "Normally, whispers only grow. But this rumor died before I could glean anything more."

"Died?" Ulric asked. "Or was killed?"

She shrugged again.

"Ash—" Inga laid a hand on his arm, her gaze concerned. "The consort binding ceremony."

Aleksi cursed. "Sneaky mortal bastards."

It took Ash a moment longer to realize what they were saying. When he did, ice flooded his veins. "We're jumping to conclusions," he said roughly. "Based on a rumor. On scraps of a rumor."

Ulric's exasperated groan shredded the night. "Don't be a fool, Ash. If the girl is an orphan, the mortal king's family will not be bound to the land. Even if you ignore their obvious plans to assassinate you, you *have* to consider that. It means the mortals are planning to do something that could harm the land."

The one thing he could not ignore. "I'll talk to Sachi."

Aleksi held out both hands. "I'll come with you."

"No." Ash started for the stairs. "I need to talk to her by myself."

"Is that wise?" Ulric called after him.

Ash pivoted, and the fierce grip on his emotions slipped. The torches erupted into flames a foot tall all along the wall, casting wild shadows in the courtyard. "I understand the stakes of this game, my lord Wolf. I will do what must be done to protect the land. As I have *always* done."

Tension sizzled between them for a dangerous moment before Ulric inclined his head. "As you say, my lord Dragon."

Ash spun again, making it halfway down the steps before he realized the sharp, stabbing ache in his chest wasn't his own pain.

It was coming from Sachi.

"Ash!" Elevia hurried down the stairs after him. "Wait."

He whirled on her, his temper straining its leash. "Do you think I can't handle myself, Huntress?"

"No, of course not. I just . . ." She bit her lower lip nervously. "This isn't a clean hunt. It isn't even war. When humans scheme, things get complicated. Dirty." She sighed. "Be sure you're prepared and ready to hear what your impostor princess might tell you."

Ash reached out to grip Elevia's shoulder. She was his oldest friend, his general in times of war, and the person he trusted most in this world. So he gave her the truth. "I'm not prepared," he said quietly. "I'm not so arrogant as to think I could be. But I know that whatever story she has to tell, we will deal with the consequences. Because we always do."

Elevia nodded. "Go. Learn the truth so you can fight it."

He turned and strode down the stairs and through the courtyard. But once he was inside the Villa, he stepped into the empty library and leaned back against the wall, willing the churning inside him to settle.

It wouldn't. The world seemed to vibrate around him. When he sank his power into the earth, he felt the tremble there, the uneasiness, as if he stood poised on the edge of a chasm and one wrong move would send him tumbling over the edge to fall forever.

In spite of everything, his every instinct still screamed that Sachi was the answer to the prophecy. The consort he had been promised, the one who would show them the path to shattering the Betrayer's chains forever.

He'd always assumed that would be a joyous thing. He hadn't considered that the breaking of chains could be violent, too.

Or that his heart might shatter along with them.

He drew in a shuddering breath. And then the Dragon gathered the courage to face his consort.

And the truth.

Chapter Thirty-Two
DRAGON'S MOON

Week Three, Day Seven
Year 3000

The knife was mocking her.

Sachi sat in the center of the bed, her knees pulled under her chin, and stared at it where it lay under the window—discarded, forgotten.

Harmless.

It *was* harmless, wasn't it? It was just a blade and a handle. Some steel, carved wood, a bit of leather. It was just there. It merely existed . . . until someone decided to pick it up and use it.

Footsteps whispered in the hall outside the door. She knew their rhythm like she knew her own heartbeat. But it took forever for the door to crack open, and when Zanya's voice came, it was hesitant. "Sachi?"

"I'm here."

Zanya slipped through the doorway. Her gaze followed Sachi's to the knife sitting beneath the window.

She shuddered.

Might as well go ahead and lay all the cards on the table. "You made me sleep, Zanya."

Zanya's hands fisted at her sides, but she didn't deny it. "I didn't want you to have to be responsible for what I did. I know how you feel about him."

Sachi's laugh felt cold and hard in her chest. "I see. It was for my own good."

"It was for your *life*." Zanya took a step forward, and she was trembling with the intensity of her fervor. "Your *soul*."

It was Sachi's turn to shudder, though she quelled the reaction through sheer force of will. It shouldn't have been possible, but that was part of who she was. What she'd been trained to be. She could swallow her emotions—revulsion, disgust, fear, panic—and smile like she was the guest of honor at a dinner party.

But they'd never taught her how to handle betrayal.

"There are worse things than dying," she finally said. "Even worse things than ceasing to exist."

Zanya rejected the words with a sharp shake of her head. "You ceasing to exist is *all* of my worst things."

"And you know that being drugged is one of mine." The words *hurt*, but Sachi forced them out anyway. "You were there, Zan. Every moment of every day. You *know* what they did to me, and you still—" Her voice broke.

Zanya flinched, flinging up a hand as if to reject the accusation. Her head shook again, then faster as she stumbled forward and dropped to her knees at the edge of the bed. "No, Sachi. It wasn't supposed to be—" She broke off. "It was like the other times. Just taking your nightmares so you could rest—"

"*No.* You know it's not the same, not at all." The more Zanya tried to justify what she'd done, the more the cold knot in Sachi's chest grew. "And what about Ash?"

Zanya's expression crumpled. Tears she was too stubborn to shed made her eyes glisten, and she looked away. "What does it matter? I betrayed you, and then I failed you anyway."

"What does it matter?" Sachi echoed in disbelief. "I saw the knife in your hand, Zanya. You were going to kill him."

"Was I?" she asked bitterly. "I told myself I could. I had the blade to his throat. I would have taken no pleasure in it, but you would have been *alive*. It's the one thing I've trained my whole life to do. It's all I'm good for. And yet—" She bit off the words and scrubbed at her eyes. "I did it again."

"Did what?"

"You *know*."

Sachi resisted the urge to rub her temples. "No, I *don't*."

Zanya gripped the tangled quilts at the edge of the bed until her knuckles went white. "The Terrors," she whispered hoarsely. "The monsters who magically appeared at the exact moment to stop me from killing him."

For one surreal moment, Sachi could only stare. Zanya was upset that she'd failed. The one saving grace in this whole horrid situation, and it was the sole focus of her ire. Zanya wasn't upset that she'd betrayed Sachi's trust or that she'd very nearly murdered Ash in his sleep.

She was angry that she'd *failed*.

Sachi clenched her fists, relaxed them again, and marveled at the numbness that permeated her body. It started in the center of her chest and spread up to her lips and out to her fingertips.

Fascinating.

She spoke, and her voice sounded so *calm*. "For the rest of the progress, you will carry out your duties as my maid. You will harm no one on my behalf. As for the situation with the Terrors, I will shield you from whatever consequences arise. For now, you will retire to your chambers."

Zanya rose stiffly to her feet.

"You will think about tonight's events, and when you finally understand how you truly fucked up, you will tell me."

Dark, dead eyes met hers. "Just because I didn't have your fancy education doesn't mean I'm an idiot, *Princess*. I knew you'd hate me for this. I knew I was giving up your love. But I was doing it to save—"

"Stop talking." Sachi slid off the bed and faced her. "I don't hate you. And love isn't so easily killed as an unwary, sleeping god. But I can't trust you right now, Zanya. Everything you're saying, all your reasons—it's only what's best for you. That's it."

"Only because you don't care about yourself," Zanya retorted in a harsh whisper. "I've *never* been able to trust you to do that."

Zanya turned and marched, just as stiffly, off in the direction of the assigned quarters they hadn't planned on her using at all.

Sachi sank to the bed, her body aching and her mind churning. She didn't expect Zanya to understand, not really. How could she? Sachi wasn't even sure she would act any differently, if it were Zanya's life at stake.

But there was more here, Sachi could feel it. King Dalvish's plotting, the Phoenix's disappearance. Even the skirmishes at the northern boundary. There was something happening, something larger than Sachi or Zanya or even Ash.

And until she understood what that was, no move was safe. Not even one to save her everlasting soul.

Chapter Thirty-Three
DRAGON'S MOON

Week Three, Day Seven
Year 3000

The numb sadness that had settled like a rock in Ash's gut told him he would find Sachi alone. The pain he felt from her had frozen over in the time it took to calm himself enough for this confrontation. The pain had been *why* it took so long, in fact—even now, every instinct screamed for him to find whatever was making her so *sad* and destroy it.

Any progress he'd made in calming himself unraveled when he stepped through her doorway. She sat small and alone in the midst of their giant bed again, but this time her unnatural pallor and the blank way she stared at him shredded his heart.

She was trying so hard to lock it down, but she *hurt*. And he was only going to make it worse. "Princess."

"Don't look so distressed, Ash." She smiled, as warm and open as ever despite the chill that bound them both. "Come in and do what you need to do."

He gently closed the door, then leaned back against it. "I have not demanded truth from you thus far because I did not want to force you to lie to me. I thought I had time to gain your trust. But now there is no more time, Sachielle. I need your honesty."

"Then you will have it." Her smile faded. "Where should I begin?"

"Travelers' Home."

He'd hoped she would stare at him blankly. Instead, she winced. But then her shoulders lifted, as if a weight pressing down on her had vanished, and she turned to face him squarely. Openly, as if all pretense and prevarication had melted away.

"I don't know if I was born there," she admitted, "but it's where I lived when I was a small child. Before."

Their bond felt different within him. Softer, less carefully contained. Relieved but *sad*. She pulled at him, and he knew why the others had worried. It was hard to stay rigid against the door when he wanted to go to her and wrap her in his arms until there was nothing left inside her but contentment and safety and joy.

Instead, he forced himself to ask the questions that needed answers. "Elevia only heard rumors. That two children had been found alive after the massacre. But then the rumors stopped."

"Of course. If word had gotten out of the two girls who had survived the Slaughter, it would have ruined his plans." She drew in a deep breath. "They weren't sure, at first, what had happened or why, so they ferried us both to the capital. The priests took one look at Zanya and knew she was Void-touched."

"Is that how the two of you survived?" He gestured vaguely toward the castle walls. "She's always been able to do that? Make them go away?"

"I don't think so. That night in the orphanage, nothing that gentle happened. I remember . . ." She trailed off and swallowed hard. "Cries of fear and pain. Blood. Shadows everywhere. And Zanya, screaming for it all to stop." Sachi shook her head. "You still don't understand. She doesn't just banish the Terrors. She *calls* them to her, Ash."

"*What?*"

"Not on purpose. *Never* on purpose. But you wanted the truth, and there it is. That night, in Travelers' Home, they found a weapon that could kill a god, and . . ." She gestured to herself. "A nobody with a pretty face who looked enough like the king to pass as his heir."

It was mad. It was *brazen*. But Ash could see how it must have made perfect sense to a king chafing under the strictures of the High Court. Take two traumatized children, mold them into weapons, and unleash them upon your enemy. Send a fake heir so that the powerful magic binding your family's fortunes to the health of the land would fade. Even if Sachi and Zanya failed—and the king *must* have assumed they likely would—if Ash had no reason to suspect Sachi's true origins, they would have had a hundred years to enact whatever foolish secondary plan they had devised.

Ash sighed and crossed the room, snagging a chair along the way to drag with him. He set it facing the bed and sank into it. She'd given him the courtesy of honesty, so he would do the same. "I had guessed you had been sent to kill me."

Sachi nodded. "They thought you might figure it out. But they always insisted that if you did, you would simply kill us."

"Then they haven't read their histories," he retorted wryly. "Haven't you ever heard of Hapless Prince Robard? Or have the songs finally gone out of style?"

"Parodies, of course. No one enjoys looking foolish, my lord."

No, he supposed they didn't. "To murder a human simply because they wish me dead would be as cruel a misuse of my power as crushing an ant because you imagine it wants to knock down your house. To murder a consort already bound to me by blood would be agony. You were always safe with me, Sachi."

She leaned toward him. "I know that, Ash. I have always known that, even when you thought I was terrified of you."

"Yet you *were* terrified, and you didn't tell me the truth. *Why?*"

"Because the situation is complicated. The priests are holding certain collateral meant to secure my cooperation, as well as Zanya's." She folded her hands in her lap. "My life."

Ash clenched his fingers around the arms of the chair. *Here* it was, the missing piece that clarified the whole thing. "How? It can't be something simple. You must have known I would destroy any threat to you."

For a moment, she was silent. Then, "There's a keepsake chest on the table over there. Will you retrieve it, please?"

It was a small box of leather and carved wood, the kind of chest where one might store letters or trinkets. Yet his fingers tingled when he touched it. "It's imbued with magic. *Strong* magic."

"Yes." Sachi gestured to a solid gold medallion on the chest. "The gold seal is the latch."

"How do I open it?"

Her eyes radiated sadness—and hope. "Only a kiss from someone who truly loves me can unlock it."

Oh. Ash held her gaze as he slowly lifted the box and pressed his closed lips to the seal.

It clicked open, and Sachi inhaled sharply.

Inside the box was the intricate hourglass he'd seen in her chambers. Only the red sand was flowing into the lower chamber despite the fact that the timepiece was lying horizontal in the box. Ash lifted it and turned it upside down with an experimental shake.

The sand continued its inexorable fall, undeterred by gravity.

"The darkest of magics." Silent tears tracked down Sachi's face. "A curse. The hourglass counts down what time I have left. If you are still alive by the time the Witch's Moon arrives, I will die, and my soul will be severed from the Dream."

The rage burning through him should have set the castle to trembling. But the world pushed back, the strength of the earth reaching up to him, grounding him in place—and reminding him of what mattered. *Who* mattered.

Sachi could not afford his rage. Nor could she afford for him to fly off to the capital in a temper and murder his way through the mortal lords until he had vented his wrath.

First, he would keep her safe. *Then* he would destroy those who had dared harm her.

He set the box and the cursed hourglass aside, then held out his arms in quiet invitation.

Sachi trembled, uncertain. "I never wanted to hurt you. And I never want you to *be* hurt. I won't let it happen."

"Shh. Come here, Princess."

She slid off the bed and into his lap, curling up against his chest with her head tucked beneath his chin. He settled back into the chair, pulling her closer, her body terrifyingly fragile against his. Or maybe it simply seemed that way now that he knew Void magic had bound her tightly—as if her essence was already draining away into the endless nothingness, making her smaller and lighter and dimmer and *less*.

He stroked her golden hair and pressed a kiss to her temple. "Only one member of the High Court has a hope of combating Void magic. But the Phoenix *can* do it. The flames at their Tower wouldn't have been enough, but their own flames will. Tonight, I'll send to Dianthe to start the search. Tomorrow, we'll sail directly to Seahold. I'll fix this, Sachi. You have my word."

"Thank you, Ash." Her hand curled into a fist against his chest, and she raised her head. "But I need you to promise me something."

"Anything."

"If you can't fix this, and I'm going to die . . ." Sachi laid her hand on his cheek. "Take care of yourself, and of Zanya. Protect each other."

He'd been doing his best not to think of Zanya, because reconciling with *her* would not be so simple. But neither could he put Sachi off with a hollow promise. "I need to know something first."

"If I know, I'll tell you."

"Why did the Terrors come? What made her call them? When you were young, and tonight?"

Her jaw clenched. "They accused Zanya of stealing something. I don't remember what—a toy, perhaps, or a bit of food. They were getting ready to whip her for it, and I stepped between them." Her fingers drifted up to her cheek and lingered there. "The matron hit me instead, and then she kept hitting me. That night, the Terrors came."

"Oh, sweetheart." The endearment came without thought, and he covered her hand with his own, gently coaxing it from her cheek so he could press a kiss to the palm. "I'm sorry."

"She called them to save me. Do you understand, Ash?"

How could he not? The one thing he had always known to be true about Zanya was that Sachi was the center of her world. "She loves you. She'd do anything for you."

Sachi gripped his hand. "She was going to kill you tonight. She had the blade to your throat when the alarm sounded. She called them . . . so she wouldn't have to use it."

The import sank in slowly. Perhaps he should be angrier about a nearly successful attempt on his life, but Ash found it difficult to blame her. Protecting Sachi was a bone-deep instinct, forged in childhood and tempered by adult love. That Zanya would choose to slay him to keep Sachi safe was no surprise.

That anything had caused her to falter in her mission—*that* was the shock. How she must *hate* him for it. By doing his best to woo her and win her trust, he'd set the handmaid at war with herself. Unwittingly, to be sure, but the agony tearing Zanya apart must be real.

And anything he did to try to ease it would likely only make her turmoil worse.

Sachi was staring up at him, her eyes pleading for the vow she'd asked of him. At least he could give her this. "You're not going to die," he promised. "But if you need to hear it . . . I will keep Zanya safe, either way. I pledge to give her whatever protection she will accept from me."

Sachi's shoulders sagged, and a quiet sob slipped free. "Thank you. I know I have no place asking you for anything, much less something of this magnitude. But I love her, Ash. Just as I love you."

The world chose that moment to *dance*. Not physically—at least, the castle didn't shake—but the dizziness inside him spiraled up from the deepest heart of the earth, and the flames danced on their candles in the rhythm of the dips and whorls.

Ours, whispered the voice he usually heard in dreams, and he cupped Sachi's cheek and traced his thumb over the lips that had gifted him with that word.

Love.

"We love you, too," he whispered.

Her brow furrowed. "We?"

He laughed softly. "Me. And the world. It has been . . . insistent that you belong with me. Did you think there are always earthquakes every time I come?"

"I suppose I did." A beat. "How does the world feel about Zanya?"

He considered that, tilting his head. The world's eager-puppy reaction to Sachi had been distracting, but beneath it had always been a quiet, desperate yearning centered on Zanya—especially when they sparred. As if the world craved another strong protector.

Or as if it craved a strong protector for *Ash*.

The thought brought a sad smile to his lips. "The world hopes that someday Zanya will love me the same way she loves you."

"Good." Sachi buried her face in the crook of his neck. "It's been . . . an eventful night. I'm so tired."

"I know. Rest, my love."

He felt her lips curve against his throat as she snuggled trustingly against his chest. He smoothed his fingers through her hair, savoring the sweetness in their bond now. Sachi had told him the truth and trusted in him to save her—or to protect Zanya from harm if he could not. So simply was Sachi's world set to rights.

He wished Zanya's would be mended so easily.

Chapter Thirty-Four
DRAGON'S MOON

Week Three, Day Seven
Year 3000

When the Dragon came for her, Zanya was sharpening her boot knife.

Not that she'd expected the thing would do her much good if the High Court turned on her. She'd already banished the only weapon that might have given her a chance against their collective wrath. This flimsy knife with a blade no longer than her fingers would be scant protection. But the whetstone was familiar in her hand, and the sound soothed her.

Any peace she'd regained scattered when Ash opened the door without knocking and stepped inside.

The room seemed intolerably small with him looming inside, and worse when he shut the door, blocking any hope of escape. Flame-filled eyes stared at her from an expressionless face, and she *hated* herself for the stab of hurt.

She'd fooled herself into thinking he harbored some affection for her. But perhaps she had never been anything more than his rival for Sachi's time and his reluctantly tolerated partner in her pleasure.

Perhaps he was tired of having a rival, and this was how she died.

"Stop it," he rasped.

"I'm not doing anything."

"Stop looking at me as if *I* am here to kill *you*." The Dragon huffed out a dark laugh. "Sachi told me the truth tonight. All of it. Including what you almost did to me. And why you didn't."

Shock held her in place for a moment—the shock of betrayal. Hard on the heels of that came the sure knowledge that Sachi could not possibly have betrayed Zanya to save herself. How she *wished* Sachi had that capacity. Whatever Sachi had said, she had done so in an effort to protect Zanya.

Which meant she truly had told the Dragon everything. Not just that Zanya had tried to kill him, but that this terrible, loathsome *tenderness* that he'd kindled in her had thwarted her plans.

She felt stripped bare before him again, only worse than in the cabin, when he'd only caught sight of the scars she'd been given by others. Sachi had revealed something far more intimate to him—the scars she had given herself.

"If you know the truth, then you know I have to try again." Zanya gripped the knife until the hilt made her hand ache. "It's her life. Her *soul*."

"I'm a *god*, Zanya! You should have told me and trusted me to *fix it*." The words seemed torn from him, and she realized for the first time that what she was seeing in those flame-colored eyes wasn't rage.

It was *pain*.

Then he stalked toward the bed, and panic overtook her. She scrambled back, bracing herself against the headboard. He froze, one knee pressed to the mattress, the pain in his eyes doubled. "What have I ever done to make you think I would hurt you?"

Her heart pounded. Humiliation that he'd seen her fear made her cheeks hot. Her own anger washed in behind it. "The world has made it clear that *everyone* will hurt me, my lord Dragon. Everyone but her."

Ash's knee slid more fully onto the bed. Pride held her stiff, not shrinking away as he reached out to push her windblown hair back from her face. "I won't hurt you, Zanya."

How seductive he could be. Warmth from his fingertips heated her chilled skin. The gentleness of his caress raised shivers. His voice was like honey, promising her things she had been too proud and too wise to crave until these fools on the High Court had offered them to her so recklessly.

Affection. Teasing. Companionship. Acceptance.

Love.

Tears pricked her eyes, and she choked them back roughly, jerking away from his touch. "How can you save Sachi? The priest told me no one in the High Court can work Void magic. It's against your very natures."

Ash let his hand fall. "True enough. But your priest doesn't know everything. The Phoenix can burn away such corruption."

For one glittering moment, hope leapt in her heart. Then she remembered what the priests from the Burning Hills had said, and despair nearly crushed her. "No one knows where the Phoenix is."

"We'll find them, Zanya. We're getting on a boat tomorrow and going directly to Seahold. The Siren is already sending word anywhere the wind or water touches. We *will* save Sachi."

He was so sure, she wanted to believe him. But her entire life had been the worst possible thing happening, every time. *Hope* was always a lie. Hoping was how you fooled yourself into complacency until it was too late to do anything but accept defeat. "What if you don't?" she whispered hoarsely.

"I will."

"What if you *can't*?"

Ash said nothing, and the silence damned him.

"You promised to keep her safe," Zanya hissed, coming up on her knees. It brought them face to face; the heat of him was tangible. The

Dragon always burned hot, but in this Zanya burned hotter. "You said you would destroy anyone who tried to hurt her. Will you still hold to that on the final day of the Dragon's Moon, if the only way to keep her safe is to die?"

He hesitated, just for a moment, and *this* was why Zanya didn't hope. Because people were selfish at their cores, even gods. They would always betray you. "And you wonder why I didn't tell you," she scoffed, letting her tone flay him to the bone. "I couldn't take the chance. I still wouldn't. You're thousands of years old. Just because you like to fuck her doesn't mean you'll give up immortality for her to live a few more decades."

"Zanya—"

"What is a mortal consort to you?" Zanya demanded, pounding her fist against his chest so hard that he swayed backward. "You've had dozens. You'll have dozens more. They live and they die and you go on. But I won't go on if Sachi dies! Her life is *everything to me.*"

"*Zanya.*" Ash reached for her, but she knocked his hand away with all of the strength in her body. No point in holding back now, and she savored his hiss of surprise and the way he rubbed at his wrist. Everything in her coiled, waiting for a counterattack, wanting this violence because the pain in her needed an outlet.

But he didn't strike back. He simply retreated, sliding from the bed to stand at the foot, an endless compassion in his eyes that made her want to strike him again. "Pack your things, Zanya. We leave for the boat at dawn."

Pain made her lash out again, this time with words. "Do you think your friends will want me on their precious boat?"

"No," Ash admitted quietly, and even though she'd asked for it, the truth cut her to the bone. Her chest felt so tight she couldn't draw a full breath, and tears stung her eyes and lodged in her throat as a lump she couldn't swallow away.

She'd become accustomed to being feared and scorned by humans. She'd almost convinced herself she didn't want their companionship anyway. But to be feared and rejected by the High Court, by those who shaped the world itself?

"Gods be *damned*, Zanya!" The Dragon was suddenly *there*, hand gripping her chin as he did so often to Sachi, possessive and protective and commanding. He tilted her head up, forcing her to meet his blazing eyes. "What they want doesn't matter. I want you with us, so you will be with us. I promised Sachi I'd keep you—"

She couldn't bear to hear the word *safe* leave his lips, so she whipped her head around and bit his fingers.

"Fuck!" The Dragon jerked back, chest heaving. That sweet, familiar darkness uncurled in Zanya, and she knew she was balanced on the edge of a cliff. If she lunged for him now, it wouldn't be a fight. It would be heat and lust and dominance and the kind of sex that broke furniture and maybe walls. She'd drown in what they could be together—a Void-touched queen of darkness and the dragon god who didn't fear her, even at her worst.

She could give in and let him help carry the impossible burden of keeping Sachi alive when she loved and protected everyone but herself.

He whispered her name and reached for her again, and Zanya scrambled back. Her body knew the answer her heart was still struggling with—muscle memory of the most tragic kind.

No one else had ever had Zanya's and Sachi's best interests at heart. On the day the Phoenix shattered the curse, maybe Zanya could believe. Until then, the Dragon was her enemy. Because while he lived, Sachi could only die.

"I'll pack my bags," she whispered, looking away.

Silence. Then the soft tread of footsteps and the creak of the door. When she looked up, the Dragon was gone.

And she was alone.

Chapter Thirty-Five
DRAGON'S MOON

Week Three, Day Ten
Year 3000

With Naia speeding their way, the usual five-day trip down the river and across Siren's Bay took just over two. The swift arrival would have soothed Ash more if Sachi hadn't seemed to fade a little with each passing hour.

Even their arrival at Seahold couldn't revive her energy, though she smiled gently and assured him she was fine as he lifted her onto a horse. The bustling port town that shared its name with the castle that sat high on the bluff above it seethed with activity—and a restless energy that was explained when the dockmaster came to greet Ash personally.

"The Kraken's sails have been spotted from the south watchtower," she confided as she led them through the carefully managed chaos. "The Siren has called everyone who can be spared to port, of course . . . but no one expected he would come."

No, nothing short of a direct order from the Siren—and *only* the Siren—could stop Einar from restlessly patrolling the Western Wall, taking any chance he could to thwart the Betrayer's ambitions. Whatever had brought him so far east would be of no comfort to anyone here.

It took surprisingly little time to traverse the maze of shops and trading outposts that cluttered the gentle climb to Dianthe's castle. The denizens of Seahold were a practical sort, accustomed to the Siren's low tolerance for pageantry and ceremony. They moved swiftly out of the way of the High Court, limiting their acknowledgment to respectful nods and a murmured "Blessings of the Dream to you" before going about their work.

Dianthe herself waited in front of the open gates of her keep, clad in her usual flowing pants and loose tunic in blues and midnights. The wind gently stirred her unbound curls as she watched Ash lift Sachi from her saddle. "Princess Sachielle, you are welcome at Seahold."

"I thank you most sincerely, my lady."

Dianthe smiled gently, then lifted a hand and gestured to Naia. The young god bounded forward to accept a warm hug and a kiss on each cheek. "Welcome home, my darling."

"Siren." Naia whispered the word like a prayer, her eyes shining.

"The consort could undoubtedly use some refreshment. Please show her to the sunrise room. There should be food waiting for all of us there."

Naia bowed and went to offer an arm to Sachi. They disappeared inside with a silent, wary Zanya trailing behind them. Only once they were gone did Dianthe cut a look at Ash. "I thought you said she glowed, brother."

Worry tightened its grip on him. He'd hoped the fading had been his own imagination. Aleksi destroyed any last illusions when he murmured, "Sachi's glow has been diminishing for days."

Sympathy and sorrow filled his old friend's beautiful eyes, but she only tilted her head as if listening to something. Then she sighed. "Einar walks my shores. We should all hear what he says. He would not have come here himself if he did not have word of the Phoenix."

A flicker of hope kindled in spite of Dianthe's serious look. "Is that not good?"

"When has the Kraken ever come bearing good news?" Ulric grumbled, only to receive Inga's sharp elbow in the side.

"It is rare," Dianthe acknowledged, then softened it with a smile. "But there is always a first time."

She led them into the castle, falling into step with Elevia as the two began a low-voiced conversation. About Elevia's informants, no doubt—the two had always worked closely to facilitate swift communication across the country. Ash knew he should care. The pain lodged high in his chest made it hard to think.

I thought you said she glowed.

And she still *did*. He saw it as soon as he stepped into the sunrise room—a comfortable place for casual meals that gained its name from the wall of floor-to-ceiling windows facing the ocean to the east. A long table was surrounded by plush chairs, and more seats were scattered on either end of the room, available for chats over tea or wine. Sachi sat at the table, sun glinting off her hair. But even the warm light couldn't return the color to her unusually pale cheeks, and the diamond brightness of her magic felt . . . muted. Tired.

She still smiled at him as he claimed the chair next to her.

She bit her lower lip, then turned to him. "Ash—"

Her words were interrupted by loud steps outside the door, a wild rush of magic that felt like a storm at sea flooding before them. In spite of himself, Ash tensed—Einar might be a much younger god whose powers were strongest on his ship, but Ash *never* underestimated the threat he represented.

Everyone fell silent as he stepped through the doors. Einar was nearly as tall as Ash and almost as broad, though his body was hard and lean instead of bulky. He had Aleksi's golden-brown skin and Inga's obsidian hair, though his was shaved on one side. The other side fell rakishly over eyes that glowed almost the same gold as Ulric's as he assessed them all one by one, mentally discarding those he found uninteresting.

He lingered on Sachi, and longer on Zanya. Then his gaze fixed on Naia, and he prowled closer as she stood, her dark eyes wide and curious. He reached out a hand to brush her cheek, then licked his thumb. "So you're the new one," he rumbled, and a wicked grin curved his lips. "I've tasted you in the sea."

"Einar!"

Dianthe's voice was all whiplash command, and he pivoted abruptly and swept a low bow to the Siren. "My queen."

"I assume you've come for a reason? One that doesn't involve lewd comments and debauchery, that is."

"Perhaps, though the sweet new song in the sea might have drawn me regardless." The Kraken winked at Naia, prompting a furious blush. Then he dipped a hand into his long jacket and withdrew a wooden circle strapped to a long, thin piece of leather—a crude necklace or medallion.

He tossed it onto the table in front of Dianthe, who picked it up and ran her thumb over the pattern burned into one side. It was her own sigil, a cresting wave within a thin circle.

"Turn it over," the Kraken told her.

She did, and Ash stiffened. Burned into the opposite side was the sigil of the Phoenix.

"They called it a mark of safe passage," the Kraken said.

Dianthe looked up. "They?"

"The refugees I found floating in a half dozen leaky boats off the Empire's eastern shore. Your steward's taken them to the great hall to find food and clothing." Einar glanced at Aleksi and Inga. "It's likely they could use healing. Of the body and the heart. They were in rough shape. Especially the children."

Inga rose at once, Aleksi a heartbeat behind her. Elevia stirred, too, and Ash trusted that whatever there was to know, by the end of the evening, she would know it. The three hurried out. Dianthe never took her gaze from Einar. "The Betrayer rarely lets refugees escape his shores. How did they manage?"

"A cloaked figure gave them that," he said, gesturing to the wooden token. "Told them it was a mark of safe passage. Told them where to find the boats, and to follow the flames. They say there was fire on the water, blue and green, and it led them between the patrols and straight to me."

Zanya spoke up for the first time, eyes intense. "If they were so close, could you sense the Phoenix?"

Einar dashed all hope with a curt shake of his head. "One of my sailors thought they caught a glimpse of the flames, but they were gone by the time we reached them. But I sensed neither hide nor hair of the Phoenix. And the flames mean little. They can operate through the Dream in ways the rest of us can't."

Gentle disappointment drifted down the bond alongside resignation. Ash wrapped a protective arm around Sachi and told himself she didn't feel any frailer. It was just his imagination. His fear. "It still gives us a place to start. I may not have the Phoenix's aptitude within the Dream, but I can still seek them out."

"We all can," Dianthe said firmly. "Einar, I know you loathe staying on land, but I'd ask you to linger for a few days. If we need a swift ship, no one is faster than you."

Einar's gaze slid to Naia again, his smile pure sin. "Perhaps I can find some way to pass the time."

Dianthe gave him a terse warning look and turned to Sachi. "Princess, you have had a long morning of travel. Naia would be happy to show you and your handmaid to the quarters set aside for you. There should be a bath drawn, and we can send up food if you require any."

"Thank you, my lady."

Ash squeezed Sachi's hand, and she paused, lifting her hand to his cheek.

"It will be all right," he told her firmly, as if speaking the words could make them real.

"I know, my lord," she whispered back, a ghost of a smile on her lips.

She left by Naia's side. Zanya trailed behind, but stopped in the doorway to shoot a glare of pure challenge at Ash. She had never been good at hiding her feelings, and now she didn't even try. Ash could read that look as if she'd shouted the words in his face.

And if all of these desperate measures fail? Will you give up your life for her?

Ash didn't know.

It was easy to imagine falling in battle in her defense. He would charge into any fight, knowing the risk was there. But he was skilled and practiced—few fights offered true risk. He accepted the possibility, but he had never been forced to come to grips with the likelihood.

Could he stand willingly and let Zanya take his life? Could he take his own? Would the warrior within allow either without a fight?

Soft fingers brushed his arm. He looked up, and it wasn't Dianthe who stared at him. It was the Siren, eyes glowing with the power of the seas, face taut with worry. "Do not even consider it."

There was only one answer he could give. "Let us find the Phoenix, and I won't have to."

Chapter Thirty-Six
DRAGON'S MOON

Week Three, Day Ten
Year 3000

Sachi was fading.

For the first few days, Zanya had been sure she was imagining it. Certainly, enough had happened since her disastrous assassination attempt to try nerves far more steady than her own. Now that her task was all but impossible, it was only natural that her fear would blow every yawn and stumble out of proportion.

But Zanya had seen this curse work before. The warmth and energy that made a person *alive* would seep away until even drawing breath was an agony so great, the body simply . . . did not.

Sachi's hands were cold when Zanya tucked her into bed. Her usually golden skin was sickly pale. Dark shadows had deepened day by day under her eyes, and she moved as if it hurt.

The curse was claiming Sachi, and it shouldn't be. It *shouldn't be.* Twenty days remained before the sun set on the Dragon's Moon. There was supposed to be time to fix this. Time for the High Court to track down the Phoenix, time to save her . . .

Unless there wasn't.

The answer sat on Sachi's vanity, mocking Zanya—that damnable chest with its cursed hourglass. Every night of their journey downriver, Zanya's fingers had trembled with the need to wrench it open and reassure herself that the sand wasn't falling faster.

Fear had held her back. Not fear of what she'd find, but fear that she wouldn't be able to open the chest at all. That Sachi had been right, and whatever twisted, possessive need Zanya felt for her was born of self-interest instead of love. The words replayed themselves in a damning loop every time Zanya closed her eyes.

I can't trust you.

All your reasons—it's only what's best for you.

Zanya had crossed a line. She, of all people, knew how much Sachi hated to have her perceptions altered, be it by drugs or magic. Her trainers had put her through seven kinds of misery, forcing her to endure every possible indignity while they taught her to control her thoughts and feelings. How often had Sachi wept in Zanya's arms after a terrible night of torment where reality and nightmares blurred?

Someone who truly loved her would have remembered that, right? And what did Zanya know of love, anyway? Sachi was the one who breathed it in like air and exhaled it with every sigh. If *Sachi*, who saw the best in everyone, now only saw selfishness in her . . .

The answer sat within easy reach, but Zanya wasn't sure what she'd do if she brushed her lips to the golden latch and found it locked against her. Loving Sachi had been the only stable rock in her life. Without it, she was nothing but a Terror in human skin.

Zanya stared down at Sachi's sleeping form and felt the first stirrings of despair.

The rooms the Siren had set aside for the Dragon's consort were elegant and beautiful. Glass doors opened to balconies with breathtaking ocean views. One large door led to the adjoining suite where Ash had his own bed. Another led to their shared sitting room and library. A third led to a bathroom that made Dragon's Keep look positively rustic by comparison. It had a deep tiled bath, clever plumbing, running water, and a skylight that showed a star-strewn sky to anyone who lounged in the heated tub at night.

Zanya walked past every luxury, barely seeing any of it. On the far side of the bathroom, a door led to a dressing room filled with Sachi's belongings and a dozen centuries' worth of fashion in almost as many shapes and sizes, all of it available to the consort if it took her fancy.

In the corner of the closet, an inconspicuous door led to the small, sparse room set aside for the consort's maid. Even with lingering pain between them, even feeling so exhausted that standing seemed to be an effort, Sachi had protested Zanya retreating to a tiny room inside a closet. Zanya had silenced her.

Banishment to a cupboard felt like a fitting punishment for how completely she'd ruined everything.

Still, as cupboards went, it was comfortable. The mattress was soft and generous, the quilts simple but clean and bright. Her small window looked out over the ocean as well, and if she cracked it open, she could hear the crash of surf far below mixed with the calls of birds who hunted by night.

It would have suited Zanya's bleak mood more if they'd found a cold dungeon cell for her. It certainly would have been more honest. Their jaw-clenching courtesy might as well have been offered at knifepoint. They tolerated her for Sachi's sake alone, and while it amused her in a dark, painful way to realize that gods now trembled in fear where she walked, it did her little good.

The shadows seemed to pull at her, twisting sickly around her. Her stomach lurched as they coalesced in the corner, and a familiar voice taunted her mockingly from the darkness. "Given up so soon, girl?"

Her boot knife was in her hand before he finished the sentence. Magic screamed around her, a grating itch under her skin as the shadows parted to reveal a tall, icily handsome man with silken golden hair, piercing blue eyes, and expensive robes of bronze on black belted in place with a massive golden chain.

High Priest Nikkon.

Smiling.

"Ahh, yes." He flicked his fingers at the knife held in her hand. "Must we go through this every time? I understand that your solution to every problem is to threaten to stab it, but your stubbornness grows tedious."

The room was so small. Zanya lunged and had him by the throat, fingers digging in enough to choke off his dismissive laugh. She shoved him up the wall and let the tip of her knife rest against his side. "You taunt me about it every time you see me, and yet you still put yourself in my hands."

"And you threaten me every time," he retorted, "even knowing that if you harm me, your precious Sachielle dies."

This time, the threat couldn't dissuade her. Sachi already looked half-dead. Zanya dug the knife in just enough to slice through his robes and kiss his skin. "I could probably find a few places to stab that would leave you alive long enough to unravel that curse."

She wanted him terrified, but he only stared down at her in disdain, his lips curled into that same mocking smile. "Haven't you wondered why she's so tired, Zanya? You must know it's too soon."

The sudden chill made her hands tremble. She eased the knife back just far enough not to stab him by mistake. "What did you do?"

"It's not what *I* did. It's what *you* did." Nikkon gripped her wrist and dragged it from his throat, fingers like talons as they dug into her skin. "I warned you, didn't I? I warned you not to tell the High Court."

Fear turned to ash on her tongue, but she told him the truth. "I didn't. I would never."

"Then why did they abort the progress and rush to the Siren's lair? Why do ships sail from every port in the Sheltered Lands, seeking the Phoenix?"

Was that tension in his voice? Zanya's heart beat faster. "So it's true? The Phoenix's fire could break the curse?"

"Perhaps," Nikkon conceded. "Not that you'll ever find out. I'm afraid I had to make good on my promise, and Sachielle's time runs short."

Breathing in felt like inhaling glass. "How long?" she whispered.

The priest laughed, his blue eyes alight with joy. He reveled in Zanya's agony and his own power. Shadows lurched around them, already gathering to steal him away.

Zanya fought against them, slamming him into the wall again. *"How long?"*

A knife materialized in Nikkon's hand, and she recognized the thin, nearly black blade and the carvings on the handle. Void-steel. The only kind of weapon that could leave a wound from which a god could not heal. "The Dragon dies tonight," he said, the words digging agony into Zanya's heart. "Or Sachielle dies at dawn."

The shadows wrapped tight around him, stealing him from Zanya's grasp. She stumbled as the whole room seemed to *lurch*, and then Nikkon was gone. The only sound that remained was the soft clatter of the knife on the stone floor.

Zanya picked up the knife. Its hilt fit her hand like it had been made just for her. The blade itself was almost as long as her forearm, made of steel that shimmered with dark ripples across the surface. Steel folded one hundred times with magic by a smith with a connection to the Void, or so the legends told.

She tested the edge with her finger, and it was so sharp that blood rose before she felt the pain of the cut. She stared at that drop of blood, her brain grasping for a way out of this. A way to save the woman she loved without breaking her.

Maybe Nikkon had lied.

Zanya threw open the door and raced to Sachi's room. The cursed chest sat on the vanity, and her hands fumbled as she grabbed at it. Dread filled her heart, but Zanya pushed it back and filled her heart with Sachi instead. Her bright laugh and her wicked smile, the exasperated way she rolled her eyes when Zanya fussed over her. The fierceness that radiated from her when anyone dared insult Zanya. The brush of her fingers, of her lips. The pleasure of seeing her pleasure, and the peace of waking in her arms.

Love. It had to be real. It *had* to be.

Closing her eyes, Zanya pressed a trembling kiss to the lock. Her fingers shook as she pried at the lid, but it popped open easily.

Exhilaration rose on a wave that broke into despair when she lifted the hourglass.

Before, the sand had dropped one grain at a time. Now, a steady stream cascaded into the lower chamber—Sachi's life draining away. Dawn might have been too generous an estimate. Zanya didn't have until morning. She had to decide *now*.

Sachi would beg for Zanya to let her go. And Zanya wanted to be the person who could, who would look at the bigger picture and understand that Sachi's death might be a necessary loss on the path to saving their world from a larger threat. She wanted to be *good*.

But the rest of the world had never cared about her. Zanya couldn't bring herself to care about it. Nikkon had been right about her as a child, and he was right about her now.

Zanya was a monster. The world could burn for all she cared, as long as Sachi lived. Maybe that *was* selfish, but it was still love. The proof of that lay in Zanya's hands.

And as for this sick, selfish affection she'd developed for Ash . . . Well, whatever she felt for him was new. Perhaps she hadn't had the stomach to murder him in cold blood. But if the Dragon came at her in battle, Zanya trusted the brutality of her instincts. With this knife, she could slay him.

She just needed to convince him to attack her.

Chapter Thirty-Seven
DRAGON'S MOON

Both moons had set by the time Ash returned to his room, his body aching with tension and his mind raw from an exhausting night of trying to use the Dream to locate the Phoenix.

The Dream itself had never been his domain. He could transport himself to the heart of the world easily enough and meet the others there. But using it more deeply?

He might have come from the Dream, but Ash was a creature of earth and stone and fire. His power never felt as potent when he couldn't feel the dirt beneath his feet and the gentle rhythms of his world. Add in the oddness from the Empire . . .

Ash frowned, rubbing at his aching head. It had been centuries since he had even attempted to reach his magic across the Western Wall and into the vast empire his former brother had conquered. There was something . . . *twisted* there. An oddness to the taste of the Dream, metallic and bitter and cold. The deeper he'd extended his senses trying to find the Phoenix, the more unsettled he'd become. Eventually, he'd given up and left the search to those better equipped to navigate this ephemeral space.

Besides, there were more mundane solutions to this problem. Einar could tell him where the refugees came from. If he started there and worked his way out, he could likely make enough of a commotion to attract the Phoenix's attention.

A dragon soaring overhead, bellowing rage and fire, usually did.

He shoved through his door, intending to wash off the lingering grime of travel before checking on Sachi. Two steps into his bedroom, with his shirt most of the way over his head, battle-tested instincts screamed a warning.

Ash didn't second-guess them. Whirling, he tore through his shirt and grabbed his attacker, flinging them back against the wall hard enough to rattle it. He had a knife in one hand and claw-tipped fingers wrapped around the interloper's throat before he recognized wild brown eyes and silken dark hair.

"Zanya?" Cursing, he recoiled. "I'm sor—"

A flash of silver burst from the dancing shadows. He wheeled back, but not fast enough. Pain blossomed across his shoulder. He stared down, uncomprehending, at the thin cut that burned far more viciously than it should. He swiped away the blood, expecting to see already healed flesh, and struggled to understand the meaning of the fresh blood welling up as his entire shoulder throbbed.

The answer came on a whisper that had him stepping back, chilled. *Void-steel.*

Zanya watched him, her breath coming too fast and her eyes almost feverish. Her usual neat braid was half undone, her hair tangled around her face. The hand holding the engraved knife trembled.

She looked half out of her mind, and Ash's heart clawed its way into his throat. "What happened?"

Instead of answering, she lunged at him.

She was so fast. *Too* fast. He couldn't play with her this time, not with that knife in her hand. He pivoted out of the way and caught her by the back of the shirt. One heave sent her flying onto his bed with so much force that it skidded several paces across the floor, the wooden legs screeching over stone.

Instead of pressing his advantage, he dropped his weapon and stood watching her, hands tensed at his sides. The impact with the mattress should have stunned her, but she shook it off and leapt to her feet.

"Damn it all, Zanya," he snapped as she circled toward him again. "I don't want to hurt you."

"You'd better hurt me," she snarled. "Or I'll hurt *you*."

The desperation in her voice scraped at him—and Zanya had never been a very good liar. She bared her teeth and lunged, and Ash held his ground, hands held out at his side, palms turned nonthreateningly toward her.

The knife came within an inch of his throat. For one heartbeat, he thought he'd misjudged her, but at the last moment her hand twisted. Instead of slitting his throat, her knuckles crashed into his nose, hitting him so hard he thought she might have broken it.

Through the pain and involuntary tears, he knew the truth. Sachi had been right all along.

"Attack me!" Zanya screamed, swinging at him again. This time he dodged out of the way, and her frustrated snarl was the cry of a wounded creature. "Fight back, you Void-cursed monster!"

Zanya was trying to kill him. But she couldn't do it.

"What happened?" he whispered, his voice as gentle as he could make it.

A mistake. At the soothing tone, she snarled again and slashed at his chest. The knife grazed him, leaving behind a thin line of blood that blazed as if he'd been gutted.

He gritted his teeth and growled her name. *"What happened?"*

Zanya's chest heaved with her uneven breaths. Her voice was raw. "Can't you see that she's dying? The priest came to me. Gave me a message."

"What message, Zanya?"

A sob tore from her throat. "They accelerated the curse. You die before dawn, or the Void takes her soul."

The pain of it tore through his chest, knocking him back a step. Then he realized that hadn't been the pain, but Zanya, slamming into him, her fist driving into the fiery cut across his bare skin. "Damn it, *attack me*! Where's the fearsome dragon who reduces entire armies to charred piles of bone? Where's the monster? Fight back! *Hurt me!*"

Because she couldn't bring herself to kill him in cold blood. And if she didn't, if she failed—

He thought of Sachi, lying pale and cold in her bed, the light slowly fading from her. And poor, desperate Zanya . . .

This curse was tearing her apart from the inside.

What a tiny, painful life she'd led. Beaten and abused, rejected and abandoned. Tormented night and day with only one goal—to turn her into this glorious, dangerous weapon. And they wielded her by holding a knife to the throat of the one person in her life who had ever loved her.

And Ash, so arrogant in his power, had done his best to woo her. To make her care for him. To make her *trust* him. He'd thought to free her from whatever trap she was in, but all he'd done was turn himself into another blade pressed to her throat. No matter which way she moved, the result would cut bone deep.

His heart ached for her in that moment. For the loneliness of her life, for the pain she'd endured. He knew what it was like to be seen as a monster, to be scorned and rejected by the masses. But he had always had the High Court. The Raven Guard. Worshippers, those few devoted who would never turn away, who pledged themselves to him *because* of what he was.

She had only ever had Sachi.

Given that stark truth, there was only one thing he could do.

The next time Zanya swung at him, he growled and jerked her off her feet. Slinging her across the room bought him a few precious moments to reach for the Dream. Not easy, with a furious assassin bent on provoking him into a killing rage, but he only needed a moment.

The heart of the world flickered into view. Dianthe was still seated at the stone fountain. She turned, her brow furrowing. "Ash?"

"Protect Sachi," he told her. "And Zanya. Whatever she does to me tonight is by my choice. She will not be blamed or punished."

The Siren swept to her feet, concern making her eyes blaze electric blue. "Ash, what are you—?"

"*Promise me,* Dianthe!"

A tremendous force hit him in the stomach, dragging him from the Dream. But he knew he could trust the Siren to heed his words, even if she never forgave him for what he was about to do.

So Ash turned his focus to the fight, snarling as he blocked Zanya's vicious kick and yanked her off balance.

It would be better this way, wouldn't it? He could have died a thousand times over the years. Over petty things. In meaningless battles. Against lesser foes. For undeserving causes.

If he had to choose who killed him, why not this magnificent warrior? And if he had to die, why not for Sachi? His only regrets would be that he'd never truly won his way into Zanya's heart, and that he wouldn't get to see the women they would become once they were given safety and love and a place to blossom into who they were meant to be.

And that he'd have to terrify Zanya just enough to convince her to kill him. Though it shamed him to the core, Ash didn't think his survival instincts would allow him to plunge that cursed blade into his own chest.

Fortunately, Zanya was fully capable of doing the deed. He just needed to encourage her.

Ash formed fangs and claws. He let flames lick over his skin. He bared his teeth in a terrifying roar.

And he lunged for her.

Chapter Thirty-Eight
DRAGON'S MOON

Week Three, Day Ten
Year 3000

Sachielle dreamt of death.

It had been creeping closer for days now, like a looming shadow cast by the setting sun. It was near enough now to touch, cold beneath her fingers. Beneath her skin.

Then, a glimmer.

Protect Sachi.

She felt rather than heard the words. They vibrated through her strongly enough to drag her from her exhausted, unnatural sleep.

Promise me.

The room was dark. Sachi swung her legs over the side of the bed, but the moment she tried to stand, her legs collapsed beneath her. She hit the floor with an agonizing thud and struggled painfully to her feet.

It took far too long, which meant she was running out of time.

A roar drifted in from the next room over. Ash's room.

Promise me!

And she knew something was terribly, horribly *wrong*.

"No." The word tore free of her throat with all the pained effort of a shout, but it landed weakly in the room, like dead leaves rustling in a soft breeze.

She lurched toward the door that separated their suites but lost her balance and tried to catch herself on the edge of the vanity. Instead, her fingers hit cold metal and smooth glass.

The hourglass. It tumbled over, crashed to the floor . . . and shattered into a million pieces.

Sachi paid it no heed, simply stumbled through the bleeding sand and shards of glass toward the door. She slipped, slammed her shoulder against the jamb. It didn't even hurt this time, and she curled her shaking fingers around the partially open door.

It swung open to reveal a nightmare.

Zanya gripped a blade of dark steel that practically vibrated with grim magic. She faced Ash, who was bleeding—*bleeding*—and snarling at her. They moved around the room with absolute focus and no hint of playfulness.

They weren't sparring. This was a fight to the death, playing out right before Sachi's eyes.

"Zanya, *no*." Sachi could barely force out the words, and they didn't seem to hear her. A sudden, irrational thought gripped her: that she'd left her body behind on her bedroom floor along with that cursed hourglass, and they couldn't hear her because she was dead, a ghost, *dead*—

A knife lay on the floor near the door. Sachi fumbled as she tried to pick it up, slicing her hand on the blade. Blood welled and dripped from her fingers, and it reassured her.

Dead people didn't bleed this much.

The blood made her fingers too slick to grip the knife, so she swiped them impatiently on her gown. The blood seeped into the white fabric, staining it—

Bright-red blood. A crown of flowers. Hands outstretched.
There is only one way.

It was so simple, wasn't it? Truly, the most straightforward remedy to the dilemma that had twisted them all into knots. Without Sachi, there was no curse to threaten Zanya, no reason for her to break her own heart by murdering Ash. Of all the paths, this was the only one that would allow Zanya and Ash to walk away, whole and unscathed.

No, not unscathed. But they would *live*.

"Stop," she said. Her voice was louder this time, strengthened by the certainty of her decision. *"Please."*

They turned, so many emotions painting their faces—shock, horror. Shame.

And Sachi could erase it all.

"I love you." It was all she could think to say, but that was all right. In the end, that was all that mattered.

Sachi lifted the dagger, pressed the tip against her skin.

Ash began to shake his head, stretching out one hand. "No, *Sachi—*"

There was one moment of blistering pain, and then . . .

Nothing.

Chapter Thirty-Nine
DRAGON'S MOON

Week Three, Day Ten
Year 3000

The world rioted.

Ash fell to his knees. Not because of the pain flooding across his bond—though it was agonizing—but because the floor was unsteady beneath his feet. The entire castle rattled, but when he thrust his power into stone he realized *he* wasn't doing it.

Sachi stood before him, a knife in her chest, and the world was screaming.

It took him a thousand years to draw a single breath. The world around him screeched a denial so fierce and shrill he was surprised it hadn't yet shredded his eardrums. But this wasn't a cry you could hear with your ears.

It was the sound of Dreams dying.

More mundane screams echoed down the hallway. The castle was shaking.

He should do something about that. Stop it somehow.

He couldn't.

All he could see was Sachi.

And the knife.

He tried to struggle to his feet, but another wail of denial screamed through him. Thunder crashed overhead. A violent gust shattered the windows. Rain rushed in, and the wind curled around him, howling in Dianthe's voice.

"Hold the earth, Ash. Hold it!"

Why should he bother?

The knife mocked him.

Sachi dropped to her knees, and his heart thudded once. He realized it hadn't even been an entire heartbeat since she'd stabbed herself. Their eyes met, the gorgeous blue already glazed.

Agony and sadness flooded their bond, twined with regret and a love so sweet it drove him to his feet, desperate to reach her, to hold her, to *save* her—

The unstable stones threw him back to his knees. Roaring, Ash slammed his hands to the floor and flooded the castle with his power, clenching a mental fist around it to stop its violent heaving.

Calm. STILL.

NO NO NO NO NO NO NO NO

"No!"

Zanya's shriek shattered the remaining windows. Heedless of the rattling castle she dove across the floor and caught Sachi before she could topple to the floor. Her body was limp over Zanya's arm, and Ash caught one glimpse of bright-blue eyes staring sightlessly at the ceiling.

Inside him, the *warmth* that was Sachi blinked out.

Zanya threw her head back and screamed.

Her scream was the sound of stars dying. The sound of the earth tearing apart. The sound of the end of everything. Her scream made the world's wild grief sound tame by comparison. Her scream brought tears to his eyes, stinging so sharply Sachi and Zanya became a blur.

When he blinked the tears away, his consort and her assassin had vanished.

Chapter Forty
DRAGON'S MOON

Blackness stretched in every direction. No light, no shadows. Nothingness, forever.

Zanya's scream died in her throat.

That she still had a throat she knew, because it hurt. She'd shredded her voice with that one despairing cry of denial. Using up her body didn't matter. Without Sachi, she didn't need one. Didn't want one.

And yet, inexplicably, she still had one. Even here, where she couldn't see it.

If only she knew where *here* was.

"Isn't it time to stop lying to yourself?"

The voice came from behind her. And with the voice came light. Zanya caught it out of the corner of her eyes, like a promise, but there was nothing in front of her to illuminate. Just blank emptiness.

Endless.

"The Void," she whispered, then turned.

And screamed again.

Sachi floated in the darkness as if it were water. Her golden hair flared above her, stirred by invisible currents. Her eyes were closed, her face pale, but the illumination was coming from her. She *glowed* here, the gentle light from her skin forming an iridescent rainbow around her. Her hands drifted aimlessly on either side of her body.

The knife still pierced her heart.

"No!" Zanya lunged, but her fingers slammed against an invisible barrier. She clawed at it and, when that failed, smashed her fists against it until they should have shattered. "She shouldn't be here. She doesn't belong here."

"But you're the one who brought her here."

The voice came from directly behind her again, close enough to raise the hair at the nape of her neck. She spun, fingers already curled into a fist, but a strong hand caught her punch in midair. Zanya's gaze followed a well-muscled arm up to a black-clad shoulder and higher to a chillingly familiar pair of dark-brown eyes.

Her own eyes.

"Yes," her mirror image said, releasing Zanya's fist. "Take a moment to catch up, if you must. But I wouldn't dither. Sachi's life is in your hands."

Zanya stumbled away until her back thudded against the invisible barrier, every instinct rejecting this changeling who wore her features with a confidence—no, with an *arrogance*—Zanya could not imagine. Because those may have been her brown eyes, her strong brows, her high cheekbones, and bold jaw, but the whole formed a breathtaking beauty Zanya had never seen in herself. Her awkward stiffness and jagged edges had been replaced with dangerous charisma and razor blades.

And she glowed, too. Not like Sachi, with the brightness of sunshine through crystal, but in the way the moon and stars could caress the land, revealing subtle rainbows within shadows.

"You're so close." Her mirror lifted a hand to her face, and she felt the soft caress across her cheek. Felt her own skin under her fingertips. "Yes, Sachi glows. She has no idea what she truly is, so she has never tried to reject it. But you, Zanya . . ." That caress became warning fingernails. "You've always suspected. You've feared. You've pushed down that darkness because you still think darkness is *evil*."

"Isn't it?" Zanya whispered.

"Darkness is simply darkness. Light is simply light. We need both, just like we need life and death. Creation and destruction." Strong hands seized Zanya and spun her to face Sachi again, and the words fell against her ear as a whisper. "The Everlasting Dream." Another rough spin, and Zanya stared into her own face as the words fell like stones into her stomach. "And the Endless Void."

"No." Not a scream this time. A plea. A prayer—to what gods, she knew not. Surely not the High Court. The Everlasting Dream was the god to whom *they* prayed.

The Endless Void was the nightmare they feared.

"Yes," her mirror said with painful gentleness. "You know the story, Zanya. Say it with me. When time was new and the world barely formed, the Sheltered Lands cried out for a protector . . ."

The words formed on numb lips by rote. "So the Dragon appeared from the flames, and the Siren rose from the depths of the seas."

The shadow version of herself nodded approval. "And for thousands of years, they were enough. But twenty-five years ago, something changed. The High Court cannot protect the world from what is coming. And more than the Sheltered Lands are at risk."

"Twenty-five . . ." She bit her lip. Neither Zanya nor Sachi had ever known the exact day of their birth. But they had picked their own birthing day—the same one. Ten weeks ago, they'd celebrated their twenty-fourth.

A warm hand cupped her cheek. "Sachi can't survive your denial. Say it, Zanya. Say the words."

Zanya spun again, filling herself with the sight of Sachi. The curve of that cheek that she loved to kiss. The soft lips that smiled so easily. The eyelashes that could shield devious thoughts from the world. The dimples that made Zanya's knees weak.

"Can I still save her?"

"If you admit what you are. If you claim your full power. But there is a price."

"I'll pay it."

"Are you sure? The price will not be easy. You will never be able to hide again. Everyone who looks at you will know what you are. And before you can pay, you have to *admit it*."

She tried, and she couldn't, because it seemed foolish. The delusion of a girl who had never been important. The power-mad fantasy of a monster.

So she'd start with something easy to believe. Something that felt so right in her bones, she was surprised she'd never suspected it. The heart and light and *goodness* in Sachi had never been a thing of humans. "She's the Everlasting Dream born into mortal flesh."

"Yes."

Impatience in the word. Zanya heaved in a ragged breath and stared at Sachi. To save Sachi, Zanya had tried to kill the only man who had ever treated her with kindness. The only man who had made her feel, even for a moment, safe. To save Sachi, Zanya had been ready to tear out her own soul and lay down her life.

Admitting to this might still do both.

But this dark mirror was right. She had always feared. She had always wondered. From the first moment as a child when Terrors had shredded their way through the village that had harmed Sachi, but lain peacefully at Zanya's feet, crumbling to dust as she begged them to stop. Violence had never bothered her. Nightmares formed and dissipated at her whim. Destruction drew her like a moth to a flame.

"I'm the Endless Void," she whispered, and her voice cracked. She swallowed and turned to face her mirror. "I am the Endless Void, born into mortal flesh."

Satisfaction flared in those dark, luminous eyes. "Yes. We are."

A sharp pain stole her breath, followed by a flood of relief. A surcease of pain she hadn't known was there. She felt light, as if she floated as surely as Sachi. When she lifted one hand, she realized she was glowing now, too.

Power. That was the feeling flooding her. Bits and pieces had always been with her—the strength, her healing, her control over nightmares. But now possibility sparked at her fingertips, a giddy rush of lush potential.

Only one possibility mattered. "How do I save her?"

The barrier at her back vanished. When she turned, the other Zanya was already next to Sachi. "First, the curse. That is easiest, because they used Void magic. That's *your* magic. In time you'll recognize it for what it is, but for now you can ask the Void to show you. Visualizing it can help."

It felt odd, but Zanya whispered a request to see the curse. Abruptly, Sachi appeared bound by thousands of thin black threads, each no thicker than a single human hair, but together enough to muffle her glow. She touched one and had the dizzying impression that it felt like—

"Nikkon?" she asked, jerking her fingers back. The certainty disoriented her, as if a sense she'd never known she'd possessed had awakened. Not touch, not sight—she hadn't heard or tasted or even smelled him. But he was *there*, and now that she'd focused on the magic of the curse, she didn't need to be touching those black strands to sense him.

Her mirror produced a simple knife of obsidian and offered it to Zanya, hilt first. "Good. You learn quickly. So break the curse."

She accepted the blade and rested the edge against the first thread. It shivered beneath the blade, taut as if pulled incredibly tight, and Zanya hesitated. "I cut it and the curse vanishes? That easy?"

"Nothing is that easy," the other Zanya replied. A fierce, dark joy lit those eyes. "The curse exists. The intent was sent out into the world, tied to the power of the Void. You can't unDream someone else's wish. But you can change its focus. Cut the threads, and the curse has nowhere to rebound but upon its maker."

Zanya thought of Nikkon's smug smile. His endless insults. The cruelty and pleasure he had taken in Sachi's suffering. The knife fell easily, slicing through the threads. Each filament she cut seemed to snap under tremendous tension before being sucked away into darkness.

She hoped Nikkon felt every last one as it slammed home.

When she was done, Sachi's glow gently lit the darkness again, and the obsidian knife in Zanya's hand vanished. "What now?"

"Now we deal with her death." Her mirror gestured to the knife. "Time does not exist in the Void, and that gives you an opportunity. You brought her here in the moment she died, which means death still rests lightly upon her. You can take it from her. Pull out the knife, *slowly*, and focus on her death the way you would call to her nightmares. Draw her death into you. Unmake it, like you unmake the Terrors."

Zanya wrapped her fingers around the hilt. It was elaborately engraved—a dragon, with a jewel embedded in the pommel serving as a vivid red eye—and warmed at her touch. Zanya let the shadows curl down her arm and touch the dagger, and it *was* like calling a nightmare. She felt the oppressive weight of impending death crawl up the blade of the knife as she carefully, *oh so carefully*, drew it from Sachi's breast. It sparked under her hand, painful little shocks that made her fingers twitch.

"I know it hurts, but don't open your hand," her mirror commanded. "Death is not as easily soothed as nightmares. You can't banish it or dissipate it. You have two choices. Take it into yourself . . . or give it a new source."

The shocks had become pain now. Zanya pulled the tip away from Sachi's skin, heaving a relieved sob when she saw unblemished skin left in its wake. "There's no one else here," she ground out, clenching her fingers around the knife until she thought she'd have the shape of a dragon engraving burned into her palm. "How do I send her back? I'll take the death into myself—"

"Foolish girl. We didn't go through all of this just for you to die." Her double leaned close, her voice a whisper. "The Void is everywhere at once. You saw how the priest traveled to you. Wrap yourself in shadows and step from them into any place you wish to be. Surely you can find someone who deserves this death. Perhaps the man who ordered it to begin with."

King Dalvish II. Sachi's impostor of a father.

The muscles in her fingers had begun to cramp, but Zanya smiled and called for the shadows. They swirled around her, as familiar as an old lover, and she closed her eyes and imagined the king's private suite. She'd been there exactly once, summoned the night before they left for Dragon's Keep, when the king had made it clear that Zanya's job was to compensate for Sachi's "pathetic weakness" if she didn't have the stomach to complete her task.

Zanya visualized the marble floor. The tall windows. The rich tapestries, the vast bed. The door by which his mistresses arrived. The plush chair where he liked to sit and sip expensive liquor.

She held the image in place and stepped forward, and the shadows carried her exactly where she wanted to be. Cold marble coalesced beneath her feet. Another step took her into a beam of moonlight spilling through the tall window. King Dalvish himself stood in front of it in a richly woven robe, a glass of amber liquid raised halfway to his lips as he gazed out over Siren's Bay in the direction of Seahold.

"Waiting for news that the Dragon has died?" Zanya asked, and was rewarded when he yelped and spun, the glass shattering to the floor.

"How did you—?" His surprise gave way immediately to arrogant rage. It always did. "What are you doing here? How *dare* you—"

If she let him get going, he'd rant forever. The agony spreading from her hand to her arm would not allow it. Death screamed for the life it was owed. In a way, Zanya regretted it. After all the pain he'd caused, Sachi's tormentor should die more slowly.

But he would die, and that was enough. Leaping across the intervening space, Zanya drove the dragon-hilted blade deep into his chest. Her weight staggered him backward, but she rode him to the floor, ignoring the pricks of pain as broken glass sliced her knees.

She straddled the king's body and shoved the knife deeper as all the pain rolled down her arm and into her hand, then melted away. Dalvish's lips parted, working for sound, but nothing came.

"That was for Sachi," she whispered, and gloried in the understanding and futile rage that lit those blue eyes. His fingers scrabbled weakly against the marble floor, but it was too late.

Death, too long thwarted, rushed to claim the life it was due. The light faded from his eyes, and King Dalvish II died.

Zanya rose from the growing puddle of blood and summoned the shadows. As they swirled around her, she felt something else. A slimy touch of familiar magic. Someone else who moved in darkness and had ties to the Void.

The person responsible for Sachi's curse.

The shadows spun tight. She had never visited Nikkon's rooms, but the rebounded curse shone like a beacon. She *stepped*, passing through the Void, and the shadows carried her to a lavish room gilded and glittering with ostentatious wealth.

He was awake and wild-eyed, doubled over in pain in the middle of his room. He greeted her arrival with a knife held in a shaking hand, and his eyes blinked three times in a sallow face before he seemed to recognize her. "Y-you?"

"Me," Zanya replied, stepping from the shadows.

Nikkon stared. His gaze was unfocused, not quite looking at *her* but around her. When his unsteady knees gave out and he dropped to a grovel, she realized what he must be seeing. The glow. Her power.

She'd been warned she could never hide again. Apparently, it was true. And High Priest Nikkon worshipped the Endless Void.

"I didn't know," Nikkon moaned, scrabbling forward. "Great mistress, I did not see. I would never have said . . . I would never have *done . . .*"

He reached for her. Zanya kicked his hand away, as disgusted by his abrupt about-face as she had been by his cruelty. "You did not just wrong me. If you had wronged me, I might have let you live."

"Please." Another moan, and Zanya didn't know if the pain was physical or spiritual. "I will serve you. I will kill for you. Tell me the names. Any names! Your old trainers. Enemies at court. I will kill King Dalvish himself."

"Too late."

That made Nikkon look up. Zanya crouched, bringing their faces nearly level, and smiled at him. "What was it you said about the curse you twisted around Sachi? Dead before dawn?"

Shuddering, the priest nodded. Zanya reached down and picked up the knife he'd dropped. "I think dawn is too far away."

"Please, my lady. I can give you money. Jewels. Anything you want."

"I only want one thing," Zanya told him, turning the blade over in her hands. "If Sachi were here, she would ask for mercy. She might demand that I spare you, even after everything you did to her. Because she is good, and bright, and loving."

"I'm sorry, mistress—"

Zanya placed the tip of the knife to his chin. "You tried to erase her from the world."

"I didn't know."

"You didn't care." With an almost lazy flip of her wrist, she drove the knife into his throat. Blood splashed her skin, hot and metallic, and she watched a decade of her worst nightmares die with the man who had created them.

Then she rose, hand still clutching the bloody knife, and let the shadows take her.

Chapter Forty-One
DRAGON'S MOON

Week Three, Day Ten
Year 3000

It felt like the world was breaking all over again.

Ash splayed his hands against the solid stone of the floor. Seahold trembled beneath him, but it wasn't just the earth this time. He could feel Dianthe's power like a maelstrom above and around him. Thunder split the sky. Lightning flashed outside the windows. Even with them closed, he could hear the roar of the sea as the Siren tried to soothe it.

There was no soothing the world, not with his own heart carved from his chest. A vacant bloody wound was all that remained where his bond to Sachi had been. Anything he tried to whisper to quiet the earth was a lie, and yet still he tried.

It will be fine. I promise, it will be fine. Just heal yourself. Calm yourself.

NO

The shriek wasn't truly a word, but it was denial, and it lodged in his throat like broken glass. Like the tears that made every ragged breath taste like salt.

He'd failed.

He'd lost her.

His scream of pain drowned out the thunder, and the walls of his room cracked. The castle groaned above him, and he didn't care. Let it collapse on him. Maybe stone would crush his bones and punish him for his arrogance.

She was gone.

He'd *failed*.

The first falling stone hit him on the shoulder. A wide wooden beam snapped above him. He could feel every crack in the walls, like the cracks in his sanity. Madness gripped him. He channeled his grief upward, shoving his magic into the stone above, and the ceiling exploded with such force that dust and pebbles clattered down on him along with the furious rain.

And into that madness, Sachi reappeared.

Lightning lit up the sky, illuminating her pale skin and white chemise. She sprawled unmoving on the dusty floor, and Ash knew by the hole inside him that she must be dead. But even dead, he couldn't leave her like that. Exposed to the rain, unprotected.

He lunged for her body, scooping her up into his arms. His dagger was gone, leaving a small tear in her chemise. It took him a moment to realize why it looked wrong.

No blood.

He scrambled for the fabric, tugging down the neckline to reveal smooth skin, unblemished.

The castle wasn't shaking anymore.

The wind stopped howling.

Ash touched the spot where Sachi had stabbed herself, and his heart learned to beat again when he felt *hers*, thudding strong and quick beneath his hand. "Sachi?"

She gasped and shivered.

"*Sachi!*" Ash gathered her close to his bare chest, willing his own warmth into her as he counted the breaths that fell against his neck. *One. Two. Three.*

The rain eased to a light drizzle, though lightning still sparked across the sky.

Four. Five.

Beneath him, he felt the tentative push of stone. The earth reaching up to him. Reaching *through* him, as fire sparked to life on candles and lanterns in spite of the rain.

Six.

"Ash?" Her voice was soft and uncertain. Weak. He hushed her and stroked her head, rocking her against him. Even if their bond had shattered, *she* was here.

How was she here?

Seven.

Thunder crashed one more time, and every hair on Ash's body rose, as if lightning was about to strike *him*. Bare feet whispered across stone in front of him, and he lifted his gaze from Sachi.

The world stood still.

Zanya stood before him, spattered with blood. It painted her face, her hands, her knees. It dripped from the tip of a knife—*his* knife—she clutched in one hand. Lightning forked across the sky, and even it paled compared to Zanya.

Because she *glowed*.

If Sachi was a brilliant iridescent rainbow, then Zanya was black diamonds. Where Sachi glowed with the sweet warmth of a hearth fire, Zanya blazed like an inferno, like a forest fire, like a glorious dark sun, the power so magnificent it hurt to look at her. She glowed with the ferocity of a newly manifested god, but no Dreamer felt like *this*. Elemental. Magnificent. Terrifying.

As powerful as the Everlasting Dream itself.

Kit Rocha

The *knowing* hit him in the gut. Her strength. Her power. The way the shadows obeyed her. Her connection to nightmares. The Terrors coming to protect her. The way she soothed them by accepting them. By loving them, as no one but the most corrupt had loved things of the Void in centuries, in *millennia*, because even the wisest of living creatures still harbored that fear of death deep inside.

Somehow, for some reason, the world needed more than the gods that served it could provide. So something new had manifested. Something they'd never seen before. A power both ancient and vulnerable.

The Endless Void, born into human flesh.

When she spoke, her voice echoed like a midnight choir. "The mortal king is dead. So is his priest. The curse is broken."

Her words hung in the sudden silence like a fading note. Then she collapsed, as if strings that had been holding her upright had been cut. She scrambled across the floor, heedless of broken stone that cut her palms and sliced at her knees. The violent power around her faded to a soft glow as she touched Sachi's cheek. "Sachi?"

Sachi's eyes fluttered open, her blue eyes dazed. "Zan?"

Her voice broke the last of the spell around Zanya. She collapsed against Sachi, sobs shaking her body, and she didn't look like an elemental force anymore. Just a broken-hearted young woman pushed past her limits, and it was Sachi who reached up to smooth back her hair, the touch achingly tender and endlessly protective.

The Dragon's consort will break the Builder's chains, and the people will dream again.

Her heart. Her compassion. The way joy seemed to infect anyone she talked to. The warmth of her inside him. The open way she greeted the world, sharing herself as if there was always more to give, even though no one had ever given her a damn thing. The way she *glowed*, sunlight through crystal. Dreams in human skin.

364

If Zanya was the Endless Void, then Sachi . . .

The Dragon's consort will break the Builder's chains, and the people will dream.

And you will never be alone again.

Sachi was the Everlasting Dream.

Chapter Forty-Two
DRAGON'S MOON

Week Four, Day One
Year 3000

She didn't even have a scar.

For the fifth time in as many minutes, Sachi touched the skin above the low neckline of her shift. It was smooth, unblemished. Unmarred. And yet, she clearly remembered picking up Ash's discarded dagger, angling the blade toward her heart, and stabbing herself with it. She could still feel the fear that had gripped her, the desperation that had driven her. The cold steel piercing her flesh. If she tried, she even thought she could remember the Void, floating in the peace and tranquility of true nothingness.

And yet. Here she was, alive, *unmarred.* As if it had never happened.

"This must be what going insane feels like," she murmured aloud to no one in particular. To herself. To the world.

She'd learned so many things since she'd awoken—*come back to life?*—on the shattered floor of Ash's destroyed chamber. She'd died, been resurrected. Her adoptive father—the man who'd cared nothing for her, who had tormented her for years—was dead, as was the priest who had cursed her. And Zanya was a *god*—

No, not a god. Something older, more primal. An elemental force with the power to shape and unmake the world. And so, apparently, was Sachi.

She squeezed her fist shut, tighter and tighter, until her nails pricked her palm and blood welled between her fingers. She certainly seemed as mortal as ever.

And yet.

"Sachi?"

Zanya's voice—so careful, so tentative—washed over her, cutting through a little of Sachi's numbness.

She turned, the question already on her lips. "Is it true?"

Zanya hovered in the doorway to the balcony. The sun hadn't yet peeked over the distant ocean horizon, but already the skies were painted in pinks and golds. In that soft dawn light, Zanya's golden skin glowed. But the new glow transcended it, a glittering rainbow that was somehow light and shadows combined. "Is what true?"

"Did I die?" Sachi whispered. "Was I *gone*?"

Zanya finally stepped forward to perch on the edge of the seat next to Sachi, her hands twisted together in her lap. "Yes."

"And you brought me back."

"Yes."

There was only one question, one answer, Sachi needed to have before she could think about anything else. *"Why?"*

Zanya's beautiful dark eyes shimmered with tears before she looked away. "I didn't even think about it. I found out I could save you, so I did. Because I love you. You're my whole world, Sachi."

"No, I—" She reached out, covered Zanya's hand with hers. "I'm glad you did. I didn't want to die, Zan, it was just . . . the only way to make it all stop."

"I drove you to it." Zanya shuddered, clinging to Sachi. "It was the high priest, Sachi. Nikkon. He traveled through the shadows and told me that they'd accelerated the curse—"

All of it seemed like something from the royal archives. Events that had happened long ago, and were now consigned to history. "That doesn't matter anymore. You were trapped. We all were."

"We all were," Zanya agreed softly. Something fiercely satisfied flashed across her face. "We're not anymore."

The words hit Sachi like a blow, painful even through the numb haze that enveloped her. She wasn't trapped anymore . . . and she didn't know what to think about that. What to *feel*.

Her entire life had been built around one goal—eliminate the Dragon. Dalvish and his priests had never even bothered to lie to her and Zanya, to insist that riches and comfort awaited their successful completion of this goal. They'd always known that to triumph or fail would bring the same fate.

Death.

Sachi didn't know *how* to be free. That was why she had to ask. "So what do we do now? Where do we go from here?"

That fierce pleasure in Zanya's eyes faded as she looked out over the ocean. The still waters reflected the golden pinks and blazing orange of the brightening sky. "He loves you, Sachi. They all love you. And you'd be safe at Dragon's Keep. You deserve that life—soft and easy and happy."

The words hurt, not because they didn't ring true, but because all Sachi could hear in them was Zanya's absence. "What about you?"

Zanya shook her head. "They were already terrified of me. And now—I can't hide it anymore. I am what I am."

"Which is why you have to stay. Zanya, where would you *go*?"

"I don't know." The first tear spilled over, and Zanya freed a hand to scrub at her cheek. "I liked the Midnight Forest. If I knew you were safe, and *happy*, I could . . ."

Sachi waited for her to finish, but she didn't. Zanya didn't know what to do any more than she did. They were merely two lost souls, their orders vacated, set to wander without purpose.

But that didn't mean they couldn't *find* a purpose, even if only in each other's arms. "And if I asked you to remain at my side?"

Zanya wiped away another tear. "What if they won't let me?"

"If they drive you away?" Sachi shook her head. "Ash would never let that happen. *Never.*"

"I tried to *kill him*!"

"And he was going to let you." Sachi felt it in her soul. "For my sake *and* for yours."

"She's right."

Ash's voice, gentle behind them, still caused Zanya to start up from the chair, fingers frantically wiping away any evidence of tears. When she turned, it was to face Ash with wary eyes. "Is she?"

"Isn't she always?" Ash's fingers brushed Sachi's shoulder, as if he had to reassure himself that she was there. "I would have died to see you both safe. And apparently Sachi felt the same way."

"I did," she confirmed gently. "I don't know what my life will be or what it's worth, but I know it wouldn't be complete without the two of you in it."

Ash smiled and touched her cheek. Then he turned to Zanya, who still stood wary and uncertain, her entire being tensed for rejection. She still didn't understand Ash, didn't see the truth beneath his words or in his eyes.

So she wasn't prepared when he wrapped his arms around her and pulled her against his chest.

She stood stiffly in his embrace, arms out awkwardly at her sides— but she didn't push him away. Ash brushed his cheek against her temple as he met Sachi's gaze. "Dragon's Keep is your sanctuary for as long as the two of you wish to stay. Anyone who insults, scorns, or upsets you will be banished from my lands. You are both safe within my castle."

He spoke of safety, of sanctuary, and it wasn't enough. Zanya expected to be shunned, *hoped* to be tolerated, and none of the noble words spilling from Ash's lips would do a damn thing to counter those pernicious thoughts.

Zanya needed to know she was loved.

Sachi rose, her eyes locked with his. "And what of your bed, my lord?"

He smiled slowly, heat filling his gaze. "To be honest, the consort's tower is quite a bit nicer than mine. So is the consort's bed. And if both of you were to extend an invitation . . ." He kept one arm curled around Zanya but reached out to cup Sachi's cheek, urging her closer. "I would not have either of you think that bedding me is a requirement. But if I had my way, we would never sleep apart again."

"Good." Sachi melted into his embrace, and it soothed a little of the uncertainty that chilled her. "I want to go home."

"Soon." He kissed the top of her head and stroked a hand over Zanya's hair as she unbent enough to curl one tentative arm around him. The other hand found Sachi's, twining their fingers together. "I need to meet with the High Court one more time to discuss plans for the fallout in the capital. Elevia is calling in her contacts now. But after that . . ." He hesitated. "Well, I was going to say we could take the barge, but if Zanya can bring someone with her when she travels through shadows . . ."

Zanya tilted her head, considering. In the distance, the sun broached the horizon, spilling golden light across the waves. But shadows curled around the three of them, cool and soft and somehow feeling of *Zanya* even as they wrapped Sachi in absolute darkness.

There was a heartbeat of disorientation, as if she was falling and yet floating, and then the shadows unwove themselves, and she felt sand beneath one bare foot and a roughly woven rug beneath the other.

Sachi opened her eyes to their little seaside cave on the Bay, the only place in the capital where they'd ever been safe. It remained as they'd left it, untouched, full of the trinkets they hadn't dared to keep in their possession. She touched a blanket, running her fingers over the luxurious weave. It was stiff with salt, redolent with the briny scent of the sea air.

Tears pricked her eyes. "I never thought to see this place again. Not in truth. Only in the Dream."

Ash turned, his gaze sweeping over the small space. With a flick of one finger, the candles set on salvaged wooden boxes flickered to life, illuminating their soft refuge. "Where are we?"

"The cave where Sachi and I used to meet." Zanya sank to one blanket. Her finger found a woven bracelet Sachi had made for her and stroked it. "I tried to go to your room at Dragon's Keep first, but I suppose I need some sort of anchor to a place. Or at least to have seen it." She glanced up at him, a hint of mischief in her eyes. "I tried to get a look at your quarters, but your steward is a little scary."

"Camlia can be," Ash agreed, taking a seat next to her. "That is still a formidable gift you have, Zanya."

She shrugged a shoulder. In that moment, she looked as bewildered as Sachi felt.

"What does this mean?" Sachi asked helplessly. "For this to happen, and to Zanya? Is she one of you now? Is she something else? Help me understand, Ash."

"I wish *I* understood." He shook his head. "Something like this has never happened before. The Dreamers . . . Our connection to the Everlasting Dream is what gives us our powers, and they are shaped by who and what we are. But each of us is no more than a pinprick of magic. A single star in the sky. The Everlasting Dream is *every* star, and the Endless Void is the sky they inhabit. What does it mean for something that vast to be born in human flesh? The word *god* was made for smaller things."

Zanya dug her hand deep into the sand and let the single grains trail through her fingers. "It talked to me. Or . . . something did." She swallowed, refusing to meet either of their eyes. "It looked like me. It said something happened twenty-five years ago. That the High Court can't protect the world from what's coming, and that's why . . ."

She finally looked up, her gaze locking on Sachi's. "It's not just me. It's both of us."

It couldn't be. It just *couldn't*. "I don't think so, Zan. I mean—" Sachi waved her hands, "—I can't do anything like this. I can't do much of anything at all. I know what you saw, what you believe . . . but I'm not *her*. It. The Dream."

"You glow, Sachi." It was Ash, his voice soft. "It's why I knew from the first night I saw you that everything was not as it seemed. All of the gods do, though the ones freshly born from the Dream glow the brightest. You're like a rainbow made of sunlight refracted through diamonds."

"The Void said it's because she never rejected herself like I did. Because she didn't know what she was." Zanya leaned forward to take Sachi's hands in her own. "You've always had your Dreams. And your *heart*, Sachi. You're like hope in human form. You're so bright."

Their belief was a tangible, breathing thing. If they'd been telling her anything else in the entire world—*anything*—she wouldn't have questioned it for a moment. But this . . . "Then why couldn't I laugh in Nikkon's face and shrug off his blasted curse? Why am I still so *human*?"

"If I had to guess? You have yet to fully manifest." Ash leaned back and exhaled softly. "Did you feel it, Zanya? The *moment*?"

"It hurt," she whispered. "But it also didn't, because it was like I'd been hurting all my life and didn't know it, and then it just *stopped*. That's when I felt the power."

He nodded. "It was like that for me, too. I'd always been a little stronger, a little faster. I had a connection to the land. But it wasn't until—" He cut off, looking self-conscious. "It's been three thousand years since I told this story."

Sachi slid her arms around him. "You don't have to."

"I don't mind. It just feels . . . odd." He exhaled. "When I was a child, the Blasted Plains were fertile farmland. But they *were* plains then, too. Endless plains with grass almost as tall as I am. We'd had two years of drought the year I turned twenty-three. And there was a grass fire. Most of the village was trapped in its path, without enough water to stop it and no direction they could run to flee it."

Zanya leaned forward, eyes intent. "You stopped it?"

"Not at first," he replied, voice amused. "I was trying to cut a firebreak to buy time. But the wind shifted, and the fire was on me before I could run. I remember thinking that I'd always been overly fond of fire, so it was a fitting way to go."

"But you lived." The proof of it was beneath Sachi's cheek—the strong, steady beat of his heart.

"The fire didn't burn me. And then the earth . . ." He laughed. "I'd been trying to dig a firebreak with a shovel, and when I realized I wasn't burning, I picked that shovel back up. And the earth split apart for me. All I could feel was the *power* of both of them. But I suppose that's where the story about me rising from the flames comes from. The entire village had gathered on the other side of the firebreak and was waiting when I stepped out of the fire. Once I did, it vanished."

"And you were changed?" Sachi asked. "Right then, at that moment, you became a god?"

"I've never liked that word," he admitted, his brow furrowed. "And we didn't use it back then. We called ourselves Dreamers, people who could hear the whispers of the Everlasting Dream. People whose hopes and will were so strong they could change the world around them. But as the ones who had known us as humans grew old and died . . . Well, to those born knowing only our power, we *were* gods."

"So it took a moment of crisis." It made sense to Sachi—at least, as much sense as any of this could. "Is it like that for everyone?"

"Most of the time. Dianthe brought her ship safely through a storm that lasted a full three days. Ulric . . ." He shook his head. "That's his story to tell. But survival was key to it, too. Though I suppose, in almost every case, we were doing something reckless to save the people we loved."

"Like me," Zanya said softly.

"Yes," he agreed. "Exactly like you."

"But not me." Sachi exhaled, partly in disappointment and partly in relief. "So you see? It can't be true."

Ash hesitated. He and Zanya exchanged a look, as if they disagreed but were willing to humor her. "I can't say for certain. Not that you didn't do something reckless." That last word came out as a growl. "You nearly stopped my heart in my chest as well as your own."

"And mine," Zanya added.

"It won't happen again." That was something she could readily promise. "And believe me, I'm perfectly fine just being *me*. As long as I have you—both of you—"

Zanya silenced her with a kiss, as sweet and hungry as ever, but when she pulled away, she cradled Sachi's face between her hands. "It doesn't matter if you're *the* Dream. You've always been my dream."

Ash stroked a hand over her hair. "And you are the answer to mine."

And that was more than enough for Sachi. In fact, it was *everything*.

Chapter Forty-Three
DRAGON'S MOON

Week Four, Day Two
Year 3000

It had been over three thousand years since the first time Dianthe had seen the Dragon.

Honesty compelled her to admit that it was rather closer to four thousand at this point. The years had felt heavy in the beginning, because none of them had truly understood what their lingering youth and increased vitality had meant. Every year in those early days had been a revelation.

Now she felt like a stone skipping over the water of time, only realizing how much had passed when a cherished brash young sailor, her face now lined with wrinkles, brought her granddaughter to court, or her favorite cook—a young genius she'd stolen from the mortal lords— took off his apron for the last time, his back stooped with age.

Mortal lives burned so bright and swiftly. But Ash was eternal, still the arrogant young warrior who had sought passage on her first ship with a confident smile and the bold declaration that the two of them together could shape worlds.

He hadn't been wrong. The sea had already sung to her in those early days, and the wind had whispered her to sleep at night. But the cool, calming depths made it easy for her to withdraw from the world. The howl of tempests and storm-tossed waves might be part of her nature, but the Siren cherished the still coldness of the deepest ocean and the peace it brought to her soul.

Ash was her opposite in every way. Some might have thought that the grounding presence of earth and stone would temper his moods, but in all the years she had known him, it never had. If anything, the stone and bones of their world had grown as restless and temperamental as the Dragon himself, with moods enough to make the sea envious. And fire lived in Ash's heart, however he tried to deny it. He burned hot and protective, and even with the windows of her tower meeting room flung open to the cool evening air, he burned so hot that sweat dotted Dianthe's brow.

She summoned a gentle breeze to circle the room, carrying in the coolness of her sea and washing away the heat of temper. But Ash and Ulric were facing off across the ancient stone council table, and it would likely take more than a soft wind to stop them.

"I'm not saying we abandon her," Ulric growled, fists planted on the table. "I'm just saying we *think* about this. The danger she represents—"

"We're all dangerous," Ash snapped back, his brown eyes lost to flames of temper. "You were always fine with it, Ulric, as long as *you* were the most dangerous one in the room—"

Inga laid a hand on Ash's arm, silencing him. Then her gaze swung to Ulric, and her eyes had gone bright pink around the irises, too, a clear warning of temper rising. "Ulric can't help his nature. His deepest instincts are warning him that danger is coming. That is not the girl's fault. The problem is what she represents."

"Something has changed," Elevia said quietly. "It changed twenty-five years ago, and we're only just now finding out. We need to know more."

Dianthe fingered the rough wooden token Einar had taken from the refugees. A mark of safe passage, they'd called it, given to them by a robed figure. Her thumb traced the outline of a wave within a thin circle—her own sigil, which flew above this castle in white on turquoise. Then she turned the token over and traced the sigil of the Phoenix.

Twenty-five years. As many years as it had been since any of them had spoken to the Phoenix.

Warning prickled over her skin. The wind tugged at her hair, anxious and uncertain. It whipped in a circle around the table, forceful enough to rattle papers and cut Ash off midsentence. Dianthe rose, then froze as her gaze fell on the door.

A man stood there, unassumingly dressed in work boots and pants and a brown cotton shirt open at the throat. His sleeves were rolled up to show off strong forearms. The seams of his shirt stretched over massive upper arms, showing off the muscles he'd developed early in life at his father's forge. Sandy hair and hazel eyes complemented lightly tanned skin.

He'd always looked like sunshine.

"I see you removed my chair," the Betrayer said, his voice cheerful as he strode into the room. "I'd say I'm wounded, but . . ."

Deadly silence around the table. Ulric watched their ancient enemy with hackles rising. Elevia like a huntress drawing on a target. Sadness laced Aleksi's sudden tension, and Inga's eyes blazed a dangerous pink as her hands clenched on the edge of the table.

Ash was the only one who moved. He rose to his feet, violence trembling in the air around him. "Leave, if you know what is good for you."

"As predictable as ever, you great brainless lump." The Betrayer—for Dianthe would give him the honor of no other name, not even in her heart—strode forward and smiled straight at her. "Dianthe, love, do tell that rabid beast of yours to stop violating my borders and kid-napping my people."

She spared a moment to be grateful that Einar had left with the morning tide. He wouldn't think twice about collateral damage if he sensed his enemy within reach. The two would have torn her castle down around them—and Ash had already done quite enough of that. "If you mean giving refuge to those desperate to leave your shores, then I'm sorry. That's beyond my control."

The Betrayer shrugged. "Not everyone is willing to make the sacrifices required of progress."

The Wolf growled. Elevia put a hand on his arm.

No one could similarly silence Ash. "You're one to talk. I assume you're behind the idiocy of the past few weeks?"

"Oh, your rebellious king?" The Betrayer's smile widened. "Honestly, no. The first King Dalvish came to me. Can you believe that? They were so desperate for help in ridding themselves of you. Sadly, his daughter was too soft a touch to do what was required. But I sent a member of my court to help raise her son, and *he* was all too willing to follow my advice. They truly do hate you."

Ash said nothing.

Obviously disappointed by this lack of response, the Betrayer twisted the knife. "Of course, I could never ignore a plea for help. Though Nikkon has fallen rather abruptly silent. I don't suppose you know anything about that?"

Ash's hands fisted at his sides. A revealing tell, and his ancient enemy pounced on it with a satisfied grin. "You didn't think you could hide them from me, did you? The world shakes at their arrival. Creation and destruction, embodied in deliciously fragile human flesh."

Ash looked on the verge of lunging across the table, so Dianthe cut in, her voice ice. "You don't know what you're talking about."

"Oh, I think I do." The Betrayer huffed. "It really is a pity one of you killed Nikkon. I would have liked to explain to him his towering idiocy in not recognizing the truth of what he'd found, and the further foolishness of delivering it straight into your hands. But no matter. She'll be mine soon enough."

That was more than Ash could tolerate. He shook off Inga's restraining hand and took a step around the table. "Zanya is under my protection."

"Zanya?" The Betrayer scoffed. "You think I want the tainted one? The Void-corrupted whelp will be dealt with soon enough. Unless one of you destroys her for me." He quirked an eyebrow at Ulric, who flushed with rage—and guilt. "Oh, don't look at me like that. I know your heart, brother. Mortality sits uncomfortably on you. Do yourselves a favor. Kill the abomination. Though if she wants to destroy a few of you first . . . Well, I won't quibble."

Ash took another step. Aleksi rose and grasped his arm, whispering something softly to him, but Ash shrugged him off with enough force that he stumbled.

Which delighted their ancient foe. Glee filled his eyes as he taunted Ash. "What's wrong, Ash? Do you want to keep her? You truly have grown perverse over the years. But I'm not greedy. You take the damaged one, with my blessing. But I'll be taking Sachielle."

"No," Ash ground out. Another step. "You will not."

"She's the light of creation made flesh. You don't deserve her." His voice trembled with true fervor, and fear twisted inside Dianthe when she realized the Betrayer wasn't taunting Ash anymore. He believed his words to the depth of his soul. "You're nothing. A simple man with no dreams and no vision, content to die in the same mud in which you were born. Do you really think you can give her what she needs? Do you think you can ever be *enough* for her? Give her to me and spare yourself the humiliation. As my empress, she can realize her true potential."

Ash lunged at him.

The first punch took the Betrayer straight in his mocking face. He slammed backward into the wall, shattering the windows on either side of him. The stones behind the wall cracked. The ceiling groaned above him. The ground rumbled.

Elevia hopped onto her chair and then the table, lunging to grab Ash's arm before he could advance on his opponent. Ulric surged to his feet and grabbed his other arm.

"Yes, put a leash on your guard dog," the Betrayer taunted, wiping blood from his mouth. "Unless you'd like to have it out now. Is she worth tearing the world in two, brother? Think hard."

Ash's chest heaved. Rage kindled in his eyes. And Dianthe realized another terrifying truth.

For three thousand years, Ash had feared nothing more than he feared another clash with the Betrayer.

Now he feared losing Sachi—and Zanya?—even more.

And the Betrayer knew it. He backed toward the door, still smiling, still bleeding. "Tell your pretty princess I'll see her soon."

Ash roared. The flames of the torches on either side of the door flared, surging toward the Betrayer. But he was already gone, leaving Ash to shake off the restraining arms and pace around the tower, violence and frustration practically radiating from him.

Finally, he turned, glaring at all of them. "We're not letting him have either of them."

"Of course we're not," Ulric grumbled, and it wasn't just a promise. It was also an apology. Ash jerked his head in acknowledgment before leaning on the table. His gaze sought Dianthe's. She stared back, knowing she was the only one who could turn him aside from this path.

Would she?

No. Because she knew the truth, the same as he did. "For the Dream and the Void to manifest, whatever is going on in the Empire must be worse than we imagined. Something that would do more than just shatter the world. Something that would unmake it."

"We'll need them," Elevia said bluntly.

"So we'll protect them," Inga added.

"How?" When they looked at Aleksi, he held up both hands. "I'm not saying we shouldn't. But you all remember what it was like to first manifest. To have that *power* and not know how much you can do. Zanya is a young woman who has been hurt and betrayed by everyone in her life, and now she's been given the power to grind the world into dust. How do we protect her? How do we protect ourselves *from* her?"

"There's only one way," Ash said quietly, his gaze never leaving Dianthe's. "We make her feel safe."

This time it was Ulric who asked, "How?"

"I'm going to do what Sachi does," Ash told them, and the possessive fire in his eyes was something new. The wind danced around him, giddy at the sheer *power* in the words that followed. "I'm going to love her."

ACKNOWLEDGMENTS

It's been over a decade since we dipped our toes into a new world. After spending so much time in a dystopian world of shattered dreams, we wanted to try something else. We wanted to visit a world where dreams had real power, and those who dreamed hardest could shape the world.

We also wanted everyone to get free healthcare and puppies. So if anyone ever has reason to call *this* book prescient, we hope it's because of the free healthcare and (wolf) puppies.

We owe many people our gratitude for helping make this book happen. First and always, our agent Sarah Younger, who encouraged us when we said, "But what if horny dragon?!" Second, to our wonderful editor Lauren Plude, who replied, "Okay, but no, really—*what if horny dragon?!*" (At the time I am writing these acknowledgments, we are resigning ourselves to the fact that we probably can't release this under the title *Horny Dragon Book*. Whatever title you are holding in your hands, know that it is still the *Horny Dragon Book* in our hearts.)

On this book, we were delighted to reunite with Sasha Knight, the editor of all our Beyond books, to help dial up the angst and tragedy. If Zanya and Sachi made you cry, blame her! She made us do it! (Just kidding, we also love making readers cry.)

Bree's capitalization is a copyeditor's bane. A million thanks to Megan Westberg, who had to grapple with whatever chaos Donna couldn't contain. Bree is sorry. She is a menace.

Thanks always go to Sharon Muha, the final defense against typos. We don't let a book out into the world without Sharon putting her eyes on it. Any mistakes that slip past her have earned their right to stay. Please respect them as the warriors they are.

Thank you always to the members of our Patreon, and to the users of the Broken Circle Discord who encouraged us and cheered this project on from the first days we were out on submission to the final days of putting edits to bed. A more supportive group of gentle chaos gremlins has never been found. And you didn't start a single cult this time! (An extra glitter thank you to Lillie and Quinn for always being the best mods.)

Thank you/we're sorry to everyone who replied to our Twitter post asking if you wanted to die in this book. We hope your fantasy alter egos did you proud, or at least died in a fun way.

Surreal but glorious thanks go to Twitter of Time and the members of the Straw Haired Chits Discord, who literally chased Bree around the internet with brooms for a solid six weeks so she would stop getting distracted and actually finish this book. Who knew being chased with broom emojis and gifs could be so inspirational? We recommend it to everyone looking for a productivity hack.

Final and forever thanks to our readers. Fifteen years into this business, we still can't entirely believe we get to just . . . write books for a living. Wow. How is this our life?

It's our life because you read our books. Thank you.

ABOUT THE AUTHOR

Kit Rocha is the pseudonym for cowriting team Donna Herren and Bree Bridges. After penning dozens of paranormal novels, novellas, and stories as Moira Rogers, they reinvented themselves by writing the nine-book multiple-award-winning—and extremely steamy—Beyond series, which became an instant cult favorite. They followed it up with two spin-off series, including the popular Mercenary Librarians trilogy published by Tor. Now they're leaping into sexy epic fantasy with happily ever afters.

Their favorite stories are about messy worlds, strong women, and falling in love with the people who love you just the way you are. When they're not writing, they can be found crafting handmade jewelry, caring too much about video games, or freaking out about their favorite books or TV shows, all of which are chronicled on their various social media accounts. Learn more at www.kitrocha.com.